Praise for the novels of Karen Harper

"The thrilling finish takes a twist that most readers won't see coming. While intrigue is the main driver of the story, the able, well-researched plotting and sympathetic characters will keep romance readers along for the ride."
—*Publishers Weekly* on *Broken Bonds*

"Haunting suspense, tender romance and an evocative look at the complexities of Amish life—*Dark Angel* is simply riveting!"
—Tess Gerritsen, *New York Times* bestselling author

"A compelling story...intricate and fascinating details of Amish life."
—Tami Hoag, *New York Times* bestselling author, on *Dark Road Home*

"Harper, a master of suspense, keeps readers guessing about crime and love until the very end...of this thrilling tale."
—*Booklist* on *Fall from Pride* (starred review)

"Danger and romance find their way into Ohio Amish country in a lively and endearing first installment of the Amish Home Valley series."
—*Publishers Weekly* on *Fall from Pride*

"A tale guaranteed to bring shivers to the spine, *Down River* will delight Harper's current fans and earn her many more."
—*Booklist* (starred review)

"Well-researched and rich in detail... With its tantalizing buildup and well-developed characters, this offering is certain to earn Harper high marks."
—*Publishers Weekly* on *Dark Angel*, winner of the Mary Higgins Clark Award

Visit karenharperauthor.com for more titles.

KAREN HARPER

CHASING SHADOWS

MIRA

ISBN-13: 978-0-7783-1952-8

Chasing Shadows

Recycling programs for this product may not exist in your area.

www.MIRABooks.com

Printed in U.S.A.

To Bill and Sunny
for their great St. Augustine hospitality
and, as ever, to Don.

CHASING SHADOWS

1

Naples, Florida
Collier County Courthouse

2014

Surely nothing else could go wrong now. As Claire Britten and her client left the courtroom in triumph, she was convinced she was on a roll. She felt like making a fist pump in the air but she kept her cool.

As a thirtysomething single mother struggling with building a career and coping with a dreadful disease, this high-profile victory had to help. Her interviews and testimony had made all the difference in the trial. A guilty man was going to prison instead of hiding out so he and his family could enjoy a three-million-dollar death settlement. Her current client, Lifeboat Insurance, small as it was, had beaten out the vaunted law firm of Markwood, Benton and Chase. She'd helped to best the best in the business.

Claire was swept outside with her boss and their lawyer, past the big pillars holding up the shaded, covered walkway. They hit a wave of humidity and reporters, washing toward them in the mid-September afternoon. She fumbled in her purse for her sunglasses amid shouted questions, the thrust of arms with recorders...padded microphones on poles... jostling, shouting...

Over the crowd noise, her client Fred Myron shouted in her ear. "That fancy defense lawyer's the one who needs a lifeboat now. I'm going with this for all it's worth. I see cameras from Ft. Myers, even Orlando! Look at that—CNN!"

A long pole with a padded microphone brushed Claire's shoulder and someone shouted, "Ms. Britten, tell us how you first knew the wife and son were lying! Hadn't Sol Sorento covered his tracks to make everyone think he drowned in Key West? What were the clues he wasn't dead?"

"As I testified on the stand," Claire answered, "Mrs. Sorento and Mario sometimes slipped into the present tense when talking about him. I theorized they knew he was alive and were in contact with him. Then a call they made was traced to the Bahamas where the insurance firm detective took over to locate him."

Another voice, a woman's: "Ms. Britten, can you explain for our viewers what you mean by a forensic autopsy you did on the accused? You're not a doctor, but that sounds really medical, and you didn't even have a body to work with."

"I am not a medical doctor or a psychiatrist, but a forensic psychologist. A forensic autopsy, which some call a psychological autopsy, means taking apart and studying a person's life—often their motives and alibi. I do interviews, not interrogations, of those close to the deceased to learn who might be responsible for foul play. Please take a look at my website and…"

Someone bumped into her from behind, pressing closer. The crowd noise and a small jet going over made her shout to be heard. Oh, it wasn't a jet but a drone. Could the media be filming from it, or could it belong to security here? Its whine was like a screaming mosquito, and it wasn't even directly overhead. It seemed to hover above the Sorento defense team. A few others looked up at it, too.

She asked the reporter, "Can we just step over there a minute in the grass in the shade of the palms?"

Surely this publicity would lead to more future clients than her business Facebook page and website had brought in. This would be a starred item in her meager resume. She'd already been covered in *The Naples Daily News* so she was banking on that to promote her struggling one-woman Certified Fraud Examiner and Forensic Psychologist business she'd named Clear Path. Despite Jace's monthly child support, she wanted to stand on her own for herself and little Lexi. Besides, she believed in her work and maybe now could start believing in herself again.

But had she remembered to take her meds on time? Spending so much time in court had played havoc with her schedule. She'd like to pop a piece of chocolate for some quick caffeine, but not with everyone watching. She'd had to miss her short afternoon nap. All week she'd had to cut back on her regular jolts of caffeine so she didn't have to run to the bathroom during testimony and so she could be there for the reading of the verdict. All she needed was to doze off or have a horrible hallucination triggered by all this emotion.

Fred kept a firm hold on her arm. No doubt he wanted in on this interview. She wondered if any of these reporters would turn up that having to pay the huge death insurance benefits for Sol Sorento would have sunk little local Lifeboat Insurance into the depths of bankruptcy. Her theory was that, desperate to prove the Sorento family's claim was bogus, Fred had borrowed money to investigate and fight the claim. She'd like to deal with larger, more reputable firms, but she needed to build her bank account.

Trailing reporters, they moved down the walk toward a patch of grass near the four-story parking garage. Claire noted the lead lawyer for Sorento, Nick Markwood, walked away from his group and made straight for her, his suit jacket slung over one arm, his shirt blinding white in the sun.

The man had been amazing in court, forceful, clever. She knew he wasn't used to losing. Was he going to shove his way in here to make his point in the interview? His law firm was a force around here, powerfully promoted on billboards and through TV spots, but with his looks and voice, she supposed he could usually sell anyone on anything. He was a commanding figure, tall and tanned with a sculpted face and physique, maybe forty, going silver at the temples, which matched his steely eyes. She'd had plenty of time to study him and she had to admit she'd enjoyed watching him work and psyching him out when he spoke in that deep, commanding voice.

"So," the first reporter, a blonde woman with a

Live at Five cameraman, was saying, "what other hints besides verb tense that his family was lying? A lot of our readers might not get that."

"As I testified, besides verbal cues, I rely on body language, the closed, defensive look liars often use with legs and arms crossed," Claire explained. "If you mention my website—here's my card—you'll find my list of other signs that can suggest a witness, acquaintance or family member is lying. I also—"

A loud crack slammed through the noise. People stopped and looked around and up. Fred let go of her arm and stepped away. Someone screamed, "Gun! Gun!"

People scattered, ducked, shouted. A voice screamed, "Oh. He's been hit!"

A second shot, a breaking of the sky. Pain, searing pain in her arm, her body, somewhere. Had she fallen into a fire? Was this a narcoleptic nightmare?

She fell back onto the green sea with royal palms swaying overhead, and she was with Jace and Lexi. At the beach by the pier. But the sun burned her skin, her arm.

"Call 9-1-1!" someone shouted.

A man's deep voice, maybe Jace. But he was flying from LA to Singapore now. No, not Jace bending over her, wrapping his necktie around her upper arm, then pressing his hand hard against her. It was that lawyer, that man who had studied and glared at her when she testified, the one who had cross-examined her. The one who had almost made her doubt her own words. Nick Markwood, still watching her, what she said, her mouth. That mouth—she screamed.

"Don't move," he said. "You've been shot. I know

I'm hurting you, but I have to stop the bleeding. Lie still. Help is coming. Is there a doctor here?" he yelled.

More screaming. Not hers, maybe sirens coming closer. Strobe lights, or was that the sun?

Someone shouted, "Is anyone else down?"

Down? They couldn't keep her down. Never. But red-sunset blood shone from the man's shirtsleeves, his hands. Hands on her.

Someone cried, "I think the insurance guy is dead. Did anyone see who shot them?"

"From the parking garage. Didn't see him. One cop car went after him when he fled…only two shots…"

Searing red burning pain made worse by the man staring down at her, bending over, pressing into her hurt arm. Did he know she could easily fall asleep? Did he know the high school bullies had taunted, "Claire Fowler, Claire Foul-up! Foul-up!" when she'd fallen asleep reading, eating, sitting on the volleyball bench, even standing up? Her disease had ruined her marriage—her fault but Jace's, too. Would her sister keep Lexi if she died, or would Jace try to take her away, far away?

She heard someone sobbing from fear and pain. It was so close. She guessed it was her.

Nick Markwood fought to keep Claire Britten conscious, tried to stop the bleeding from her upper left arm. Maybe all the blood made her wound look bigger than it was. He'd seen gunshot wounds before, in his worst nightmares of finding his father, even worse than this.

Now, both of them and the grass were spattered

with her blood. She was slender, maybe didn't have much to lose. Too slender. And that bounty of stunning red hair and alabaster skin stood out in this sunny South Florida of bottled blondes and bronzed skin. With her green eyes, he'd thought she looked like some Irish colleen off a St. Patrick's Day card, here among the snowbirds and native Floridians. But she had those eyes tight shut now in pain.

In court, he'd had to fight to keep his mind off her looks and on her testimony so he could tear it apart, but she'd torn their case apart. He didn't need the loss, hated losses. Too many from too far back. But maybe it had all worked out for the best—if she'd trust him and if she didn't die like her boss who'd been standing close to her. The shooter had been really good. But had he meant to kill them both and just wounded her? He'd evidently blown away Fred Myron with one hit. A shooter out for revenge from Sol Sorento's big family?

Or—and this scared and angered him too—since he'd been moving close to the two victims, Nick's next thought had been that the bullets could have been meant for him. Clayton Ames had his ways of ruining things. He must know Nick would never give up his crusade to nail the bastard. Ames and his lackeys managed to wreak havoc and then disappear just that fast. Talk about Sol Sorento vanishing for two years to try to pull off this fraud. The master murderer Clay Ames had reeked of deceit and danger for years but stayed too slippery to prosecute or even locate lately.

Shrill sirens came close, drowning out other voices, even the ones in his head. The court staff and reporters shouted and pointed to bring the rescue squad to Claire. Running steps; the joggling sound of the equipment in their bags. Reporters' cameras still rolling.

Though they were heading right for them, like some damn idiot, Nick shouted, "Here! Here! She's shot in the upper left arm and bleeding bad!"

They knelt, bent over her. "Should I let go?" he asked them. "I don't want to let go."

"Good job, sir. We'll take over now," a medic said. Nick watched as they put a better tourniquet on her and some sort of a plastic patch over the wound. Tears streamed down her cheeks so she was conscious.

Nick sat back on his haunches. His muscles ached. He was a mess. He stood, moved away, ignoring questions shouted at him by the press. He usually kept his comments—especially after losses—to a minimum. They'd done him and his mother no favors when his dad died. Talk about blood on someone's hands…

Sean, one of his associates, pulled him away, but he didn't want to go. Nick wanted to know she'd be all right. If he hadn't wanted to talk to her, he wouldn't have been near her when she was hit. But he needed to make her an offer she could not refuse.

Police pushed everyone back, wound some police tape between a courthouse pillar and two royal palms. He watched the second rescue squad bend over the dead man, feel for a pulse, then stand, whispering, shaking their heads. One guy got on his cell, probably to the ME. A police officer of the growing number of them covered Fred Myron with a body bag, but they didn't move him yet.

They were getting ready to move her already, Claire Fowler Britten, the sharp little expert who had done his case in with her clever questioning of Sorento's family and her steady testimony he couldn't shake. He wanted her for that.

He let Sean carry his briefcase and started dazedly toward the parking garage before he saw that was being cordoned off, too. He got only a few steps before one of the officers hurried up and asked, "Did you see the shooter, counselor? Anything that would help?"

"Nothing. I was going to talk to her—the forensic psychologist. Tell her she'd done a good job. I—I was looking at her. I saw her go down from the shot, tried to help her."

"You did. They're taking her to the hospital downtown."

"Did they say she'll be okay?"

"We'll know soon. We've got to notify Mr. Myron's next of kin, then notify hers. It's bad when NOK learn things from the media, and they're all over here."

"You know I'm available if you have more questions," Nick said.

He had already checked out where Claire lived, an attached villa in the Lakewood area, evidently so she could be near her younger sister, Darcy, who did her daughter's child care. He'd researched Claire's family, education, marital status. Divorced for a year with a four-year-old daughter. Her ex, Jason "Jace" Britten, was an international airline co-pilot living in Los Angeles and sometimes Singapore, though he kept an apartment here in Naples. Nick had wanted to move on his plan—on her, but this was sure screwing up his schedule. Claire Fowler Britten might have gotten the best of him in the courtroom, but he had to get the best out of her and soon.

Jace Britten yawned and stretched out in the back-seat of the taxi as it pulled away from Changi Airport where he'd just left the Airbus after an eighteen-and-one-half-hour flight from LAX. A great airport here, a great destination where he spent his time when he wasn't in LA or making a quick trip home to see Lexi. Smooth flight as usual with a pilot he liked, but, as first officer, he was always itching to get into the captain's seat.

He glanced down at the three stripes circling the sleeves of his uniform jacket on the seat beside him, and thought about Claire. When he'd gotten this promotion, the two of them had celebrated at Stoney's Restaurant, and the next day at McDonald's with Lexi. Slender, like her mother, that little kid could put food away but never seemed to gain weight. He hoped like hell that was all his girl had inherited from Claire.

He tried to put his past life—and past wife—out of his thoughts. She'd betrayed him, though not by being unfaithful. A woman with a career exposing liars had lied to him, hid things, and he couldn't take that. Absolutely unacceptable. He'd have tried to take Lexi if the child hadn't been so close to her mother and her aunt Darcy, if he hadn't always had wander-lust for exotic places and Claire had argued that Singapore or even LA wasn't the place to rear a child. Hell, Singapore was just a foreign version of Naples: heat and humidity, tourism, traffic, beaches, great restaurants, crocs instead of gators—that's all, if you ignored the mosques and Buddhist temples.

"Very nice day," his taxi driver said. "No monsoons yet in 'Garden City.'"

"I like the nickname 'fine city' for this place," Jace told him, partly to head off the next punch line he figured was coming. "A six-hundred-dollar fine for littering, a twelve-hundred-dollar fine for speeding."

"I not speeding. No, sir."

So much for that conversation. English might be the main language here, but the place was a real scramble of people, just like the mix of skyscrapers and sampans they drove past right now.

At his favorite, familiar hotel on busy Orchard Road, he paid his fare, hefted his small bag and walked past the gorgeous garden with flowers and a fountain. Under the spray of water was a statue of the so-called merlion, the mythical beast that was the symbol of the tourism industry here. Its top half was a lion and the bottom half a fish. A couple of years ago, when he'd taken a stuffed merlion home to Lexi, she'd insisted on calling it Lion King Little Mermaid from her two favorite Disney movies at that time.

Ginger at the desk saw him coming, smiled and winked, then handed him a key card and a note. *Call Darcy,* it read.

His stomach flip-flopped, especially when he remembered he hadn't even taken his phone out of airplane mode after the flight. What if something was wrong—really wrong?

He hurried to his usual room and linked into the hotel Wi-Fi. He looked at his list of numbers, Claire's at the top. Once a week, he Skyped with Lexi and

Claire just to keep in touch with Lexi. He hit the line with his former sister-in-law's cell number. Darcy answered right away.

"Darcy, it's Jace in Singapore. What's up? Everyone okay?"

"I thought you should know Claire had an accident so they won't be Skyping with you tonight."

His voice rose with his pulse rate. "An accident with Lexi in the car?"

"No, not exactly an accident. Someone shot her in the arm, coming out of the courthouse after that trial which she—they—won. I still have Lexi, so don't worry. It's just that it got a lot of publicity here, and I thought you might stumble on it in the news somehow."

Claire hurt. That hit him so hard it scared him.

"In the arm. Is she okay? How bad is it?"

"I don't really know yet, but not life-threatening. Just a day or two in Naples Hospital. They want to be sure infection doesn't set in. And they haven't found the shooter, who killed her boss—you know, from that insurance company—and they aren't yet sure who was the intended victim."

Jace swore under his breath. Just like Darcy to hold back the worst news. Claire's boss was shot to death? Why did Claire insist on being in this type of business? Why didn't she just stick to online consulting? She was just looking for trouble, hanging around shady characters like frauds and liars. Damn, it took one to know one, so no wonder she was good at that.

"Jace, are you there?"

"Yeah. So they didn't get the shooter?"

"Escaped. The theory is it was a member of that

Italian Sorento family that won't be getting the millions in death benefits. They're thick as thieves."

"Did Claire ask you to call me?"

"Yes. Yes, she did. And I told Lexi a version of events. Steve took her and our two to get ice cream so she's not here right now."

"I'm not scheduled to fly back to LA for two days this time. I'll check in, though, try to change off. Maybe I can get a jump seat back sooner."

"I'll take good care of Lexi. It's not a crisis. Claire's done with that case. Nothing dangerous on the horizon, and this was just that she was in the wrong place at the wrong time."

"Yeah," he said, fighting to keep his voice level. "Tell the little mermaid I love her, okay?"

"Sure. She misses you, Jace, wants you back."

"Thanks for letting me know," he said and ended the call. Though he fought it hard, as hurt and angry as he still was, he wished she'd said that about Claire.

2

Claire's wounded arm hardly hurt at all, that is, until she tried to move it or her shoulder. Then, too, she was on pain pills. Despite this accident—this assault—she was blessed it wasn't worse.

They had her sitting up in the hospital bed. No cast, since the bullet had missed her bone. Only one of the three major upper arm muscles had been impacted. In the ER while she was sedated, they'd given her a transfusion, probed for and extracted the bullet, irrigated the wound and put her back together with some sort of blue adhesive and a bandage, all supported by a pink sling, no less. The doctor had said her skin would get sticky and itchy but should heal well.

"I see you've finished your breakfast. Feeling reasonably okay?" the nurse named Mandy said as she swung the tray table aside and took Claire's temperature again with an electronic thermometer. Why did doctors, nurses and dentists always start to chat or ask a question when they had something in your mouth?

"Mm-mm," Claire said.

"Good. We gave you a tetanus booster in your right arm if that's a bit sore. Sometimes in the panic and pain in the ER, memories can be strange and I know you missed your dosages of meds before we realized you were narcoleptic. You really should wear a bracelet with that info. Your sister had to tell us, you know."

"Mm-mm."

Actually, that was a good suggestion, so maybe something positive would come from this mess. She'd been so sedated that she didn't recall much either from the ER or last night. But she didn't want to be explaining to people what a NARC bracelet around her wrist meant. The fewer people who knew she was narcoleptic, the better. Thank heavens, she hadn't had one of her terrible dreams from being even slightly off her meds but she just bet it was the hospital sedation that had saved her from that. Regularity of her meds, her naps and daily stimulants were essential.

Taking the thermometer out of her mouth and squinting at it, Mandy said, "Good, no fever. Now, before we release you later today, I want to warn you not to be upset by major bruising. Your skin will be black and blue like crazy, following lymphatic channels under the skin, maybe looking like a series of stripes."

Claire heaved a huge sigh. "A small price to pay, considering my client was killed. He's Jewish, so his wife will want to bury him soon. He has two adult children. I'm so sorry for all of them."

"They won't be burying him before the next sunset. An autopsy. Standard procedure for a—a tragedy like this."

Claire nodded and sniffed back the urge to cry, for

Fred, for herself. Dreadful, the thought of a physical autopsy, instead of the psychological ones she specialized in.

Someone called out in the hall, and she jolted. Pain shot into her shoulder. That sound was hardly like a gunshot, but it brought it back. But no way was she going to suffer from post-traumatic stress disorder, not with everything else she'd been through.

She asked Mandy, who was typing into her small laptop, "Do they know if I'll need physical therapy to get everything working again?"

"To be decided in a week or so. The Tylenol 3 with codeine you're on should handle the pain if you don't use the arm much, but Dr. Manning has also written a prescription for stronger stuff, should you need it. With the powerful meds you take, remember, use the stronger pain meds sparingly, if possible. And no driving for a while."

Claire sighed again. "I'm used to that, off and on, though I've been cleared to drive again recently since I have my narcolepsy meds calibrated just right. Cab fares add up. I can't have my family always running me around as if I were a kid. And, yes, I'll be careful. Believe me, I always am. I was just in the wrong place at the wrong time. I think the shooter meant to hit Fred, or even someone else nearby."

"I think that's what you told the officer who questioned you last night."

"Oh, right. That's vague, but I remember it. Not the same man who was guarding my door. It was a detective working on Fred's murder. I wish I could have helped him."

"If you don't mind me asking—well, I've never

come across someone with narcolepsy before, only read about it in textbooks. The meds keep it under control? Do you have cataplexy, too, lose muscle control when you wake up or get emotional? Do you think that's why you fell to the ground so fast?"

"I have mild cataplexy that's controlled by one of my medications. I think I fell to the ground because the bullet spun me around—maybe instinct to get down. Unless I get overly tired or overly excited, the meds plus a mini-nap or two and stimulants like caffeine, even in the form of chocolate, work wonders. I've had the disease since eighth grade, and it took a while for it to be diagnosed. It was really hard going when I was a kid. I had terrible nightmares, actually thought I was haunted by ghosts. People thought I was lazy or stupid. I took some ribbing—bullying."

"I'll never understand cruel people. I think they're insecure and strike out at others to make themselves feel better, stronger than someone else."

"I usually hide my disease from people, because it's hard for people to trust you when they expect you to just fall asleep at any moment—be out of it," she admitted, more to herself than to Mandy. Here she was talking freely with a nurse about the nightmare of her life, and she'd kept it from her own husband. She pictured Jace—the handsome blond, athletic, perfectionist Jason Andrew Britten—shouting and stomping around when he finally found her stash of hidden meds and learned what they were for.

"Sorry," Mandy said. "That must have been really tough."

Claire whispered, "I never expected to end up in the hospital where my diagnosis would matter. It helps now, to talk about it with someone—someone who understands, like the doctor who eventually helped me. My sister and parents knew, too, but no one else."

Mandy patted her good shoulder and they were silent for a moment. "By the way," Mandy said, "there's major coverage of the shooting on TV and in the papers, even national. It's in *USA TODAY* and I caught a story on *Good Morning, America* before I left the house. 'Fatal courthouse shooting… Man supposed dead for two years now out of the grave and into prison for fraud,' that kind of thing. What a way to be famous, huh?"

Claire just rolled her eyes. Suddenly, they were the only part of her that didn't feel sore. "Is the police officer still outside my door?" she asked as Mandy typed something else into her laptop.

"A new one this morning. Just until they catch the killer," she said as she went out and left the door ajar.

The killer. She'd been shot by a killer. Hard to believe. Poor Fred and his family. But had one of Sol Sorento's family been the shooter? Of all the interviews she'd done to try to figure out if Sol was dead or alive, not one of his family or friends had seemed like a killer, even if some of them were temperamental and deeply distressed. But losing hope of a fortune, with Sol going to prison and others up for perjury, their lives ruined, who knows that desperate people couldn't turn deadly? But that was all she'd been able to give the detective when he'd questioned her.

A knock on her door interrupted her agonizing. A middle-aged, bald and bulky officer stood there with a huge bouquet of red roses in his hands. "For you, with a visitor, if you're up to it, Ms. Britten," he said. "It's been cleared."

Her first thought was that Darcy and Steve should not have bought expensive roses, even if they were supposed to be from Lexi. Maybe they'd even brought Lexi! Surely, Jace hadn't sent the flowers, though Darcy said she'd call him.

"Yes," Claire told him. "Yes, of course, they can come in."

But it wasn't her family. It was a senior partner of Markwood, Benton and Chase, Attorney Nick Markwood, not decked out in his lawyer suit but in gray casual slacks and a bright blue golf shirt. He took the roses from the cop and came in to sit in the chair beside her bed, laying the bouquet beside her sheet-covered leg. Like an idiot, she hoped her hair looked okay. At least she had a robe over this stupid-looking hospital gown.

"I know that officer," he said. "I asked him not to say it was me, or I figured you might not see me. We were adversaries, and I know you probably hate me for grilling you the way I did. But I have a proposal— a job offer—if you'll just hear me out."

"I don't hate you, and I want to thank you for helping me yesterday. They gave me a transfusion, but it could have been worse if you hadn't stopped my bleeding." Still, she thought, that didn't mean she trusted him. But if he was going to offer her a job at that prestigious law firm...

"Okay, here's the deal," he said, crossing one ankle over his other knee. "I intended to talk to you about this just before you were shot. I could use your help immediately on an important issue in St. Augustine."

"St. Augustine? Do you have an office there? With this situation—I have a young daughter, too—I can't really work outside this area."

"I need your expertise and talents and so does an innocent woman who's a friend of mine. If we don't move fast, she may soon be indicted for murder. Her mother is dead, and the daughter's innocence hinges on whether the death was an accident, suicide or murder. It will not only impact her, but the state of Florida. Needless to say, I'll make it worth your while. I'd like to retain you as a consultant, have you conduct some interviews on-site there. We need to prove that her daughter did not commit murder."

"If it were a local case, maybe, but St. Augustine's about as far as you can get within the same state. As I said, I have commitments here."

"I hear you're being released later today. I'm sure you'll want to get home to your daughter, but can we meet to talk this over again soon, and I'll give you more details? I saw your physician in the hall, and he said not to stay long right now."

Her eyes widened and her lower lip dropped before she got hold of herself. The reach of this man amazed her. He knew the cop on her door; he'd consulted with her doctor. Wasn't anything about her condition or release privileged? Was this master manipulator the kind of client she could trust? She really should not have trusted poor, dead Fred Myron, either. But, she sure needed that job, and this one could be an entrée to others. It sounded high-profile.

"Claire, could I pick you up tomorrow and take you over to Lake Avalon midday? I'll bring lunch. We'll talk, so I can explain everything. The case, the people—your fee, of course. Unless you'd rather not go out into open spaces right now."

"I'm not going to cower under my desk. Besides, those bullets surely weren't meant for me. Really, I don't have any enemies...not someone who would do that."

Just yesterday, she would have said this man was her enemy from his trying to tear her testimony to shreds. She shouldn't trust him now. No way she was going to leave Southwest Florida to work for who knew how long in the northeastern part of the state. She might as well be going to Alaska for all she knew of that area. And this was something that would affect the entire state? This guy was good with words, with convincing people, but not her.

"I don't really want to do profiling of possible murderers," she told him. "That can be tricky and dangerous. That's what you're looking for, isn't it, I mean if it's an alleged murder? In *Lifeboat versus Sorento*, I was only trying to establish that Sol Sorento was alive. I turned up nothing to prove his friends and family wanted him dead or would have committed murder."

He put both feet on the floor and his elbows on his knees as he leaned closer and fixed her with his riveting, silver stare. "Think of it this way then. I'm not asking you to profile a murderer, but a victim. Surely, this woman's daughter would never have hurt her. The deceased had panic attacks and was on powerful meds, so maybe she accidentally or intentionally overdosed. It would be what you called on the stand a forensic autopsy. I want you for this. And then we'll go from there."

I want you... And then we'll go from there... And the woman had panic attacks...powerful meds... Claire closed her eyes for a moment. She felt for this poor dead woman and her daughter. And, she hated to admit it, but she was moved by Nick's passion for this case.

She amazed and scared herself by saying, "Call me first. But why don't we meet at your office?"

"This is *ex officio*, not under the aegis of the firm. It's a kind of charity I sponsor, a low-profile company I call South Shores that only takes on certain suicide-versus-murder cases."

Now she was sure she was crazy to even talk to him about this. But she was curious, too, totally tempted—not by his charisma, of course—but by the mystery of what he'd shared so far.

"I'll call tomorrow morning," he said, standing. "I have your number from your website." He lifted his hand and walked out, probably trying to leave before she had time to change her mind again.

At least, she'd only agreed to hear him out. Too late she realized she'd been gripping the florist paper wrapped around the rose stems. She crinkled it so tight she'd stuck her thumb with a thorn. All she needed was to lose more blood, even a drop. And was it an omen?

She had to admit she wasn't doing well lately choosing clients. Nick Markwood fit the description of something Claire's mother, who always had her nose in a book, had said about romantic poet Lord Byron: *mad, bad and dangerous to know.*

"Darcy, thanks so much for bringing Lexi and me home, but you don't have to stay," Claire told her younger sister that afternoon when they got back from the hospital. "You've gone above and beyond the call of duty."

"Not duty, big sister. Love. *Love is the key*, like in that song our munchkins keep playing over and over. I swear, I'm going to scream if I hear it one more time."

They hugged—that is, Claire hugged her one-armed and Darcy encircled her very gently, before they sat at Claire's kitchen table. Darcy had driven her home with Lexi and her own four-year-old Jilly in the car. Lexi had cuddled up to Claire the whole way in the backseat, and she'd managed lots of hugs despite her sore arm.

It was a Saturday, and Darcy's husband, Steve, was at their house with their six-year-old son, Drew. The girls were in Claire's living room, playing the song "Let It Go" from Disney's *Frozen* over and over. *Frozen*, Claire thought, that's how she felt. Like her wounded arm was frozen to her side, like her thirty-two years of life were frozen and on hold. Like her feelings for Jace were frozen. She shuddered, remembering how horrible it had been when she used to lie awake and feel frozen for a few minutes, unable to move, helpless...

"But I'm telling you," Darcy went on, "that you are out of your everlovin' mind if you even hear out Superman Lawyer, man of steel, able to leap tall buildings in a single bound. You need your rest, not some new assignment gallivanting all over the state."

"I didn't say I'm taking him up on it. I only agreed to a chat, across the Trail at Lake Avalon. You know I can use the money from a new assignment, and I need to build the reputation and publicity for Clear

Path. I have big plans for it, not just to be the only Certified Fraud Examiner for consult or hire, but to have a staff."

Darcy rolled her eyes. She'd heard all that before. "One more warning," she said, then took a sip of the strong tea she'd fixed for the two of them. "I'm telling you, Nick Markwood's a ladies' man. He's not married, shows up in the society pages all the time with a string of different, beautiful women. Last week it was some 'Stomp in the Swamp' dance for an Everglades reclamation charity. Can't recall if that was in the newspaper or that glitzy mag *Naples Illustrated*."

"Everglades reclamation? Well, see? A lot of charities are worthwhile. Besides, he needs a high profile to be a rainmaker for his firm. But—what? Stop looking at me like that. You think this request for my help is a come-on? I hardly move in his circles. He has some friend who's in trouble, and he was impressed with how I handled the Sorento interviews, that's all."

Claire amazed herself to be defending Nick. No way was she admitting to Darcy that this assignment was not actually for his law firm, but for a sort of secret charity. Actually, didn't his dedication to such causes mean he was a nice guy after all? But she was too tired to argue that now.

"Okay, okay," Darcy said, looking hurt. She ran her fingers through her pixie-cut hair.

When Darcy got emotional, it had always seemed to Claire that her freckles popped out. Her hair had never been as red as Claire's, and her eyes were blue, but anyone could tell they were sisters.

"Listen," Claire told her, "I know I pay you next to nothing for child care, but I want to thank you again for all you've done for me and Queen Alexandra in there." She nodded toward the door to the living area. "You've been a second mother to her, and Jilly's like a sister. It should be the older sister taking care of the younger, but you've always been the steady one. You've stuck with me through—through everything."

"Well, with a hard-driving, hard-drinking traveling salesman father and our nearly unresponsive mother, we needed to hang together, that's all."

"It isn't all."

Darcy's lips crimped into a smile, and she crinkled her nose. Here came her make-light-of-their-sad-childhood routine when Claire had always wanted to psych it out. Darcy had majored in elementary education at Florida State while Claire had immersed herself in linguistics and psychology there.

"I mean," Darcy went on, "maybe you should just psychoanalyze me and be done with it. How many girls do you know who were named for someone's favorite *male* character in an English novel of manners, no less? At least she didn't name me *Mr.* Darcy. How did you ever escape with Claire?"

They held hands across the corner of the table. Darcy managed a smile, but Claire blinked back tears. "Remember, I got Claire from 'Clair de Lune'—Claire de Looney." They smiled at one of their old childhood jokes. "But I have to admit—" Claire went on as their daughters' song floated in again with both girls singing along "—I still prefer the Hans Christian Anderson story *The Snow Queen* to Disney's rendition of it in *Frozen*. What did she not read to us when we were growing up? At least we had that. You do remember that fairy tale is about two sisters who learn to stick together?"

Pieces of the lyrics floated in again, maybe the tenth time it had been played. The words of the song about the past being in the past and wanting to move forward, despite being unsettled in one's heart...

Maybe, Claire thought, as they rose and went to join their girls, that song that was driving them crazy was exactly what she needed to hear.

3

"Let's sit at the picnic table over there," Nick suggested as they got out of his black BMW at Sugden Park just across US 41 from where Claire lived. The traffic sounded muted here. It seemed like another world.

He carried a cooler and a tartan blanket, no less, when the temperature must be in the high eighties. She couldn't wait for the weather to break to the clear coolness of autumn days, but the oppressive humidity and the cloudy sky seemed appropriate somehow. She was sure she would—at least should—turn him down.

A warm Gulf breeze rippled the man-made lake that was set back a mile or so from the shore. The park service was giving kids waterskiing lessons today, and several small sailboats zigged and zagged across the surface. The screech of ospreys sailing overhead reminded her of the drone in the sky at the courthouse.

Then, high above the lake, she saw there was a drone, a white one, hard to see in the sun against the sky. She'd read those might be used to spray for mosquitoes, but surely over the Everglades, not in a populated locale like this. She scanned the area to see who might be controlling the drone. Maybe the man way down where the bike trail disappeared into the woods.

She watched Nick flap the blanket over the worn wooden surface of the picnic table. He took soft drinks—with plastic glasses and ice—and two plastic deli cartons out of the cooler. Plastic utensils, napkins, dark rolls and tiny tubs of butter. She saw everything was from Wynn's, a market uptown she loved but usually avoided because she'd walk out of there with a bill twice what she'd intended.

"Lobster salad," he said, sitting across from her with his back to the lake, when she was hoping he'd sit beside her so he didn't seem to be interrogating her. She was really sensitive about body language, and his said impatience and controlled aggression right now. Worse, since his back was to the sun, he took off his sunglasses and regarded her with those disturbing silver-gray eyes. "Hope lobster's okay."

"Great. I'd eat that even if I had no hands instead of just one that's working well. So how is the state of Florida involved in this St. Augustine situation, other than, if your friend is indicted, she'll go on trial there?"

"So you have been thinking about this case. Good sign."

"Maybe, but I'm not ready to sign up."

"Let's not do a contract per se, except for this."

He fished a piece of paper out of his shirt pocket, unfolded it and turned it toward her. He was eager now, in a hurry. And he had not answered her question.

She took off her sunglasses to read the paper better. It was not a contract but an offer letter, for two hundred dollars an hour for interviews! And fifty dollars for "general consultation" time! She'd never earned more than seventy-five dollars for an entire interview. It also offered a daily rate of three hundred dollars while in St. Augustine (St. Johns County) and someplace called Palatka (Putnam County) to be paid weekly to her account. Her stomach cartwheeled as she read on. If she helped his South Shores company prove that Jasmine Montgomery Stanton did not murder her mother, Francine Montgomery, there was a $10,000 bonus. He'd signed the paper and had it dated and notarized.

She just stared at the document at first, a forkful of lobster salad halfway to her mouth. She put the fork down and stared into his intense gaze. He moved across from her to block the sun from streaming into her eyes.

"This means a lot to you," she said, her voice almost a whisper. "You said she—this Jasmine—was a friend. Is that why?"

"It's not the only reason. Through South Shores, I usually take cases in which I believe a so-called suicide or accident is actually a murder. I don't want to sway what you'll find out but I don't think this woman would kill herself. She was influential in St. Johns County, owned Shadowlawn Hall, one of the largest pre-Civil War plantation houses in the area—not a working plantation anymore but a real historic and cultural treasure. It's been handed down in her family for generations. For financial reasons, she came to the difficult decision to either deed it to the State of Florida or auction it privately. But her daughter Jasmine disagreed with letting it go from the family, despite the financial crunch. I'm convinced Jasmine did not kill her mother, so someone else did. People who knew the deceased are the ones who need to be deposed—I mean, interviewed."

"And Jasmine herself, of course."

"Indirectly. She's been through hell with the authorities, and they still may indict her. She has a small staff and there is at least one other acquaintance who needs to be interviewed."

"Then let me start briefly with you, since you know her well enough to be quite assertive that Jasmine is innocent. She and her mother did have a disagreement on the fate of the property, which some could construe as a motive for murder."

"See, I knew you were good. But it isn't like that," he insisted, hunching forward. "She loved her mother. I've known her—both of them—for years. Francine was a friend of my father, which makes this case more important to me. He thought the world of both of them."

"I read your father started your law firm."

"True."

She'd thought a slight change of subject would calm him, but he seemed even more agitated. And she needed much more information than he seemed willing to share. He gripped his plastic fork so hard he snapped it in half. He sighed deeply, frowned and put the fork down.

"After founding the firm," he told her, "Dad got into some real estate investment problems that ruined his reputation, but this isn't about him." He narrowed his eyes. "So, have you been reading up on me like I have on you?"

"Not yet, but you're not exactly a private person around here."

"No, but I'm a deeply concerned person. Claire, I need your help on this. Maybe on other cases, too. I saw how damn good you are. Besides being a Certified Fraud Examiner, I see on your website you've trained to be a Forensic Document Examiner, too. I don't think any forgeries are involved with this case, but that could be important for the future."

The future, she thought. *We're already talking about a future?*

"You're strong," he went on, "but you can come off as gentle and nonthreatening. There's something about you people like and trust, but you're wily and clever in psyching out and piercing through their armor of lies. Let me ask you the same question I overheard a reporter ask you. Besides verb tense and body language, how *do* you psych people out?"

She nodded, on familiar ground now, even though she was well aware he'd shifted the conversation from himself. She took a bite of the lobster salad—delicious—though she wasn't tempted to take a second one right away because he was asking her about her passion. People. People who built walls the way her parents had, people who could help or hurt others and too often did the latter.

"To summarize six years of working my way through college with a double major in psych and English, here it is. When people are lying, they seldom refer to themselves and they tend to talk around direct action. They don't say, 'I unlocked the door,' but 'The door was left unlocked.' They speak evasively, try to answer a question with another question like, 'Why in the world would I kill my own brother?' They use you've-got-to-believe-me language with oaths or vows like 'I swear,' or 'God as my witness.' They either leave out details or talk too much, often off the subject. So in court, as you saw in the trial, explaining this as I testify makes me an expert witness—hopefully a credible one who can sway the jury."

"As I've seen close up and personal," he said. He nodded and rapped the table with his knuckles. "You should have gone to law school. And that psyching people out is the way I'm trying to learn to think. Maybe after this St. A case, you can do a workshop for my associates at the firm."

"I'd rather do that than go to St. Augustine, Nick, because I should stay home. Besides, my sister and doctor will have a fit if I go with this shot-up arm over three hundred miles away anytime soon. You said soon, right?"

"Are the terms suitable?" he countered, pointing at the paper still open before her.

"Oh, yes," she said. "And evasive people sometimes counter a question with another question."

"Touché," he said. "I need to know you're on board before I tell you everything. Some of this is privileged. But I should have said the offer includes room and board. We'll be staying at the Bayfront Hilton in St. A. It's a drive from Palatka and Shadowlawn, but we'll need our creature comforts. I'll drive you there, get you settled, help set up your interviews, introduce you to the right people, then be in and out."

"You're assuming I'm going with you."

"Aren't you? Jasmine needs your help. Shadow-lawn Estate does—I do."

"I'll need a doctor there to check my arm if it takes over a couple of days."

"No problem."

"Nick, there is a problem. It's leaving my daughter behind for a while, even though my sister's family is great to her. I need to know exactly how I'll get around if you're not there since I can't drive safely right now with one arm. I can dictate into a computer, but can't use a keyboard easily without two hands. In short, I'll need some sort of transportation and digital backup."

"Heck," he muttered.

"What? You didn't think of that?"

"No, Heck—Hector Munez, goes by Heck. He's my South Shores geek genius. I plan to set things up with you, run you around, but he'll be available to help you with anything digital and drive you if I'm not there for a while. I'll have you meet him before we head out tomorrow."

"Tomorrow? I couldn't!"

"Day after tomorrow at the latest. I'll make things work out for the best. You'll see."

The sun came out from the clouds and blazed brightness and heat on them. Their gazes snagged and held. *Mad, bad and dangerous to know...*

But shouldn't she tell him her other caveats? Not that she had trouble even dressing herself, couldn't so much as hook a bra, but she'd get around that some-how. He needed to know that, like some darned little kid, she needed her naps, that she had to get her sleep at night. She absolutely had to calibrate and balance her meds. She had hidden all that from Jace and, since he was gone so much—actually, was so self-centered—she had managed for a while. But all that had caused her downfall, the blowup between them. But this was just a business deal, not a life shared.

"I'll do my best to give you an answer soon," she heard herself promise him.

"Your best is all I'm asking."

At home while Lexi took the short afternoon nap Claire always insisted on—she watched her daughter like a hawk for early signs of anything—Claire forced herself to take her twenty-minute power nap, at least that's what she liked to call it. With a cup of p.m. coffee it perked her right up. Of course, she'd rather have dark chocolate, especially from Norman Love's shop up on the Tamiami Trail, but once she started on that, she couldn't stop. She might be narcoleptic, but she was also a chocolate-holic.

She played with Lexi for an hour, and yes, read to her as well, since that had been one good thing "She," which is often what she and Darcy called their mother, had done for them. Claire had a great American and English lit education before she even took English 101 her freshman year.

Today, when Darcy stopped by to take Lexi grocery shopping with her and Jilly, Claire called a cab to take her to Port Royal to give her condolences to Fred Myron's family. She'd phoned Fred's widow to be sure it was all right and had been told the family had already gathered in preparation for the funeral tomorrow. They were getting Fred's body back today from the Collier County ME, and then they'd be sitting *shiva* for a week.

At the Myron home with its backyard on a canal, everyone greeted her and commiserated. Repeatedly, she was asked if she knew why anyone would shoot at her, because "our Freddie had absolutely no enemies." Though she felt exhausted by the visit, she was glad she went; that is, until she started to leave, driven home by Fred's brother, because they wouldn't hear of her calling a cab again. A small group of reporters, some of whom she recognized from the courthouse, had assembled on the front lawn.

"We're not talking to them, not one word," Jerry, Fred's brother, muttered as he backed out of the driveway past their shouted questions. "I'd like to get poor Sarah away from them for a while. Those vultures keep circling, trying to prove poor Fred did something wrong when he was only standing up for the truth and the business he'd built up with his own hands. You going to get away so they don't bother you?"

"Maybe I should now that they know I'm out of the hospital," she said. "Yes, I guess I may get away for a while."

"Get some good rest. Put everything bad behind you, right? Forget the reporters and that lawyer that tried to rip you apart."

"I'm sure that's good advice." It was the only thing she could think of to say that wouldn't be a lie. She hadn't actually decided she was going to trust Nick Markwood yet. But she was going to do two things before she agreed to go north with him. First, she would research him to death—so to speak. Without talking to him or his contacts directly, she was going to do an online study of him. Then she was going to risk telling him the real reason she was afraid to accept his offer, and hope that he would be the one to back out of the deal.

Jace never liked riding in the so-called jump seat that was available to pilots. Hard to see out the windows. Rode backwards. Could hear the flight attendants chatting when they were in the galley. But worse, he was close to the cockpit but not in it, so he felt completely out of control. And he hated that.

He tried to doze but he kept replaying the last time he'd been with Claire, seven weeks ago, when he'd flown into Miami and rented a car there to go see Lexi. But that had meant seeing Claire, too. She'd changed since their divorce. She'd always been kind of quiet, almost private, probably because of all she was hiding—she and that sister clone, Darcy. Man, Claire had put one over on him, however quick their courtship had been. If he hadn't been flying so much, he would have sniffed it out earlier.

"Narcolepsy with mild cataplexy!" he'd exploded a little over a year ago when she'd finally come clean with him, after he found her stash of pills and that gross-looking liquid stuff she took at bedtime. "No wonder you sleep like a rock! No wonder you want sex in the daytime but not at night like a normal woman! I thought it was me!"

"It isn't you, except I know you can't stand weakness, can't stand anyone being sick. You're a driven perfectionist, Jace, and I'm not perfect."

"Oh, try to blame me for your lies and hiding things. You hiding anything else—anyone?"

"Of course not. Can you keep your voice down? I don't want Lexi to hear us."

"Oh, yeah, hear her mother never trusted or loved her father enough to come clean about—about this sleeping sickness and getting paralyzed at times!"

"These pills you're freaking out over keep me from falling asleep or getting paralyzed at times. I'm dealing with my problem. I'm on an even keel."

"You could have gone to sleep when Lexi was in the tub or the pool! You could have nodded off and dropped her."

"I told you, it's all under control."

"Well, hell, I'm not. You may not have lied to me, 'cause I didn't ask, but we've been living a lie! Is it too much to ask the person who's supposed to be closest to me not to lie?"

"I knew it would upset you and drive you away. I didn't want that. Look, Jace, our romance and eloping happened so fast, and you're gone so much. I know this is about me, but I found a note to you from someone named Ginger on hotel stationery from Singapore in the pocket of a shirt I laundered, so don't lecture me on not telling everything. It was a come-to-my-room note. I know you're gone a lot but—"

He'd slammed out of their condo. He'd divorced her soon after, and she hadn't contested it, a Marital Settlement Agreement with a Parenting Plan, the state of Florida called it. Looking back, he supposed they'd done it just as hastily and recklessly as they'd decided to get married.

But the kick in the gut was that he still felt for Claire, even after all of that. Too often, even now, he recalled their sunset dinners on the beach, how they would dance in the dark in their own living room. How insanely happy they were when she told him she was pregnant and the first time he saw her holding Lexi. How Claire felt curled up against him, or under him...

The airplane intercom kicked on. The voice of Don Thomas, a pilot he'd flown with many times, interrupted his agonizing: "Good afternoon. We're beginning our descent into the Los Angeles area. Local arrival time should be 2:14 p.m. with a temperature of eighty-four degrees, cloudy with a light northwest wind. Flight attendants, please prepare the cabin for landing. Welcome to or back to the United States."

Someone in the plane actually clapped. An attendant began announcements about tray tables, seat backs and turning off electronic devices. *Yeah,* he thought, *welcome back to the United States,* but he was going to soon head out on yet another flight, to a state far from California, to see Lexi, of course, but also to see the woman he couldn't get out of his head and his heart.

Frustrated she had to move so slowly, typing on the keyboard with one hand, Claire had switched to her smartphone to find websites and articles on a variety of subjects: Nick's law firm; Francine Montgomery; Jasmine Montgomery Stanton; Palatka, Florida; on and on. There wasn't much about Shadowlawn besides brief mentions of it. Kingsley Plantation near Jacksonville, rather than the little town of Palatka, got all the publicity, but then it was already open to the public and evidently thriving. Pressed for time, Claire gave everything a mere skim read.

She searched references to Nicholas Markwood, Jr., but she had not found one hint about his under-the-radar company he'd called South Shores.

Still, she could patch together why such an entity probably existed. Nick's father, Nicholas Markwood, Sr., had committed suicide when Nick was ten, evidently over a bad land development deal that had swept him into debt and ruined his reputation and the reputation of his law firm, which Nick had resurrected later. Nick Markwood, the father, had left investors holding the bag for his bad deals, though he'd claimed he'd been duped. His world—and, no doubt, young Nick's—had collapsed.

Nick was an only child who had been born with a silver spoon in his mouth that was evidently, she assumed, tarnished by the scandal and his notorious father with the same name. But he had put himself through the University of Miami undergrad and law school on scholarships and hard work, even bought his mother a property in Naples before she died, quite young, of cancer. He lived in that same house in the Aqualane Shores area of Naples when Claire had imagined he at least owned a place in tony Port Royal or Quail Creek West. She looked up a photo of his house on Google. It wasn't pretentious or even very big, though it was on a canal. And the boat moored behind it was hardly a yacht, more like a fishing boat with an inboard motor.

So—surprises all around about Nick. Still, she was going to use her last ploy to see if he would really trust her to take the case he offered and to let her handle it her way, not his. No coddling Jasmine Montgomery Stanton just because Nick wanted that. Shadowlawn Plantation and the generations of women who had run it, including most recently Francine Montgomery, intrigued her. Nick intrigued her. And if he accepted her restrictions and rules when she told him the truth about herself that she'd shared with few others in the past twenty years—only Jace, who didn't understand, and a kind nurse, who did—she'd take Nick's South Shores case.

4

Nick could not believe he was paying to get into the Naples Zoo. He hadn't been here for years, not since it was small and called Jungle Larry's and he used to spend time here with his dad. After he lost his father, he couldn't bear to come back. But he hadn't protested when Claire had told him that, if she was leaving with him tomorrow, she was spending this day with her daughter, niece and sister, doing something special for her child—bringing her here.

He'd left his suit coat and tie in the car and rolled up his sleeves, but he still felt warm, overdressed and out-of-it with this casual crowd. Running shoes and flip-flops were the order of the day, which made him feel like these Italian leather loafers were screaming, "Look at me!" The crowd was heavy with grandparents doting on kids, especially in the playground area called the Cub Corral. It was a big, much improved zoo over Jungle Larry's, that was for sure. Hell, this whole mess with Jasmine—and now Claire—was turning into a zoo anyway.

He followed the signs toward the Primate Expedition Cruise where Claire had said she'd meet him. She had to tell him something important, and if that was okay with him, she'd said she'd sign on the dotted line and leave with him tomorrow morning. He admitted to himself that he could have employed any of the three what he privately called psych-out-the-bad-guys consults the firm had used but he wanted Claire. He supposed, if he was honest with himself, he wanted her in more ways than one.

He took the right-hand path that skirted Alligator Bay. Across the small stretch of water, zoo workers were feeding the alligators. The whole thing reminded him of how his father's former friend, a man he should not have trusted, had turned into a carnivorous beast. The man he'd grown up calling Uncle Clay had turned out to be a monster. Nick had been only ten, but those memories still haunted him.

Haunted: that reminded him that he'd better tell Claire about the ghosts that supposedly inhabited Shadowlawn before he took her there. He'd never seen them, but Francine and Jasmine had sworn they existed. Supposedly, the one who had thrown herself from the balcony only appeared to women. Francine had joked that would be a big draw if the plantation was opened to the paying public: "If you have ghosts, tourists will come."

He scanned the area near the cruise dock where people were waiting for the boat to leave. Screeches of monkeys pierced the sound of children's chatter. Claire had a sun visor on, but her red hair shone like a beacon. She spotted him, too, where she was waiting in line with her little group. She said something to the other redhead, obviously her sister, and came over, holding her little girl's hand.

The child was cute with blond hair barely tinged with red. "Nick, I'd like you to meet Alexandra, whom we call Lexi."

He smiled at Claire and squatted to get to Lexi's height. "Are you having fun with your mom today?"

"Lots. We're going to see everything here, but I don't like the snakes. Their place here is called Snakes Alive. My cousin Drew threw one at Jilly and me in the backyard. He's in school today—first grade."

"Drew should not have thrown the snake. You know, if you pretend you're not scared of them, maybe tell Drew you really liked seeing them at the zoo, he won't do that again. He probably just likes to scare girls. Alexandra is a pretty name. There was a Queen Alexandra once."

"Well, Mommy said so, but I'd rather be a princess. You know, like Cinderella, Snow White, Ariel, Belle, Pocahontas and Jasmine."

At that last name, he stood. He had business to attend to here. "She's a walking Disney encyclopedia," Claire put in. For the first time, he realized Claire was fairly tall at about five-ten. At six foot two, he was used to towering over women.

"And she's bright, like her mother," he said. "Your sister's gesturing. I think the line to get on the boat is moving."

"I'll get Lexi to her and be right back. We can talk while they take the little cruise," Claire said and ran, holding Lexi's hand, back to deliver her to her sister, who kept looking their way.

He snagged a bench, and Claire came right back.

"I don't know what I'd do without Darcy—even when we were small," she told him and sat on the bench, angled toward him. He turned to her. The hot breeze ruffled her blue sundress above her knees and she smoothed it down. A moment of silence passed while they just looked at each other. He almost tilted toward her, as if he were drawn to a magnet.

"Shoot," he said. "Well, I shouldn't have put it like that," he added with a glance at her arm. "By the way, I have a doctor lined up in St. A who can check the wound in three days, which is what you said you'd planned to do here."

"Thank you. Nick, I am intrigued by your offer. I love the challenge of it, and I'm sure the heritage treasure, as you called it, of Shadowlawn, is worth saving—as is your friend Jasmine, if she's innocent. But I have to level with you about something first, something you may consider a deal breaker."

She actually looked as if she were going to cry. This must be serious. His stomach knotted. "I checked your CFA credentials, and they're fine," he tried to assure her.

"It isn't that." She took off her dark sunglasses and looked squarely at him. "I just need to tell you that, since I was thirteen, I've had what is a fairly rare but demanding disease, though I have it under control with meds and watchful behavior."

"The disease is?" he prompted when she seemed to hesitate.

"Do you know what narcolepsy is—with mild cataplexy, actually?"

He sat up straighter. "Exhaustion? Dozing off? No, I don't know the catalepsy part."

"Cata*plexy*. Yes, dozing off big-time with narcolepsy. Those of us afflicted with it prefer to call ourselves PWNs—Persons With Narcolepsy—rather than narcoleptics. That sounds too much like alcoholics, and *narcs* reminds people of narcotics. But yes, being exhausted continually for no apparent, normal reason. Cataplexy, which often strikes a PWN, is a brief, sudden immobility or paralysis that can occur on waking or dozing off—or when one's emotions get too strong, so I have to watch that—involvements with that, sudden rushes of feelings…"

Her voice kept trailing off, her gaze darting away. It surprised him, for she usually spoke well and seemed so self-confident. But again, their gazes locked and held. Could she read his mind that he felt a rush of feelings for her, right now, and it wasn't just that he'd been afraid when she was shot. Watching her in court had almost done him in, and not just because she was ripping his defense of Sorento apart bit by bit. But despite all that—and this—he had the feeling he could trust her. He'd seen her in action.

"Okay," he said, "but it is, as you said, all under control with your meds? I watched you in court for four days—no apparent problems."

"Strong meds, pills and a liquid I take at night keep me going. I need one or two brief naps and regular sleep, as well as stimulants like caffeine from coffee or chocolate. No alcohol, or it can mess me up. I need to be disciplined. Another problem, one I've coped with well, is hallucinations, nightmares. When I was young—before this was diagnosed—I actually thought I was haunted by ghosts, by things I'd see and feel that weren't there. I seldom have these waking nightmares now. I tell almost no one all this, but I thought—considering your trust and investment in me—that you should know."

He reached for her good hand. She held his. She was trembling. Well, he thought, all this complicated things, and he for sure wasn't going to tell her about the Shadowlawn ghosts right now like he'd intended. But she'd done a great job with the Sorento case—and she'd leveled with him about this. He wouldn't worry she'd hold other things back, however bad the going got.

"So," he said, still holding her hand, "we can shake on it." They did. She managed a firm shake and even a tight little smile. "And if you need some sleep, I won't think it's your work or my company that's boring."

"Hardly that," she blurted, obviously relieved he was still all in. She actually blushed. "Nick, just one more thing. Well—when my mother used to say that, it was always time for a double whammy," she admitted.

"Go on," he prompted.

"It's just that—well, I know you're used to being a senior partner, and you're the boss here. But I will need to do these interviews my way, with my expertise and knowledge."

"Agreed."

"But that means not giving someone a pass just because you have your own theories or prejudices—your favorites, or maybe someone you owe a favor to. I'll need access to Jasmine, whether you think she's guilty or not, for example."

He sat up a bit straighter. "Sure, I get that. I'd want that."

"Without pressure from you, no matter what I find. I realize you must be tied to her emotionally some-how—"

"Was."

"All right, was. But I can't do my job unless it can be mine—then I'll report to you, of course."

A strong woman, delicate appearance or rare dis-eases be damned, he thought. But that was what he wanted, wasn't it?

"So, let's make some plans," he told her. Realiz-ing he still held her hand, and much too hard, he let go. She put her sunglasses back on, but not before he saw her blink tears off her long lashes. He cleared his throat and tore his gaze away, as if he were just scan-ning the area. He noted a small, white drone over-head, probably one taking pictures for the zoo to sell later. What he used to call monkey island was an ap-propriate place to be, with the way this woman scram-bled his emotions. She really got to him on a personal level when this should be all business.

"Then, fine," she said. "I'm in. Tell me what time you and your man Heck will pick me up tomorrow."

"Right. He'll drive the second car, and I'll brief you on the people you'll interview—the ones I know, at least, though you may want to do others. Nine a.m., okay?"

"I'll be ready."

But she wasn't ready for who rang her doorbell at seven that evening. She'd gotten Lexi, whose head was nodding from exhaustion, bathed and settled down for bed and, since it was easier to have as-sistance undressing and dressing, she'd taken her shower, too, so Lexi could help her into her cotton nightgown and robe. They were going to have cookies and milk and cuddle, and then Claire had to finish packing for—for how long?

But Lexi heard a car door, looked out the window and went berserk, screaming. "Daddy! It's Daddy! Daddy's here!"

And sure enough, there was Jace at their front door.

Furious with him for getting Lexi riled by suddenly showing up, Claire went to the door where the child was already unlocking the knob and bolt. The safety chain snagged until Claire closed the door and slid it free.

Lexi hurled herself at Jace, and he picked her up and walked in. "Glad I caught you," he told Claire, bouncing Lexi up and down. "How's the arm? I figured you could use some help for a couple days. They catch the idiot who shot at you yet?"

That quieted Lexi. "Did someone mean to shoot you, Mommy? Aunt Darcy said it was an accident."

"It *was* an accident," she said, glaring at Jace who mouthed, *Oops!* "No one meant to hurt me. Jace, I wish you had called. As you can see, we're just settling down, and I have a business trip tomorrow."

He frowned at her and started to dig small gifts for Lexi out of his pockets as they went into the living area. He hadn't shaved. Golden stubble dusted his lean cheeks and half-moon shadows hung under his blue eyes. His shirt and pants were mussed, and he was missing his co-pilot suit coat, but he still somehow looked put together, his short hair cut perfectly to frame his broad face. He always had looked that way, especially in the navy pilot uniform he'd worn before she knew him, the picture Lexi kept on her dresser because of "Daddy's pretty pins and ribbons on his coat."

She stared at him now, the perfect physical specimen. How many times had she and Jace just fallen into bed together when he'd returned from a flight? How many times had she forced herself awake to wait for or respond to him, so he wouldn't know she was about on par with the walking dead? She'd even fallen asleep under him once in the throes of passion, slumped like a dead doll, he'd said, and he'd patted her cheeks to wake her up. Sexual desire, just like any other intense emotion, used to set her off before these newly calibrated meds, but she'd never tell him she was better now. He'd relinquished his right to know anything intimate about her.

She left the two of them together and went down the hall to pack for a half hour while he regaled their daughter with tales of foreign places, and she chattered on to him about the zoo and starting preschool after the Christmas holidays, about wishing she'd lose her teeth and get some big ones and how Drew scared her and Jilly with a snake. Claire kept the door to her room open, though, of course, she trusted him not to fill her head too full of travel temptations. But it was sure going to be a battle to get the child settled down in bed tonight when Claire, too, needed her rest—right now.

But Jace knew that. Surely, she could get him to leave soon. Wishing again she could get dressed without help, because she would have changed out of her nightgown and robe, she went back in to join them.

"I forgot, Mommy, you need to go to bed."

"Yes, but Daddy's leaving soon. How long a leave this time, Jace?"

"Because of what happened to you, I took a week off. You said you're leaving on a business trip? With that arm? Like—to where?"

"St. Augustine for a few days on assignment."

Lexi said, "With Mr. Nick, who is very nice. He said if I pretended to like snakes, Drew wouldn't try to scare me again."

Jace's brows rose. His eyes and lips narrowed. "You're taking out-of-town assignments now, Claire?"

"This one. Very worthwhile in more ways than one. If you'd like to tuck Lexi in, that's fine."

"You're right, it is," he groused and stood to take Lexi's hand and lead her toward the hall.

But Lexi pulled away from him and came back to hug Claire. "You're the best mommy ever."

"And you are my best and only sweetheart." Claire finished their usual good-night with a kiss, despite Jace's scowl behind Lexi's back. Who did he think he was, coming back like this and judging her, trying to take over?

At least, she thought, he got the hint not to take long with Lexi. He came back out, and Claire stood so he wouldn't sit and try to make himself comfortable as he had before when he'd dropped in.

"I'll be seeing a lot of her this week," he said, his hand on the front door knob.

"That's great. She'll be staying with Darcy, so please clear times with her. If you spoil her as usual, please don't let her eat all the junk food she wants."

"So what's this St. Augustine gig?"

"I'll be interviewing people about cause of death."

"What you used to call murdercide?"

"Evidently."

"Who's Mr. Nick? He's obviously met Lexi."

"Nick Markwood, a lawyer, my client. I had an interview with him today at the zoo, because I wanted to spend the day with her."

"Next assignment New York City? Paris? Rangoon? Marrakech?"

"You know, that sounds like a list of places you'd rather fly out of than Ft. Lauderdale or Miami, so you could see your daughter more. Look, Jace, sorry to say, this is none of your concern. I'm building Clear Path, this is a good assignment, and you're not involved."

"But you just said, 'sorry to say,' Ms. Word Maven. So, are you sorry I'm not involved anymore?"

"Don't be ridiculous," she blurted. But had he caught her there? No, that wasn't what she'd meant. But, darn the man, he still had that swagger, that I-own-this-room attitude, that almost swashbuckling aura that had first attracted her.

"Good night, Jace. And, as I've said before, now that you have really, permanently 'left the building,' please call before you just appear next time with gifts like—like an off-season Santa Claus or the Ghost of Christmas Past."

He opened the door, then turned back and put one hand on the frame, almost as if he were blocking her in her own condo.

"I'll see you soon," he said. "One place or the other. One way or the other."

She couldn't decide if that sounded like a promise or a threat.

5

A light rain glazed the pavement as Darcy's car pulled away. Claire waved goodbye to Lexi until it disappeared. She'd filled Darcy in on Jace's *abracadabra* appearance, but Darcy was used to that, too. Feeling suddenly unsure and alone, Claire was still standing outside under the overhang when Nick pulled into the driveway and another car came right up behind—a black SUV—evidently driven by South Shores' tech expert, Hector Munez, alias Heck.

The two of them stepped inside where Claire had her luggage ready. Nick made the introductions. Heck was young—maybe midtwenties, but then, weren't all cyber gurus young? He was short and wiry with slicked, coal-black hair, trimmed beard and dark eyes under thick brows. He spoke with a slight Latino accent. He seemed a little jumpy, probably nervous like her to be heading out on an important assignment.

"I hear I might be a chauffeur, too," Heck told her with a broad smile.

"And, perhaps a second pair of ears and recorder in interview sessions," she told him. "It's important I watch as well as listen. Besides, I can't type with one hand, and there are lots of legal drawbacks if I record every word, chain of custody and all that. I have to admit you'd be a lot less threatening than Attorney Markwood sitting there, glaring."

"But I can glare with the best of them!" Heck said and elbowed Nick. Claire saw under the TECH-TOCK T-shirt he wore a thick gold chain to match his earring, which made her remember she hadn't worn hers.

Nick shook his head and told Heck, "Your suddenly sitting in on interviews, my man, is probably just the first of many surprises from our new partner. But she's the one calling the shots—on that, at least."

"You will get used to my name," Heck told her, while tossing his car keys from one hand to the other. "It always sounds like mild cursing, yes? But where you been, boss?" he said and hit Nick's shoulder lightly with his fist. "Ladies—they all like that, full of surprise—surprise!"

Heck asked for her cell phone and punched his and Nick's regular and his emergency numbers and email address into her phone logs in case she needed them, then hefted her single big suitcase and put it in the trunk of Nick's car. With a wave, he got in his own vehicle and backed out, windshield wipers spitting rain.

Claire got it: they were in a hurry. Nick carried her laptop bag and she grabbed her purse and slung it over her good shoulder. While Nick waited in the covered entryway, she locked up, relieved that Jace hadn't shown up at the last minute. She'd half expected him to. The first assignment she took after their split, he'd actually followed her to be sure she was safe when she drove into an area he didn't like.

"I told Heck he doesn't have to follow us, since he's a fast driver," Nick said with a nod at the departing SUV. She saw the back was covered with bumper stickers but they were too far off to read. "*Too* fast, so if he runs you around, keep an eye on him," he added. "South Shores doesn't need his speeding fines rolling in."

"And where does South Shores billing roll in to?" she asked as he held the car door for her and she ducked in out of the rain.

He closed her door, hurried around and got in. "I'll explain all that. We've got a long drive, and I brought a lot of background information for you to look over so we can hit the ground running. By the way, Heck is staying in a B and B in St. A, because he hates big hotels. I think it's the fact his grandfather used to own a small hotel in Havana which Castro took over in *la revolution*, and he really loved the old man. He died just recently in Miami."

As they left Naples and headed north on I-75, Nick kept his word, not about explaining South Shores, but about briefing her on everything else. "Not a good way to start a long drive," he admitted as they headed into more rain, and he raised his voice over the thwack-thwack of the windshield wipers. "So, anyway, I think you should look at the Putnam County ME's autopsy report on Francine first. You have everything you need to read by?"

"I'm fine. Don't need magnifying glasses quite yet in my dotage."

He smiled at her, and his gaze seemed to take her all in for a split second before he looked back at the road. "Nope," he said. "I think you've got a few good years left in you. Look in the top folder in the accordion file by your feet."

Annoyed that that split-second look from him scrambled her brain, she pulled the thick report out one-handed. She'd seen such before and was familiar with the layout. *Francine Anne Montgomery, age 61, female, Caucasian...* Claire skimmed to the estimated time of death. Her daughter Jasmine Stanton (nee Montgomery), age 41, had discovered her unresponsive at 8:04 p.m. exactly one month ago today, sprawled on her bedroom floor near the French doors to the balcony on the second floor of Shadowlawn Hall overlooking the St. Johns River near Palatka, Florida. Daughter called 911, and the squad pronounced Francine Montgomery deceased at 8:45 p.m. Date and time of the autopsy were listed with the attached, handwritten note that "The deceased's daughter Jasmine Stanton insisted her mother must have died of a drug overdose and did not want Francine 'to be dissected like a frog.' Daughter was distraught and belligerent."

"Not only poor Francine, but poor Jasmine," Claire said.

"Yeah. Losing her mother, finding her mother..." His voice trailed off. For one second his deep voice snagged before he went on, "Then being investigated for her possible murder. If we can turn something up fast, it may keep her from being indicted. Did you get to the forensic findings yet?"

"I am now. External Examination. No needle marks, no unexplained scars or bruising."

Claire flipped pages one-handed, balancing the papers on her knees. *Internal Examination.* "Stomach contents, food and beta-blocker drug, all listed.

Death from cardiac arrhythmia," she read aloud. "But it says here that leaves no autopsy evidence, so why did the ME put that down?"

"His best guess at first. She was on Propranolol. Ever hear of it?"

"Actually, I have," she said, looking up at him. "It can calm panic attacks or anxiety syndrome. And, yes—it lowers blood pressure and heart rate, so you have to be careful with it. I only know about it because a friend who does amateur theater in Naples uses it to calm her stage fright. But it says here it didn't show up on tox reports."

"Not the first one. Keep reading. Propranolol has to be screened for specifically and, knowing Francine has been prescribed it, the ME ran another test and found it. Lots. Too much. Serious overdose. Otherwise her death could have been declared a heart attack or cardiac arrhythmia, and we wouldn't be going through all this."

"Which—if she was murdered—the killer could have been banking on." She kept skimming the lines of print. "So the question is, did she accidentally overdose—or intentionally—or did someone help her to overdose? Someone who knew the power and danger of this panic attack drug."

"That's it. And because Jasmine happened to find her, and they had rather publicly disagreed on whether the mansion and estate should go in trust to the state, be sold or be kept in the family…"

"Jasmine's their number one suspect, but they can't prove it."

"They're working on it, though. And now you've

got the case. I won't say this again or try to push you on it, but I'm telling you, Jasmine's not a murderer."

"You've evidently known her for a long time and well. Maybe I should interview you first."

"If I can help—be a character witness, whatever. But I knew Jasmine best years ago. My father's ties to Francine, not Jasmine, go even further back. He and Francine were romantically involved before he married my mother."

"You said earlier you aren't emotionally tied to Jasmine now."

He cleared his throat, glanced back out his side window, signaled and did a lane change. She saw the sign ahead to I-4 toward Orlando that would take them across the state to the other coast.

"The fairest thing to say is I'm involved with proving her innocence. I still care for her deeply. But not romantically—free as a bird."

Claire recalled how Darcy had said he was a ladies' man. He was avoiding her question again. She'd told him that was one way people avoided the truth, so was he testing her tenacity? She had to admit she didn't really know him, except he seemed a sort of knight in shining armor to want to help Jasmine, evidently others, too, through his shadowy South Shores company. If she didn't need another quick nap, she'd question him again on that, but there would be time enough. Riding in a car always made her nod off, so if she was the one driving, she prepped herself with stimulants—not only coffee, but her favorite, hand-made-in-Naples dark chocolates.

She skimmed the death certificate itself. *Mode of death: cardiac arrest from cardiac arrhythmia.*

Cause of death, overdose of beta-blocker Propranolol. But under *Manner of Death* where the boxes to be checked were *natural, homicide, suicide* and *accident* was written, *UNDER INVESTIGATION.*

As they left the series of Disney World exits behind and passed the tall buildings of downtown Orlando, Nick stole quick glances to watch Claire sleep. He'd done a lot of fast reading last night on narcolepsy and cataplexy. A weird and dangerous disease, but she obviously coped well with it. And with being a single mom and starting her Clear Path consulting firm. He knew how hard it was to get something off the ground from when he fought like hell to resurrect his father's tarnished law firm.

Claire Britten was innocent-looking, almost angelic, as she slept. Her trust in him moved him deeply. He prayed he would not betray it. She'd shared with him about her Achilles' heel, so should he tell her about his? That he was hiding one of the real purposes of South Shores, something that was a risk for him. Hopefully, not for her.

One of the secrets his dad had hidden from most people was that he loved writing poetry. Didn't fit with the image of hard-hitting attorney-at-law. The so-called suicide note left beside his hand holding the gun had one line which read, *I will be safe on those South Shores forever more.*

No way his dad had shot himself, however bad it looked, despite that poetic touch in the note! If it was the last thing Nick ever did, he'd prove it and nail who killed him. He knew who that was, or thought he did. Trouble was, Nick knew he, too, was being stalked.

But by his dad's killer or by someone else he had let down? He had enemies. Most criminal lawyers did.

Claire stirred so suddenly he wondered for a second if he'd said that out loud. He shot another fast glance at her. Waking, she looked dazed, upset, maybe surprised she was here with him in a rain-coated car. Was that look of dismay she quickly hid part of being between the worlds of sleep and wakefulness? He'd read that PWNs sometimes had terrifying waking nightmares.

"Still raining, I see," she said, shifting her hips in her seat. She arched her back and stretched her good arm.

He shifted in his seat, too, and cleared his throat. "Letting up a little."

"I warned you about my naps. That beef sandwich hit the spot. Lexi would have a fit if she knew we were that close to Disney and didn't visit the Magic Kingdom."

"Yeah, well, when you see Shadowlawn, that will be enough magic kingdom for now."

For a few minutes, they talked easily about everything and nothing, though he knew they should be back on track about the interviews she would have. Still, she'd been touchy about choosing those herself. He should have known she was tenacious, because she suddenly asked him in the midst of talk about their *alma maters*: "So at the University of Miami—is that where you met Jasmine?"

So, no more skirting around that, he thought. Actually, he didn't trust lawyers who had a personal stake in a case, and here he was, with exactly that.

"That's where and when I dated her," he explained.

"We discovered our parents' past connection by accident—that her mother and my father had once been in love but had broken up. She figured it out when her mother met me, and wasn't too pleased Jasmine and I were a couple."

"Nothing like a bolt-from-the-blue coincidence—though I've learned chance meets often aren't. Did you two ever figure out why they didn't end up together?"

"No, but as for Jasmine and me, her mother seemed like a tyrant back then, raising her alone, and the scholarship boy didn't fit in until later when I'd made good—then too late because Jasmine was married. It was hard to forgive Francine about that for a while, but I didn't want to marry an heiress and move to north Florida anyway. All the Montgomery women from way back ran the roost and Shadowlawn. I mean from *way* back. They seemed to devour their men after they mated, like a male gator tried to if it got too near its hatchlings and, hopefully, was run off by the female. By the way, I have a small pamphlet Francine put together on the history of Shadowlawn in that packet with the other information—interesting reading for later."

"Great, because that's one thing I couldn't research yesterday. I found info on a place called Kingsley Plantation but not Shadowlawn. And I can sympathize with Francine being overly protective of her only child and a daughter."

Curious, she paged through the pamphlet. It included a family tree. The Montgomerys were a matriarchal family with the men dying young of disease or in wars, including the Civil War. Right after the

Civil War, one man had met his death suddenly and violently, but it didn't say how.

"Wow," she said. "My actor friend Liz is always looking for a plot for a play. Couldn't do much better than this. What interesting facts if Shadowlawn would become a state site."

"Which Jasmine doesn't want. Keep that in mind."

She stretched and put the book aside. "The rain is letting up a little, isn't it? Look at that large lake off to the right. I'll bet this view is great on a sunny day."

"That's Lake Monroe on the Volusia-Seminole County line near Sanford, the little town that made national headlines in 2012. Remember the Trayvon Martin shooting by George Zimmerman, who called himself a neighborhood watch coordinator?"

"I do. And Zimmerman got off."

"The seventeen-year-old was wearing a hoodie and looked suspicious. I always tell myself looks aren't everything, but I know you read body language and that was a part of the case, too—witnesses were important. Anyway, we'll soon pass over part of the lake on this elevated bridge, but I don't know how much you'll glimpse of the lake or Sanford in this weather."

"So you've driven this stretch a lot."

"Lately, yes. About two years ago, Francine hired me as a backup lawyer for the estate, so I've been back and forth. She still retains her longtime family lawyer who did her will, too, but he's quite elderly and has been ill, so I'm slowly taking over. I can't see hiring a plane when I can drive it in half a day. Look, Claire, I don't want to alarm you, but I swear the white car behind us has been following us and he's driving too damn close. No—don't turn around.

Just look in your side rearview mirror. Speaking of hoodies, it seems the driver's wearing one, but it's a warm day, and in a car…"

"I wish Heck had followed us. Want me to call him, see how far ahead he is, if you really think—"

"Wait. Maybe I'm wrong. The guy is going to pass us, I think. Must have been my imagination about some kind of nut or road rage. But— What the hell!"

They were on the outside lane on the elevated bridge over the water. The white car came abreast of them and swerved close. Nick jerked the wheel, moved them nearer to the edge. The barrier between them and a fall was barely door-handle high.

"Nick! Nick, look at him—the driver!" Claire cried and sucked in a ragged breath. "Am I—am I seeing that?"

Nick twisted his neck for an instant. Within a dark hoodie—no, a black shroud—was the pale, elongated and contorted face of a demon from an old horror movie. Claire screamed.

If that fiend face shoved them any farther, they were going off the edge.

6

Instead of trying to outrun the car or slam into it, Nick glanced behind and hit the brakes. *Drop back! Get the idiot's rear license plate...*

But the other vehicle dropped back even slower, moved over, hid behind another vehicle—a big UPS truck, which blew the horn at the shifting confusion. Nick swore under his breath and accelerated. Claire craned around to try to see the white car in the spew of water from their car and the truck.

"I don't see it now," she said, her voice shaking. "Should I call 9-1-1 or the highway patrol number?"

"I can't block a lane or go back. Maybe he'll get off at the next exit. And what would we say? There's some nut who thinks it's Halloween over a month early, some damned kid, and, by the way, we don't have his license plate, not even sure of the make of the white car. Or someone's en route to an audition for a slasher movie like that old one, can't think of its name."

"It—it reminded me of that painting. I can't think of its name, either. Actually, it brings back some of the cataplexic nightmares I used to have where I thought I saw dead people stalking me, leaning over me. Do you think it's some sort of warning to us?"

"I think it's some SOB jerk who just happened to choose us—and probably some others here where it's elevated and scary. I'm not stopping, but I'll contact the highway patrol later to report it and see if anyone else saw the same thing."

He shook his head and flexed his hands on the wheel. "Maybe we've both fallen asleep together and had a bad dream," he tried to joke, but it came out flat.

"You okay?" he asked. "I still can't believe that happened."

"More or less okay. You know, a lot of places are now giving ghost tours. I read St. Augustine is. Maybe he was loose from one of those—or driving home from some Disney haunted-house job and he thinks it's funny to freak people out."

He could tell she, too, was trying to make light of it. He appreciated the fact she was made of pretty stern stuff, so now or never.

"In the autopsy report," he said, wishing his pounding heart would calm down, "you noticed Francine was found on her bedroom floor near the French doors that opened onto the balcony. Actually, it's a wide gallery that goes around all four sides of the mansion on the second floor."

"Yes. I thought that was an interesting, very specific detail."

"I think the ME included it for a reason. I was going to tell you later, but considering what happened, I'd better mention that Shadowlawn is supposed to be haunted—but not by some moron in a car. One of

Francine's ancestors threw herself off the gallery to her death from those French doors."

"Oh, that's awful. Then there's a history of suicide in the family! And that woman supposedly haunts the place? People have seen her ghost?"

"Both Francine and Jasmine say they have. There's a second one—ghost—supposedly on the premises, one whose story is evidently unrelated. Some kind of overseer was hanged from one of the huge live oaks there on the front lawn, evidently lynched for murdering the owner after the Civil War, maybe late 1800s. When you interview some of the house staff— well, they'll bring it up. It's in that history book of the house, too."

"I saw the mention of an early, violent death, but it didn't say much else. I really don't believe in psychic phenomena. As I told you, once I got over thinking I saw dead people and learned it was just my meds and my disease, I was so relieved. Is there a possibility that Francine or Jasmine are unstable or taking some other kind of meds that could make them delusional?"

"If so, their female ancestors and estate workers were, too. Jasmine said once that only the women in the family see the woman on the balcony. The other ghost supposedly wanders the grounds and riverbank at night and has been seen by at least one of the men you'll interview—Gates. Be sure to ask about that when you talk to him. And the artist Win Jackson."

She dug out the interviewee list. She'd merely skimmed it because it was only names and titles. "By the artist, you mean the photographer, Dr. Winston Jackson, PhD."

"Right. His photos are works of art. Wait until you see them."

"And the house manager Neil Costa and the groundskeeper guy, Bronco Gates? Bronco, really? A cowboy in North Florida?"

"He busts St. Johns River gators and Everglades pythons, not horses, but I'm going to let you make your own judgments on all of them."

"'*Stranger and stranger*,' said Alice in Wonderland."

"Yeah. Shadowlawn and its people are a world unto themselves, maybe more like that *Wizard of Oz* movie."

"Ever read the book that came from, a children's novel? My mother read it to us. It's darker and scarier than the movie by a long shot. Darcy and I used to have bad dreams over it. Crows trying to peck out eyes, horrible spiders. A lot more than just those flying monkeys. That kind of book and those grotesque fairy tales with ogres and wolves in the woods haunted us."

They were both silent after that. Even when the sun finally broke through, Nick felt a chill. He should tell her more, warn her about some things, but then he'd be not only prejudicing a witness to whatever might happen, but he might scare her off.

St. Augustine charmed Claire from the first. It seemed compact and welcoming with the small-town ambience that Naples had outgrown. The old, historic part of town where they'd be staying was lovely, with restaurants, shops, a walking mall and Spanish architecture. St. A, as Nick called it, laid claim to being the oldest continually occupied European settlement in the United States, since the Spanish had settled it—the signs boasted—in 1513.

As they took advantage of the valet parking at the hotel on the bay, the sun devoured the shroud of rain and their unease from what they'd been calling the attack of "Fiend Face." Nick checked both of them in at the Bayfront Hilton, telling her he had some calls to make, including Heck, his home office, the Seminole County Highway Patrol and Jasmine. He said he'd meet Claire in the lobby in an hour and a half, gave her his room number and sent her upstairs with a valet he'd already tipped.

Her spacious room with a balcony overlooked the sparkling bay crowded with boats. She unpacked a bit and took a fast nap. She'd done next to nothing yet, but she felt tired. She knew it was her emotions that needed calming as much as her body. For starters, merely being with someone as compelling and attractive as Nick was a challenge, let alone the task she was facing. She popped a dark chocolate ganache as if it were a pill.

She took a lightning-fast shower, changed her clothes and spread her notes out on the king-sized bed. She'd written four pages of them on her lap as Nick had described the people he wanted her to interview. And first thing in the morning, they were going to Shadowlawn to meet Jasmine.

She called Darcy's number and talked to Lexi, telling her there were tourist trolleys here just like the ones in Naples they'd gone on last summer. Lexi was going to play miniature golf and eat out with

Jace later that evening, but they hadn't seen him yet today. Then Claire hurried downstairs to meet Nick.

He was waiting for her in the lobby, still on the phone, but he got off as she approached. "Hey," he said, "don't want to rush things for you, but Jasmine says Winston Jackson's art photography shop just down St. George Street is hosting a series of St. Johns River pictures, including some of Shadowlawn. You could see them, meet with him informally before setting up an interview. It's a short walk from here, but I'm starving, so how about we grab something on the way?"

"Sounds good. I'd like to schedule an interview with him. He may be more objective than the two men who worked for Francine, and it's best to start with a neutral witness. I know he was a sort of advisor to her about the mansion, but he wasn't on her payroll. On checking out Winston Jackson and on the food, you read my mind."

He did seem to do that sometimes. Which, considering how attracted she felt to him, was not necessarily good in this still awkward, strictly business partnership.

"You mean, you aren't coming in?" Claire asked Nick as they approached the Jackson Photographic Art Shop after grabbing salads and pizza at a picturesque place called Pizzalley's.

"I might set off alarms. You can say you're working on Jasmine's behalf to get an interview without a lawyer present. But you can say I've retained you if he starts asking questions. I'll sit on that bench over there and get caught up on phone calls."

"That's fine," she told him. "Thanks for not hovering. You're right that I need to do this myself, with you and Heck assisting when needed. I won't report everything I'm thinking to you as I work on this. I need objectivity for my report to mean much. Enjoy the sun and the tourist parade."

The first of two large, framed photos in the window of the shop was of the famous Spanish fort Castillo de San Marcos that still guarded the waterfront here. Each detail of shade and sun, each crevice on the parapet of the solid stone blocks—the photo was a work of art with the blue-green bay, crystal sky and banks of clouds behind it.

Before she went in, she took off her sunglasses and studied the other large, framed photograph labeled simply, *St. Johns River Scene.* It seemed panoramic with its depth and details. The silvery Spanish moss drooping from the gnarled cypress trees hanging over the curve of riverbank, the patterns of mottled shade on the gray-brown water. She could almost feel and smell the place. There was something otherworldly about it that gave her the shivers.

A man's voice behind her said, "Immense beauty and primeval rot. Taken last month yet timeless."

She turned to face a man her height. His hair was shoulder-length and mussed, and he wore dark-rimmed glasses and a flower-patterned shirt that looked Hawaiian.

"Lots more like that inside," he said. "I'm hosting a juried show, but I never reward my own work."

"You are Winston Jackson."

"Guilty. Win Jackson, photographer, collector, movie buff, local historian. And you are a lady with a pink sling that clashes with your stunning Titian hair."

She hooked her sunglasses over the sling and extended her hand. *Bright! Talented! Eccentric!* were the words that buzzed in her brain to describe him. He wore the sort of glasses that darkened in the sun because here, under the awning, they were lightening to show intense brown eyes. His mouth was full, his nose a bit crooked, but he emanated intelligence, like a slightly mussed professor.

"I'm Claire Britten. I've been retained to gather information about the loss of Francine Montgomery in the hope of helping settle certain legal issues for her daughter, Jasmine. I've been told you knew—and know—them both, and I'd be grateful if you could spare me time for an interview, not today, but soon, perhaps tomorrow afternoon or evening."

He held her hand a bit too long. His grip was steady. Were long, thin fingers part of being an artist? He gave her a little courtly bow from the waist.

"Of course," he said, releasing her hand. "Anything to help Jasmine, the estate and the unique treasure she's now been entrusted with. Have you seen Shadowlawn yet?"

"No, I haven't. Soon."

"Well, at least let me introduce her, that is, the mansion in some of my work inside. Shadowlawn's ambience and provenance are definitely feminine. Several others are viewing the photographs, and I only stepped out for a moment, when I realized they weren't going to buy. Even artists must be practical, you know."

They went in, and he introduced her to his assistant, Len, a young African-American man who was cleaning what appeared to be a large antique camera with accordion folds behind the lens. Three people perused the hanging works, and "Please call me Win, not Winston," escorted her to the back of the large display area with two huge photographs of the most magnificent white-pillared, two-story plantation house she had ever seen. It looked as if she could walk from under the gnarled live oaks framing the photo, push aside the Spanish moss and stride right up the velvet green grass into the double doors.

"*Gone with the Wind* revisited," she whispered, awed at the stunning photograph.

"Better than Tara," he insisted. "This place is real. And endangered. I'll do whatever I can to help Jasmine save it. And save herself."

7

The next morning, Claire and Nick crossed the St. Johns River on the Palatka Bridge and drove south on River Street around the loop of Wilson's Cove, following foreboding road signs labeled Devil's Elbow. That was where the river narrowed, a fairly uninhabited area. Nick had warned Claire there wouldn't be a Starbucks in sight. Since gas station coffee tasted like tar, she'd come prepared with her own from the hotel. She felt perky this morning, because she didn't want to miss a thing in this beautiful but primeval area, as Win Jackson had called it. And she had found that, in general, just being with Nick was like a jolt of the best java.

They were grateful for the sunny weather. But humidity hung heavy in the air like a sponge ready to be squeezed, so Nick had the air-conditioning on despite the midmorning hour. Heck had stayed behind to work on other assignments, although he'd drive over to join them if she could set up any interviews today. Nick said he was certain Jasmine would agree to talk but he didn't want her to be recorded in any way. That way, if she was indicted, whatever she'd said to Claire could not be subpoenaed.

"Win Jackson is knowledgeable about a lot of things," Claire told Nick. "No problem getting him to talk about anything and everything."

"He's very talented. But, just remember, you said that's one way suspects can avoid answering the real questions."

"I haven't asked him any real questions. And verbosity is only a tip-off if the person usually speaks in fewer words. There are tests for that, but it usually scares people from acting naturally. Anyway, I'm doing interviews, not interrogations, and I think I built some good rapport with him. He said he'd be willing to do an interview this evening. 'Anything to help Jasmine,' as he put it."

"He does know a lot about this area."

"Do you know anything about some sort of little museum the estate manager, Neil Costa, runs?"

"Win mentioned that? It probably has about six visitors a year, mostly classic movie experts like Win himself. Costa's so-called museum focuses on the old series of movies tied to *Creature from the Black Lagoon*, which was actually filmed on this stretch of river."

"You're kidding! I've heard of that oldie, but—really? From the sixties?"

"Fifties, I think. I've only looked inside his place once. Francine was willing to let him use the old kitchen block area just down a covered walkway from the house as long as he didn't put any signs up on the property. He advertises in local papers and draws in a film fanatic from time to time."

"But that means strangers could have come on to the estate."

"Right. The police are aware of that, but Costa says no one unusual came the day of Francine's death, if that's what you're thinking."

"How old is Neil Costa? Was he around when the movies were made?"

"No. I'd say he's early fifties. He had a relative—an uncle, I think—who worked on the movie set of a couple of the films, so he has inherited some memorabilia, movie posters, the monster's suit, stuff like that. Costa comes off almost like a displaced English butler, but he's been the estate manager for years. Still, he's obviously got a strange side."

"Don't we all? Including his friend Bronco Gates?"

"Yeah, they're both Florida crackers, as people used to call them. But once again, I don't mean to color your thinking."

"I'm just trying to get a fix on those two before I talk to them. Don't worry, I'll form my own opinions, and I've been through too much to be easily shocked."

"I'm counting on that."

Their gazes met and held a moment before she sighed and looked out her side window across the fields at the line of dense trees clinging to the twisting river. "It does seem like another world here. From seeing Win's photos, I assume Shadowlawn will be set back in those trees?"

"Right. When you see the detail in his pictures, remember that's the detail he knows about this region."

"I saw no people in his photos."

"You're right. Jasmine once called the photos 'Florida Gothic' with Shadowlawn as the forebod-

ing, crumbling castle. Then her mother scolded her
for saying the mansion was crumbling. But no, he's
refused to do portraits for years—family and wedding
photos—and he could make a mint doing that. I'm
glad you two hit it off because he obviously doesn't
get along with some people."

"Jasmine?"

"He seems to."

"*Seems* is a really big word. Did he with Francine?"

"See, you're interviewing me again. Why don't
you hit Jasmine and Win with that since you're talking to them today?"

"I thought I'd let her do most of the talking without establishing a Q and A atmosphere with her. I'd
like to at least start out that way—with all of them."

"Next turn in the road, and we're there," he said,
pointing. "It's a narrow drive that goes a ways in before you see the house."

She leaned forward in anticipation. As they turned
in between the remnants of a rusted iron fence, the
creamy white pillars and facade of the mansion
emerged through the screen of large live oaks. The
drive was paved only partway back and became a dirt
road that must have been here from the beginning.
Taken last month yet timeless, Win Jackson had said
of his photo of the house and river.

"Win said this place is a treasure, and it is," she
whispered as details became more distinct. They
drove through the tunnel of trees with their tresses
of Spanish moss shifting in the warm breeze. French
doors with open, dark green shutters appeared between each pillar on the ground floor and the second

level. Under the roof were dormer windows she had to lean forward to see.

"There's an old ballroom upstairs, now an attic," he told her. "And, so I've been told, the distant sound of music and dancing feet some nights."

"Oh, great. Remind me not to do any interviews here at night. But what a beautiful place. From a little farther back, the mansion almost looked like a person peering out with those dormers for eyes and that filigree railing like a stubborn mouth. But those pillars, like teeth or fangs then."

"The place does cast its spell. You can see where it got its name with all the shadows and shade. The river's just on the other side, and those buildings off that way are the old kitchen block and the ruined slave quarters."

She shuddered from a chill, despite the heat that hit them when they got out of the car. "Of course, it was a working plantation with slaves once," she said. "For cotton?"

"Indigo, but I'll let Jasmine fill you in on all that since she's promised you a tour. There she is now."

A petite but voluptuous woman came out onto the front entrance and waved. She wore a long black skirt with a handkerchief hem in what looked like layers of chiffon. Her long, swept-back hair was blond, almost white, as she stepped out into a flash of sun. Until Claire came closer to her, she would have sworn she was a young girl, but no, her years sat heavy upon her posture and face, so that first impression must have been a fleeting glance, a trick of light and shade.

"Nick," Jasmine said and stood on tiptoe to kiss both his cheeks and hug him. He hugged her back.

She had a lace handkerchief in one hand, and her eyes looked swollen and red. "Claire," she said, extending her hand to Claire's good one as a strong floral scent wafted from her. Heavy, heady—could it actually be the aroma of jasmine perfume?

"Welcome to Shadowlawn," she told Claire. "I can't tell you how grateful we—all of us—are for your help. Please come in. I would love to show you around and I have some iced tea inside Neil fixed and left for us before he went into town. He takes such good care of me now just as he did my mother. Please," she repeated, "come in."

Claire's mind snagged on the words *we. All of us*. Perhaps Jasmine meant others on her staff like Neil Costa, even Bronco Gates. But, in this ambience of the place, Claire couldn't help thinking the *we* included the imaginary ghosts.

"So what do you know about this Nick guy your mom is with?" Jace asked Lexi as they walked out on the long Naples pier midmorning. Despite the early hour, it was a busy place with fishermen casting their lines over the railing and tourists strolling on the sand beach below. Hoping for scraps, pelicans hovered overhead or treaded water as several fishermen cleaned their catch.

"Well, Mr. Nick is tall—taller than you," Lexi said, stopping to lick her ice cream cone. "But he, like, kind of bent down to talk to me. That's when he said Drew was wrong to throw the snake at me and Jilly."

"Did he already know about that or did you tell him?"

"I told him. Daddy, maybe you can meet him if you

want to know about him. I think he's rich or something like that. And I heard Aunt Darcy tell Mommy
he's a ladies' man, so I think he's already married to
someone. I wish you and Mommy were still married."

She put her free, sticky hand in his. Thinking
how Nick Markwood had evidently stooped to his
daughter's height, Jace sat down on one of the wooden
benches and lifted her next to him. He bent close.
Kneeling for him wasn't easy anymore, not since his
high school football injury, let alone years of rigorous
navy demands. The damn thing sometimes stiffened
up on long flights.

"You know," Jace told her, "I might just drive up
north to see your mommy before I have to head back
out west. I'll have to talk to Aunt Darcy about exactly where she is."

"But she's working. Talking to people to help Mr.
Nick, that's what she said. But I got her phone number right here, wrote it down, see? The hotel number,
'cause I got memor—memorized her cell number."

"Yeah, I know that one, too," he said and watched
his darling girl—he could see Claire in her and that
haunted him—pull a folded piece of paper out of her
shorts pocket. She gave it to him and he opened it.
ST. AUGUSTINE BAYFRONT HILTON it said in
Claire's bold printing, and then a phone number. He
studied it, then gave it back to Lexi.

"You're right, she'll be working," he said, "so I'm
not sure if I'll go. But I'll tell you this. Next time I'm
here, I'm going to take you and Mommy to Disney
World, if you can talk her into going, okay?"

"Okay! Yeah!" she cried and almost lost the scoop
of chocolate ice cream out of her cone. "Will you

fly us there in your plane? It's not as far as Singing-poor, is it?"

He smiled and pulled her baseball cap down over her eyes to her nose. "No, not that far. Better finish that ice cream before it falls out, and we have to let the pelicans eat it."

"Oh, they don't like that, but the ants do."

Jace didn't like it that Claire had gone off to a fancy hotel with Nick Markwood. And, though he promised Lexi they'd go to the Sun-N-Fun Waterpark Lagoon tomorrow, he just might drive north again the day after that.

Claire was in awe of the interior of Shadowlawn mansion. The place obviously needed serious resto-ration, but it was a time warp with fabulous antiques like a rosewood piano with a shelf for oil lamps, and a massive mahogany dining room table. Cypress wood trim from trees that once lined the river now edged the hand-painted, twelve-foot-high ceilings. Despite the humidity outside and even without the iced tea with mint crushed in the bottom of the tall glasses Jasmine served them, Claire thought the sixteen-inch-thick exterior walls of stuccoed brick kept the rooms amazingly cool.

"They knew what they were doing in the 1830s when this was built," Jasmine told Claire as she gave her a tour. Nick was on his cell phone in the library since there was no Wi-Fi here for his laptop. "Would you believe out by the back—in the original part of the house," Jasmine went on, "the walls were made with a mix of mud, deer hair and Spanish moss, and they're still standing strong?"

Her voice still seemed husky, as if she had a cold or had been shouting—or maybe crying.

"It's a real treasure, as Win Jackson put it."

"Did he? Yes, he would. The staircases are unique, three of them which were each built in different eras and have a history lesson of their own. I'll tell you before Dr. Win Jackson lectures you on that."

Ah, there was an edge to her voice, an attitude about Win. But he'd seemed so pro-Jasmine. Interesting, but Claire knew she'd stepped not only into the long-ago past, but the recent past that had somehow led to the death of this mansion's matriarch—and now she was talking to the next in line of Montgomery women, one who didn't have a daughter or heir to bequeath the place to.

"There's another staircase outside, around that way," Jasmine said, gesturing, and wafting out the heady scent she wore. "It was built very early because the Spanish, when they held this area, used to tax staircases inside the house. Tricky and excessive government taxes, so what's new, right? It's one reason Mother wanted to donate this place to the state, but I thought—and still think—that private ownership with carefully controlled public visitations are best for Shadowlawn. But if the state didn't take it on, with all the money they'd have to put into it, I just couldn't imagine it going up for auction. I'm sure Nick has told you Mother and I disagreed on that."

"He mentioned it."

"But it doesn't mean I wished her ill," she said, rounding on Claire. For a moment, the muted tones and calm demeanor changed. An explosive temper perhaps? "I didn't!" she plunged on. "But," she added, more quietly, "I'm sure you will discern that for your-self. Now, this interior, hidden spiral staircase," she said, opening a door in the dining room, "could be used by the family privately, or servants—slaves, though I hate that part of the house's heritage. The thought of that is as bad as the voices here," she said, indicating the upward reach of the winding staircase before she closed the door on it.

"The voices?"

"That's what we've always called them. Just echoes that carry at night from one floor to the other through the stairwells or the chimneys that connect the fireplaces. Owls, even bats in the attic, or the wind or weather howls a bit. Now, the third staircase, of course, the grand one at the front of the house, was built just before the so-called Civil War which we Southerners still call the War of Northern Aggres-sion. Remember that from your high school days—if you attended school in Florida?"

"I do, though in South Florida, the war of choice is also the Seminole Indian Wars."

Jasmine took her upstairs where there was a cen-tral hall. Downstairs the parlor, music room, library and dining room had all connected directly with no hallway. Another stunning crystal-and-bronze chan-delier hung at the top of the staircase.

"I know you'll want to see Rosalynn's bedroom," Jasmine said. "Why Mother made it her own after my father died, I'll never know."

Claire wanted to ask "Who is Rosalynn?" but she kept quiet. Like Win Jackson, Jasmine seemed to do quite well answering questions without being asked.

But as Jasmine swept open the second door in the

hall and Claire stepped into a spacious room which opened only to the outside gallery, she saw Rosalynn—that is, a commanding, life-size, full-length oil painting of a Civil War–era woman. *Oh, that's right.* There had been a Rosalynn in the family tree, a woman who, with the help of an English-born indigo expert, had saved the mansion from being burned by Union troops during the Civil War while the master was away fighting for the South.

And the oddest thing as Claire went closer but Jasmine stayed at the door—no, several strange things. The portrait seemed to smell of the same overpowering, sweet scent as Jasmine did, but of course, Claire knew that was her imagination. Rosalynn's hair was pale blond, almost the hue of Jasmine's, and there was even a slight resemblance. But the most compelling thing was that the woman's painted eyes, staring straight out, seemed to follow her.

Claire walked to the side—yes, how had the artist done that? She turned back to Jasmine to comment and saw her own reflection in a full-length mirror with a gold frame and the portrait of Rosalynn reflected from behind.

"Yes, everyone notices that about her eyes," Jasmine said, as if Claire had spoken. "Even if you look at the portrait in the mirror, the eyes follow you. That's called a petticoat mirror, by the way, since women would check their skirts all around in it before going out. No flash of underskirt or ankle allowed, of course."

Jasmine looked as if she were going back out in the hall. Tearing her gaze away from the portrait's reflection, standing by the huge, high rosewood bed with the carved pineapple motifs atop the four posts, Claire asked, "Is this the room where you found your mother?"

Jasmine stopped and turned back. So she was not going to tell about that?

"It is," she said. "As I said, it was her bedroom, like the Montgomery women before her, but I can't bear to sleep here. I'm down the hall. It's just as she left it. I haven't even had the strength to go through her things yet. I did have to clean the places the police fingerprinted and scrub the carpet where they had their tape around the outline of—of the body. I'm sure you read the newspaper articles, so full of sensationalism, purple prose at its best and worst."

"Actually, I haven't. I like to see things for myself, talk directly to the people involved."

"There was no blood, so don't stare at the floor. But I want to show you where Rosalynn Montgomery is now, still on the grounds. She killed herself off that gallery, right there. She's dead and buried so it angers me to no end that people with vivid imaginations say she still walks here just because a flash of light flitters past like the bats that live around here. I'm telling you the truth on that! Rosalynn may have killed herself, but I don't think Mother did. If I were lying, I'd say, 'Yes, Mother was suicidal' so I could keep the county sheriff at bay. So, doesn't that prove I'm not guilty of harming her?"

Claire only nodded. But *methinks the lady doth protest too much*, a line from a Shakespeare play Mother had read them, danced through her head. Yet Jasmine's comments about the ghost surprised her, too. The female sighted in the house and the male spirit who supposedly stalked the grounds at night were mentioned in the small booklet Nick had given her to read. And hadn't he said that both Francine and Jasmine had seen the female ghost here? So who was telling the truth about that?

"Come along," Jasmine said, "then we'll sit down with Nick for lunch and we can make plans to continue our talk later. That would be best, wouldn't it?"

"I— Yes. Before I talk to your staff or Win Jackson, anyone else you might suggest?"

Claire was surprised that this woman had somehow unnerved her. She'd talked to more distraught and certainly more dangerous people than this. Or was it Rosalynn, the woman in the portrait, in the mirror, in the atmosphere of this place, who rattled her? The painting made her look as if she would say something. If she could talk, it could solve what happened to Francine in this room. And it could explain what had happened to Rosalynn herself to make that beautiful, commanding-looking woman commit suicide. Mysteries seemed piled on mysteries, as heavy as the perfume in this room.

Claire hurried out, and Jasmine closed the door firmly behind them, then pulled a key out of her skirt pocket and locked it. She rushed down the front staircase with Claire close behind, out the back door onto a slate courtyard. The humidity and heat slapped at them. Strangely, even in the air, the floral scent Jasmine wore was prominent. But then, Claire saw a nearby cluster of bushes, oleander and hibiscus, but also a white bloom that might indeed be jasmine, or maybe gardenias. Too late for magnolias, anyway. She would have asked, but she didn't want to steer the conversation with her own questions—yet. She was still trying to get a fix on this woman.

As they left the courtyard, Claire glanced down a stone path toward the river, draped with cypress, live oaks and other trees. It was just as Win had captured it in one of his photos, so he must have been right here when he took it—last month he'd said, which must be about the time Francine had died.

"A small, old family graveyard," Jasmine was saying as she led Claire a little ways from the house. "Of course, no one else is buried here these days. Mother wanted to be, but I couldn't see it and put her with my father in the Palatka cemetery."

"I see," Claire said, but she wasn't sure she really did. Why hadn't Jasmine honored her mother's wish on that? Had there been some deep resentment between them? Claire had to admit she could understand resenting the way one's own mother had reared a daughter.

Jasmine went on, "I don't want anyone coming in here. But of course it would be on the tour if Shadowlawn is opened to visitors or is ever sold." She nearly spit those words out. "Over my dead body, not my mother's," she added under her breath.

"Forgive me for asking, but can you afford to keep this place? Keep it up?"

"Investors? I don't know. I have to get clear of suspicion first. She wanted to let the State of Florida, or the National Registry of Historic Places, have control, even possibly a wealthy outside buyer. There is no reason why this can't remain in family control and still be profitable enough to fund restoration and upkeep. But that disagreement, as I said, is no motive for murder, I don't care what they say. Over here, this brick tomb with iron grates. I can't abide the place, but Mother found some sort of strength and solace here."

"Oh, you can see the old cast-iron caskets inside," Claire said, stooping slightly.

"Yes, Rosalynn and her Civil War–colonel husband. Hers is nearest to us. See, marked Rosalynn Montgomery? Years ago, I once thought I'd seen her in the house at night, throwing herself off the gallery, but it was just alcohol and teenage raging hormones—and I'd been smoking pot. You know, Mother said, *If we open this place*—the house, not this tomb, she meant—*they will come. Visitors to learn about our past, paying guests to keep things going.* Strange how a family fortune can disappear. But if anything would raise the dead and have poor Rosalynn spinning inside there, it would be letting Shadowlawn pass from family hands. Mother thought it best for the past to be preserved by deeding it or selling it away, but I could not accept that and—and Rosalynn wouldn't, either."

"Nick said this was once an indigo plantation. Could the fields be worked again—not that I know what indigo is worth now."

"Most of the land has been sold off. You're looking at what is left. And you're looking at the Montgomery woman who is left to carry on the legacy—the burden—and I hope I'm looking at the woman who is going to help me and Nick prove I did not harm my mother, any more than she would overdose accidentally or intentionally on her medications. I swear to you," she said, coming closer and gripping Claire's good shoulder in a rush of emotion and flowery aroma, "someone murdered my mother, and you have to find a way to help Nick and me prove it."

8

Neil Costa served Jasmine, Nick and Claire lunch at the massive dining room table where a long board hanging above served as a swinging fan.

"It's automatic now," Jasmine explained, "but I hate to think of some small slave child standing in that corner working it by a cord years ago while everyone ate a delicious meal in front of him."

"And," Neil put in as he collected their chicken salad plates, "they had bowls of ice from the old ice house sitting in the center of the table to cool the room—instant, old-fashioned air-conditioning."

Claire was pleased to find that Neil Costa, the longtime house manager, appeared to be calm and easygoing. He did not seem like a servant but a family friend. His demeanor and manners were a bit old-fashioned, an impression which his thick Southern accent enhanced. Nick had said he was like an English butler, but he was dressed casually in white slacks and a short-sleeved silky white shirt. He was a big, clean-shaven man with a high forehead and close-cropped, salt-and-pepper hair. He had a mellifluous voice, and Claire knew she'd enjoy interviewing him. He'd agreed to that tomorrow afternoon, so she'd be coming back here with Heck. Neil was evidently a jack-of-all-trades in the house, while Bronco Gates, who was away for a few days, took care of the lawns, landscaping and outside repairs.

It seemed that Neil was also chief cook and bottle washer, as they used to say. Part of his realm was the modern kitchen which had been added just beyond what used to be a huge library at the back of the house. No more hustling hot foods under silver domes from the old kitchen house through the covered walkway to the table. Neil also lived at the back of the house in renovated servants' quarters. Jasmine had mentioned he had a small living room, bedroom and bath in his private realm.

After lemon sponge cake and iced coffee, Jasmine escorted them out onto the shaded veranda to say goodbye.

"I look forward to later discussions to learn more about your mother," Claire told her. "And thank you for the very personal tour of this beautiful home."

"You know, I need to think of it again that way now. I've lived so long in other places, St. Augustine, Tampa, Denver."

"Denver?"

"Yes, actually the town of Evergreen outside Denver. My husband had a business there before he died much too early of a sudden heart attack. I did miss this when I lived away. The graciousness of it, the fabulous past, the scents…"

But, Claire noted, she hadn't said she'd missed her mother, and here she was an only child, a daughter. And since Jasmine had mentioned *scents,* Claire saw her opening.

"I've been meaning to ask about the unique perfume you wear. Is it gardenia, or is it made from your namesake flower?"

"It's jasmine, Mother's fragrance she distilled from flowers here on the grounds. It has a reputation for being an aphrodisiac. Karma, the god of love in India, tipped his arrows with jasmine, they say." She took Nick's arm, leaning into him a bit.

"Their answer to Cupid?" Nick put in.

She nodded. "But I wear it for its antidepressant properties—yes, really. Research it, as I'm sure you will do much else on this assignment, won't she, Nick?"

"With all you and Win Jackson are teaching her, she may as well toss her laptop and smartphone in the river," he said with a tight smile.

"Well, you asked about indigo earlier, Claire," Jasmine went on, "but you just look up jasmine. The flowers must be picked at night because the sun drives the scent from the blooms. I guess for that reason and its white color, some call it the ghost flower. But, truly, it's a popular essence for aromatherapy for more than its aphrodisiac associations. Shadowlawn matriarchs have grown and distilled it here since the Civil War, though I'm just using what Mother...what she left behind.

"So anyway, it's her legacy to me—besides this place," she added with a sigh. "How I wish the jasmine had kept her on an even keel without having to use her mood-enhancing pills. Honestly, we ought to all wear jasmine not only because it lifts one's mood, but, they say, also leads to mental alertness."

"I could use that," Claire said, though she didn't explain why, even though it seemed that Jasmine was now almost baring her soul. And did the fact that Francine made and wore a scent that was an antidepressant mean that she was depressed enough to be suicidal? Even someone who seemed to be on an even keel, as Jasmine put it, could tip so far as to attempt suicide, the perfect but dreadful storm of wanting to escape from life for some reason.

Now Claire empathized even more, not with Jasmine, but with Francine. She must have fought depression as well as anxiety, and Claire could totally sympathize with that. After all, the woman had been taking drugs to fight a frightening health problem, just like Claire.

She realized she was no longer only on this assignment for a fee or even to help Nick or to save Jasmine from suspicion or arrest. She suddenly felt close to poor Francine, and, whatever it took, she was going to learn what happened to her.

After an early dinner that evening in St. Augustine, Nick and Claire walked the seawall overlooking the mooring area for boats near the hotel. Many were sailboats but yachts bobbed at anchor, too. The owners rode in to shore on small motorboats or rowed.

Heck would be meeting them at the hotel soon to escort Claire to interview Win Jackson. For now, Nick was glad for some private time with her.

They laughed at some of the names on the bigger boats they could read from here: *Retired and Rejoicing. Roaming and Juliet. Sailor's De-lite*, and what Claire claimed was her favorite, *Billable Ours*.

"Definitely owned by some rich lawyer," she told him. Their gazes snagged and held, as happened so often—too often, he supposed. He always had the craziest urge to touch her.

"I have a fishing boat that seats four, but that's it," he said. "With an outboard motor. I hardly have time for it anymore."

"I believe you. When I checked out your place to see if it was huge, I saw you have a reasonably-sized house and boat, especially for where you live."

"You drove by?"

"I let my fingers do the walking. Google browser for Street View Maps. Well, don't look at me like that! It's just another form of research. I had to check you out."

"If I'd had a place the size of Shadowlawn and a massive yacht, you would have said 'yes' to working with me faster than you did?"

"I just wanted to know more about you."

"I get that. I like that."

He studied the beautiful *Billable Ours*, then Claire's profile. Her hair was almost the color of the flaming sunset behind them.

"So ask away," he said. "If there's something that's privileged info, I'll take the Fifth."

"Are you working on a defense for Jasmine already?"

"Ah, always business," he said, pretending to pout. Was it his imagination or did she subconsciously thrust out her lush lower lip to match his? That little movement hit him below the belt. "Okay," he said, forcing himself to look out over the mooring field again, "yes, I am. And I'm banking on what you find in your interviews to help me."

"But what's your strategy? I mean, in general, how do you protect clients? You were ruthless—well, maybe that's the wrong word—defending Sol Sorento, and you didn't even have emotional ties to him like you do—did—to Jasmine. I know one thing you did was give an alternate theory to what the prosecution was pushing, that Sol had suffered a head injury and wasn't to blame. That's kind of like an insanity defense, right?"

When he turned toward her, their faces were close and neither wore sunglasses. He shifted his feet. Even in court she'd gotten to him, and here came that caveman feeling again. Before Claire, he had never wanted to just pick a woman up off her feet and sprint away with her.

"Right. Ah, yes. More or less." Some clever lawyer, he thought. He sounded like a stammering teenager. He cleared his throat again. Her eyes might be green but they swam with golden flecks. "Another tactic is to discredit evidence or key witnesses."

"Which I was, not an eyewitness but an expert witness. You did an almost-good-enough job on me."

"Distracting the jury is the name of the game," he admitted. "I can try to convince them the prosecution's case is flawed, the truth can't actually be known, that evidence is inadmissible, that the chain of custody for evidence was tainted, et cetera."

"What I don't understand, counselor, is how you can defend someone you think is probably guilty, and I don't mean Jasmine."

"Everyone has a right to a defense in this country. I try not to take a case in the first place if I think the person's shady. Sol—well, I took him on partly because he'd once invested in a business my father had and I wanted a chance to interview him about that. But I'd have trouble defending someone like the Boston bomber or someone I was sure murdered his family or—"

"So you do truly believe in Jasmine's innocence?"

He looked her right in those stunning eyes. "I do."

She nodded. They leaned closer together. A boat motor started nearby. No, it was a sound from above, and they both glanced up.

"Is that what I think it is?" she asked, sounding suddenly breathless. "I've see those in Naples lately, too."

"A white drone, small one. Can't tell if it has a camera or not. Those are everywhere lately, and novice users are going to cause a problem, especially near airports where they could bring down a plane."

"So my ex says. He was flying out of Los Angeles when one was almost in their flight path."

Lifting a hand, Nick shaded the setting sun from his eyes. "It's hard to see against the western sky. I've heard people are flying in cocaine from boats offshore on those. Since 9/11, our government has justified them for self-defense against terrorists, but those who hate us can use them, too. Eventually, the bad guys think of everything."

"Nick," she said, touching his arm, then quickly pulling her hand back, "I'm really committed to Francine's case now—to Jasmine's, I mean. I know you are doing it for her, but I'm doing it for Francine, too."

He nodded, leaning nearer to her again. "Then we're really in this together."

They drifted closer, inches apart. His entire body went into overdrive. Even with the evening breeze from the bay, he felt hot.

"Yes," she said. "Good. That's good." She took a step back and looked away.

"Let me walk you back to the hotel to wait for Heck," he said. He'd almost said, *to your room*, but then he'd do something to prove he needed an insanity defense, and it was against his rules to mix business with pleasure. Physical attraction—it was only that with Claire, wasn't it? He didn't want to screw up their still tentative working relationship. Heck should be here any minute, and he'd turn her over to him as assistant and escort. He only hoped he could concentrate on work after they left for Win Jackson's art photo shop which was closing up in—Nick glanced at his watch—fifteen minutes.

Claire could tell Win Jackson didn't like Heck here, taking notes, though he'd agreed to it earlier and said he understood with her injured arm that she needed help with an interview log. She didn't tell him she'd been shot, and he didn't ask. Or perhaps he knew. He could have seen the news, researched her as she had him.

Heck, who had been talkative on the way over— especially when he'd learned she could speak some basic Spanish—knew enough to keep quiet unless spoken to. He had his laptop open on his knees and sat behind Win's big office desk, almost in the corner.

Claire had managed to maneuver Win to sit in one

of the two chairs in front of his desk while she took the other. It provided a more informal setting, helped her to watch his body language and, in general, it was good to position the person being interviewed where he or she didn't feel boxed in.

After some preliminary questions for the record and the usual formalities—that this interview was voluntary—Claire said, "By the way, I saw the exact spot at Shadowlawn where you must have shot that amazing first photo you showed me. You said it was taken about a month ago, so was that before or after Francine died?"

"A couple of days before. I was here at the shop developing it when I got the phone call from Neil Costa that she had died."

"Was that a shock to you, or had you seen any signs she was ill or weak?"

"Neither, but she was always nervous. We'd served on several local charity and historical preservation committees and fund-raisers together, so I knew her in different situations. I was all for her turning Shadowlawn into a living museum if that's what it took to save and restore it. It was sad that she and Jasmine disagreed about the options, but you know that."

"Did you advise Francine one way or the other about Shadowlawn?"

"I didn't think it was my place to do so, though I admit, it could have been tricky and dangerous to find a private bidder who would preserve it if the state didn't take it over. But I think it was right to let the public share in its history and beauty. It needed funding for a lot of restoration. I would have photographed or even filmed that step-by-step."

"Filmed? I didn't know about your talents in that area."

"Purely amateur compared to my large-format landscape work, but I am an old film buff. Everybody's an amateur filmmaker these days with their phone cameras, YouTube and all—which I pretty much ignore. Have you seen some of the stuff on there that gets millions of hits?"

He ignored YouTube but had watched it? Contradiction. And off the topic again, but then she'd given him the opening. No, she figured Win Jackson, PhD, just liked to show he knew about anything and everything, not that he was trying to distract from her intent here. He'd given his take on Francine, but now it was time to see what he thought about Neil Costa.

"So," she said, "have you seen that little film museum Neil Costa has in the estate's old kitchen block? He said he'd be glad to show it to me."

"There won't be a crowd. It's a little creepy and pretty dusty. Of course, he would lose what he has there if the place goes public. I can't see someone else wanting that so-called museum focusing on that old B-grade movie, *Creature from the Black Lagoon* and its sequels, for heaven's sake."

Ah, she thought, *there's something not right between Win and Neil Costa.* More importantly, he'd just subtly given her a motive why Neil might want to stop Francine from going public. But maybe it was just that the snobbish Win looked down on Neil's shoddy collection. As if to back up her suspicion, Win was nervous talking about Neil. He had crossed one ankle over his knee and was bouncing his foot. If Heck didn't write that down, she'd add it later.

"You know," Win went on, "the truth is Francine and Shadowlawn remind me of another old movie, not a B-grade cheapie like *Creature* and not *Gone with the Wind,* like you mentioned yesterday. Have you heard of the noir classic, *Sunset Boulevard*? It's a 1950 Billy Wilder black-and-white with Gloria Swanson and William Holden, about an aging silent film star who lives in a decaying mansion and thinks she can still have her fame and fortune. Now don't get me wrong. I'm not saying Francine was over the hill, but there's a murder in the film."

"No, I haven't heard of it. How fascinating. Are there other parallels?"

"You might be more familiar with the Andrew Lloyd Webber musical of the same name that was made from it in the early 1990s. But the point is, the Gloria Swanson character has a loyal butler/chauffeur who reminds me of Neil Costa. It all ends badly, too. I have the film if you ever want to see it."

"Does the *grande dame* of the film die? Who kills whom?"

"Oh, it's nothing like Francine's life in that respect. The aging diva, Norma Desmond, shoots her young lover when he tries to leave her. She's living in the past and is quite demented, which, of course, Francine was not, although I think Jasmine thought Francine was off her rocker to let Shadowlawn slip from family control, despite financial problems."

"Do you think Neil Costa did a good job for Francine?"

"He's quite the chef and loyal as the day is long, as they say."

When the interview ended, Claire had a new piece

of the puzzle but she had no clue where it fit. Win Jackson resented or mistrusted Neil Costa. And he was well informed about the differing opinions of Francine and Jasmine over Shadowlawn.

As they were leaving, Win warned her to beware of Bronco Gates because he was a loose cannon. So did Win suspect either of her employees had harmed her? After she questioned them, she'd interview Win again.

Well, she told herself, as they walked back toward the hotel on the dimly lit streets, she already knew this case would not be a walk in the park—a walk she'd agreed to have with Jasmine tomorrow in the local Fountain of Youth Park after she saw the doctor about her bullet wound. Right now, she had to take her night meds and get some sleep, if she could only stop everything she'd learned so far from rioting through her brain.

On St. George Street, she didn't know whether to laugh or cry when a large van passed them with the words on the side, St. Augustine Ghost and Graveyard Tour: Come Get Acquainted With the Night!

9

Claire heard a sharp sound. She tried to drag herself from sleep. A siren? The emergency squad was here? She'd found her mother on the floor and called the squad. No, that was years ago. A fire alarm? She had to save Lexi!

Oh, she remembered now. She wasn't home but in a hotel on assignment. With Nick. Nick, who was a stimulant to her whole system in a way the meds and caffeine never could be.

She realized the sound was the hotel alarm clock. Groaning, she rolled over and hit it off. Her alarm app on her phone started to sound. She sat up and reached for it, shut it off. Groggy. Almost dizzy. At least she'd had no nightmare as she fought her way from sleep to reality.

Then came the courtesy wake-up call on her hotel phone. She fumbled for the receiver, picked it up. Not a live person, a mechanical voice. She hung it back up to silence it. All her alarms were working, but she'd wanted to be sure she woke up for her second dose of her night medicine.

She used to dread the dark. Feared nightfall. When she was first diagnosed, she'd set three alarm clocks to wake up for her night meds, but she'd had to improvise when she went away from home. When she was pregnant, she'd stopped taking the strong night medicine at all, and her mild cataplexy had made a comeback. When she got excited or overly emotional, she'd get weak in the knees, sometimes stumble or collapse. Then the half-waking, dreadful dreams returned, too.

But now, something was wrong, because she felt exhausted and hung over, and she thought she'd conquered that. She'd awakened easily lately. Too much activity, too much thinking, too much stress—a dangerous emotion. Never again did she want to hallucinate about those horrible, dead people trying to touch her, take her.

Then it hit her: she'd slept through until now when she should have taken the second dose of her medicine last night. There it was, waiting. The daytime narcolepsy pill stimulants were easy, but the second middle-of-the-night dose from that horrid orange bottle with its syringe to measure out the amount— ridiculously expensive stuff—needed to be taken not only when she went to bed but four hours later, too. When she was married and Jace was home, it was a real trick to take the second dose without rousing him—worse, making herself wake up to take it.

No wonder he'd left her. Though he wasn't home much, he must have felt he was living with a secretive madwoman at times. She should have told him about her disease, should have told him before he swept her off her feet and they practically eloped.

"Ugh!" she greeted the day, putting her head in

her hands. Without that second night dose, she'd have to really concentrate to keep on an even keel. Nick was taking her to a local doctor to look at her bullet wound, then she was meeting Jasmine for lunch nearby in a wide-open park Jasmine had insisted on, though why they couldn't just walk down together by the river at Shadowlawn, Claire wasn't sure. In the afternoon, she and Heck were going to interview Neil Costa back at the mansion. So she had to get herself together, plan her questions for Jasmine and Neil.

Claire got up, steadied herself and headed for the bathroom to work a miracle on how she must look.

Nick drove Claire into the parking lot at the Fountain of Youth Park where she was going to meet Jasmine. "You know," he told Claire, "there's a guy in Goodland who claims he has the real Fountain of Youth in an old cistern on his property there."

"In that little, old-fashioned enclave between Naples and Marco Island?"

"Right. It's in old Spanish records that Ponce de Leon did stop there for water and named the area Good Land, in Spanish, of course. So this guy wants me to take a lawsuit case against a big pharmaceutical firm that's been advertising bottled water called Youth Do and a related cosmetics company promoting Youth Dew, which uses the water in its lotions. Both brands claim they use 'a hidden secret from times past.' It brings him visitors but very little money, because he doesn't know how to market himself. I told him I'm a criminal lawyer who specializes in capital murder cases and not corporate lawsuits and that I'm tied up, but he's adamant. I'll take you down there to meet him sometime."

"All right. I suppose, if the people behind this park thought he was a threat or if he bugs those businesses too much, you might have another murder case on your hands—just kidding. But it's very brave of him to try to stand up to the big boys, so maybe you should help him."

"I don't like to lose cases. But what I'm really thinking about," he said, as his voice became quieter, and he touched her shoulder once, lightly, "is the good news about your arm."

That was the second time he'd said that after leaving the doctor's office, she thought, as if he had to reassure himself instead of her.

"And good news I can quit taking the pain pills. I don't need those mixing with my other meds. I am so glad to lose the sling and just have this bandage and wrap, but I still don't have the use of this hand without discomfort. It's tough to even dress myself without Lexi's help."

He returned his right hand to the back of her passenger seat. She hoped he didn't think that comment was a plea for help. He'd insisted on taking care of her co-pay at the doctor's. He hadn't gone in with her to see the doctor, but he was hovering like a—a worried spouse. But then, of course, he needed her to help Jasmine.

"Thanks for going above and beyond the call of duty," she told him as she unlocked her door and took her purse off the floor. That was a phrase Jace often used, *the call of duty*. This moment felt both comforting and awkward: it was as if Nick were her man, dropping her off at work and they'd been lingering, chatting in their car. It reminded her of when she and Jace were first married and she'd take him to the airport, wishing he wouldn't be gone for so long. Lexi had said on the phone last night they were having a great time, but that "Daddy misses you and wants to see you." Now, wouldn't that be all she'd need?

"Good luck with Jasmine in round two," Nick said as she unlocked her seat belt. "If she can't drop you back at the hotel, call me."

"It's not a long walk. I could use the exercise. Things are laid out pretty close near the Old Town area."

He reached carefully for her left hand. "Still, be careful," he said. "And go easy on Jasmine—if you can."

"I will," she said, getting out. "After all, she's Francine's daughter."

Jace was pleased that Darcy trusted him enough to let him bring Jilly with Lexi to the Sun-N-Fun Lagoon water park today. What Darcy thought always went a long way with Claire and vice versa. He felt bad Drew was in school and couldn't come, but then he might not want to hang out with squealing little girls anyway—no, not a big first grader. As much as Jace loved Lexi, he wasn't sure he wanted to hang out with them either as the three of them floated along in a big tube on the lazy river in their swimsuits. The girls kept whispering and giggling. Their chatter almost sounded like a foreign language. He wished he had Claire here to translate.

"Not lots of people here like on Saturday." Lexi finally said something that made sense. "I like it. Starting in January, too bad Jilly and me are gonna be in preschool and can't come weekdays."

"I know," Jace said. *I'm paying for it, or most of it,* he thought, but didn't say so.

There were still some families here. He'd noticed one set of parents where the woman reminded him of Claire, not red hair but slender build, kind of tall. And graceful. The one time he'd seen Claire off her meds, having a hallucination, collapsed on the floor, he thought he'd seen an alien.

The girls were talking about something called *Frozen*, probably some kind of ice cream treat they sold here. He had to admit he sometimes tuned them out. He kept thinking of Claire being shot, of Claire off in the boondocks with some silver-tongued guy— silver-eyed, too. He'd looked up his picture online. Expensive-looking suit, probably custom-made. Would Claire go for that over a pilot's uniform?

Yeah, maybe he would call in to see if he could fly out of Jacksonville instead of Miami to head back to LA. St. Augustine was close to what the pilots called "Jacktown." He wanted to see Claire again before his next assignment, and he'd better not tell Lexi or she'd tip her off. He'd just show up, so she wouldn't tell him not to come. He could say St. Augustine was just on his way to JAX en route to LAX.

"Daddy, can we go to that water fountain place here that squirts people?" Lexi's shrill voice cut through his thoughts. "Me and Mommy like that part best, and we keep laughing all the time!"

"Yeah, that sounds good. I like to laugh all the

time," he said and tickled both girls until they squealed and tried to splash him. So why was he still sad—and mad?

Claire and Jasmine walked into the spring house at the Ponce de Leon Fountain of Youth Park where the underground aquifer burbled with water that supposedly gave eternal youth, though the sign said Spring of Eternal Hope.

"That's more like it," Jasmine said, pointing at it. "My hope springs eternal this nightmare is going away. By the way, they sell bottles of this water at the gift shop. But I've drunk it more than once over the years, and you can see it's not doing much for me. So—we can either walk way out past the Ponce statue to the inlet or sit at one of those umbrella tables by the café. I just don't seem to have much strength in my legs today, and I could use some coffee."

"I'm with you on that. Are you sleeping all right at night?" Claire asked the question she'd been asked by doctors over the years.

"Not really," Jasmine admitted as they went inside the Five Flags Café to order sandwiches and colas, then sat at one of the round tables with the white umbrellas. "I keep replaying things in my mind. Of course, I deeply regret the falling-out I had with Mother that everyone is making so much of to try to blame me for her death. I regret we argued in front of a local historical preservation committee. But I could not believe she even considered letting outsiders— supposedly altruistic bidders, or government, no less, the way it is today—control our family heritage. It's bad enough to open it up to 'the paying public,' as they say, if we kept control."

"So that's how you would propose to fund it?"

"Yes, that and maybe donations. Or maybe I should marry again, a very rich man," she said with a bitter laugh. She went on, "Anyhow, the state of Florida already has Kingsley Plantation up near Jacksonville on the same river, for heaven's sake, so isn't that enough to control? Mother should have seen we should remain private."

"So you can't keep the house and land if you don't get some sort of additional financial support?"

"Not for long. Restoration and repair bills loom. Legal fees and all that, which will get worse if I'm indicted. I refuse to let Nick do my case completely pro bono. By the way, how is it for you, working with him *under counsel*, as they say?"

Hopefully, she didn't mean that as a double entendre, Claire thought. She answered carefully. "Our team of Nick, his data guru Hector and I is working well, though we're just getting started." And wasn't she supposed to be the one asking searching questions?

They both jumped when one of the peacocks wandering the ground screeched at a squirrel which skittered past. "Well," Jasmine said, "who needs watchdogs with peacocks around? They used to use them on grand estates for that. If we walked a little farther here we'd listen to reenactors, you know, people who re-create the old days. Claire," she said with a sudden sob, "I keep reenacting, replaying in my mind finding my mother dead. Can you understand the horror of that, finding your mother on the floor, dead?"

Claire almost blurted out that she had done exactly that, but she needed this time to focus on Jasmine, not herself. "I—it must have been terrible for you," she said, putting her good hand on Jasmine's arm. The older woman brushed a single tear from her cheek under her sunglasses.

"Truly," Claire said, trying to comfort her, "I can't imagine anything worse. Well, except losing a child," she adding, suddenly missing Lexi terribly.

"Claire, it's just that, besides fearing I'll be arrested, I would hate to see Shadowlawn go to the state by default if something happens to me. I mean, if I'm sentenced for a crime I didn't do and sent away…like prison, damn it, or the death penalty."

"Nick won't let that happen. They would never go for the death penalty."

Jasmine whipped off her sunglasses and leaned closer to Claire. "Don't bet on it. You haven't met local law enforcement yet. Kent Goodrich, the county sheriff, is a cowboy, kind of like Bronco Gates, only pushy. I admit I'm afraid. Goodrich is politically ambitious and arresting me would raise his profile. I have to ask permission from his office to go out of the county, even just to drive here for the day. It's almost like bed check from the old dorm or sorority house days. I feel I'm under house arrest already. And here both Neil and Bronco are depending on me, and the estate needs them, too."

"I understand," Claire tried to comfort her, but she needed to get back on track. "You're living under a lot of pressure. So your mother lived there supported by Neil and Bronco? Not financially, I mean. Did Neil do the housecleaning, too?"

"Oh, that was a bit below Neil, though he's excellent in the kitchen and with repairs," Jasmine said, taking a lace-edged handkerchief out of her purse and wiping her eyes. "Lola did all that as well as serve, more or less, as Mother's maid."

Claire twisted her paper napkin on her lap so hard her left hand ached. She sat up straighter. "Who is Lola? Where is Lola?"

"I let her go. I felt bad about it, but I had to let her go. I didn't need her hovering and watching."

Hostility? Claire wondered. Resentment? Well, she was feeling both of those things right now, so she tried to calm down, modulate her voice.

"I need her entire name, Jasmine. Nick didn't mention her. You didn't—no one did."

"Oh, I—well, I suppose you could put her on the list, but she wasn't there that day. She helps her family with their puppet shows at times. Marionettes for children's birthday parties, appearances here and there in town."

"In town here?"

"They have a shop in Heritage Walk off St. George's Street. Although I hated to let her go, I can clean the few rooms of the house I use myself, and she did have that other family business and support. I'm sure the police must have talked to her, and I suppose she resented me. I—it's just an oversight that she wasn't mentioned, but I'm telling you, she's painfully shy. Doesn't say much, very private. People think she's stupid or autistic at first, but she isn't. It's as if the marionettes do the talking for her. You'd probably get more out of her twin sister. They're really tight but at least Cecilia has some social skills. I never understood how Mother and Lola hit it off so well—as if Mother sometimes took care of her instead of the other way around."

Yes, resentment. And Claire had to admit, another motive for Jasmine to have possibly hurt her mother. Claire was astounded and angry. With Jasmine. With Nick. This Lola was like one of the house ghosts then, sometimes seen but not heard!

"Jasmine, I'm sure you understand that I'll have to interview her," she said, trying to keep her temper in check. "How did you get along with her?"

"She made herself scarce when I was there to see Mother. Now don't be upset with Nick, as I'm not sure he saw her, or even knew of her."

"Please give me her full name and address."

"Lola Moran, but I'm not sure where she lives in town. But, to make up for my oversight, I can take you to their Party Puppets Shop."

"I'd appreciate that. If your mother did not accidentally overdose on her pills and you didn't harm her, someone did, someone who probably had her trust, knew their way around the house and about her medication. We have to find that person before that sheriff interrogates your staff again. Now let's finish up here, you talk me step-by-step through the day you found your mother on the floor, then I'll just take you up on going to see Lola Moran."

"Heck, Nick here," he said into his cell phone, staring at files on his laptop screen about another case. "Any calls from Claire about what time you're supposed to pick her up to head for Shadowlawn?"

"Not yet, boss. It's not set for Neil Costa 'til 4:00 p.m., so we got time. What'd the doc say?"

"She's healing well. Listen, I'd like for you to research whether or not my father's old 'friend'—and I use that term loosely—has any corporate ties to a company that makes quad copters, two-foot-square drones. This one I saw was white and, I think, had a camera. I swear it was hovering over Claire and me."

"He could've just bought one of those for his guys if they're still tailing you."

"I haven't seen any sign of 'boots on the ground,' but it's his style to buy companies just the way he buys people. You have any way to check into that?"

"I can try, but the guy's slippery as an eel."

"Damn, but he is. I swear I'd almost rather have him make a move than stalking and tormenting me."

"You're not thinking that ties into that weirdo you told me tried to scare you off the bridge?"

"A long shot, I guess. I don't know. There's too much I don't know right now."

"Don't let it get to you, 'cause we got a couple feelers out on locating Ames. Oh—sorry, you said not to use his name on the phone. Thing is, I guess money talks, and he's got it."

"Yeah, the bastard. Some of my father's money. Thanks, Heck. And take good care of Claire, keep your eyes open, even along that pretty river at Shadowlawn."

"Yes, boss, will do. I'll be in touch."

Nick punched off and stared at the phone log on the screen. Heck was working on his English but he always said *jes* instead of *yes*. As for *I'll be in touch*, that's what he wanted with Claire, to touch her. It had never hit him so hard, so fast, no matter how many women he'd known and dated, including his early-twenties passion for Jasmine years ago.

But he'd told himself, he couldn't risk having a wife or kids until he was sure Clayton Ames was dead or in prison. It would be just like that bastard to try to hurt Nick's family to get to him. He was positive Ames had killed his father and staged it to look like a suicide, maybe bought off the ME or the judge. Sometimes, the fact Ames had not struck yet obsessed him. He must know Nick was after him, was dedicated to nailing him if it was the last thing he ever did.

Jasmine, still apologizing for not mentioning Lola Moran before, parked her car near Old Town, then led Claire down the walking mall to a covered alleyway called Heritage Walk Mall, across St. George Street from the Catholic Basilica. It was 2:00 p.m., and bells from the steeple echoed here. The mall was a covered lane with shops on both sides. Claire noticed one where a man sat inside rolling cigars; she smelled tobacco even out here. On the other side was a display of great-looking leather purses, connected to a salsa shop called Mara's Hotter Side.

She saw ahead there was a back exit to the mall. They went farther toward a small shop with a sign that read Party Puppets and, staring at them out the window, many posed marionettes on strings: Spanish soldiers, Native Americans, princesses—how Lexi would love one of those!—and figures for Halloween over a month early, ghosts, witches, black cats, a skeleton, goblins. The sign said Closed, but there was a light on inside, so Jasmine tried the door, and it opened.

Looking nervous, Jasmine stuck her head in. The bell above the door jingled. "Lola! Cecilia! Anyone here? It's Miss Francine's daughter, Jasmine!"

Claire followed Jasmine in. No sound but a gust of wind from the open door shifted the marionettes hanging in clusters from the ceiling behind the counter. Their strings swayed; their loose limbs rattled. A few blinked their painted eyes.

"Someone must be here," Jasmine muttered. "The door was unlocked, and look at the price on these things."

Jasmine went to the back of the display room and called through the saloon-style doors, "Anyone here?"

"Maybe someone just went to the restroom," Claire said.

She closed the door behind her, but a breeze still blew in from the back room. "Maybe she smokes, or someone stepped out the back door for a breath of fresh air. Look, there's a plastic glass of soda here, and the ice isn't quite melted in it."

Claire looked around, remembering that Jasmine said Lola was always hovering and watching. With all these puppets here, she felt they were being watched.

"I think I have Lola's cell number," Jasmine said, peering through the saloon doors. "I'll just phone her and tell her we're here, that is, if she answers the phone." She whispered, "I repeat yet again, she is painfully shy. I always thought she needed counseling. It was almost as if she was like one of the puppets and not really there."

She took out her phone and punched in a number; Claire heard muffled musical ringing in the back room. "I hear it. I'll bet she fell asleep." She tiptoed to the doors and quietly stepped through them. "Hello! Lola or Cecilia? Could we talk to you?"

She followed the phone music. It was playing that song from *The Sound of Music* where Maria works the puppets with the children. How clever, how—

Among the hanging puppets in the back room, Christmas angels and Easter bunnies, Claire saw, half hidden, a woman's body. No puppet, no strings but a cordlike noose around her neck, suspending her from the rack attached to the ceiling. Hovering and watching…hovering and watching… Her tongue out, the dead woman stared blankly at Claire, silent now, silent forever.

So Claire screamed for her.

10

The dead woman's phone kept playing that bouncy tune. Jasmine ran into the back room where Claire stood gaping up at the corpse.

"Oh, dear God, no! No!" Jasmine cried.

"It's her—Lola?" Claire gasped out. Wavering on her feet, shaken and dizzy, she could barely stand. Those dead people of her nightmares…this was—this was real!

She told Jasmine, "Hang up your phone. I'll call the medics, the police and Nick." Her legs nearly gave out. She leaned against the wall by the back door. "Don't touch anything. The murderer's fingerprints could be anywhere." She stared at Jasmine's hands clasped together and pressed to her lips.

Jasmine turned, almost leaped at her and seized her shoulders. "No, we can't call the cops," she cried. "Do you know how this will look? Like I'm finding a dead body every month? They'll have my head. We've got to sneak out the back, wait 'til someone else comes in, finds her. We can't do anything to help her. Please, Claire. You—we'll sink Nick's case if this gets in the papers, too, the fact that I fired her, then she ends up like this."

Claire raised her good arm to break Jasmine's grip. The woman was strong in her panic and passion. Still pressed against the wall, Claire held her hand to her forehead as if that would force her to think.

"No, we can't lie. That would be worse. Someone could have seen us come in here—recognized you. She—I don't think rigor mortis has set in yet, so maybe someone just did this, ran out this open door. A forensic team will work this place, find out who—"

Jasmine doubled over, sucking air, crooning, moaning. She slid down to sit on the floor. Claire sat beside her, took her own cell phone from her shoulder purse and punched 911. She gave her name, told them what they'd found and where they were, asked for a medic squad and the police. They tried to keep her on the line, asking questions like what was her age, her address.

She told them she'd handle all that later. She punched off and called Nick. He didn't pick up, and it went to voice mail: "Attorney Nick Markwood here. I'm not available right now, but please leave a message, or if this is a business call or emergency, phone my office in Naples at…"

She wanted to throw the phone against the wall. She called Heck. He answered right away. "Heck, it's Claire. Jasmine and I need Nick. You have to find him, tell him where we are. He has to come at once. We've found a body, the woman who was Francine's maid. The police are on the way." She told him where they were.

"Okay, okay. He's taking a break in the pool about

twenty feet from me. He'll be there. I'll call Neil Costa and postpone the interview. Like they say on those forensic TV shows, don't touch anything..."

Don't touch anything... That was a good one. Jasmine's prints were all over the doorknob and she'd made a call from here to the dead woman. Claire's cell phone records would show calls from here, and her 911 would be recorded. Neil or even Bronco might know that Jasmine had words with this woman and resented her, and if so, there went Nick's case and hers, too. Even if they didn't prosecute Jasmine for her mother's death, now there was this.

Oh, damn. Just when Claire was trying to fly under the radar, this was going to blow up. And Nick was, too.

The police and the squad arrived almost at the same time. Because of the walking mall, they came in the back way. Jasmine was on her feet and somewhat subdued. One of the officers recognized her right away. At first even the medics stood in awe at the bizarre sight of a human body dangling among the marionettes. Then the police taped off the front of the store and the back room and took Claire and Jasmine out to separate squad cars to await questioning.

Great, just great, Claire thought. She was the one who was supposed to be doing interviews, and they were both going to get grilled. She kept looking at her watch. The hotel wasn't that far away. Where was Nick?

After what seemed like forever—but was twenty minutes—she heard his voice and craned around to see him talking to the detective in charge. Nick must have put his slacks and shirt right over his bathing suit because she could see the damp, darker outline of it.

"Yes, representing both of them," he said, his words floating to her.

It was hot in this squad car. The back alley was shaded, but the windows were barely cracked. She was getting dizzy. She still pictured that poor woman hanging inside, dead, dead, dead…like those terrible hallucinations at nightfall, deceased people chasing her, reaching for her, dragging her back…

She sucked in a breath and tried to get control. Rampaging emotions always did a cataplexic in. Her meds last night…needed to take both of them and hadn't…

It made her angry that Nick went to talk to Jasmine first. She needed to prep him. Who knew what Jasmine would say when she was interviewed? Actually, who knew if she was to be trusted, despite Nick's constant vouching for her? But, after a moment, leaving that squad car door open, he strode toward Claire and opened her door.

"I'm your lawyer now as well as your boss. I can't believe when you knew you had to protect Jasmine, you two found a body."

Fury and frustration poured through Claire. She got out of the car, pushed him back a step. How dare he blame her!

"Look, counselor. Yes, I stumbled on the body of a woman no one told me about—a key witness either for or against Jasmine. Don't you think her maid might know what happened to Francine, and she was MIA as far as you knew. You said you gave me a complete list of Francine's staff!"

"I swear I didn't know about Lola Moran."

"You mean that Francine never mentioned her and Jasmine didn't, either? Nick, the poor woman was Francine's aide around the mansion, her *personal* maid."

"Jasmine says Lola wasn't there when Francine died. And that she barely talks and would be a terrible witness."

"Yeah, well Win Jackson talks all the time but he also says he wasn't there. I'm sure whoever is guilty would just blurt out the truth. I shouldn't have to tell you I need all the key interviews to put the puzzle together. I believe that's what you hired me for."

"All right, all right. I screwed up but I didn't know about this woman."

Claire exhaled hard. "Jasmine said Lola often made herself scarce and was here sometimes at this puppet store or giving shows. I didn't mean to jump on you, either. But Jasmine should have told you and me about her. What else hasn't she shared? Does she have an alibi for the time frame in which Lola died?"

"You don't suspect her?"

"I'm trying to think like the police if they learn she fired Lola, and I can tell Jasmine resented her, maybe was jealous of Francine's attention to the girl."

"Look, I hear rigor mortis hasn't set in yet, and Jasmine's been with you. You are her alibi. Besides, she wouldn't agree to bring you here if she'd harmed her. In these warm ambient temperatures—it was poorly air-conditioned in that back room—"

"Maybe because we found the back door open."

"My point is, rigor mortis sets in faster in warmth,

and I overheard the detective say it hadn't set in on Lola yet."

"Actually, I observed that."

"So someone killed her quite recently, and Jasmine was with you. Claire, I need you to be on my and my client's side! You should have called me from the park, first thing before coming here."

"Never mind changing the subject. I always watch for that when someone feels guilty. Nick, that poor woman inside was suddenly at the top of my list to talk to, so of course I hurried here! And she might have been a hostile witness against Jasmine!"

"Keep your voice down. This place is swarming with cops."

"You know, I noticed that."

Another wave of anger poured through Claire. She wanted to please Nick, and he blamed her. This wasn't her fault. And surely, this murder wasn't Jasmine's, either. She never would have agreed to bring Claire here right now if she'd been the one who had harmed Lola—would she?

A woman—she looked almost like Lola—ran past the squad cars and the rescue squad down the alley, toward the back entrance of the shop. An officer grabbed her, turned her back.

"No," she shrieked, "let me in. They called me. My sister, my store!"

They watched the officer speak quietly to her. The woman began to sob. Tears blurred Claire's sight of the scene.

"That's obviously Cecilia, her twin sister," she told Nick, but she suddenly sounded strange to herself, as if she were underwater. Before she could stop herself, she blurted out, "My sister screamed like that when I found her—our mother. And Jasmine found hers and…"

Her knees buckled. She didn't mean to argue with Nick. She had to watch her emotions, fighting for the truth, fighting him… She tried to grab the car door and get back inside before she collapsed. His hands came hard on her waist, and he half lifted, half pushed her to get in the backseat and put her head down between her knees.

"One of the medics—send one here!" he shouted, pushing her across the backseat and getting in beside her. "This woman's fainted."

Shades of when she was shot. Poor Nick.

But she hadn't fainted. She heard him. It was her missed meds…missed her mother, missed Lexi, maybe Jace, too.

"I'm fine," she told him. "Tell them I'm fine and to stay away."

Just like Lexi curled up in her arms, she curled against Nick in the backseat of a car or somewhere good, somewhere he could keep bad dreams away.

Jasmine and then Claire managed to make it through the detective's questioning at the police station. Nick sat with each of them during their separate interviews. Jasmine finally received permission to drive back home, but, Nick told Claire, she was really annoyed that the detective here had called Sheriff Goodrich back in Putnam County to tell him what had happened.

"She's afraid Sheriff Goodrich is going to put her under house arrest, though it would be better than being in jail there," he explained. "He's like a pit bull, looking for evidence against Jasmine, when I keep telling him—other than a family disagreement on how to handle the house—there isn't any."

"Is it too late to call Heck and have him take me to interview Neil Costa? We've got to get ahead of Sheriff Goodrich. Jasmine says he's not good and not rich, but wants to be both. A politician at heart—if he had a heart, she says."

"No way you're going to interview Neil Costa right now fifty miles from here! After you've been through this and almost fainted? I'm taking you home and up to your room. Can you walk to my car?"

"Of course I can. See, the thing is I messed up my meds last night and that made me a little tired and gimpy today."

"Gimpy? Did you trip or fall over?"

"Not quite," she said as they walked out of the police station to his car in the parking lot. He put his arm around her waist. He felt so good—solid to counteract her shakiness. If she did fall today, she thought, it was just that she fell a little more for him, but she'd never let him know. It had also shaken her to have Cecilia Moran thank her for finding Lola and calling for help. Claire couldn't fathom how it would feel to lose Darcy, so she totally sympathized with the poor woman.

Cecilia had also said Claire could call her later if she had questions about Lola's job at Shadowlawn. As Cecilia put it, "Francine treated her like a daughter but Jasmine had treated her like someone selling something at the door—'Goodbye. Get out!'" Since Cecilia, in place of her twin sister, could obviously be a hostile witness against Jasmine, Claire was half-afraid to question her, but it had to be done.

Nick put Claire in the passenger seat, even hooked her seat belt, leaning in over her. He smelled of swimming pool chlorine, but on him it was better than aftershave or cologne. He got in and started the car, pulling slowly out of the parking lot.

"They let me have a glimpse of the scene," he said. "Bizarre with all those hanging puppets. The murderer has a sick sense of humor. If Bronco Gates was back now, I'd talk to him right away."

"I'd expect Neil, with his *Creature from the Black Lagoon* museum, to be the one with the strange sense of humor."

"Wait until you meet Gates. And he's got tall tales and funny stories about everything. Like I said, he supplements his income by hunting not only alligators on the river in season but pythons down in the Everglades. I wanted you to see and talk to him for yourself, but consider that a warning. Though Gates works on the Shadowlawn grounds, he lives in one of those old Airstream trailers down by the river. But all that aside, who would silence a shy, quiet domestic worker and children's puppeteer by murdering her?"

"Maybe the same person who killed Francine."

Nick insisted on taking her up to her room to get her settled. From there, he ordered taco salads and iced tea from room service and sat on the balcony until she washed up. It was breezy but warm. He'd taken off his damp trousers and wore his swimming trunks. When she joined him, she kicked off her sandals and put her bare feet up on the lowest rung of the balcony rail.

"What a day," she said with a sigh. "I'm glad Heck can go with me in the morning to see Neil."

"He rescheduled you for 10:00 a.m. That will give you a chance to get a good night's sleep—and get back on all your meds."

"I haven't messed up on those for such a long time. My goal is to try to switch myself off my doses of that powerful stuff to herbal sleep remedies like melatonin, valerian, chamomile tea, even lemon balm liquid extract. But with all that's going on, I can't experiment with any of that now."

"Claire," he said, turning toward her and taking her right hand in his left, "you said something about finding your mother on the floor, and your sister screamed. Can you talk about that?"

"I try not to even think about it," she admitted. "I know I blurted that out. My mother—she didn't take care of herself. Ate too much, little exercise. She was heavy—which is—it's why I try to watch my weight. She had a sudden, fatal stroke when Darcy and I were in high school. I found her—gone, with the book she was reading in her hand. And that was that. Dad stayed home more after that but, from then on, Darcy and I kind of raised each other. And maybe we had before that."

"I'm sorry. We have something in common. My father—he died really young." He looked as if he'd say more about that, but instead he asked, "Claire, are you sure you can handle all this right now?"

"Yes. I told you, yes."

"I don't like it that someone just upped the ante

by silencing a voice who could have been—probably was—a key witness. I blew it not to know about her, and Jasmine made a big mistake not to tell me. I know this sounds heartless, but I'm actually hoping the police—and your talking to Cecilia Moran—turn up that someone completely unrelated to Shadowlawn in Lola's life did that."

She sighed. "Jasmine did keep trying to convince me that Lola wouldn't know anything anyway, that she wasn't there that day, that she didn't talk much and was painfully shy. But what if someone didn't want her to talk to me? There's no way that poor woman committed suicide, whatever problems she faced. I don't see any way she could have lifted herself up there without a ladder—or help. Nick, I'm not making any deductions from all that, but we need to be careful. I will and you, too."

"Deal," he said and, though she thought he would shake her hand, he leaned closer and kissed her mouth, lightly, quickly. It took her by surprise. She blushed, felt her skin heat from her throat to her cheekbones. They stared at each other a moment before a knock resounded on the hall door.

"Room service with food and caffeine," he said. "I'll get it."

Claire got up and went in, too, opened the drawer on the table next to the bed and took a pill from the bottle there. She watched Nick open the door and gasped. Not room service but Jace standing there, fists clenched, glaring at Nick and her.

11

"Jace!" Claire cried. "What are you doing here?"

"Breaking up a private meeting, I guess."

"Nick Markwood," Nick said, thrusting his hand at Jace. "We're going over our case on the balcony, waiting for room service. But since you're here to surprise Claire, I'll leave you two alone. Is that okay, Claire?" he asked, turning back to her.

"It's fine. He's probably just passing through as usual. But I'd love to hear how Lexi's doing."

"I'll be sure Heck picks you up for the interview about nine tomorrow," Nick said.

Claire marveled at how calm Nick seemed. At least Jace hadn't made a fool of himself by some sort of crazy accusation. Still, she blushed again to think that Nick had just kissed her, and she could still feel his lips on hers, however quick it had been.

But Jace's demeanor was another thing, more like a ticking time bomb. He glared at her as Nick walked out. Jace closed the door, came in and did an obvious once-over of the bed, evidently to see if it was mussed or unmade. Arms crossed over his chest, he walked to the balcony and looked out at the view of the bay. When he came back in, he had Nick's slacks in his hand.

"Your 'employer' left these out on the balcony," he said, his voice barely leashed as he faced her in the room. He threw them down on the bed.

"Well," Jace went on, "perhaps he just took these off so he could dive into the swimming pool from way up here. And room service rather than eating out? Tea for two or something to celebrate? I looked his picture up, knew who he was the minute he opened your door."

"Just cut the innuendos."

"How about this one, then? I see you lost the sling. Both arms free now."

"Whatever you're thinking is wrong. And how did you get my room number? They don't give those out."

"I was down there by the pool," he said, pointing at the balcony. "I looked up, and there you were. With him."

She figured he didn't see the kiss, but she was so upset she almost didn't care. "Would you like to sit down for a little while?" she asked, gesturing toward the balcony. "Salads and iced tea will be here shortly."

"Compliments of the big-time lawyer. No, thanks. Just wanted to know how you were." He was still frowning, and he made no move to head for the balcony. She decided not to either, but to avoid staying so close to the bed she sat down at the desk where she had her laptop and folders spread out.

"This is hardly the place to fly out of to get back to Singapore," she said, pleased her voice sounded somewhat controlled.

"I'll drive to 'Jacktown,' get a connector to LAX

there. You should have been home these last couple of days. Lexi and I had a great time."

"She told me. That was special for her and you, too, but I need to make a living and build my business."

"Yeah, right. But we should do something together next time. Maybe Disney."

"Darcy and her two can go with us. Any way you look at it, you'd have to pay for two rooms."

"They have suites, you know. And I meant just the three of us."

"I know Lexi would love it. If I'm not on an assignment and you and I could come to a good post-marital working relationship, maybe."

"You know you're starting to sound like a damn lawyer. Look, Claire," he said, walking toward her, "I know part of our problem was my fault, being gone so much. In the future I might just get cross-country, Canadian or South American flights when this contract is up."

"Lexi would love that."

"Would you quit saying that? What about you? Us?"

"Jace, there is no 'us' except as Lexi's parents who want the very best for her. You left, you wanted a divorce. So why did you come here? You could have called."

He propped his fists on her desk and leaned toward her, stiff-armed. "But then I wouldn't have found you and your employer all cozy together, would I?" he demanded, his voice rising.

Suddenly, this was all too much. Trying to figure Jasmine out. Finding a body among those bizarre puppets. Did Jace still think she was a puppet, and he could pull her strings?

"Please keep your voice down and calm down," she said.

"You know, you're as good—or as bad—as a regular shrink," he insisted, his voice rising. "You gonna pull one of those psych-out interviews on me?"

She was surprised—and suddenly a little afraid—of how upset the usual automatic-control pilot was. If he knew what had happened to her earlier today, that the police were involved, and that she was starting to feel personally involved with Nick as well as professionally—

"Jace, I don't think you're in the mood to tell me about the nice time you had with Lexi. Why don't you just text me and send the photos to my phone?" Grateful when a knock sounded on the hall door, she got up and walked around him to answer it.

"Ah," he said, "saved by the bell."

She ignored that and opened the door for a woman with the tray. It annoyed her that Jace whipped out a five-dollar bill as she put the tray down. "That's the going rate for a room service tip in Singapore," he told Claire. "I think we're done here. Enjoy!"

He stalked out.

"He not want his salad?" the woman asked.

"Not right now," Claire said, fighting fatigue, tears and anger.

After the woman left, Claire slid the room bolt and the chain lock in place. She picked at one of the salads and drank both iced teas, while she talked to Lexi, who said Daddy had flown away again, so the child had no idea he'd come here. Sitting at her desk, she forced herself to go over her interview questions for Neil and Bronco, and wrote out some for Cecilia, until it was time for her night med and bed.

Instead, she called Nick.

"I worked quite a while after you—and he—left," she told him. "Sorry about Jace's surprise visit."

"Everything okay?"

"Yes. He didn't stay long."

"He wants you back," Nick said, surprising her when she didn't think anything could after today. She hadn't seen that—didn't want to believe that.

"Not going to happen," she told him.

"I don't like to see families have problems, but good."

Her insides cartwheeled. What to say?

"I need to concentrate on this case."

"Right. Me, too. We'll get through it together. But any more surprises—I don't mean Jace—you call me and don't go walking into some place that hasn't been checked out."

"I agree."

"I like the sound of that, too."

And she liked the sound of his voice. Smooth. Silky. Comforting, yet downright disturbing. Hard to believe she'd only known Nick for a little over a week.

"Good night," she said, shocked her voice was a throaty whisper. "See you tomorrow."

"Call me anytime you need help," he said. "Anytime."

Like an idiot adolescent—well, she had somehow missed her teenage years being so sick and bullied, too—she sighed as she got in between the sheets.

Jace still had two days to kill before heading to LAX, but he sure as heck wasn't going to spend them around northeast Florida. He watched TV in the hotel room he got not far from Claire's ritzy one—in the Best Western—and fell asleep early, though he kept waking up and remembering Claire with Nick Markwood. Jace had to admit he'd been a jerk, but she'd almost made him lose his temper, after years of working hard to keep it reined in. That delicate but strong woman always did push his buttons.

In the morning, he went down for breakfast before checking out, ordered coffee and grabbed a copy of the local paper, the *St. Augustine Record*. Waiting for his sausage and eggs, he opened it and read the front page headline, Local Woman's Body Found Hanged Amid Her Puppets in Old Town Shop. And the second, smaller headline read, Lola Moran's Body Found by Suspect in Another Murder And Her Forensic Psychologist Friend.

He studied the captioned photos. An old one of the dead woman working marionettes with her sister while kids about Lexi's age watched. Another of police cars and the EMS vehicle parked behind a building with an open door to a shop. And, wouldn't you know—Claire standing next to one of the cars in heated conversation with Nick Markwood. Had to be; it was a distant shot, but he could pick out both their profiles.

He skimmed the article: "Jasmine Montgomery Stanton…undecided cause of the death of Stanton's well-known mother and wealthy benefactor of local causes, Francine Montgomery…" And then—yes, damn it. "Police summoned to the murder scene by Claire Britten of Naples, Florida."

Man, she was in way over her head this time! He

scrunched up the top sheet of the paper in his hand, then got hold of himself. He smoothed it back out and bent over it. Yeah, here was Nick Markwood's name, too.

"More coffee, sir?"

"Yeah, thanks. I thought I was in a hurry, but I'm not going anywhere."

"So, Neil Costa's *Creature from the Black Lagoon* museum sounds like a pretty *loco* place, yes?" Heck asked as he pulled into the long drive to Shadowlawn. "I'm gonna watch my back if he does the interview in that place."

"I hope he'll show it to us," Claire said, "but I'm not doing the interview there—unless I need to keep Jasmine from hovering when I talk to him."

"I'll take care of that," Nick said from the backseat where he'd been on the phone and working on his laptop. After the chaos of yesterday, he'd decided he needed to see his client while Claire and Heck spent time with Neil. She was glad to have him along. Besides, Nick had been right that Heck tended to speed and, at least with Nick in the backseat with an occasional comment, she hadn't needed to scold Heck.

Nick went on, "If Jasmine says anything about her or Francine's relationship with Lola, I'll let you know, Claire, but I won't question her on that."

Heck looked through the SUV's windshield at Shadowlawn with the same rapt expression Claire figured she must have had when she first saw it.

"Wow, this place is somethin'," Heck said. "My grandfather, he had a mansion in Havana, big and *muy bonita*, seen pictures of it, growing up. 'Course, never saw it in person. Yet. Want to, though, even if it's in ruins, even if the damned Castros gave it to their cronies. Some big deal *jefe* living there now, so's I hear."

"I'm sorry about all that, all that your family lost," Claire told him.

"Like to get it back. Might someday. The Castros, they bad and crazy, too."

Not only crazy, but hated, Claire realized. Among the scattering of bumper stickers on the back of Heck's SUV—sayings like What Are You Driving At? and Nonconformists, Unite!—the one that stuck out in her mind said simply, Kill Castro!

Heck pulled in near the front portico. This time Neil Costa came out to greet them. Claire wondered about his last name. Could he be descended from Cuban refugees, too? It certainly wasn't on her list of questions for him.

"I hear yesterday didn't go as planned," Neil told her as he greeted the three of them. Heck was introduced as her assistant who kept her interview logs and was a data expert. "Poor Lola! Who would do that to a quiet, unassuming woman? Sheriff Goodrich questioned both Jasmine and me here last night, but nothing we could say would help. But today, anything to help Jasmine," he concluded in a rush with the words that seemed to be his motto as well as Win's.

"Yes," Claire said. "Now there are two deaths to be investigated."

"I've got to warn you," Neil said, "the sheriff asked both of us when you'd be back here, and I felt I had to tell him. He probably wants to talk to you, too."

Nick put in, "That figures, but he has no jurisdiction where Lola's death occurred, unless he thinks it happened in this county and she was moved, which I doubt. I'm glad I came along today. I'm familiar with his tactics. He has no real case, so he puts pressure on everyone, hoping something pops free."

"All that aside, please come in," Neil said. "Jasmine will be down for a late breakfast in a few minutes. Usually, she's up early but it's understandable after events. I have coffee and pecan rolls for all of you, then we'll get down to business. I'd like to show you my movie museum."

Claire said, "Win Jackson, movie buff that he is, told me about that. I'd love to see it."

Neil's worried expression lit up before he frowned again. "Dr. Jackson told me once it was 'small potatoes.' He thinks he has a way with words and with the history of old movies, but I'm telling you, the man is a cinema snob. So what if other snobs labeled *Creature* a B-grade movie? I'm thinking of advertising my collection online, pulling more people in. I would never sell my things on eBay like some have suggested. They are family heirlooms from my great-uncle who helped with lighting for the making of the trilogy. After all, if we could just promote the ghosts who live here, my creature display could tie right in to creatures of the night!"

Claire thought he was making a joke, but evidently not. So, she thought, Neil was not necessarily against the mansion becoming a public attraction. And the tension between him and Win went both ways.

Claire's gaze snagged Nick's as they went inside. Behind Neil's back he mouthed to her, "Ghosts and creatures? I just want a murderer!"

"At least," she whispered as Neil and Heck walked on ahead toward the dining room, "after the surprise and horror of yesterday, what worse could happen?"

12

"No doubt, mistakes were made on both sides," Neil told Claire with a shake of his head and a shrug.

She had asked him whether Francine and Jasmine had ever disagreed about the future of the estate in his earshot. As they sat in the library, facing each other in high-backed leather chairs, he seemed eager to help, but he was in the flight-mode position and he hadn't answered the question. His upper body was turned toward her, but his feet toward the door. It was one of the basic body language giveaways that a person wanted to escape being questioned.

"Disagreements in families—of course, we all have that," he went on. "I was aware of their differing opinions. And I must tell you, I prefer your calm mode of questioning over my dealing with the county sheriff after Francine's death and then, briefly last night, when he came to see Jasmine over both of you finding Lola's body. So hard to imagine—so hard to get over seeing her like that."

His eyes teared up. Perhaps Lola had meant something to him as well as to Francine. For one who studied each word a person spoke, Claire noted well he'd said, *so hard to get over seeing her like that*, when he hadn't seen Lola like that. Had he? He frequently ran errands, but could he have gone clear into St. Augustine, visited—and killed—Lola and come back?

Claire tried another tack. "So, who could have known where Francine's anxiety medicine was kept and how dangerous an overdose could be?"

"Other than Francine herself, Jasmine, I suppose, but you'd best ask her. Lola, of course, God rest her soul. It was known by her—me, too, of course—that the pills must be in her bathroom, down the hall from Rosalynn's room—that's what we've always called it. Oh, I did pick up Francine's prescription in Palatka a couple of times at a pharmacy, never at her doctor's. Well, the doctor who prescribed the Propranolol was in St. Augustine anyway."

He'd smoothly spit out the difficult name of the drug, but then, if he'd had to pick up prescriptions, that was understandable. But did it mean he could have taken a few of the pills from a fresh prescription to add to her food later? Sometimes Claire had a flash of hating this job: she was obsessed with looking for lies and guilt.

Besides that, Neil was trying to assert that he was telling the truth by repeating *of course*. But she still didn't feel he was lying—perhaps just nervous. He had his whole future at stake here, whether it was only that he and his museum would be kicked off the property or whether he was guilty of harming Francine. Not only did he want to protect himself, but Jasmine, too, if she wanted to keep the estate in the family. That is, unless Neil knew that, even if Jasmine kept Shadowlawn, she wanted what Win had called a "small potatoes," shoddy museum off the grounds.

"Could Bronco Gates have known where Francine's meds were?" she asked.

"Only through overhearing, though it is pretty logical where the pills were. He does know the house as well as the grounds, so he could have searched for them. As you'll see when he returns, the man seems to appear out of nowhere and is silent on his feet. A hunter and killer at heart—well, I didn't mean of people, of course, just of beasts like gators and pythons."

Claire's pulse pounded. Neil was trying to cast suspicion on Bronco. Once she talked to Bronco, that all had to be probed.

"Do you consider Bronco a friend?" she asked.

"To Francine or to me?"

"To you."

"We've worked well together for years. Each knows his bailiwick, his part of the kingdom, so to speak. You know, back to a question you asked earlier. I believe Bronco did know about her medications, at least that she was on edge and that she was better when she 'popped a pill' as he put it. He said that when she took him to task about a month ago over his skinning an alligator out back, leaving the skins stretched on the ground. But I'd say everyone got along well on her staff, as different as we all were."

So much, she thought, for a possible conspiracy theory among these two men, though selling or deeding Shadowlawn to the state might have disenfranchised them both. For a conspiracy to work well, the plotters needed to have close connections and try to cover for each other, and Neil seemed to be giving hints that Bronco was a loose cannon—as Win had, too.

"So you were here and upstairs part of the time on the day Francine apparently overdosed," she prompted.

"My own house records will show that. I don't have them here now, though, because Sheriff Goodrich told his detective to take them into evidence. But I recall that Lola had just left to help with a birthday puppet show in St. Augustine, and Bronco was on the grounds somewhere. Jasmine came and went. There was a decent wind that day, and I was airing out the upstairs, opening windows. Installing air-conditioning for the mansion would be exorbitant, but even with all the shade here it can get warm upstairs. Francine was aware we'd need AC year round if we brought in an audience, so that cost might also have gone into her thoughts about turning the mansion over to the state or even selling it the right way."

"An audience—an interesting word for a movie buff like yourself. Would it have made any difference to your museum if the family opened the grounds and house or the state took over and did that?"

"Shadowlawn should and could remain in family hands if Jasmine could just find funding. Whatever happens, I would hope that my unique, if small, museum could be sponsored by the state or by anyone who bought or opened up the house. After all, the river near here was the black lagoon in a series of cult and popular culture movies, and the state of Florida ought to be proud of that."

Neil sat up straighter and finally shifted his body out of the flight mode. His voice rose as he declared,

"If mistakes were made, I regret it, concerning this long legacy of the family I serve!"

"Employees are often not loyal these days, so that's very admirable," Claire tried to assure him. It was the second time he'd said *mistakes were made*. But he hadn't said by whom. Had he done something rash he was regretting? Her job was to ponder and parse every word, but was she getting too paranoid, too personally involved in this case? She felt for poor Francine, and she certainly wanted to please Nick—her own self-analysis right now.

"Let me ask if you saw any signs that Francine was more distressed or nervous than usual just before her death."

"A bit. No doubt, her public disagreement with Jasmine set her off, but you can strike that out, Heck," he said, turning toward him. "Pure opinion on my part. But she did say to me she was sleeping less. Yes, I guess she did seem a bit depressed and irritable."

Signs of suicidal thoughts, Claire noted. And, if distressed, she might have upped her dosage of the pills and accidentally taken too many without help from anyone else. Or she might have meant to end it all and let Jasmine have things her way, despite the financial struggles she would face.

"Do you think she might have taken more of her panic attack pills to counteract how she felt?"

"I wouldn't know. The sheriff took her pill bottles to, no doubt, count the pills and consult on her dosages with the pharmacy. Poor Lola might have known, of course. Again, I'm trying to stick to facts for you, not impressions or opinions."

"I appreciate that, but from such a close friend and

observer of the deceased, those can be valuable, too. You haven't been sworn in, and we're not making an affidavit or testifying in court here. Now, if it's a good time with your duties, I'd love to take a break and see your museum—and Heck would, too."

Jace parked his rental car about a hundred yards down the road from where the GPS on his smartphone indicated Shadowlawn Plantation should be. He hadn't gotten much info from either the newspaper article or his map, but he'd picked up the location from Google searches. It made him angry that Claire had taken an assignment that brought her way out here, hundreds of miles from home. Palatka wasn't exactly Podunk, but this road along the river reminded him of some travel channel show about the past, and he much preferred living in the present.

He guessed he got that from his gung-ho marine dad, though he hated to admit he'd inherited any traits from him. His father might shout *Semper Fi*, but he'd never been faithful to Jace or his mother. In and out of their lives, sometimes call of duty, sometimes just restless—or chasing women. Jace had been raised by a drill sergeant who wanted perfection. He'd demanded complete trust and honesty, then the lying bastard had taken off for good. It was for good; Jace always told himself he was glad to be rid of him and his mom was better off, but she'd never really gotten over him. Finally ready to retire, Master Sergeant Jason Britten had died in Iraq taking care of young marines like he was their father. Jace might have flown for the navy—trying to connect with his Dad—but he'd refused to become a gung-ho marine.

But, hell, Jace still had to admit he both loved and hated the man.

Walking down the road—after a driver of a pickup had stopped to ask if he needed gas or help—he found the long lane with the small sign Shadowlawn at the end, and decided to walk toward the house. He'd listen for guard dogs, didn't want to be caught on the private entry lane and no way was he going to tip off or infuriate Claire or Nick Markwood by just driving in if they were here. He'd get back to St. Augustine by nightfall, call Claire and ask her to meet him in the restaurant or lobby downstairs in her hotel. After she found a body yesterday, surely he could pull her strings—Lexi, danger—to get her back home. He'd up her child care support, anything to get her out of here and away from Markwood. Jace wouldn't trust a rich lawyer as far as he could throw him.

He hated to admit it but he still loved—well, at least, cared deeply for—Claire.

He moved away from the narrow lane that headed toward the house, walking about five yards off it, going from tree to tree where he wouldn't be spotted. He gasped when he glimpsed the place. Huge. He crept a lot closer and peered around a live oak close to the mansion.

Jace heard a sound behind him and started to spin around. But the jolt to the back of his head sent him facedown into the grass. Then there was only night.

Saying he'd make them all lemonade, Neil had disappeared about fifteen minutes ago out toward the kitchen, so Claire and Heck sat and talked. She had felt more tense than she usually did in interviews, so she took the time to unwind. She was surprised Neil was gone so long, but they were interrupting his regular duties, and he'd said he'd take drinks to Jasmine and Nick. Claire thought of going to find Nick to ask if he'd like to tour the Creature museum with them, but he'd said he'd seen it once and she hated to butt in on him and Jasmine right now. She and Heck went over his notes, but when Heck wanted to discuss them, she told him, "Not here. The walls might have ears."

"Ghost ears?"

"Someone told you all that, huh? No. Do you believe in ghosts?"

"In the spirits from the past that haunt us in our hearts, yes," he said as Neil finally came back in with the lemonade, ginger cookies and the key to the museum. Perhaps he'd ducked out to arrange things there.

After their refreshments, they followed him down the old brick walk to what was once the outdoor kitchen block. He unlocked the door with a flourish and led them in, snapping on a switch that lit three overhead lights. So he had put some money into this place, she thought.

The interior was one large, high-ceilinged room with curved partitions which funneled visitors into narrow passageways that spiraled inward. The entire room was painted black—no, that was some sort of inner lining, maybe painted drywall. She noted, as they stepped farther in, the lighting system sent shivery, silver waves onto the walls and ceiling, no doubt to give the illusion they were underwater. The curved entryway displayed posters and explanatory signs.

Neil said, "The creature—Gill-man—had a bad habit of taking kidnapped women down to his underwater sanctuary. I've tried to re-create that."

On the first wall, he pointed at a series of movie posters under glass.

The first one was from *Creature from the Black Lagoon, 1954 in 3-D!* A printed sign next to it read, "Outdoor scenes filmed on the St. Johns River near here." Another read, "Mention of the monster in Stephen King's book and horror movie of the same name, *It*." The creature was grotesque-looking, with amphibious, clawed hands and a finned face. The woman wearing a bathing suit being abducted was, of course, terrified.

The second poster advertised *Revenge of the Creature, 1955.* "The St. Johns River stood in for the Amazon River during this filming," a sign read. There was a second sign, "First movie role by Clint Eastwood in a bit part as lab technician Jennings."

Claire jumped when Heck spoke close behind her, "Well, everyone who makes it big got to start somewhere."

They shuffled along to the third poster. It advertised *The Creature Walks Among Us, 1956.* This one had been filmed in 2-D, whatever that was, and the creature looked changed.

"He mutated," Neil explained, touching her elbow to lead them farther in. Around the turn, the creature reared above them, seven feet tall, claws uplifted, mouth open. Claire sucked in a gasp.

"Looks real, doesn't he?" Neil asked, beaming.

"He was greenish in the poster, but now he looks—yellow."

"They had to make one yellow suit for the underwater filming," Neil told them, looking, she thought, like a proud father showing off his new baby. He pointed to the second mounted creature farther in, this one green. "That's airtight, molded sponge rubber. For the underwater scenes, air was fed to the actor through a rubber hose. In the story, Gill-man keeps killing members of an expedition one by one to protect all he holds dear. You can watch the last movie—*Revenge*—on YouTube, but I have it here, too, ready to run over in that corner, if you have time. I have many other photographs about the filming, pages from a script, diagrams of the sets, much more, over here, see?"

They walked along a wall of pictures, most black and white. She wondered what Win Jackson would think of the river shots. Several pictures were of Neil's great-uncle who had worked on the lighting for the film, as well as other cast and crew members.

"I wish we had time, Neil," she told him, "but I have a few more questions for you. You said Bronco would be back this afternoon, so I'd like to schedule talk time with him."

"Oh, sure. Business before pleasure, always. On the way out, we can see if he's back yet."

Claire couldn't believe how relieved she was to get outside. That crazy place cast a spell. She'd have to walk down by the river soon to see if it looked like the photos here.

As for the woman clutched in the monster's arms, she wasn't quite a redhead but had auburn hair. And her screaming mouth—Claire's memory of Fiend Face jumped at her again.

She wondered if the undulating light waves had made her a little queasy. She sucked in a big breath. Glancing down at the river lined by ancient trees with moss hanging over it, she could almost imagine the Creature there.

Neil asked, "Did Jasmine or Mr. Markwood tell you Bronco lives in a trailer on the grounds—over that way? I tell him if my museum Creature ever gets loose, his trailer would be the first place he'd visit. Oh, I see him now, his truck, that is, driving in," he said, pointing at a black pickup truck that had seen better days. "Let's give him a little time to get settled, and I'll explain about your interview with him. If he hasn't heard the news about Lola's murder, he's going to freak out, so I'd better let him know and give him time to settle down before you talk to him."

"Good," Claire said. "Good idea." Besides, she was the one who needed time to get herself settled down.

13

"I still can't get over finding Lola like that," Jasmine told Nick as they sat on the second-floor shaded veranda at the back of the house with the lemonade Neil had brought them.

Her hand went to her throat, and the sight of the puppet strings cutting into the woman's neck slammed at Nick again. He'd only had a glimpse of the scene from the back door of the shop, but it haunted—no, wrong word around here—it sickened him.

"I was so glad Claire was with me—not to walk in there alone," Jasmine went on, turning toward him in her canvas deck chair. "I suppose she told you that my first instinct was to run—to let someone else report her death. Claire talked me out of it, but our finding Lola like that isn't going to help with Sheriff Goodrich and his detective on my tail."

"No, she didn't tell me. And don't obsess about the sheriff. I've held him off so far."

"But I'm sick of questions and accusations, however subtle. From him, even from Claire."

He sat up straighter and turned toward her. Her

gold bracelet kept rattling against the wooden arm of the chair, and it annoyed him. He took a swig of lemonade, then said, "Claire is on your—on our—side. Her job is to establish and, through others, to corroborate you did not kill your mother, that either she overdosed accidentally or on purpose or someone—not you—harmed her."

"But, I mean, if I'm indicted, and you call her to the stand in my defense, can we trust her?"

"What are you talking about?" he asked, his voice rising. "She's good, she's well-trained. I've seen her in action in a high-stakes, tense trial, so what do you mean?" He felt a flash of fear that—no, that couldn't be. He believed Jasmine did not kill her mother.

"Well, here we are with the fact that Mother's meds did her in, with or without outside interference," Jasmine plunged on. "At lunch at the park yesterday, when Claire took a pill, she admitted to me she has narcolepsy and what she called 'mild cataplexy.' I'm sensing she wants to accuse someone of hurting Mother because she sympathizes with her. Did you know about Claire's illness?"

"She told me up front."

"Well, did she tell you about the powerful medication she takes day and night to control it?"

"Not in so many words, but—"

"I knew it. And you're so taken with her you're giving all that a pass, aren't you? Nick, the stuff she takes at night is so dangerous that if someone else gets a sip of it, you have to call poison control. It can cause hallucinations if not properly handled, so can she even recognize reality if something goes awry with her treatment? One of the ingredients in her night medicine is the so-called 'date rape' drug, and I'm telling you that just because they're more or less 'knock-out' drops. And get this. Since she's on this case about Mother possibly being depressed enough to commit suicide, I figure you should know that liquid med she takes has that side effect—depression and thoughts of suicide! I like Claire, but I'm afraid you do, too, in quite another way, and you're trusting her too much."

Nick was steamed but he tried to keep control. No, he didn't know all that, but he trusted Claire and her judgment.

Jasmine's bracelet rattled again as she reached to grasp his wrist. Was he being played here? Did she really have a point? Was she jealous? Damn it, was she innocent?

"Nick?"

"Jasmine, get this through your head. You're not the one doing the research, putting this case together. I am, with Claire's help and Heck for backup. You want to replace your lawyer, that will get all three of us out of here. Otherwise, trust me—and her."

But he was shaken. Surely, he hadn't given away how attracted he was to Claire. If so, he was losing it. With this second death of Francine's maid, he couldn't afford to lose time, Claire's work, or this explosive case.

The opening bars to "Don't Worry, Be Happy" sounded on Claire's cell phone. She hoped it was Darcy so she could talk to Lexi. But her caller ID said it was Jace.

She told Heck, "I've got to take this," and walked outside onto the first-floor front veranda.

"Jace, are you ready to fly out of Jacksonville?"

"Don't I wish. I had an accident—hit my head on a tree branch and fell. I went to a walk-in clinic and got stitched up. No concussion as far as the doc and I can tell."

"That's terrible. Where was this?"

"More later. Listen, I hated for us to end on a bad note right now—always hate that when I'm flying. I'd really appreciate it if you'd just meet me in the lobby of your hotel this evening, so I can say a couple things when I'm not so upset. You know, shades of 'the greatest marine who ever lived,' fly-off-the-handle Master Sergeant Jason Britten in my genetic code."

"Well—all right." She pictured Jace's favorite photo of his dad in full marine uniform. Actually, it had always reminded her of the one of Jace, Jr., that Lexi loved so much. He'd had such mixed feelings about his father, about being Jason, Jr., that he had always insisted on being called by his nickname. "I'm not sure when I'll be back to the hotel though," she told him. "Can I call you, and we'll be a little flexible? But are you sure you should fly? Is your head okay for sure? You know you had a couple of football injuries."

"Back in the dark ages. Other than a killer headache, I can tell I'm all right, and, like I said, I got checked out. Listen, Claire, if you're out at that plantation estate they briefly mentioned in the paper—"

"In the paper? What paper?"

"You and your employer are in a photo in the

St. Augustine Record this morning with the story about your finding that woman's body and—"

"And that's why you want to see me?"

"No, it isn't. I know my work can be dangerous, but you've had two strikes against you now on two cases—two dead bodies too near you, sweetheart—so maybe your work is getting dangerous, too."

Sweetheart?

"Jace, I'm all right. Fred Myron's death and now Lola's are not strikes against me, just coincidence."

"Yeah, but sometimes so-called coincidences might not be. You know that."

"There is no link between the two cases or what happened with the shooter and now this woman's murder. I am going to keep working this assignment and—"

"Let's not argue. Not now and not when we talk in person. All for one and one for all—and that one and all is Lexi, right?"

She sighed and leaned against a porch pillar. "Right."

"It's just I have something to tell you—and you can tell your lawyer friend, too—maybe about your case."

"What? Jace, like what?"

"Call me as soon as you can when you get back."

Claire saw the sheriff's car coming up the lane before she went back inside after talking to Jace. Poor Jason Allen Britten, Jr. Something had shaken him up, maybe even something about her case, but that didn't make sense. She ducked into the house to summon Jasmine and saw her coming down the staircase with Nick.

"Everyone's favorite local sheriff is here," she told them, wondering where they'd been upstairs.

"Loco sheriff, you mean," Jasmine said. "He might want to interrogate you to corroborate what I told him about finding Lola's body." She kept smoothing her hair and her blouse, though—thank heavens—Claire didn't notice that either were messed up.

"Maybe I should make myself scarce," Claire said, looking at Nick. "Counselor, what do you think?"

Standing a bit away from a front window, Nick looked out at the approaching car as Claire stood behind him, peeking around. The sheriff got out and slammed the car door. He must be alone. When he took off his hat, she noted he was gaunt-faced and bone-thin, when she'd been expecting a fat-cat look.

Nick said, "I don't think it would be a good idea to really hide from him, but we can let Jasmine's explanation of what happened at the puppet shop stand unless he asks for you."

Claire knew Heck was still in the library working on transcribing notes from Neil's interview. Neil had walked out to Bronco's trailer to talk to him. "I'll be out back if you—or he—needs me," Claire told them and hurried toward the rear of the house as a knock resounded on the front door. She heard Jasmine greet him and his strong, sharp voice.

Knowing she'd probably have to talk to him eventually, though he could just get her statement from the St. Augustine detective, she went out the back door and walked past Neil's *Creature from the Black Lagoon* pride and joy. *The black lagoon, indeed,* she thought. Some of Win Jackson's photos showed dark depths in the foliage and water on the river, but it was hardly a lagoon.

She walked to the edge of the clearing and saw Bronco's black pickup parked next to the silver Airstream trailer Neil had described. Sleek, shiny aluminum, retro-looking, but then she'd read somewhere that the design never changed, so it could be brand-new. Despite the fact it sat in the shade of a huge, peeling gumbo-limbo tree, wouldn't it be hot in there?

But as she went a bit closer, she saw and heard a generator, so maybe that provided air-conditioning. Over that whine, she heard men's voices.

As she watched, a man she didn't know—no doubt Bronco—came into view, pacing, hitting the tree trunk and the trailer each time he passed. Unlike how she'd missed a guess about the sheriff's appearance, she had imagined this is how Bronco Gates, gator and snake hunter, would look. He was a big, bearded man, though he moved like a much smaller one.

"She didn't deserve that!" She overheard the man's loud voice. "I got her favorite food here. She was gonna drive out here tonight, and we was gonna cook it, all the fixin's. Jasmine never should've let her go from here! I'm gonna find who did that!" His words were punctuated by a string of angry oaths.

Claire surmised he hadn't heard about the murder on the news, hadn't called Jasmine or anyone else to learn about it before just now. This was fresh anger and pain.

"Look, man," Neil was saying, his voice raised, too, "keep a low profile about the two of you. No good you go on a rampage or a hunt for whoever did it. The cops are on it, Jasmine's lawyer Markwood and his special interviewer, too, and she wants to talk to you soon. And don't you go telling her you two had a spat, either. Just keep it cool."

Claire stepped back against a palm with coconuts in a huge cluster looming above. She hoped one of them didn't conk her on the head, but she wanted to hear the rest of this. That big, blustery Bronco Gates and petite, shy and quiet Lola Moran? And they'd had a spat? Well, all's fair in love and war. But did what she just learned impact her interviews in any way? Here was Neil, playing support man to Bronco's anger and grief when he'd seemed to be setting him up before—or was he doing that now, too?

Bronco's voice still carried to her, though she couldn't see him now. "I got to talk with Miss Jasmine and that woman Clara."

"Claire. Claire Britten. Yeah, well, like I said, she wants to talk to you, too."

Thinking Neil or even Bronco might come looking for her right now, Claire took a few steps away and hurried back to the house so they wouldn't know she'd overheard.

Claire went to the library at the back of the house, watching out the window to see if Neil or Bronco had followed. Leaving his laptop and papers on the table, Heck had gone out near the river and was talking on his cell, gesturing wildly. He usually came off as calm and controlled, but occasionally she sensed he was hiding a temper. Maybe something about this house made people lose control.

Pressing her nose to the window, looking in the other direction, she peered out again toward Bronco's trailer. No one coming after her. Even though she was in another room, she could hear the sheriff's ringing tones but could only make out a few words of what he said. Occasionally Nick's calm voice, or Jasmine's strident one chimed in.

Despite the thickness of the walls, the high ceilings and hearths, this house carried sounds quite well. She recalled Jasmine had said she thought the ghost voices at night were just wind in the connecting chimneys. That meant Neil could have overheard Jasmine and Francine arguing even if he was not in the same room or hovering outside a door. Right now, Claire could tell the sheriff was on the subject of why Jasmine fired Lola and something about money—did Jasmine owe Lola any backpay, or had Lola taken something from the house she should not have?

Well, Claire thought, she was getting to be not only an interviewer but an eavesdropper. One of the rules she'd learned about being an effective forensic statement analyst was not to get personally involved with the witnesses. But, in this case, for Nick—with Nick—she'd done exactly that.

She bided her time until she heard the sheriff leave. Nick came looking for her. "Where's Heck?" he asked.

"Out back on the phone."

"I wanted you anyway. The sheriff said he got your deposition from St. A, so you're off the hook with him for a while anyway. He said your rendition of things synced with Jasmine's."

"I could hear a bit of what he said, even in here."

He came to stand behind her at the window and put his hands on her shoulders. His touch was comforting, and she needed that. Again, he seemed solid, someone to lean on, and how she'd missed that since she'd lost Jace.

"It's part of the sheriff's MO to come on like that, I guess," Nick said, his voice low. "He needs a big case to help him run for state office."

"And," she said, leaning back just slightly into his hands, "maybe if he could deliver the treasure of Shadowlawn to the state, that would get him big PR, too."

"You never cease to amaze me." His breath ruffled the hair at her temple. "I intentionally didn't match his tones, but kept my voice low, though Jasmine, unfortunately, doesn't follow my lead."

"I can see why he upsets her. Nick," Claire said, turning toward him, though that made him drop his hands from her shoulders, "Bronco Gates just drove in a short time ago, and Neil's out with him. I went out and—overheard something."

"I don't deal in hearsay, but tell me."

"Bronco got pretty distraught when Neil told him about Lola. I think he and she were sort of a pair, before some sort of argument—spat, he said."

"Bronco involved with her, not Neil?"

"Right. And Bronco was saying he wanted to talk to me, so there's a switch, but I want to take him up on it."

"Let's initiate that, because the way that cocky son-of-a-gun sheriff is acting, I think we're getting more pressed for time. But if Bronco's distraught, you'll have to take Heck or even me with you."

"All right. Not Neil for sure. We all have agendas, but his is starting to matter. I don't want one witness in on what another one says."

"Here comes Neil now, so let's see how this goes."

Nick sat and Claire was still standing when Neil came in. Before he got a word out, Heck hurried in, too.

"Bronco's pretty distraught," Neil said. "Usually, not much riles him, but he and Lola were good friends. He's not all bluster. He has a loner streak— hunters are like that, used to lying in wait, I guess— and she was quiet, too. Well, anyhow, he'd like to talk to you before you leave today, Claire. Said he was 'fixin' to have a memorial service' with the frog legs and hush puppies he planned to cook for her tonight. I told him you've got a shadow, takes all your notes," he added, looking at Heck, "but he said, no shadow, no notes."

"Well," Nick said, getting up, "that all sounds great, except she's not going alone. I'll walk her out, and if I'm told to leave, we'll reschedule with him another time. All right, Claire?"

Although she said, "You're the boss," she realized her talking to that big, bearded man alone could almost be worth the risk.

14

Nick and Claire approached Bronco Gates's Airstream trailer slowly. "Bronco?" Nick called out. "Neil said we could come talk to you."

The big man poked his head around the curved corner of the trailer so fast that Claire realized he must have been outside. For one moment, as a sliver of sun caught his face, she wondered if he'd been crying. He was not quite as tall as Nick, but seemed larger with his muscular shoulders. It was almost as if his head sat directly on them with no neck.

"I'm Nick Markwood, Jasmine's lawyer," he told Bronco as they came closer and Bronco walked to meet them.

"How you both?" Bronco said. The men shook hands and he nodded at Claire.

"This is Claire Britten, who is helping me to be sure Jasmine and Shadowlawn are protected."

"Tragic no one done that for Lola," he said, frowning. His thatch of unruly brown hair dipped almost into his eyes when his brow furrowed. "But who would've guessed she needed a bodyguard? Miss

Claire, Neil told me you was with Miss Jasmine and found her—like that."

"Yes. I was hoping she could help me, but we were too late to help her. I'm sorry—for her loss and yours, too."

"Neil told you we were close, huh? You two mind settin' out here?" he asked, turning away and gesturing toward several beach-type chairs set in a circle. So did this man have regular visitors out here?

"Don't want to be cooped up right now," he went on. "Got a smoke pot out here to keep the skeeters off."

"Yes, this is fine," Claire told him. "I realize this is a difficult time, so I could come back tomorrow to talk."

"Could use the company now. Tonight, I was going to fix us—Lola and me—some food I convinced her to like." He bit back a smile and shook his head. "Frog legs I got me upriver with a little gigging on the way back from the Glades, lookin' for pythons got loose down there. I cook these legs in peanut oil, eat 'em with hush puppies and hearts of palm. That's better known as swamp cabbage 'round here. Gotta be careful cutting that outa the tree, 'cause rattlers coil up in the palms if they can, so keep an eye out."

Claire and Nick locked looks as they followed him to two of the plastic-woven chairs near where he was cooking over an outdoor pit filled with wood. Yes, he really was cooking frog legs in a sizzling iron skillet set on an iron grate.

Claire elbowed Nick, then answered for them. "We're honored. I've never had that, have you, Nick?"

"Actually, I have. My friend who lives in Goodland fixes them."

Bronco said, "Tastes like chicken, don't it, real Florida cracker food. See you boogied up your arm there, Miss Claire."

"Yes, I hurt it last week." This man was being so honest with her, and she wanted to build on that. "I was accidentally shot by someone from a distance, and he hasn't been caught. He killed the man standing next to me."

"Whew!" he said, but he didn't look surprised or upset. "But then, I didn't think Lola had no bad friends neither, quiet and sweet like she was."

"I suppose you're disappointed Jasmine asked her to leave Shadowlawn," Claire said.

"Real sad, but she loved the puppets, Lola did. Was fine with just doing that with her sister. Folks don't know what another soul really wants from the outside—got to get to know them and listen real careful like when the gator you want rustles in the bushes on the shore or the copperhead shifts through the thick grass. Lola and I liked to hear the leopard frog chorus on cool winter nights, but she's not gonna be here for that anymore. I don't want to go to her funeral, see her laid out and all. I'll just think of her here—settin' right where you are now, Miss Claire. I'm just trying to do what I got to so I can survive."

Claire was astounded the man was such a talker—almost poetic—when she'd expected she'd have to pull things out of him. How many times had she been taught not to stereotype someone, she scolded herself. She could tell Nick was surprised, too. Bronco Gates was what her mother would have called *the noble savage* as in some of the James Fenimore Cooper books she'd read her and Darcy.

"You must love this area and this river," Claire said as he turned the frog legs in a spatter of peanut oil. She could tell Nick was letting her do the talking but was hanging on their every word.

"Sure do," Bronco said. "Neil thinks he's got ties to it 'cause his great-uncle helped make them movies 'round here, but yeah. My kin go back farther'n that— and some say one still lives hereabouts. Miss Jasmine tell you about the other ghost, not Miss Rosalynn in the house? The one walks the grounds was an ancestor of mine, some kind of overseer, expert on growing indigo, not the slave overseer, or I wouldn't even mention him. Got himself lynched in a tree out front, maybe for attacking the master here once, somethin' like that."

He straightened from bending over the sizzling skillet. "I'm not real sure those ghost tales about Miss Rosalynn's true, but I seen my kin's ghost a-hangin' from the tree, can show you which one. Well, too much talk about the dead, but with Lola gone—"

The big man sniffed hard. "You mind steppin' inside, fetchin' plates from the cupboard, Miss Claire? We'll have us a meal in honor of Lola. Then you can come back tomorrow, and we'll talk. We'll just set outside here, or we can walk to the hanging tree. Oh, when you go in, don't you pay no heed to the palm fronds hanging just inside to keep the skeeters out. If I had me a grand house, it'd be called 'the losing' room, 'cause that's where to ditch them suckers."

Claire got up and ducked and brushed her way through the rustling, dried palm fronds hanging over the door. Inside, the place was tidy, when she hadn't expected that, either. No wonder a shy loner like Lola liked Bronco Gates. Despite hunting gators and snakes, when it came to people he seemed gentle and kind. But then, she reminded herself, *seemed* was a pretty big word.

But Claire almost dropped the dishes on the floor when she saw, staring at her, sitting primly on the single bunk, a life-sized marionette that looked just like a picture Neil had showed her of Lola Moran.

Claire could tell Nick didn't want to leave her that evening. He'd been on edge since she told him about the life-sized doll on Bronco's bed. Nor did he want to leave her alone with Jace, even in a busy hotel lobby. Maybe she shouldn't have told him about Jace's phone call and their meeting.

"I'll be fine," she assured Nick. "Jace sounded calm and reasonable. If you're so worried, why don't you just sit over in the bar where he won't see you? Besides, he said he had something to say that might help the case."

"How could he know anything about that? We just read the newspaper article, and nothing was mentioned there."

"I don't know. He said he'd be here soon, and I'd rather not greet him with you at my side again."

"Okay. Right," he said, putting up a hand as if he was being sworn in in a courtroom. "Far be it from me to come between a man and his ex."

She glared at him. He was annoyed. She was, too, at him, at Jace, at how slowly she felt her work on the case was going. But, she thought, looking at the dark half moons under Nick's eyes, she was not the only one exhausted.

He walked away, and she went over to a seating arrangement of chairs with no one there right now and sat. She refused to even look over to see if Nick had gone to the bar or left. Feeling suddenly belligerent, she changed seats so she had her back to him—or where he'd been. She hoped Jace made it here fast and then was quick with what he had to say. He knew she needed her sleep.

"Hey," Jace said two minutes later as she stared at her watch, "thanks for being prompt." He sat next to her; the square, padded arms of their chairs made a barrier between them.

"How's your head?" she asked.

"Hard as ever. I'm all right—see."

He did a quick turn to show the back of his skull. The ER he'd been to had shaved a bit of his hair. A bandage about three inches square covered his scalp where he'd...

"Jace, a tree limb did that?" she blurted.

"For all I know. Okay, it's 'to tell the truth' time. I didn't want you to get upset on the phone. When I read that newspaper article this morning, I wanted to see Shadowlawn. I had a day to kill. I wasn't going to get in your—or Perry Mason's—way. I parked down the road and walked in."

"Onto the grounds?" she asked much too loudly.

"Keep it down. Yes, a ways off the private lane. Got to that last set of live oaks, near the house, the one on the left side of the front entrance. What a place! Anyway, that was it. Lights out. Someone gave me a good crack from behind. I swear, it's as if someone dropped out of the tree on me, because I didn't see or hear anyone on the ground. I woke up facedown and got the hell out of there—and to the hospital ER in Palatka where they stitched me up."

Claire finally remembered to close her mouth. "You—shouldn't have."

"Someone else evidently thought so, too. You have any idea who could have hit me? I swear, I heard no one. It's as if he—she, it, I don't know—came out of thin air. Is there a gardener or groundskeeper, or an estate guard?"

"What time was that?"

"Ah, 10:00 to 10:15 a.m."

"So Bronco wasn't back yet."

"Who's Bronco? Sounds like a cowboy."

Her mind racing, she ignored that. Neil had seemed to disappear for at least a quarter of an hour about then. Surely, the sheriff had not set up surveillance or a guard on the place.

"Claire?"

"So that's what you think might be information for the case I'm working on? That there's someone sneaking around the grounds? Maybe an eavesdropper—a kind of spy? And he attacked you."

"Yeah, right. Like I said on the phone, you're a magnet for trouble lately. Danger. You get shot when Fred Myron gets killed. You and your client—or Markwood's client—find the body of a woman who worked where you're working now. Then I come to check the place out and get blasted. Look, I know you're deep into this assignment, but for Lexi's sake and your own, you've got to resign and leave for home. Did you sign any kind of a contract with Markwood, because we can get a lawyer and—"

"Jace, please, not so fast!" she said, putting her

head down and spearing her splayed fingers through her hair as if that could keep her head from exploding. She didn't know whether to laugh or cry. Get some little lawyer to take on super lawyer Nick Markwood when he was the only one who'd signed a contract? But all that was none of Jace's business.

In as calm a tone as she could manage, she told him, "I'm just starting to make headway on this case and a woman's future is at stake."

"Yeah, yours. But Jasmine Montgomery Stanton's, you mean?"

"Yes, and the future of that estate, and maybe whether poor Lola Moran's murder is solved. I don't feel in danger."

"Oh, great," he said, standing abruptly and hauling her to her feet. "I'm sure you can trust female feelings over facts."

"Let me go! I'll tell Nick what you said, try to figure out who could have hit you. You could report it to the local sheriff, though we don't like or trust him."

"In Putnam County, you mean, not here, where you and Jasmine 'were questioned' by the St. Johns County Sheriff Jim Parsons. Amazing how much an innocent bystander can learn from a little newspaper article when the mother of his child won't tell him anything. And who is the 'we' that doesn't like or trust the sheriff?"

"I said, let me go." She stepped back and tugged her wrist free. But he came closer and clamped his hand around her upper arm. Several people in the lobby stopped and stared. "Jace, I need to get upstairs. Thanks for letting me know what happened when you were trespassing, and I'm glad you're not hurt more seriously. If I learn anything about who assaulted you, I'll let you know. I wish you good flights to Singapore and back."

She wasn't as afraid that he was going to make more of a scene as she was that Nick was going to rush over, which he did.

"Hey, Jace," Nick said, gripping his wrist that held her upper arm, "I thought you'd be wheels up by now, halfway across the Pacific."

"Well, look who's hovering and don't you wish," Jace said, letting Claire go but not stepping back. She felt sandwiched between the two of them. "I just came to warn Claire to be careful. She's living too close to someone else's problems and dangers—maybe yours."

"My problem is preparing this defense case, but suddenly my problems seem to have more to do with you."

"That's enough from both of you," Claire insisted. "Please leave, Jace, and good night, Nick. As you both know, I need my sleep."

Jace turned on her. "As you *both* know?" he repeated, his voice rising. "It took me years while we dated, were married and had a child for you to tell me about your disease and meds. And you told him after—how long, Claire? A couple of days? A few, intense minutes?"

Her insides cartwheeled. What she'd kept from Jace had ruined everything between them. And, yes, she had trusted Nick with that almost right away, and she'd even shared it with Jasmine.

She looked Jace straight in the eye. As angry as she was with him, she had the strangest urge to smooth the loose lank of blond hair on his forehead. He looked not only angry but hurt, and she didn't want that.

She turned toward him and said, her voice low, "Let's just say I learned to tell the truth the hard way. Good night, both of you. Jace—safe flying."

As she turned away, she prayed they wouldn't get into more of an argument, but before she stepped into the elevator, she glanced back. She saw Nick, alone, heading toward the bar. His shoulders were set, and she could almost see steam pouring out his ears. Jace was stalking out the front door of the hotel. So at least that was over.

At least, over for now. She was still working Nick's case, but she was thinking Jace might be right that she was a magnet for trouble.

15

Claire glanced at her watch as she and Heck walked into Win Jackson's Photographic Art Shop the next morning. She had a half hour before her appointment with Cecilia Moran, but they'd be driving to her house. Then they needed to head back to Shadowlawn so she could speak with Bronco again. She and Nick had agreed that Heck would sit in on neither of those interviews. She didn't want to scare Cecilia, and Bronco still said, "No shadow!"

Heck held the door to the shop open for her. The bell rang, and Win appeared. She had not intended to see him again, but he'd phoned this morning to ask her to stop by.

He'd explained on the phone, "Bronco Gates called me all upset about Francine's maid's murder. He insisted that before you go out to talk to him again, I show you a couple of photos."

"Ones with Lola Moran in them?" she'd asked. "I've seen one of her."

"No, these are fairly recent ones of the ghost, the one Bronco claims was his ancestor."

"Really? You photographed a ghost?"

"Let's just say it depends on the eye of the beholder."

Win escorted her into a back storage room while Heck stayed in the display room. She asked Win, "Why didn't you mention these ghost shots when I was here before?"

"I couldn't see the point. Still can't, but Bronco helped me set things up when I took my river photos, so I owe him a favor. He also let me take shots of gators, one he was *rasslin'*, no less. And Claire," he added, turning to her from where he was flipping through photos in a file drawer, "you should know I've called Jasmine to ask if I can shoot more at Shadowlawn, not the grounds, but inside the house—soon. If it's restored, redone or sold, I'd like to preserve all that, too, living history, before someone else gets their hands on it. Exterior landscape and panoramic photos are my forte, but this is important."

"I can see why," she said, wondering how big a stake this man really had in Francine's and Jasmine's disagreement to keep, sell or deed Shadowlawn. She couldn't think of anything he would gain if it went public or stayed private. He surely had enough shots of the river to last a lifetime. And yet, he must not be rolling in money, because he had mentioned needing to keep the shop open, even when he wasn't there.

"Would you sell copies of the pictures?"

"Actually, I'd love to do a photographic homage to Shadowlawn. Take a look at this." He handed an eight-by-ten photo to her. It was taken at night, a glossy print with one large live oak illumined by a flash. And, yes, there appeared to be something—

someone?—hanging from a tree branch partly ob-scured by Spanish moss.

"See that light grayish body?" he said pointing it out before he slid another photo on top of the one she held. "Here, from another angle. This one looks more—"

"More like a man's body," she finished for him. "Ugh. It makes me recall poor Lola hanging amid those marionettes."

"I can't imagine. Poor girl. Reading between the lines in the newspaper—and having known Fran-cine—I'll bet Lola was just an innocent bystander. Maybe someone thought she knew more than she did." He slid a third photo in. "So sad. Here—I've taken ones in the daylight and others at night where there was nothing to be seen, like in this one. A trick of the light, I think, but Bronco's convinced. I've taken it from other angles, too. Some show it, some don't."

"The form only shows up at night?"

"Evidently. When Bronco or I walked up to the tree, we saw nothing where it appeared something had been. Nothing at all by daylight. Even Bronco admits that. Sometimes I think he stalks the grounds in the dark, part of his definition of a groundskeeper. But in these night pictures—see here?—some ambient light comes from the front house windows, if lights are on inside. Especially lights, I think, from Fran-cine's room, the one where they say the female ghost comes out and jumps off the veranda."

"They say? So you've never seen or photographed that one?"

He shook his head. "I suggested to Francine once

that we invite that *Ghosthunters* TV show there, but she'd have no part of that."

She noted he'd said *we,* but then it was possible in working with and maybe advising Francine, he'd thought of them as working partners. He had, no doubt, been Francine's friend.

"If the mansion does go to the state or someone else at auction," she said, "I suppose advertising a 'haunted house and grounds' would help promote it." She handed the photos back to him. "So why do you think this is so important to Bronco?"

He slid the photos back in the file drawer. "He wants to know why his great-great-great, etc., relative was lynched, I guess. He only knows the when and who. He's asked around, even tried the local library, which was a stretch for a man who reads nature's signs and not much else. But I'm hoping he'll help me by carting my equipment around if I shoot in the house, so my assistant can stay here and keep the store open."

"You're waiting for Jasmine's permission to take interior shots?"

He nodded. "I'd give Shadowlawn a share of the profits, which might help with the restoration." They went back out to join Heck who had put his laptop on the counter and was looking at pictures labeled Old-Time Havana on the screen before he saw them and closed the lid.

"That project sounds like a great idea," Claire told Win. "I'd love to know what Jasmine thinks about that."

As they went out, she thought to herself, *Among a lot of other things I'd like to know from her.*

* * *

Cecilia lived in an area called St. Augustine Shores on Deva Street to the south of Old Town. Heck drove a curving road near a park along Moultrie Creek until they found it. She had a stucco home painted bright aqua with a plaster swordfish attached to the front, one that looked as if it was arching out of the water, pulling puppet string rather than a fishing line that had snagged it.

"I'll go up to that restaurant we passed for a while," Heck told her as she got out. "I'll be back in a half hour and just sit here 'til you come out, so don't worry, yes?"

"Thanks, Heck. I don't know what I—or Nick—would do without you."

Claire wished Nick had come along today, but he was going to meet them at Shadowlawn this afternoon. She had the feeling the presence of Nick or Heck would have spooked—well, wrong word, after seeing Win's photos—Cecilia, but the woman was obviously much more social than her twin sister had been.

Cecilia opened the door before Claire knocked. The woman had a doll-like face, which greatly resembled Lola's. It was difficult to tell how old she was, though Claire knew the twins' ages from the newspaper. Besides round, painted eyes, her most dominant feature was a cupid-bow mouth. And her light brown hair—so much of it, the length halfway down her arms.

"You saw me coming," Claire said. "I appreciate your inviting me to drop by at such a difficult time."

"I've been keeping an eye out, hoping the reporters don't come back again. And better you by far than more visits from the detective working on her case. I'm grateful and want to help him, but he's just a reminder of how awful it must have been for her. But when you said you were working to learn if someone harmed Miss Francine... Well, I know Lola would have wanted to speak with you."

Claire blinked back tears as she went in. If something that horrible had happened to Darcy, she'd never get over it.

The house seemed as if it had been draped for mourning, the way Mother had read to them in some of Charles Dickens's novels. Not swagged in black but with colorful cloth over the windows and half of the furniture. Claire guessed the material must have been used for puppet show curtains. Some had animals or flowers on them.

"I covered her part of the house," Cecilia said. "We shared everything here but bought our own furniture."

"I wish I could have seen her work the puppets."

"She had many voices for them. Now they are all silent forever."

Cecilia indicated a sofa that was undraped. They both sat. Claire sensed she should not take notes, so she put her purse on the floor.

"Her own voice—few heard that," Cecilia went on. "She didn't talk much, but she did talk to Miss Francine."

"I understand that went both ways."

Cecilia wiped under her eyes with her index fingers. "Yes, she was so good to Lola. And Lola honored her by taking good care of her and by doing her voice for our kindest marionettes in the show."

"Doing her voice?"

"Yes, imitating her voice."

"Did Lola do men's voices, too?"

"Yes, and I think she had her friend Bronco Gates's lingo down. He had the most quaint backwoods way of talking. She was much better at voices than me, but my part was painting the faces."

"I saw the one you must have done of Lola herself."

"Oh, yes, the one she gave to Bronco, because she would not give herself to him. You know what I mean."

Claire didn't, exactly. In bed? In marriage? But Cecilia was doing such a great job of explaining her sister, Claire just nodded. Some of the earliest interview rules she'd learned were to never interrupt, never say the word *but*, or *you're wrong* or *that's not right*. Encourage, always encourage.

So all Claire said in the little lull was, "Bronco thinks highly of her, misses her but said he would rather not come to the funeral. He'd like to remember her as she was."

"I, too. It wouldn't do to have a funeral. I don't know adults that would come with Miss Francine gone. And I don't want the many children she entertained to attend a dreary funeral. When the ME releases her body, I'll show you what I'm going to do, to have a special memorial service here."

She popped up and started toward a back room, so Claire followed. At the back of the house, a screened Florida room with sliding doors opened onto a patio. In the crowded room, at least thirty marionettes were all seated or standing by strings hooked onto a cross-hatching of boards on the ceiling. They were all turned toward a small table with a wooden, painted head on it that looked just like the one on Bronco's bed—Lola's.

"I'm going to have her cremated and put her ashes in that for a sort of urn," Cecilia explained. "Then I'll have a private party here for her with all our children."

A chill raced up Claire's spine. She meant these elaborately dressed and painted wooden people. And there was one, seated close to Lola's head that looked like the photos Claire had seen of Francine.

"But I'll show you one who is not invited, who will be broken up and thrown away during the service!" Cecilia cried, her bland, sweet voice sharpening. She pushed aside several hanging bodies. They clattered and swung. Claire tried to steady herself. These figures were suspended just as Lola had been.

"I know you recognize her!" Cecilia said, pointing at a figure that looked so much like Jasmine that Claire gasped. "I painted that face from a photo Lola borrowed from Shadowlawn. That woman told her mother more than once to let Lola go, and she fired her the day after Miss Francine died. If you hear her say anything about my sister harming Francine, she lies! Or maybe she thought Lola knew too much about how she treated her own mother."

"Too much—like what?" Claire asked.

"That Jasmine wanted control of the house and to pull her mother's strings! I can't prove it, but I hope you do. When Lola stood up to Jasmine, she was horribly angry."

Letting the puppets come together to hide the figure of Jasmine, Cecilia turned back toward Claire. She had suddenly gone from shy girl to spitfire. "I didn't say it in so many words, but no one had it in for Lola," she said, her voice subdued again. "Except for Jasmine. I think she learned Miss Francine had invested big-time in our store when their wealth was fading."

Now *that* was news, Claire thought. Nor had Jasmine shared that with her or probably not with Nick. "So, you told the detective all that?"

"Yes, and he told me Lola drank something put in her drink in the store that drugged her before she was lifted up to be hanged. If they put me on a witness stand, I will say who did it. Lola was small. That woman could lift her. If the puppets in the store could talk, they would say so. That woman hurt her mother and my sister, too!"

16

En route to Shadowlawn, Claire did not tell Heck Cecilia's accusations against Jasmine. It wasn't that she didn't trust him, but she had to tell Nick first, then help him strategize how to proceed—if he wanted help on that. If this turned into a murder case and she had to testify, she dreaded being away from Lexi for weeks when she'd already been gone four days this time.

She did use some of their drive time to assure Heck that she'd be safe alone with Bronco. He was going to give her a tour of the river and estate, so she could ask him questions in an informal setting, which she thought was good.

"Okay," he said. "I'll hang around outside and keep an eye on you from a distance. Boss's orders."

As Heck pulled into the lane to the mansion, she told him, "I imagine Neil will greet us with drinks and baked goods again. Even though I sometimes inhale caffeine, I think I'll pass and go right out to see Bronco, so please let me know if Neil says anything of interest. Do you know what time Nick will get here?"

"Not sure. I might call him."

"Good. I need to fill him in on some things."

Again, as they approached the house, Claire leaned down and looked out the windshield at the line of live oaks.

"Looking for what you told me about earlier—the 'ghost' tree?" Heck asked. "I wouldn't be scared to check that out at night if you and Nick want me to."

"I don't think that's part of our case building here." Her voice trailed off. As she stared at the last tree, a thought hit her like a punch to the gut. Jace had described the place where he'd been knocked out as *the last set of live oaks, near the house, the one on the left side of the front entrance.* He'd said he'd been hit on the head by someone who just suddenly appeared as if he'd dropped out of that tree, someone he didn't even hear!

No, ridiculous. Ghosts don't hit living people on the head when they trespass. But who had hit him? This entire place was getting to her. And she didn't look forward to telling Nick that Cecilia's accusations against Jasmine would probably fall right into Sheriff Goodrich's hands, and that he'd use them to charge her for Lola's death, too.

Nick put the incoming call on Speaker so he could keep both hands on the wheel. "Heck, hi. What's the update?"

"I'm drinking coffee on the back patio, keeping an eye on Claire who's with Bronco down by the river."

"Good. How did she do talking to Lola's sister?"

"Shook up over something, you ask me. But she didn't say. We stopped at Win Jackson's shop again 'cause he wanted to show her pics of the ghost tree, you know, where Bronco claims his old ancestor was hung by the neck until dead, like they say. Fidel and Raoul preferred fast firing squads, but don't get me started on that."

"I won't. I'm glad you were with her. I'll be there in about a half hour. I was hoping you had some news for me about our slippery mystery man."

"Yes, something new. Not that I could trace him to a drone company or big new corporate buy, though. But in looking for that, I found a link to possible investments on Grand Cayman Island, under one of the aliases he uses."

"Good work! Any details? I mean, don't give me names over the phone, but that place reeks of offshore banking and semi-legal investments. Can he be living there?"

"Some expats are, but can't find a trace of him in George Town. You know, during the last presidential election, the press got all over candidate Mitt Romney for huge investments there, though he proved he'd paid taxes on it, like, I mean, millions of dollars. It's big bucks there, so that sounds promising for your guy."

"And that would be chump change for him. But don't call him 'my guy.'"

"Right. But what's chump change?"

"*No mucho pesos.* Keep following that money trail, Heck. That bastard's going to be at the end of it and probably into schemes just as illegal—and lethal—as what he used to bilk my dad. Make sure you don't leave a trail."

"No, boss, don't worry. I'm lots smarter than that."

* * *

Bronco Gates was giving Claire her first real tour of the grounds of the estate. The roots of primeval-looking cypress trees crouched in the river, and egrets perched in the branches. In the shade of the massive, hunched trees, the water looked almost tea-colored in the splotches of sun, black in the shadows. But even the foreboding aura here couldn't dampen the amusement she'd tried to hide at his straw hat with alligator teeth stuck in the brim. Not Crocodile Dundee but Gator Gates.

She told him, "No wonder they got away with passing this off for the black lagoon, though that was supposed to be the Amazon River."

"This river's really brown from goin' through all the saw grass and tree roots. Some say it's endangered too—industry and pollution, all that. Bet you didn't know it's one of the few US rivers flows north. It's a mighty strange, special river, all right."

"Oh, is that your airboat?" she asked, pointing at the twelve-foot-long, flat-bottom aluminum craft pulled up on the bank in a small clearing and chained to a tree trunk. It had one elevated seat—a plastic, molded chair—which made the interior of the craft look homemade. The driver steered by a long vertical stick while its aircraft-type propeller shoved it through shallow water. She recalled how loud they were from the one she'd been on with Lexi and Darcy's family, whipping through the "river of grass Everglades" south of Naples.

"Yep, it's mine. Good for hunting gators at night, strictly in season, almost over for this year. The hunting license for them says you can take only two, use the meat, sell the hides. Even catching and keeping a little gator for a pet's a crime in this state."

"A pet? But they aren't endangered, are they?"

"Not anymore. Not as much as human beings 'round here lately," he said with a grimace and a snort.

Since he'd said "human beings," he was obviously shaken not only by Lola's loss, but by Francine's, too. He'd said "'round here lately," so he wasn't thinking about his ancestor who was hanged on these grounds so many years ago. Although Claire had witnessed a show of temper from him, he seemed to be fairly stoic now. But that didn't mean he couldn't explode. Could he have lost control when Lola refused to "give herself to him," as Cecilia had said?

"But you got to be careful," he went on, "even when you think you killed a gator. No such thing as a dead one, 'less you hit it in the back of the head with a bang stick."

She pictured the back of Jace's head. Had someone—surely, not a ghost—banged a stick into the back of his head? These weren't the kind of questions she had for Bronco, but she asked, "What's a bang stick?"

"An explosive charge set up at the end of a stick. An underwater bullet—to the brain in this case. Gator brain's as small as a poker chip. It's kill on capture, no kill and release. Meanwhile, think I see one."

He pushed aside a palmetto leaf hanging over the water. With a swish of its tail, a four-foot gator wriggled into the current and soon became only two wary, protruding eyes.

"That's the way to find them at night," Bronco said, pointing. "Shine a light in their eyes at night, and they show up reddish. That one's a kid. Biggest one I ever seen was fourteen feet. But if you ever come on one with a heaped-up nest or babies, get away fast."

"I think I'll leave the gator watching to you."

"So Win Jackson showed you those ghost pictures, right?" he asked, suddenly changing the subject. She sensed that was what he'd been waiting to talk about. "Not quite gator eyes gleamin' in the dark, but a body swingin' under that tree out front. You want to see it close up?"

"All right. Did you show it to Lola? I hear you researched it some."

"I swear I seen the ghost—that thing—walking on the grounds, checking things out at night like I do. He did once oversee the crops here, you know."

Now why hadn't he answered the question she'd just asked? He certainly had his own agenda.

"Don't believe in reincarnation none," he went on, "like I'm him come back to life. But I got to learn why he was lynched, if he was a thief or did really— maybe accident'ly—kill the master, Miss Rosalynn's husband. That's a rumor. And then, weird that Miss Francine died almost in the same place as Miss Rosalynn. You seen that big painted picture of her hangin' up there? Now, talk about hauntin's…"

So Bronco had been in the house and upstairs. Well, why not, as he'd been here for years.

He said, "Let's cut around the side of the house this way. You see that empty field a-stretchin' out far from here?"

Her gaze followed his as they walked toward what must be the northern property line. "Yes, but that's not Shadowlawn land anymore, is it?"

"No, but it's one a the fields my ancestor William Richards oversaw, thick with indigo, not cotton."

"I heard that's what was grown here."

"I picked up stuff about that, trying to track him down at the liberry."

She didn't correct his pronunciation. She fell easily into the rhythm of his words and unique grammar. Lola had evidently found it charming.

"So indigo used to be a good cash crop?" she prompted, scolding herself again for getting off the subject of Francine's demise. But she had picked up earlier that Bronco admired Francine and was even grateful to her for helping Lola. She wondered if he knew about the investment in the puppet shop, but she didn't want to ask him yet. She needed Nick's advice to pursue that.

"Made beautiful blue dyes the slaves extracted right here. You know," he said as they reached the so-called ghost tree and they both looked up into it, "I learned some of it can be used for more than dye. To kill pain, like stings and snakebites, even ulcers. Wisht I had some, 'cause I'm sure missin' Lola and Miss Francine."

"Bronco, if Shadowlawn goes to the state or is sold at auction, you'd be in pain over that, too, wouldn't you?"

"For sure," he said, gazing upward toward the branch where, she supposed, he imagined his ancestor William Richards had been hanged. Gator hunter or not, she thought, this was such a gentle man.

He suddenly kicked the tree as hard as he could, then punched it with his fist without so much as a flinch. "We don't need lots of folks here!" he shouted.

"Someone sells this place is gonna answer to me! If I find out who hurt Lola, they gonna do more than answer to me!"

So much, she thought, for all her supposed skills at reading people.

When Bronco went back by the river, Claire walked out the lane a ways to think things over. She had a lot to digest but felt pressure to get this over, to report what she'd learned to Nick—especially what Cecilia Moran had told her about Jasmine. Both Neil and Bronco had to be worried they'd have to leave Shadowlawn. Neil came off as nervous; Bronco, full of suppressed anger, but over Lola or at Lola? Would either of them have tried to get rid of Francine so that the land would go to Jasmine, who wanted to keep the place?

Win Jackson, too, obviously wanted to protect Shadowlawn, and not have it lost to outsiders. In talking to Jasmine, Nick had learned that Win was not in the store the day Francine died. He'd been on the grounds here, photographing the river, though he hadn't exactly told Claire when he took those photos. At least he now had new plans to preserve Shadowlawn the best way he could.

A car horn honked. Nick's BMW had turned in down the lane. He stopped next to her and rolled down the window.

"I'm glad you're here," she told him, walking to the car.

"I like the sound of that."

"Because I have a lot to tell you, and you won't like some of it."

"Great greeting, Claire. Let's talk before we're back with the others. I'm a big boy and I can take it."

He pulled the car off the lane between two trees, killed the engine and got out. He brought a burst of air-conditioning with him. Was it just the weather and her stroll that made her feel suddenly flushed?

They walked a ways deeper into the trees. He shoved his sunglasses onto the top of his head, maybe to see her better. "So hit me with the worst," he told her, his fists perched on his hips, his legs slightly spread.

Claire leaned back against a tree to steady herself. "All right. Cecilia Moran hates Jasmine and has told the detective working on Lola's murder that Francine heavily financed, I don't know for how much, their puppet shop because, I've learned from other sources, 'Lola was like a daughter to her.' Needless to say, with Shadowlawn in financial danger, Jasmine could have been furious with Lola and might have confronted her. Lola was drugged with something in her drink in the store—which I saw when we were there, the ice hadn't even melted completely—before someone hanged her. In short, Cecilia believes Jasmine killed her sister."

"Damn it all! Wait until Sheriff Goodrich pounces on all that."

"Exactly."

"But you were with her—you're her alibi, especially with unmelted ice in the drink."

"If the detective took note of that."

"I know you'll work up formal reports to me about the others, but any more bombshells?"

"Neil and Bronco don't want to be forced off the

grounds. I had Bronco pegged as a gentle man, but his Clark Kent turned into Superman and he nearly punched out a tree a few minutes ago. Also, Win Jackson's going to be back here—if Jasmine gives the okay—to photograph inside the mansion. So, not him, but I believe the others had access to Francine's pills—as did Jasmine."

"That Lola-Cecilia complication with Francine's funds could have really set Jasmine off," he admitted.

"She was upset by her mother's affection for Lola for starters…"

He sighed and put a hand on the tree she was leaning against. "If there's anything else, let's have it," he said.

"All right. Not about one of our possible suspects, but when Jace read in the St. Augustine paper about Shadowlawn—since he knew I was working here—he wanted to see it."

"He's here?"

"Not now, but he came out yesterday around 10:00 a.m. or so. He parked out on the road and walked in—and got knocked out by someone he didn't see under that so-called ghost tree near the front of the house. He came to and left for an emergency center to get stitched up."

"So that's partly why he wanted to meet you in the lobby last night. He's got to steer clear of all this. Did he refer to it as the ghost tree?"

"No, I got that from Bronco, who believes it's haunted by an ancestor of his and from some pretty scary pictures Win took of it at night."

Nick looked furious. "Well, maybe you can just write up that one of the ghosts killed Francine because she wanted to sell this place. Wouldn't that be a great defense when they charge Jasmine, which I'm expecting any day. They're just getting all their ducks in a row first, and now they may try to indict for a double murder."

"I will write things up for you, as much as I know. So who's left to interview? No one new, as far as I know," she said, answering her own question. "I'd like to be around when Win photographs the interior, though, get a closer look at that so-called Rosalynn's room and Francine's bathroom, the places she might have kept her pills. I was hoping to convince Jasmine—with your help—to let me help her go through some of her mother's correspondence, anything else I can find. Who killed 'Miss Francine' may still lie with 'Miss Francine,' even though she's dead."

Staring intently at her, he nodded. "I hate it—hate it!—when someone who may have been murdered has the slur of suicide dumped on them."

The slur of suicide? she thought. He was speaking with such passion, so that was personal. It must have been horrible for him when his father supposedly killed himself, which a young boy could see as desertion or rejection.

"Claire," he said, seeming to focus on her again instead of looking through her, "about Jace. Is he still around—not around here, but around you?"

"Except that we both love Lexi—no."

"But to come here... I'm telling you, he still worries about you and cares."

"Only for Lexi's sake, and maybe old time's sake, too. He's en route to Los Angeles and then Singapore right now, that's really where he wants to be, trust me."

He nodded. They stared deep into each other's eyes. She felt warm and her words *trust me,* echoed in her mind. Did she trust Nick? Right now, she felt they teetered on the edge of a cliff.

He pressed her gently against the tree. His free hand lifted to cup her chin, caress her cheek with his thumb. Her hair snagged on the rough bark. A breathless moment hung between them as he lowered his head and brushed her cheek with his. She felt the slight rasp of his beard stubble clear to the pit of her belly.

He took her lips. No, she gave them. It was as if a bolt of lightning leapt between them. His free hand dropped to caress her bare throat, then skimmed her shoulder. His thumb slid beneath her V-cut cotton shirt and snagged in her bra strap. He tipped his head so their lips met. She opened her mouth slightly as he tasted her. Though she was pressed between the tree and his hard body, she felt dizzy, spinning. They breathed in unison as the kiss went on endlessly, but much too short a time, before he stepped back.

"Didn't mean to do that, but I've been wanting to."

"Yes," she whispered.

"Against company rules."

"Mine, too."

"You wouldn't want to work for a boss who does this."

"Absolutely not."

"I'll take that for a yes."

He kissed her again, gently, then harder, not touching her body this time, with his hands on the tree trunk on both sides of her head. But she pressed closer, her arms around his neck, kissing him back again, her breasts flattened against his chest. For that moment, nothing else mattered. But this time, she grabbed for sanity and, out of breath, broke the kiss. She either stepped or fell back against the tree, bumping her head. And that reminded her of reality.

He whispered, his voice rough, "You think this will get it out of our systems so we can concentrate on this case? Except for this, things are getting worse."

"I didn't think this time was wasted," she said, amazed she could say something that made sense. As he had said, this was such a bad idea, so why did it feel so right and good?

They were about to kiss again, when something rattled or rustled nearby. And had someone sneezed? They turned their heads. That sound—dry leaves? About twenty feet away, only one frond in a palmetto thicket shivered despite the still air. Footsteps crunched something, then ran fast, faster away.

"Maybe Heck?" she said. "He was watching me before."

"Not if he saw us together. Stay here, get in the car—all my important stuff's in there." He thrust his car key into her hand and took off at a mad sprint toward the thicket.

17

Nick went to a full sprint. He saw no one ahead or off to the side. He went by sound, someone crashing through brush, feet flying.

This was the direction where Bronco lived. Claire said he'd been on the grounds this morning. But whoever he was chasing was heading along the river, away from Shadowlawn.

Damn, the guy had a big head start on him. He saw nothing, heard nothing now but his own ragged breathing and crunching strides through cypress needles and dried leaves. Not only had he not glimpsed anyone, but the guy seemed to have vanished, as if he'd gone into the river. Nick stopped, panting, still looking around. When he leaned over with hands on his knees and sucked in huge gasps of humid air, his sunglasses fell off the top of his head and hit the ground. He'd taken them off to get closer to Claire and he had to get back to her now. What if this was some sort of diversion? But he still felt he was the one being watched, not her. If he thought she was in danger, he'd send her home.

Swearing under his breath, he jammed his glasses on his face and jogged back toward where he'd left Claire. As he skirted Bronco's trailer site, he saw the big man, raking ashes out of his fire pit. He didn't look out of breath or sweaty. So much for his number one suspect spying on them. He bet Neil couldn't run like that. Or Jasmine? Some outsider, the same one who had hit Jace Britten over the head when he got too close to the house?

He couldn't bear to admit what scared him most, not out here, far from southwest Florida. But he had to admit that Clayton Ames's reach was long and dangerous. When those shots had killed Fred Myron and wounded Claire at the courthouse, Nick had been near and moving toward them. But surely, if Ames sent someone to take him out, he'd send the best. Ames liked to toy with his prey—torment and torture. Nick knew he'd been a thorn in the man's side for years, and he wasn't going to stop. Unless he was stopped.

As he emerged from the trees near his car, Claire tapped his car horn. Good girl! She was peering out at him from the passenger side. He was relieved to see she was safe, along with his traveling office of files and laptop he kept in the car.

She popped open the locks as he hurried to the car and got in.

"See anyone?" she asked.

He shook his head, still out of breath. "Heard him running for a while. Lost him by the river near Bronco's camp. But it wasn't him, because I saw him calm and quiet there. You sure Jace flew west?"

"Of course he did! Don't be ridiculous."

"Nice to hear you defending him."

"I wasn't. You might as well blame that darn ghost again."

"Don't kid about that."

"Could it have been a woman?"

"Jasmine can't run that fast."

"You're so sure you know her. I realize you did once, but do you anymore?"

Frowning, he grabbed his water bottle from the console between them and took a long swig. "You're not caving on my client, are you?"

"You well know there are other possibilities besides Jasmine being guilty, including Francine accidentally—or intentionally—overdosing." She bent her left leg under her and turned toward him. "Nick, someone possibly spying on us is putting the pressure on. Who knows Sheriff Goodrich doesn't have some deputy out here, watching our every move?"

"Okay," he told her. Despite her being a big distraction for him, he valued her smarts and opinions or she wouldn't be here. "I'm listening, because I know you have something to say."

"I've taken a close look at everyone involved in this except one. I've only studied Francine through hearsay. But my forensic autopsies have included 'interviewing' the dead before—through not only the people but what they left written behind."

"For a minute there, I thought you planned to talk to that big portrait upstairs."

"Very funny, but never mind avoiding this. I'd like to push Jasmine to let me look through her mother's correspondence, business letters, her personal papers especially. Neil seems to think the sheriff only took her meds. If Jasmine tries to claim her papers are private or it doesn't matter, I'm going to tell her she'd better help me because of Cecilia's claims. And that we and the authorities know about the money her mother put in Lola and Cecilia's puppet shop, which must have upset her mightily. Jasmine needs a jolt to open up more and that may be it."

He nodded. He was sweating from his run, from how bad this case was starting to look, from just being near this woman again. He turned the motor on and started the air-conditioning. "You want me to push her on that so you can keep a neutral interview relationship with her?"

"No, I think I need to do it. Of course, if she tries to stop or fire me—"

"I won't let her. You're right, we have to dig deeper on this. We need a break and—"

His cell phone rang with a buzzing sound. He opened the top of the black leather console between them and took it out, staring at the screen.

"The Naples office," he muttered and answered it.

It was Sean, one of the firm's junior partners. "Nick, a Spencer Clawson, Attorney-at-Law, retired in St. Augustine, called here. He's quite elderly and has been recovering from open-heart surgery, but he'd like to see you. This guy was Francine's mother's longtime attorney, then Francine's before she went to you."

"Yeah, I know, though I've never met him."

"Well, he wanted to tell you something about a new will Francine was planning to make."

"Any details on that?" Nick asked, as his heart rate picked up again.

"He only has it in draft because of his illness and

her death. He couldn't even attend her funeral. He lives someplace near St. Augustine called Vilano Beach. I've got the address here."

"Okay, good. I just said I need a break," he said with a quick look at Claire. She was listening intently. He realized, though he hadn't put it on speakerphone, she could probably hear, but he was okay with that. He told Sean, "Give me the address and phone if you have it, and I'll stop to see him this evening if it's convenient for him, when we get back to town."

After he jotted down the information and ended the call, he told Claire, "I'd like you to go with me this evening to listen to what Francine's old lawyer has to say about some new will she wanted to make and never got to. It scares me she never mentioned it to me, nor did Jasmine—if she even knew. We can eat on the way back to St. A, then go see him. Heck can head back to town early if he wants. I've seen a copy of her will, one about a decade old, and I'd counseled her to make a new one if she was thinking of deeding Shadowlawn away." He frowned. "But she didn't tell me she'd acted on that. Maybe Jasmine didn't know, either."

"Or, maybe she did. Sure, I'll go with you. Any port in a storm to help us."

He turned to her and took her hand. "It's starting to feel that way, isn't it, like we're in a storm and not making much headway? I know you miss your daughter and want to get back to her soon, but I feel something—or someone—is going to break. I just hope it isn't Jasmine. Yes, go ahead and put some pressure on her, and I'll back you up. Don't mention to her about our going to see this Spencer Clawson. I've been so sure about trusting Jasmine. But now, I'm wondering if she's working against us."

"Hey, I'm on your flight to Singapore!" Amber Dixon, a stacked blonde flight attendant told Jace as he got off the flight at LAX. Rolling her suitcase behind her, she fell into step with him down the crowded concourse. When he only nodded, she snagged his arm. "How long is your layover in Singapore this time?" she asked with her tooth-whitener-ad smile. She was what pilots politely called "a clinger."

"Two days."

"Oh, me too. You know the area so much better than me. I'm at the usual hotel where they keep us, in case you want some company."

"Thanks, Amber."

"Oh, what happened to your head?"

"Just an accident. See you later," he said and kept going, but as usual, she clung like tape.

"I sure hope so!" she called after him as he headed into the men's room.

When he checked into the airline desk to get his assignment and a cab for his overnight here in LA, the woman at the desk said to him, "You know, I think there's something that came for you with the overnight mail."

She bent down and drew out from under the desk a brown, square envelope addressed to him. No return address but it was postmarked St. Augustine. He didn't think it was Claire's printing, but who else would know how to reach him here?

"Thanks," he told her and went over to lean against the wall and rip it open.

Inside were five-by-seven photos. The first one was evidently taken from above, like in a low-flying plane. Yet it was a clear close-up of Claire with, damn it, Nick Markwood. He muttered a curse. He even knew where this was. They were having an intimate picnic at what looked to be Lake Avalon at Sugden Park near where she lived. The second one—oh, yeah, he recognized this place for sure even with the overhead shot. It was also of the two of them, shoulder-to-shoulder, faces close, at the mooring area near their hotel in St. Augustine.

And the third one, also an aerial picture: someone was on the ground with someone else laid out nearby. Lots of people. A man bending over a woman?

He squinted at it, tipped it away from the light which blurred its glossy surface. His stomach heaved when he realized what it was: the lawn between the courthouse and parking garage. That must be Claire on the ground next to the body of Fred Myron! And bending over her, he wasn't sure, but Darcy had said something about the opposing lawyer helping her. So that was Nick Markwood close to her, too, in all three pictures.

But this one was put last, out of order. Almost expecting to see more photos of them in intimate poses, he shuffled through the pictures. That was all. He flipped them over. One had a handprinted note on the back:

YOU CARE ABOUT THE MOTHER OF YOUR CHILD? DON'T TRUST THIS MAN WITH EITHER OF THEM. GET HOME AND GET WHAT'S YOURS.

It was signed, A FRIEND.

* * *

"Jasmine, it's absolutely essential that you trust Nick and therefore trust me," Claire began as the two of them sat on the back, shaded veranda over iced tea and lemon cookies.

"Well, what's this about? I'm sorry I didn't mention Lola, but I told you why. I do trust Nick and realize you have your job to do."

Claire put her glass down on the table between them a little too hard. "I know this is all painful, but it's necessary. There is a possibility your mother did overdose, you know, either by mistake or intentionally. She was very distressed for several reasons."

"Of which I'm one, you mean."

"I mean I really need to have access to her most recent papers and correspondence since I can't interview her."

"You hardly interview the subject of any death investigation, only those the deceased leaves behind."

"But often the *what* as well as the *who* the deceased leaves behind is key. So I'm asking you—with Nick's permission and agreement—to let me go through her things that might cast light on her state of mind. You have everything to gain from that."

"And much to lose if you decide to testify that she was so angry with me that she was afraid of me."

"Was she?"

"God as my judge, of course not!"

Classic guilt—or at least a guilty conscience, Claire thought.

"Jasmine," she said, leaning closer to her and looking her straight in the eyes, "we have to move on this fast. Now. Cecilia told me—and more importantly, told the detective investigating Lola's death—that your mother invested heavily in the Moran sisters' Puppet Store. They didn't lease it, they bought it. It's in a great tourist area in a historic city. You should have told us she did that up front, and about confronting Lola over it. You did, didn't you?"

"Yes, of course I did! You would have, too. But that doesn't mean I hurt her. I was with you when someone killed her, for heaven's sake!"

"You were and I will testify to that if need be, but Nick recently received a copy of Lola's autopsy report. With the rigor mortis, body temperature and lividity timing, you would have had time to visit her and then meet me. Then, I'm sure you realize, our sheriff duo can theorize that you and your mother might have had words over that money, too, let alone over how she doted on Lola, on top of the public knowledge that you two disagreed on what should happen to Shadowlawn."

Jasmine gasped and raked her spread fingers through her hair. "All right! I know it looks bad I didn't mention Lola at first, but you're grilling me like a lawyer. Whose side are you on?"

"I'm on your lawyer's side, and therefore, on yours. Complain to Nick if you want, but he agrees. I need to go through anything that can throw light on your mother's state of mind."

"But she was angry with me and taken in by that quiet little mouse of a maid who more or less bilked her out of money she didn't have when Shadowlawn and I should have come first!" She stood as if she'd flee. If Jasmine got on the stand in her own defense, it could be a disaster.

Claire grabbed her wrist. "Sit down and calm down. To survive this—and thereby preserve this treasure house for yourself and others—you need to think rationally, to help Nick and me defend you, if it comes to that."

"You believe it will, don't you?" she demanded, but she sank back in her chair and Claire let go of her wrist.

"Not if we head it off first. Learn all we can. Plan to fight Sheriff Goodrich, Sheriff Parsons and their plans."

"All right," she said with a sniff. She gripped her hands in her lap and stared at them. "Mother was distraught that I was so upset. She was depressed. Yes, she could have overdosed, but not intentionally."

Claire agreed. The fact that Francine had talked to the family's longtime lawyer about changing her will—would she kill herself before taking care of that? And if she thought Shadowlawn should go to the state or a buyer who could afford to restore it, would she overdose, even accidentally? What if someone helped her along before she could change her current will?

"Then you'll let either me or both Nick and me go through her things—without sorting through them first?"

Jasmine looked up again, glaring. "If I haven't already, you mean? How dare you! But yes, let's get Neil out here right now and tell him to bring everything down from the attic where I had it taken because I couldn't bear to look at it in that room where that dead woman stares down all day and night!"

"Let's leave Neil out of this for now. Take me up there right now so I can assess what's there."

Jasmine sat up straighter and turned toward her. "Look, Claire, this is all one horrible nightmare where I feel like I'm fleeing, like I'm fighting for my life, like dead people are grabbing at me! You can't know how that is."

Actually, Claire thought, she did.

18

Claire didn't see Nick or Neil in the house as she followed Jasmine up the center servant stairs toward the attic, lit by only their two flashlights.

"Of course," Jasmine said, "since they had pre-Civil War dances up here, you can go up the staircase at the end of the upstairs hall, but I prefer to keep that sealed. By the way, bats get in somehow, but you won't see them in broad daylight unless they are hanging upside down."

Claire shivered, though it was warm here. The stairs creaked. The very walls reeked of dust. A strange whisper buzzed, evidently the wind. Claire recalled Nick saying something about voices or music emanating from the attic at night, but in such an old house, strange sounds were understandable. Still, her pulse began to pound.

The attic walls were cypress wood. The vast room did not have a high ceiling and was lined by the dormer windows, which had wooden window seats under each. With long-gone cushions, they must have been tiny alcoves for flirting and chatting. Yes, ghosts seemed to hover here. The room had obviously never been electrified, for three, dust-shrouded antique chandeliers still hung from the ceiling. She looked for bats but didn't see them.

Strange, Claire thought, but the scent of jasmine perfume was back again, hanging heavy here. She hadn't smelled it on their hostess since that first day. Perhaps Jasmine had worn it out on the veranda, too, but it just hadn't hit her until they were closed in here. Or she might have put some on when she went into Rosalynn's room to get the flashlights. And why did she have two flashlights in there? It was where Francine had slept, not Jasmine herself, who was in one of the five other bedrooms.

As Jasmine began banging shutters open, they turned their flashlights off. Daylight fought its way through dancing dust motes. They both sneezed. It was pretty obvious that Lola, even if she cleaned house downstairs, didn't do much up here. But at this end of the large, open space, light revealed the extent of the clutter.

It reminded Claire of the TV show she and Darcy liked, *The Antiques Roadshow.* Here was stored a keyhole desk with a broken leg, a worn velvet settee, the headboard of a bed, a roll of carpet, an umbrella stand, humpbacked trunks, crates, boxes—all with a velvety cloak of dust except for two large cartons.

"Where to start, right?" Jasmine asked. "Those two boxes over there," she added, pointing to the ones Claire had noted, "are her most recent things I brought up. It was like—once she was buried—I wanted this to be buried, too, that is, what I didn't need to settle her will and the estate, which is still ongoing. It hurt so much to go through them, to know that she's gone forever, so I just stored them for now. Actually, I just threw things in these boxes, so I suppose they're a mess."

That sounded so sincere, Claire thought. But was she sad because Francine was dead, or because she regretted causing that?

As they walked toward the boxes, Jasmine went on, "She remade her will from time to time. The last one—Nick's seen it—is ten years old and keeps the property in the family." That much was true, Claire thought. But she'd let Nick confront Jasmine later about whether she knew of the new will Francine had planned.

"Then I'll start with those two boxes and go back a bit from there if necessary."

"Exactly what are you looking for?" Jasmine asked, suddenly turning toward Claire and stepping between her and the boxes as if to protect them. Her voice rose; she propped fists at her hips. That sudden change in body language seemed to scream at Claire.

"I'll know it if I see it," Claire told her. "How about I get Heck and Nick to help us carry these down to the library? These boxes look heavy, and we'd need to be very careful on the stairs."

"Yes, well, I guess I'm glad you dragged me up here," she said with a sigh. "I've got to face things, not just store them. By the way, I've given Win Jackson permission to photograph the interior of Shadowlawn for a book project he has in mind. We'll share the profits, and he doesn't need to see all this clutter when he works up here."

She heaved a second huge sigh that seemed to deflate her stiff stance. She walked a few steps away and sank carefully onto a leather, iron-banded trunk. "This attic is like the head of this place, the stored memories, just like people keep in their heads..."

Her lower lip quivered. Her shoulders shook. She began to cry silently. Two tears slowly started down her cheeks, but, gripping her hands together in her lap, she made no move to brush them away. Sincerity or a clever plea for sympathy? Claire had come to be skeptical of Jasmine and her lightning mood changes, but this seemed real. She knew not to try to comfort her. She needed to stay neutral. It wasn't her place to be pulled in emotionally—which seemed a stupid thought considering how she was falling so fast for Nick.

"You have a child, don't you?" Jasmine asked.

Surprised at the shift in subject, Claire said, "Yes. A four-year-old daughter."

"Well, Shadowlawn is my only child, and I'm its daughter. I couldn't save my mother, but I need to save this place, do what's best for it as I see it, so please keep that in mind as you go through these things."

"Yes," Claire promised. "I will."

"Hey, Bronco," Nick called out as the big man came around the tree guarding his trailer. "Didn't want to startle you, but I wanted to ask you a question."

"Sure," he said, walking toward him with a fishing pole in his hand. "Shoot."

"I thought I saw someone on the grounds a while ago. I couldn't tell who it was. He ran past here, toward the river," he said pointing. This close, Nick saw Bronco had gator teeth stuck in the brim of his hat.

"Wha'd he look like?"

"Couldn't get close enough to tell."

"I find someone like that, I'd kick him out," Bronco muttered. "I sometimes run off kids—haunted house and all—but that was at night."

Nick had meant to ask him about Jace being knocked out over by the so-called ghost tree, but he didn't want to suggest Claire had been asking outsiders in here, so he said, "This might sound crazy, but have there ever been any incidents under the lynching tree near the front door?"

"Like you mean, seein' the body? Claire tell you she seen it in Dr. Jackson's pictures?"

"Yeah, she did."

"He's coming here tomorrow to do some pictures for Miss Jasmine and I'm gonna help him, cart his stuff around and all that. Done it before when he took shots of the river and outside the house. Neil just told me he'd like to hire the doc to do some photos of someone in one of those monster suits he's got, maybe get publicity for his museum, start putting stuff online which I don't mess with none."

"The internet is a blessing and a curse. A great way to stay in touch and do business, but it can be abused really bad, too."

"Like live people," Bronco said. "But I'll keep a sharp eye out for strangers, daytime and night."

Nick thanked him and started to walk away, but Bronco called after him, "You think I should help Neil by puttin' on that monster suit or not, if that's not askin' for free lawyer advice?"

Nick turned back. "He wants *you* to wear it?"

"While he films—or talks Doc Jackson into doing it while he's here. Making a short flick, not sure."

"I think you should only do it if there's something in it for you, Bronco, and tell him no otherwise. Say," he said, walking farther back and seeing a good opening for a question he hoped wouldn't tick Claire off, "do you and Neil plan to still live on the grounds if Jasmine keeps this place? Has she said one way or the other about that?"

"If'n Miss Francine would have let it go to outsiders, we figured we was both done here. Miss Jasmine, we're not sure. When I'm cartin' the doc's photo equipment around, I'm gonna ask him to put in a good word with her, even if the one he was pretty close to was Miss Francine. 'Preciate it if you'd do the same, 'cause Miss Jasmine prob'ly listens to you."

"I'm sure she'd listen to you, too, Bronco. She's fighting hard to clear things up right now. Claire and I are helping her. But I'm sure she'll take your ties to this place into consideration if she can keep it."

As Nick turned to walk away again, he saw the puppet Claire had mentioned of Lola Moran had been moved outside and was sitting primly in one of Bronco's old lawn chairs. A shiver snaked up his spine. For some odd reason, his dad's voice leaped at him, teaching him the Twenty-third Psalm when he was small. "Yea, though I walk through the valley of the shadow of death, I will fear no evil."

Shadowlawn and its people were getting to him. There was something evil here. He stretched his strides to go find Claire.

That afternoon Claire and Nick commandeered the library. Working from opposite ends of a long, narrow table before the back window, they each took a box and went through it, unpacking it first to assess what was there, then sorting and prioritizing what to read. Heck was sitting on the veranda just outside with his laptop, reading through newspaper articles about Jasmine's case he'd downloaded back in St. Augustine as well as working on files from Nick's other pending law cases.

"Wow," Claire said, paging through a small, leather-bound book from the bottom of her box. "A diary that goes way back, looks like she kept it for years! Yes, way back. Maybe there's something in it about your father and her."

"Old love affairs are not of immediate use here, partner. Keep digging."

"Oh, I will. I shouldn't take anything off property, but I don't trust Jasmine not to go through this stuff herself when we leave. Do you think she'd let us take these boxes with us?"

"Like you said, not a good idea. But you're right about chain of custody. I'm surprised the illustrious Sheriff Goodrich missed this stuff. He should have searched the place and come up with it—unless it wasn't visible at the time. If there's a trial, we'll have to enter this as evidence and let him see it, if we intended to use any of it."

"He was probably too busy planning his campaign for state senator to look around much. I swear, Nick, it's only that he doesn't want to share the glory with anyone else that he's not working closely with Sheriff Parsons in St. A, or we'd have a murder indictment against Jasmine already."

"Why do I bother with law partners when I have you?"

"Very funny. But one more thing to convince you I'm whacked out lately. Do you smell that jasmine perfume on any of the things in your box?" she asked, sniffing at the diary as she fanned the pages.

"No, but maybe that's a woman thing."

Claire flipped to the back of the diary to see how recently it ended. Lots of spidery writing but no dates. She'd have to establish that by references when she studied it.

"Nick, give me a couple of papers with her signature on it, or maybe some other writing of hers. Despite how authentic this diary looks, I'll need to compare her writing with other signatures and script to get a standard—rule number one in the forensic document courses I took."

He handed her several papers. She folded them carefully, putting them in the diary. When a knock sounded on the door, and Neil poked his head in, she slipped the diary in her purse to go over tonight with more time. Although she'd previously decided not to take things off-site, this was too good to pass up and she'd need time to evaluate it without Jasmine or Neil hanging over her shoulder.

Neil announced, "I'm preparing a late lunch on trays for you all since you seem busy— Oh, that stuff from the attic. I carried it up there for Jasmine. She packed it away rather hastily a couple of days after Francine died."

Darn, Claire thought. So he knew these documents were there, could have gone through the boxes, pulled things out—if he had any reason to. Neil had been so nervous when she'd interviewed him, and he had a lot to lose.

"We'd certainly appreciate the lunch," Claire told him.

"Yes, well, I'll be feeding one more mouth tomorrow with Win Jackson here again, this time in my territory instead of only outside. Frankly, I plan to watch the man like a hawk because Jasmine gave him permission to stage things—rearrange them for best effect, so to speak—and I pride myself on that."

Nick spoke up. "You don't think he'd put them back?" Claire clutched her purse with the diary tighter; she needed that to discover and settle things, so she could get back to her own daughter.

"Let's just say the man's had his eye on things here for years. Enough said," Neil concluded and went out and shut the door.

"I wouldn't put a lot of stock in those innuendos," Claire told Nick. "Win and Neil don't get along, though they obviously work together when they have to."

"According to Bronco, Neil wants Win to make a promo film for his museum," Nick said. "Are you listening?"

"Of course, but I do think we should consider asking Jasmine if we can take these things with us. I have the diary, but I mean both boxes. She and Neil know we have access to them now and, if they haven't been tampered with already, they could be. We can work on boxes after we talk to Francine's old lawyer."

"Okay, boss. What would I do without you?"

In the end, Jasmine let them take the two boxes, so they carefully listed the contents on an inventory—including the diary—Heck typed up, dated and had her sign temporarily into their possession. Nick carried the boxes out to the trunk himself. Jasmine had fussed some about the diary—said she didn't know about it and what could be in it—but Claire had been adamant about looking at it. She could tell that Jasmine had caved on that just so she didn't seem to be making a scene over it.

Neil had given them such a hearty lunch that they decided to drive straight to see Francine's old lawyer, retired attorney Spencer Clawson, then have dinner later. If Claire wasn't too tired, she said she'd planned to study Francine's diary. She was desperate to understand the woman more. The business memoranda, bank statements and minutes of committee board meetings, which Nick planned to go over, didn't look promising to her.

"Look, Nick," she said, pointing as they approached the St. Augustine Usina Bridge which spanned a wide stretch of the Intercoastal Waterway en route to Vilano Beach where the attorney lived. "It reminds me of the bridge over Lake Monroe where we saw Fiend Face."

"You're right, but don't remind me."

They drove over the arched bridge without a problem. Beach traffic was coming out, not in, this time in early evening. They found Shoreside Drive and the address. Nick drove into a curved, brick-paved entry and parked under an arch alive with hot pink bougainvillea, its colors fading as evening set in.

"A bit more house than your favorite attorney has," he told her. He made sure the car was locked. He was nervous about the boxes in the trunk as well as all his business things in the car. It was almost nightfall, but he scanned the area for a drone, then scolded himself as he took Claire's upper arm—she still favored her wounded one—and rang the doorbell. A young woman with long blond hair opened it.

"Nick Markwood and Claire Britten to see Attorney Clawson."

"Hi, I'm his granddaughter, Lindsey. He told me to bring you right in. Could I get you a drink? Water? Coffee? Some of the expensive Scotch he still sneaks despite his surgery?" she asked with a big smile.

"Ah, coffee would be fine, right, Claire?"

"I'd appreciate that. Thanks, Lindsey," she said, then as the girl led them into the house, she whispered, "and thanks, Nick."

"Caffeine for my favorite PWN," he told her.

A thin, white-haired man sat in a recliner he had tipped back, looking out over a dimly lighted pool, some dwarf palms and the beach before the big, Atlantic Ocean reached away into the growing darkness.

He shook hands with them and asked Nick about his law firm, evidently glad to have attorney talk. Lindsey served them coffee and disappeared before Nick managed to turn the conversation to Francine's will that was never made.

"I jotted some notes," Spencer said, shuffling under a newspaper from the table next to his chair. "Now where is that?"

Nick's gaze slammed into Claire's. So how competent was this elderly invalid? Man, he was starting to read her thoughts and he was pretty sure she read his—some of his.

"Oh, here we go." He put on a pair of reading glasses. "Oh, yes, the really new thing here was, if she died or became incapacitated, the oversight and care of the estate was to go jointly to her daughter,

Jasmine, and to Dr. Winston Jackson but to be deeded to the state or possibly sold to an altruistic owner."

Nick's head snapped up. He drew in a sharp breath.

"Really? The care of it to Jasmine *and* Win Jackson? But not financial control?"

"Not included. Both of them were to be advisors to whoever controlled the estate. You know, as much as Francine loved Shadowlawn, I believe she thought there was a curse on it from the past. I don't think she wanted her only child to have to shoulder that. Oh, I didn't put it down here I see, because we never got as far as the wording before my heart attack—and Francine's sad demise—but I believe Jasmine and Win Jackson were to have input on something like artistic control. That's it, artistic but not financial since ownership would have passed from Jasmine."

"Artistic control could mean indirect money," Nick said. "A salary for advice."

"But Jasmine and Win working together is not the thing that really surprised me, since Francine had known and trusted him for years—why, I know him too—but it was that she talked of considering a buyer. And not Win Jackson."

"The State of Florida?" Nick asked.

"If that didn't work out, some private investor who had heard about the estate somewhere—knew you were her new lawyer for it, too, as I recall, though I must admit, all that major surgery and anesthetic has dulled my brain at times. They say I'll make a good recovery, but I don't think so. Good would be going back to work, having my wife back, my son living closer than Milwaukee."

"So what do you know about this other buyer,

the one who might have known I was taking over as her lawyer?" Nick prodded. Should they trust everything this man said, especially since he seemed shaky? Nick was racking his brain to think who he might know who would invest in something as huge as Shadowlawn.

"She didn't give me his name, said he wanted to remain private through some sort of trust. But this buyer had sworn to keep the history and integrity of the estate alive, redo the place, control public visits. I don't believe she had discussed it with Jasmine and was hesitant to do so. But I do know Francine said the possible buyer was living somewhere on Grand Cayman Island in the Caribbean."

Nick just stared at the man. Then out the window toward the ocean, now a black mirror that reflected the three of them. A coincidence, when he'd learned not to trust that?

"Nick?" Claire prompted. "Are you all right?"

"Sure. Fine. I just wish I had the investor's name or contact information, because I'd like to—check him out. Sir, if you recall anything else about this, please call my number here."

"I have your Naples number."

"This is my private cell. You've been a big help to us," he told the man, scribbling his number on the back of a business card.

They left after a bit more small talk. The moment they stepped outside—it was starting to rain lightly—Claire said, "Do you think Win could be more involved than we thought?"

"I'm glad he's coming to Shadowlawn tomorrow. Maybe he knows something about this investor."

"Does it matter now? Spencer didn't think Jasmine knew of it. And if she did, she's too stubborn about keeping control to let a stranger in on things. Is that what you were thinking when you—you went blank for a minute?"

"Yeah, exactly," he said, feeling guilty for the first time that he wasn't leveling with her about his past, his father's death, his pursuit of Clayton Ames. But he didn't want to confuse things with his crusade against Ames, or scare her off. Still, he had to protect her in case her growing closeness to him put her in danger.

He said, "Let's head back to the hotel and get over that big bridge before we stop to eat. You've got me spooked now about it."

"Do not use the words *spook, ghost* or *haunted*, please."

He breathed a sigh of relief as they passed the bridge and headed toward town. The back-from-the-beach traffic had ended now, and they were pretty much alone on the road. He was glad to see only a ditch with water on their right side rather than the wide Intercoastal or the ocean. He had to call Heck as soon as they got back to dig deeper into Ames's ties to Grand Cayman. It could be that Ames had learned Nick was working for Francine and checked her out. He'd obviously contacted her so why hadn't she told Nick she was thinking of a buyer/investor?

It began to rain hard. Nick turned the windshield wipers up another notch. Damn dark on this stretch of road. Trees, the ditch off to the side and not much else.

From nowhere, a car without lights on behind them crashed into their rear. Again, hard. Sudden. So sudden. He'd been looking ahead, hadn't seen it coming. He tried to veer away, control the car. Claire screamed.

Nick clenched the wheel as their car jumped, shuddered and seemed to leap into the blackness of the ditch, front down. Water slammed into the windshield.

"Brace!" he shouted much too late. "Brace!"

19

Claire thrust her good hand toward the dashboard to brace herself, but on impact, their airbags exploded, crashing into their upper bodies. They deflated fast, but Claire's seat belt also held her hard. Blackness but for the car's headlights in the murk. Nightmare? No, this was real.

The car, front down, sinking, hit bottom, jerking them again. Not too deep here. Was it? Water like ink smeared the windows. Gurgles. Bubbles, going up. Car lights, dashboard too, still on.

"We have to get the windows down before the power stops," Nick said, his voice loud. "Too much pressure to open the doors. Don't panic. We have to get out and up."

At first she could not believe he was going to let the water in. The road had been deserted but someone would come. They had to keep the air in!

"Claire, do as I say," he commanded, as he started to roll both windows down. "Unhook your seat belt. We have to get out or we'll drown."

Lexi! She had to get out of here for Lexi!

The windows were coming down too fast, she thought, as water started to pour in. They were going to die! She wanted to scream at Nick, cling to him.

But somehow she found courage and a lot of anger that someone did this to them. "Yes," she cried. "Out and up."

She remembered her meds. She'd brought the day ones in her purse and had started to carry the night liquid with her, too. Trained to never leave them, she fumbled for her purse by the dimming lights of the instrument panel. She pulled her purse over her shoulder. Never do that in a plane crash, she recalled. Take nothing with you, but this could mean taking her life with her.

"Hold your breath." Nick's voice still sounded steady. "When there's enough water, we'll get out. I'll help you."

Dear God, please help us, she prayed as water poured in. It was cold. Some things in it. What if a gator...?

She held her breath, then floated higher in the car to grab the last of the air. Nick's face broke water. He gasped in the air, too. He reached for her, squeezed her shoulder.

Then the lights all went out to leave them in utter darkness.

They were going to lose the things in the trunk— maybe proof Francine killed herself—or Jasmine did it for her. Is that why someone...

"It's too hard," she cried. "The water—too hard to get out."

"It won't be in a minute. If you can't get out that

window, I'll come around for you, pull you out. Don't be afraid. Hold your breath—now!"

She did. Endlessly as the last of the air in the car was washed away. But he was right. The water stopped pouring in. She was already floating. Her lungs were going to burst. Now! Nick had said now!

She felt her way through the open window, started to push out. Then he was there, outside the car, hard hands on her, pulling her, then pushing and kicking them upward. They quickly broke the surface in a gush of bubbles. They sucked in air.

As they struggled to get out of the water, their feet did not touch bottom. It wasn't far to the steep bank of the ditch. The night was as black as the water, stars overhead, beautiful stars.

"Watch your bad arm," he said, but she paddled with him to the edge. There was no shore, nothing to hold on to. Nothing but Nick, which seemed enough. They were out. Alive. And together.

As he boosted her up to cling to a tree branch, headlights approached on the road but went right past them. It could be daylight before someone saw the car, if then. No lights, no houses around here. It might have been days—weeks—until someone found them.

"Who would have done that?" she gasped, still out of breath. "Not just by chance—like Fiend Face."

He didn't answer. He struggled to get a hand-hold and crawled up on the grass, then dragged her after him until they leaned, panting, on level ground against a tree. They looked back at the car. The left side of the back bumper was barely visible above the surface of the water. That car could have been their coffin and the ditch their grave.

Though she wasn't cold, she began to tremble. Nerves. Shock. She watched as he craned his neck to look all around. He finally spoke. "No, we weren't hit just by chance." Sitting on the grass, his back against a tree, he pulled her into his arms, onto his lap, and held her tight with her head tucked under his chin, much as Claire sometimes held Lexi to comfort her—or herself. She clung to him hard. They stayed like that, silent, breathing. She began to shake harder. He held her tighter.

"The car behind us had no lights," he whispered. "I didn't even see it until too late. I just want to be sure whoever did it isn't coming back to check that it did the job. It's so damn deserted on this stretch right here. We must have been followed and this—this attack—was planned."

"Nick, my cell phone may work. It's here in my purse," she said, when she realized it was still over her arm. "I grabbed it for my meds, but…"

He loosed her and shook his head. "It's probably doomed, but try it. I can't believe you have your purse when I lost so much in the car. Maybe someone knew that," he said, muttering a curse as Claire dug into the damp interior of her purse and pulled out her cell.

"Oh, I put Francine's diary in here, too, so it wouldn't get knocked around," she told him. "I hope it's still legible." She pressed the button on her phone. Its face lit.

"Thank God," he said. "For everything. Call Heck."

"What about the police?"

"I'm going to get you out of here with Heck, then get the police, then get the car out. This is getting too dangerous for you, so I've got to send you home."

"You mean to the hotel."

"Yes, then home. If the police need your version of this, they can talk to you, but I was the driver."

"But I can't just go home. We're obviously getting somewhere. Someone is really shook we're getting close. I'm going to read the diary."

"There are things you don't know," he said. "Things I haven't told you."

She shuddered. For the first time, she really felt cold. "About Jasmine or someone you suspect?" she asked. "You need to tell me. If you've been holding things back about this case…"

"I don't think it's related to this case. Or at least, I didn't until something Spencer Clawson said tonight."

"What? You angered someone in an earlier case?"

"Call Heck. Let's get him out here, see what we can salvage of my car, the boxes in it—and this case."

"I'll call him when you tell me what you're talking about, what you're afraid of. Nick, you owe it to me."

"I do. But we need help now. I'll have to report this to the police and tell them I have no clue who did it."

"But you do. And not someone tied to Francine's murder?"

"Probably not, but with that man I never say never. Just trust me for now. I want to get you back safely, and we'll talk tomorrow, I promise."

"All right, but you're not sending me home like some kid who's been bad in school."

"Claire, you've been nothing but good for this case and for me."

His voice snagged. It sounded like this big, bold man might cry. She wanted to hug him but she punched in her phone log, touched Heck's number and handed the phone to Nick. The only light for miles around seemed to be her phone, shining on his wet face. Was that a tear? As he told Heck what happened, she turned away so he wouldn't see she was crying, too.

"It's been one hell of a long night," Nick told Claire as he joined her on her hotel room balcony for breakfast the next morning. He hadn't shaved. Beard stubble might be in style, but he'd always hated feeling grubby. A much-needed shower and finally a change of clothes took the little time he'd had in his room after spending hours with the police and the tow truck driver. And laying out damp paper after paper from the boxes to dry in his room.

"The car's a disaster," he told her, "but some of the documents in the trunk may be salvageable. My laptop and phone are dead, but Heck had copies of some things, and I can get much of it restored from the cloud. He's getting me another laptop and phone. The report I filed with the police states that I don't know who did that to us or why."

"Which isn't quite true?" she asked as she lifted her orange juice from the room service tray. "What if they find out you reported our being jammed by a car with a masked driver on our way here just four days ago?"

"They won't. I don't know exactly who was behind the wheel last night—and maybe before—but I have a theory. When I explain, you'll see why I still think I should send you back to Naples. You've done a lot here already."

"But I have plans to do more. Go through the diary

I verified was hers and started to read this morning, though some of the earliest and latest pages are damp and the ink has smeared. I want to help you with those papers. Certainly, I need to talk to Win Jackson again at Shadowlawn since Spencer Clawson said he was to be appointed with Jasmine to oversee the estate—despite the fact it didn't entail money."

"But there may have been a salary or bequest—or fame—involved. Maybe we'll turn up something about that in those wet papers."

Cheered by her resilience and loyalty, Nick ate his omelet and bacon fast because he was starved, but as he toyed with the bagel, his mind was racing fast, too. Most women would have cut and run after what happened last night. He knew Claire could be stubborn and strong, and she was giving him strength now. Except for Heck and a couple of people he used as resources for South Shores, he hadn't bared his soul to any outsiders. But, somehow, Claire wasn't that anymore.

"Okay," he said, almost as if to bolster himself for this. "You heard Spencer mention a possible buyer for Shadowlawn from Grand Cayman Island last night."

"Right. You looked like he'd hit you over the head. I was going to ask you about that again today."

"Heck, who works for my South Shores pursuits on the side, recently linked someone I've been trying to trace to Grand Cayman. To put it mildly, this man has it in for me, a very rich, dangerous man with a long reach."

Nick knew his voice had turned bitter. Man, what would she make of listening to all this? And her obsession with body language? He saw he was gripping his butter knife as if he'd stab his bagel with it. She was waiting patiently for him to go on. She reached over and put her hand on his knee.

He took a deep breath and told her, "I've been trying to track a man named Clayton Ames for years because I believe he ruined my father financially, then killed him and made it look like a suicide."

Her head jerked, so he knew he'd surprised her. "I'm sorry. That's horrible—to live with, and for him to die that way. You mentioned 'the slur of suicide' once. Someone your father trusted?"

So just how perceptive was this woman? He cleared his throat and nodded. "A former business partner, and, supposedly, a friend. I even used to call him 'Uncle Clay.' He knows that I know. He could have had me killed a long time ago, even when I was young, but he enjoys the cat-and-mouse game. He likes to toy with his prey. He thinks I'll never prove it. Because I was walking close to you after the Sorrento trial, for all I know, the shots that killed your boss and hit you could have been meant for me, though I doubt someone Ames hired would miss. Or he just meant to torment me more, to remind me he could have me taken out at any time. If I'm actually to blame for Fred Myron's death and your arm—"

"But, even if it was to warn you, it wasn't your fault. Did you hire me just to help me out because you felt bad about my being shot?"

He gripped her wrist. "No. No, I was walking over to hire you because you're good, and I needed your help."

"So South Shores—is that a front to track this Clayton Ames?"

"No, it's a charity I fund with money, time and expertise to help others who are going through hell over someone's suicide, especially if it might be a murder instead—like trying to help Jasmine. But now, what if this whole thing is a setup of some kind? I mean, Ames found out I was representing Francine, he learned Shadowlawn was in financial crisis, made her an offer to buy just to defy me—I don't know. It's a damned spider's web."

"But he wouldn't be behind Francine's death, would he? Tormenting you because he killed her and made it look like suicide? He'd want her to go through with that new will, one maybe he promoted, so he could buy Shadowlawn. At least that's a possibility."

"Yeah. Yeah, I know."

"So you can't locate him but you think he's in Grand Cayman? Isn't that where a lot of fortunes are hidden? Do you remember John Grisham's book *The Firm*? The bad guys were all hanging out in Grand Cayman."

Still holding her hand, he sat back in his chair and sighed. This woman not only excited him but she could calm him. He wanted to hold her, protect her—he wanted her.

"Sorry," she said, scooting her chair closer to his. "I don't mean to bring up fiction, but then 'truth is stranger than...' You were blessed to have a wonderful father, and it's the tragedy of your life you lost him so early and in such a horrible—and dirty—way."

"He made some mistakes. But, yeah."

"My parents did, too. Talk about fiction. By reading all the time, by escaping to fictional worlds, my mother hid from reality—her bad health, daughters who needed her, her unfaithful husband. I think characters in her books were more real to her than Darcy and I. All that to say I understand childhood loss and pain that never quite goes away."

Staring down at their linked hands, he nodded. "Sorry to unload all my trauma on you, but it helped. We have to get going. Let's finish up here and head out. I have damp papers all over my room to, hopefully, dry in the air-conditioning I'm running full force. The car trunk was fairly sealed when the tow truck pulled it out, but things are damaged. I'm putting a Do Not Disturb sign on my room door so the maid doesn't have a fit when she sees the mess. I'll go up and shave and be back here to get you in a half hour. And, however fast Heck likes to drive, he can just follow my rental car to Shadowlawn today. Besides his replacing my equipment, I'm going to have him call my insurance company, because, as Bronco would probably put it, I've got other fish to fry."

"Or other frog legs in peanut oil."

They stood over the remnants of breakfast. He'd devoured his; she had eaten little.

She walked him to the door. "Claire, I know I should send you home."

"I'll go soon, but I want to talk to Win again—and Jasmine. You need me for that."

"I need you for more than that," he blurted. Hell, he shouldn't have said that. Nor should he make a move, but he pulled her to him, just meant to hug her, but when she responded, they were kissing again, holding tight, he pressing her against the door, and the bed was so near and—

"We can't," she murmured when they came up for air.

Damn, could she read his mind? "I know. Not now anyway." He held her shoulders hard as if that would help him to control himself. "Listen, I didn't realize how much support you'd be to me, not only in this case, but personally."

"You put yourself in all your cases, I can tell, but this one's very important."

"Especially now if that bastard is involved from Grand Cayman or whatever luxury hole he's crawled into lately. But I don't want you to get hurt by being too close to me—like at the courthouse, like last night."

"Nick, what if it's not even him? What if it's the person who harmed Francine who thinks we're getting too close? We just have to be sure we're not followed or spied on—drones or whatever."

"Yeah, I didn't tell you, but Ames could be behind that, too. You're right that he'd want Francine to live to make that new will, but he's very good at staging a suicide when it's murder. I don't mean to sound paranoid, though he's made me that way. Maybe he just wants a beautiful Southern home to fix up, but that's not him to be out in the open. I've made his life enough of a living hell, and he's made plenty of illegal foreign investments so he has to hide out."

"But, as you said, a man that rich and devious can have a long reach."

He nodded. "I'll be back in a few minutes, and we'll have Heck follow us. Don't let him know you're in on all this about Ames because I've sworn him to secrecy. If there's a reason we all need to work together on that, too, we'll tell him then."

"All right."

"Anytime you feel you should leave here, I'll get you home safely, I promise. But if I decide it's time for you to go, you're out of here, understand?"

She nodded.

Maybe one more day here, and he'd send her home, he tried to convince himself. He wanted to keep her with him, but that might not keep her safe. He bit his lower lip and nodded back at her, when he wanted to do so much more.

20

When Win Jackson arrived midmorning at Shadow-lawn to photograph the interior of the house, it was quite a production. Claire thought it seemed like the arrival of royalty, or as nervous as Neil seemed, at least a visit from a Hollywood producer.

Jasmine greeted Win on the front veranda with air kisses on both cheeks. Claire knew they were close, but how close? Maybe Francine had known what she was doing when she planned to soothe them both over the loss of Shadowlawn by appointing them joint advisors to the State of Florida or what Francine's old lawyer had called an "altruistic" buyer—and Nick feared might be his archenemy.

Neil stood back, leaning forward but arms crossed in the mixed body language of welcome and wariness. Bronco hurried to help Win with his gear. Claire was surprised to see that the large, old-fashioned camera his shop assistant had been cleaning was evidently his camera of choice. A tripod followed with suitcases of gear, then lights with collapsible stands and poles.

Neil finally greeted Win as "My favorite movie buff."

"Cinephile is the latest buzzword for that, my man," Win replied, rather too grandly, Claire thought, and Nick, standing behind her, gave a short snort.

From where they were seat-belted into the back-seat of his SUV, Win produced two huge, cut glass vases of pinkish-lavender blooms. Was that lilac? This time of year? In Florida?

"Indigo from my garden," he announced. "Hugely symbolic for this place, of course—right, Bronco, since your ancestor oversaw the cultivating of it here? I've agreed to let Jasmine put out jasmine in vases—" he pronounced it *vahses* "—but indigo was once the lifeblood of this plantation, so these will be in most of the photos." With a flourish, he handed one vase to Jasmine and one to Bronco, who looked so nervous suddenly that Claire was afraid he would drop it.

Neil served lemonade and cranberry muffins to everyone in the dining room, then sat with them himself. Win offered a toast to the plantation and announced the name of the picture book would be *The Shades of Shadowlawn*.

"After all," he declared with his goblet raised, "the word *shade* used to mean a disembodied spirit or ghost. Nothing like a double entendre for a title, right, Bronco?"

The big man, who seemed somehow out of place in this dining room with the damask tablecloth, china and glassware, said only, "Right."

The house, Claire thought, had turned rather festive, which was a change in mood around here. Perhaps Jasmine and the plantation staff were hoping a

picture book would bring in needed funds for Shadowlawn's restoration so she could afford to keep the
place. But could she then afford to keep her staff?
And would she want a retro-looking metal trailer and
a monster museum on the grounds?

As Win left the dining room to set up for a shoot in
the parlor, Claire overheard Neil ask him, "Will you
have time to make that short movie for me to advertise
my museum? I see you don't have the movie camera."

"It's in the SUV. Best refer to your promo piece
by the proper term of 'trailer' now, Neil. Not really
my cup of tea, but I told you I'd do it for a small fee.
Depending on how much staging I have to do with
the way you keep things arranged here, this shoot
will take me two days and then we'll get to it. After
all, I'm not Superman—though I guess I could don
that old costume you have. Yes, I'll do that and film
your collection of fright masks, too, for the trailer."

A Superman costume and fright masks? Neil
hadn't showed them masks or costumes except the
Black Lagoon monster's. What else hadn't Neil
shared? She planned to ask Win some things later,
so she'd work that in about Neil, then ask him directly,
too. Francine's right-hand man Neil Costa was sounding stranger all the time.

Nick walked Jasmine upstairs to the bedroom that
had been Francine's, because she was nervous about
how Win would "stage it," as he said, and she wanted
to put some things away before he took over here.

"I know he'll take several shots of this portrait,"
she told him, gesturing at the large painting on the

wall. "But I don't want him to play up our ancestor's suicide off that veranda, so close to where Mother died. I know he's going to do a section in the photo display on the ghosts—everyone agrees ghosts sell—but it just makes me upset."

"You're afraid the connection between this Rosalie—"

"Rosalynn," she corrected him.

"Right, Rosalynn. You're afraid linking her and your mother would suggest that your mother committed suicide, too? But, I've been telling you, that's your best defense, Jasmine. Either that or an unintentional overdose so—"

She turned toward him. "How can you scold me for not admitting she'd kill herself after what you've been through with your father?"

"I wasn't. I just—"

"You were going to. You've struggled for years to prove your father didn't kill himself, and I don't want that stigma on my mother. Ironic our parents were once a couple, and this hangs over both their heads. Someone tampered with my mother's meds, I swear they did, but who?"

"Motive, opportunity—you tell me. Neil? Bronco?"

"You left out Lola. She got what she wanted and knew I'd make Mother choose between us—her conniving little 'foster daughter' and me, her flesh and blood. That's what you should be working on, clearing me!"

"Then who killed her? Who maybe thought she knew too much? Jasmine, haven't you thought Lola might resent you, too—might have accused you in court of your mother's death? So who killed her?"

For a minute, Nick thought she'd heave the two flashlights she was putting in the bedside table drawer at him. But she turned away from glowering at him to stare at the portrait as if it had answers.

Damn, he wished Claire was here to translate all this smothered female, mother-daughter angst. This grown woman had been so hurt by Francine's care for poor Lola that she was willing to accuse her of biting the hand that fed her, so to speak?

And Lola had pointed the finger at Jasmine, so wasn't that, literally, a dead end? He knew time was running out. Lola's ashes were in that puppet head Claire had described, but this woman, his client and friend, could be arrested at any time for murder one—maybe for two murder ones. To defend her well, he sure as hell wasn't going to ask her directly if she had harmed her mother. He still believed in Jasmine—didn't he?

And he wished in all this, that damned portrait of the Civil War matriarch of this blasted haunted house would quit staring at him. He looked away from Jasmine and glared back at long-dead Rosalynn.

"Don't look at her, or she'll get to you." Jasmine interrupted his agonizing as she rearranged some photos on the dresser and put several others in the drawer. "How Mother slept in here, I don't know. She said she felt protected here—ha! A lot of good it did her. But you know," she said, turning back to him again, obviously relieved to be changing the subject, "I guess I'll have to let Win have his way when he photographs here." She shrugged. "I know Win. He'll have it anyway."

* * *

Claire bided her time, waiting to get Win alone. Meanwhile, she tried to read Francine's diary, sitting in the back corner of the parlor where he was setting up his shots. Besides parts of the diary having smeared ink, Francine's handwriting was hard to read, small and loopy, some of the earliest entries faded—and still damp, as was the last section—but Claire was getting more familiar with it. She wasn't sure what she was looking for, but she felt she was getting so much closer to her. Here, years ago, Claire had deciphered, poor Francine had worried that Jasmine was not only too independent but rebellious. Though Lexi was only four, how Claire sympathized with that concern, with Francine in general.

Win fussed endlessly with lighting and the angles, ordering Bronco here and there. But when he finally got what he wanted, he sent him out and said he'd call for him later. She wasn't sure she liked Win anymore. He was not quite snobbish, but definitely elitist, however fine a line that was.

It had amused her to see that Win actually disappeared under a black drape behind his large-format camera at times, as if he were some Civil War–era photographer. She had come to feel that was the essence of the man, someone who could pop in and out of any situation, who could hide his innermost thoughts but then be quite generous and grandiose with sharing what he knew. Well, she hadn't known many artists, and she considered him to be one so maybe she should cut him some slack.

"Should I leave, too?" she asked.

"You evidently have something to say."

"Maybe I'm just trying to learn from a master."

"Learn what, pray tell?"

"More about Shadowlawn and how you view it. I trust your vision."

He disappeared under the black drape and clicked away as several of his klieg lights, or whatever they were, popped to nearly blind her.

When he emerged again to move his camera and the vases of indigo, he said, "What is it you want to know, Claire? For starters, Bronco's a lot deeper and brighter—and more explosive than he seems."

"I've noticed that. You should do my job. And Neil?"

"Deep and borderline devious, whereas everything about Bronco's right on the surface. So what's that you're reading?"

She thought about lying, but time was getting short. Whoever ran from Nick and hit Jace over the head could be the same person who shot her and shoved them in the water. So she decided to push Win a little more.

"It's Francine's diary she kept for years, from way back."

"Recent, too, I hope, so it might throw light on what happened to her."

"It's very revealing, but sadly, that's the hardest part to decipher." She didn't tell him why and he didn't ask. "I'm only up to the part where Jasmine is in her teens."

"But you must have peeked at the end. Anything to help the sheriff? Or more importantly, to help you and Attorney Markwood? But my only interest in it is whether it could be used for my shoot in Francine's bedroom, if you'd trust it to me for a while. An interesting artifact."

"You could use it later if I stay right there, then take it back. It could be key evidence."

"You're teasing or taunting me, but why?" he demanded, turning toward her but keeping one hand on the camera.

"Just observing. You see with a keen eye. And I can learn from that."

He said nothing else but didn't ask her to leave. The next time he popped out from under his dark cloth, she asked, "I overheard something about Neil's Superman costume and collection of fright masks. Does he have illusions of grandeur—or terror?"

"He didn't show you everything then? Best take that as an omen. Besides the suit from *Creature from the Black Lagoon*, the man has a second cinema costume of note—old-time TV, rather. You're much too young, but in the 1950s, there was a television show called *The Adventures of Superman* starring an actor named George Reeves, who, by the way, had played one of Scarlett O'Hara's suitors in an early scene of *Gone with the Wind*."

"Shades of Shadowlawn?"

"I told you the first day we met that Shadowlawn is real, and, therefore, so much better than Scarlett's Tara."

"I remember. So he wants to display that costume, too?"

"If he gets his way with his museum, which the State of Florida or any buyer would probably kick off the grounds. You know, the ironic thing about the actor Reeves who portrayed Superman? First of all, it was really a dumb show. They expected the kids watching to believe a so-called 'mild-mannered newspaper reporter' could just take off his glasses, slick his hair back, change his clothes and not be recognized for who he was in real life."

"But it's amazing how people can con each other, isn't it?"

He shrugged. "The older you get, the more you realize how brilliant or stupid people can be. Anyhow, there was a huge scandal over whether the Superman actor committed suicide or was murdered. But back to the masks—Neil paid big bucks for the famous one from one of the *Phantom of the Opera* productions. I believe he said he has one from an early *Batman* movie and one from that horrible slasher *Scream.* I told him he was crazy to buy one of those *Scream* so-called Ghostface masks on eBay because you can get them in any store selling Halloween things. What? You look—actually, scared."

"I've seen that *Scream* mask, but I couldn't remember what it was from. It reminded me of some famous painting."

"Did it? That's by an artist named Munch. The character in the *Scream* horror movies runs around murdering people who deserve it since they're so stupid, treading where they should not."

But Claire was thinking she'd have to tell Nick she'd finally learned what had inspired Fiend Face's mask. And that Neil had bought one of those masks on eBay when he'd initially given her the impression he wasn't internet savvy. Perhaps he'd never showed her that mask—or his others—because he didn't want them to link his Ghostface mask to the person who threatened them the day they drove here from Naples. Win had said that Neil was deceptive and borderline dangerous, though she knew not to believe everything a witness said, especially one so verbal and helpful as Win.

Claire had named her small company Clear Path, because, as she'd said on her website, she could help her clients find their way to answers, to better solutions in their problems and their lives.

But in this case of Nick's, it seemed she was fighting her way through the underbrush along the river, at night, with someone she couldn't see chasing her. It was like running, running, making progress but still being lost in the mud and the thick foliage. Those narcoleptic nightmares she'd had years ago with ghosts and dead people chasing her...it was just like that.

21

Claire was surprised to see Nick peek in the door of the parlor while she was watching Win. He gestured for her to join him in the hall. Win was draped to his shoulders by his black curtain again. The camera was clicking away, and the lights were popping. Claire put the diary in her purse, rose quietly and joined Nick who closed the door behind her.

"Let's walk down by the river," he said. "I think it might rain, but not yet."

"It's that time of year. You can tell it's 4:00 p.m. when it starts to rain, at least in Naples."

"I saw there's a bench off to the side beyond Bronco's airboat. I get the feeling these walls have ears," he whispered with a glance toward the front door, then the back one.

"There was a gator near that spot on the river," she told him, digging her sunglasses out of her purse. "But I'm game."

"Don't say that too loud around here or Bronco may hunt you. I thought he'd be in there with you two," he said as he held the back door open for her.

"He was, but Win told him to take a break for a while. Win didn't even like me sitting there. Bronco may be out here somewhere," she told him, looking around, as they crossed the patio and headed for the river.

She wasn't a bit afraid out here with Nick, though along the water it seemed so—well, primeval. A dinosaur might just as well lumber out of this thick foliage, and the St. Johns River reminded her of that narrow, dark ditch last night. She realized, as terrified as she'd been when the car went in the water, that being with Nick had made all the difference. He'd told her not to panic, and she hadn't—at least, not for long.

Besides, the struggle she'd been through with her disease, the dreadful nightmares that had seemed so real before she was properly medicated—what could be more horrible than that? More than once in her sleep before she was diagnosed, she'd been certain she was going to die.

"Claire—" his voice interrupted her thoughts "—I said, any more ideas? I mean about who looks suspicious."

"I'm writing up my final conclusions for you tonight about those I've interviewed. Jasmine, Win, Neil, Bronco—even Cecilia Moran. I'll have Heck type it from my notes, though my handwriting can't be as bad as Francine's in this diary. I was hoping to learn more about her in it so that I could give you my opinion on whether she might have committed suicide. But it's slow going with faded and blurred ink, mostly from the early and late parts getting wet, not to mention her small, cursive writing. She sometimes refers to people I don't have a fix on. But I just feel there's something here that will help us."

"You just feel? If you have to testify about all this in court, since you've begun to sympathize with her so much, will you claim woman's intuition?"

She knew he was teasing but that riled her. She was on edge and frustrated and she wanted to get home to Lexi.

"Hardly," she said. "I'll swear to experience and knowledge from my Certified Forensic Fraud credentials and document examiner training. I don't mean to sound defensive, but Jasmine and everyone else I've interviewed here are sounding that way, and it's catching, like some powerful plague."

"Sorry. I have the problem of seeing you as a dynamic, desirable woman as well as a dedicated colleague."

She felt herself begin to blush, of all things. Had they almost had another argument? But she was a woman, too. They'd blurred the lines between professional and personal and, as dangerous as that was, it was partly her fault, too.

Nick took her elbow and steered her toward a wooden bench. It was rustic, almost crude, a log sawed in half for both the seat and the back, but the surface had been sanded smooth. She hadn't noticed it when she was out here with Bronco, so his airboat must have hidden it. She saw the chain that secured the boat to the tree was off and the boat rested closer to the river. Was Bronco planning to go out on a day Win was here, or had he gone for a ride already? Airboats made quite a racket, and she hadn't heard anything. She wondered if he'd been out in the boat with poor Lola or sat on this bench with her.

They sat close together, turned slightly toward each other. "So, you'll give me an opinion on murder versus suicide after you read the diary," he said in what suddenly sounded like his lawyer voice. "After some agonizing, I'm holding to my original position that Jasmine can't be guilty, and I want to explain why. I know she's done some things that look bad." He cleared his throat, then went on.

"She refuses to admit or accept that Francine might have committed suicide. I told her flat out that would be her best defense if they indict, but she won't budge. She even pulled the guilt card on me—that, because of my father's death, I should understand that she won't accept that Francine killed herself."

"Her refusal to try to take that way out is strong in her favor. But she probably knew you'd go for it the way you did, that it would help to convince you of her innocence. Does she know about South Shores?"

"No. Do you have to see every side for everything, Claire? I'm trying to build a waterproof case here!"

"You hired me to do this job, and we agreed I would do it my way. I'm struggling to stay objective, but that's getting harder the more I know these people—and you."

"Maybe you shouldn't stay objective about me, at least not when we're done here. Look, I need to get what information and insight you have, then send you home. After last night, I'm worried something will happen to you."

He angled his body more toward her and slid his arm behind her shoulders on the back of the bench.

A piercing scream overhead made them both jump. Surely not a drone in this thick tree cover.

"Sounds like an osprey way back in here," he said, looking up. "But I don't see it." They were silent a moment. In her ears echoed her own scream when they'd plunged into the water last night.

"Nick," she said, "I do have something more to say before I write things up. Win says Neil has a Superman costume that belonged to some 1950s actor who either killed himself or committed suicide—big scandal over that. Neil seems to have a dark, secretive, maybe borderline psychotic side. But something more."

"Go on," he urged, frowning. His hand behind her gently clasped her shoulder as if to steady her. That was the Nick she knew and had come to like, maybe even love a little bit—strong yet sensitive, even vulnerable.

"Neil has a collection of so-called monster masks he did not show Heck and me or even mention during our tour of his museum. Win's description of one of them is just like what we've called Fiend Face, so could that have been Neil? The mask is inspired by that horror movie franchise called *Scream*. So if Jasmine could have told Neil that I—maybe even we— were coming, and if Neil wanted to scare us off…"

"That's a lot of ifs. Bronco was not here that day or the day after, either. Could you see Neil and Bronco in cahoots to get rid of Francine before she asked them to leave, if the mansion was sold or deeded out from under them?"

"Not really, but desperation creates strange bedfellows. Bronco was supposedly hunting pythons in the Everglades when she died, just like he was when we came here."

"And the Glades are near Naples. Now you've got me thinking that way. But I agree they don't seem the type to work together. Then again, how many Americans own one of those stupid masks, and Halloween is about one month away. I know some people start getting their masks and costumes ready way ahead for theme parties. It could have been anyone—completely unrelated to this—in that car."

"Once again, none of this is proof. It could be coincidence, but after last night, we know someone is following us, at least sometimes, and wants us either off this case or—"

He finished for her, "Or dead."

Jace couldn't decide what to do about those three photographs a so-called "friend" sent to him in LA. The guy tormenting him should have signed it *Fiend* instead. Out over the Pacific now, night had fallen, and he had the controls while the pilot took a restroom break on their long flight to Singapore. As on all American-based flights, there had to be two people in the cockpit at all times, so a flight attendant sat behind him. He was glad it was Lance, because the women always wanted to talk. As the Airbus flew on automatic pilot, the wraparound lighted control panel also kept him silent company, that and the huge wing lights outside that probed the darkness.

He couldn't get those pictures of Claire and Nick Markwood out of his head. Why would someone take photos, he guessed, from a drone? Why warn the ex-husband about an ex-wife and Markwood? Obviously, someone had a beef with her or the lawyer. And then that printed warning. Should he email or call Claire about that? Even contact Markwood? Were either of them really in danger? He sure didn't want it to be Claire.

He rechecked the altimeter and cruising speed, though he'd just done that. Piloting this big baby was a lot more complicated but physically easier than controlling the Cirrus SR22 he still co-owned with a friend who rented him a small beach house in Naples. The Cirrus was a far cry from the F-16s he'd flown in the Middle East and was way different from this Airbus.

Flying at night was symbolic of life, because you never quite knew what was out here, but you had to be prepared for anything. Here at least you had GPS and radar. Living life day to day—not even that.

He'd fallen so fast for Claire, practically eloping, though they did have a small wedding because her sister had a fit over them just running off. Then Claire hiding her illness, especially never sharing the nightmarish cataplexy with him… Had he been that busy or distracted? Uncaring? Self-obsessed? He should have known, but she should have told him.

He did love her still and not just because she was the mother of his child. He still felt responsible for Claire, no way around that.

He let the huge monster of a plane fly him and the nearly six hundred souls for which he was responsible through the vast, black night.

As Nick and Claire started back into the house, Bronco suddenly appeared on the river path, though a ways from them. Nick jumped and noticed Claire was startled, too. So had they been watched? Overheard? Despite this man's denials, had he knocked out Jace Britten under the so-called ghost tree? Was he in good enough physical shape to run away after spying on them and not appear to be tired or out-of-breath when it seemed he was just working at his trailer?

"You know," Bronco said, "that bench marks the spot where the indigo used to be loaded onto river rafts. So I know my kin, William Richards, spent time there, too. Right now, I gotta go back to check if Win needs me again."

Nick said, "Have you decided whether you'll be in that monster movie Neil asked you about?"

"Monster movie?" Claire said, making Nick recall he hadn't told her about that.

With a look not to say more, Nick told her, "Bronco said it's just a short promo piece Neil wants with Bronco wearing the *Creature from the Black Lagoon* suit. With Win producing, directing and filming."

"Aha."

"I think your idea's good to forget it," Bronco told Nick. "But Neil—he got Miss Jasmine's ear more'n I do, so I don't want to tick him off. 'Sides, that rubber suit would be so hot, and he says you can hardly move in it. Fall in the river in that thing, you don't swim real fancy down under with a girl in your arms like in the movie—you prob'bly drown."

Without another word—was he just upset, or had he glared at them?—he went into the house.

"Nick—"

"Never mind scolding me. He asked me for legal advice yesterday, and we had so much going on I forgot to tell you. I don't think it means much, do you—like some kind of subtle threat to us? The guy's not that clever."

"What's that about still waters run deep? No, I think it shows Neil's the master of manipulation to get what he wants to protect and promote his museum. And that Bronco—if left to his own devices without your input—might go along with Neil. Win said Neil's devious and deep but, with Bronco, everything's on the surface."

"Even the way you describe that makes me feel we're underwater with this case," he said as he held the back door open for her. "But again, thanks for seeing things in people I miss. I need that from you."

As if the heavens stressed that thought, deep thunder rumbled overhead and shook the back windows of the house.

22

"Mommy, I just Skyped with Daddy, too, and he's got jet bags, bags under his eyes, I think. You know, from flying a long, long time to Singing-poor."

Bags under the eyes: Claire knew how that looked and felt. But, however tired he was, Jace had always seemed so alert and resilient to her. She hoped he wasn't sick. Who knew what he could catch in exotic places like that—Singing-poor, as Lexi always called it.

"Maybe he meant he had jet lag," Claire told her, trying to sound perky and keep a smile on her face. "That means, since you're not at home and in a different place, you feel kind of sleepy."

"But, Mommy, you know people on airplanes take bags. I think it's jet bags. Are you having a good time there?"

"I'm working hard, hon. And missing you, so I hope to be back in a couple of days. Any other news from the preschool you and Jilly are going to start after Christmas?"

"I think Aunt Darcy got an envelope but she said she's waiting for you."

They chatted on about everything from a cut on Lexi's knee to how Claire's arm was healing.

Darcy jumped into the session when Lexi scampered away and updated Claire on things. At least with Darcy she could tell the truth—truth she didn't know she was going to say before she blurted it out, like how beat she felt—but not why. She was determined to finish her reports for Nick tonight and slog through more of this diary before she took her meds and went to bed.

"Lexi's doing okay," Darcy said, "but she misses you. And Jace."

"I know she does," Claire admitted. "He's very good to her and I—I admire him for that, at least."

"That's what I thought," Darcy said, with a head bob. "Of course, you'll have to get along with him for Lexi's sake. Meanwhile, any doubts about taking this assignment with Mr. Charisma?"

"He's been very supportive, thank heavens, because I'm not sure which way to turn on this. Listen, Darce, gotta go. I'm kind of burning the midnight oil tonight to get through this. I hope to finish up tomorrow and head home the next day. I'm not sure if Nick or Heck will bring me, or they'll put me on a plane from Jacksonville or Daytona, but I know better than to drive that distance alone."

They said their goodbyes. Still drinking coffee, when she'd ordinarily lay off it this late Claire sat stubbornly at the desk, huddled over the diary under the best light in the room. The latter part of this handwritten document had taken the most water and was the hardest to read. But as soon as she finished this earlier section, she was going to try that part again. There was something intriguing here about Civil War–era Rosalynn's story, and she'd seen Bronco's ancestor William Richards's name in this entry. Bronco had always seemed so desperate for information about the poor man, that if she could just decipher something here, it might get her some leverage with him. Lately, she'd had the feeling he knew more than he was telling.

Her cell phone rang, and she knew it must be Nick. Or what if it was Jace?

She reached for it and stared at the number calling. Cecilia Moran. She took the call.

"Cecilia, this is Claire Britten. How may I help you?"

"By coming over here now. I think I might have said the wrong person hurt Lola."

"I'm glad I gave you my private number. Tell me. I'll be glad to help."

"I have to show you something, so you'll see what I mean. Oh, I can't believe Lola would do this, but— Can you come now?"

Claire glanced out the window. It was dark but for lights by the shops behind the hotel.

"Can you just tell me over the phone, and I'll see you tomorrow?"

"This is too important. I have to show you the proof."

"I'll have to see if I can have someone bring me. But I can come into your house alone if you want."

Adrenaline poured through Claire. She'd been almost weaving on her feet with exhaustion, wanted to go on with Francine's diary, but this could be huge.

"Yes, please. I can't sleep a wink 'til I tell someone and I trust you. I have to ask what you think before I tell the detective on Lola's case."

"I'll call a friend and be there as soon as I can."

Claire ended the call and punched in Nick's cell number. Heck was transcribing her scribbled notes tonight to give to Nick tomorrow. Besides, she'd feel better if Nick was with her. She only hoped they wouldn't be driving by any water, but now that they knew someone could follow them, they were careful—almost paranoid.

Cecilia had said "the wrong person hurt Lola." That could really help Jasmine.

"Look, Claire, I still say this woman sounds shaky to put it nicely." Nick was still arguing in the car as they pulled into Cecilia's driveway and he turned off the headlights. They both craned to look up and down the street to see if another vehicle had turned in, too, but saw nothing. It was still sprinkling, and they'd driven through patchy fog.

He put a strong hand on her wrist, so she wouldn't hop right out. "You need me in there with you. This may seem to be a blessing out of the blue. But the sisters could have had a fight over Bronco's attention to Lola, and Cecilia could be dangerous, maybe regrets what she told you before. Or the sisters disagreed how attached Lola was to Francine and vice versa, so Cecilia struck out at her. You really don't know this woman."

"I think I do. It's what you hired me for, Nick, psych people out, remember?"

"Then who maybe killed Francine with an overdose? Who knew Lola would be in the puppet shop, knocked her out with an overdose of something first, then killed her? Lola sounded like a skittish person, right? Don't you think it had to be someone she knew and trusted who was with her right before she died?"

"Like Bronco?"

"Damn it, are you listening to me? Like her oddball sister for all we know, the one who stages a funeral with a bunch of puppets, the one who, you said, hates Jasmine!"

"All right, I hear you. How about I call you on my phone, then leave the line open when I go in to talk to her? You kidded me about woman's intuition earlier today, and I took offense, but that's partly what's telling me this woman can be trusted, however eccentric she is. I think she's going to give us Bronco on a silver platter and save Jasmine in the process before Sheriff Goodrich arrives at Shadowlawn with bells on—and big media coverage—to arrest her. Is that what you want?"

"You know I want Jasmine exonerated. But I want you safe, too!"

"I'll be all right. I refuse to be a liability to you. Here, I'm calling your number, so pick up. I just hope what she tells me in private she'll repeat to the authorities to get at least Sheriff Parsons here in St. Augustine off Jasmine's back. Nothing ventured, nothing gained, remember? I'll be careful."

Nick muttered something she didn't care to hear as he answered his phone and she got out of the dark car.

When she approached the porch, a single light over-head popped on, so again, Cecilia had been watch-ing. There she stood, no heavy eye-and-lip makeup this time, so the Barbie-doll look had muted, but her wild hair still swirled around her shoulders.

Cecilia gestured for Claire to step inside. She nod-ded but her stomach flip-flopped. So their voices would pick up, she slid her phone into the outer, short pocket of her purse. She'd keep it over her shoulder this time, chest high. She had to admit Nick's argu-ment had gotten to her.

The interior of the living room was dimly lit. A few of the marionettes had migrated out of the back room and sat here. The one that looked like Lola sat on the end of the sofa where they had talked before. For once, without Win's prodding, this reminded Claire of a horror movie: as old as it was, she'd seen *Psycho* on TV last year. That crazy Norman Bates kept a sort of mummy of his long-dead mother around.

Claire tried to get hold of her fears. "That pup-pet looks a lot like the one of Lola that Bronco has," she observed, trying to paint a picture with words for Nick.

"Identical. I'd like to take his back. He said he keeps it on his bed."

"You've spoken to Bronco?"

"He called. Said he was sorry for my loss—and his. But come into the back room, and I'll show you what I learned. I was so hurt—angry, too."

Claire scuttled close behind her, hoping her words were loud enough for Nick. "Okay, let's go out to the Florida room. Do you mean you're angry at Bronco?"

Cecilia didn't answer but pointed to a marionette

hanging from the ceiling in the Florida room. The crowd of other puppets was gone now but the Lola puppet head identical to the one in the living room still sat on a small table, the head with her ashes in it.

"Look," Cecilia cried. "Look at this!" She thrust a photo at Claire. Claire stared at it. Taken at night of the same view she'd seen before in Win's studio, it was the shot of the so-called hanging tree, the one which looked as if a man's body was dangling there.

"Oh," Claire said, turning toward the phone in her purse, "a picture of the tree at Shadowlawn where Bronco believes his ancestor was lynched."

"But look at this puppet!" Cecilia insisted, giving the bare-bodied puppet overhead a shove, so it rattled and swung. "Then look at this. Come closer!"

Claire hesitated as Cecilia yanked open a drawer and dug down into it. For one panicked moment, Claire feared Nick might be right. She almost screamed, *Gun!* but only managed to jump behind the woman to see what she was digging for as she pulled out a—what looked to be a man's historic suit of clothes, Civil War era, though it was in such good shape it could not be authentic.

"Oh, a man's historic outfit, maybe from around the Civil War," Claire said, still speaking toward her phone. "But why—"

"I can't believe she did it, but she loved that man. I told her not to trust anyone, and you shouldn't either, especially Bronco Gates! Lola must have made this puppet for him, then sewed this outfit for it. Look at this picture she had hidden in another place in her bedroom! Bronco—or someone—hung this puppet from the tree to try to prove there was a ghost there.

I'll bet he thought people didn't believe him about that. Lola said that Neil made fun of him, too. Maybe Bronco just wanted a reason to hang around if Shadowlawn was sold, and that ghost would get him attention and give him ties to the land and a reason to stay."

"These photos—did you get them from Win Jackson?" Claire asked, though she saw they weren't the quality of his work.

"Who's he?" Cecilia demanded, her voice rising. "Lola said she had a big argument with Bronco about sex. She must have also argued with him over this, since she couldn't have known he was going to pull a trick with it."

"Go on. I'm listening."

"She must have brought it back here, but I only figured all that out going through her things after she died. Now, I'm thinking Bronco went to our shop when she was there. She wouldn't sleep with him or marry him. Why, he could have lifted poor Lola up to hang her with one hand. If he hurt Lola, maybe he hurt Miss Francine, too! Maybe Miss Francine knew he was putting pressure on Lola and that Lola helped him fake that ghost."

That was a jumble of ideas—all speculation—but Claire hoped Nick heard it. "So who took this photo then?" she asked.

"Why Lola, with her cell phone. Printed it out, too. Makes me wonder what else is on her phone."

"Haven't you looked? Do you still have it?"

"The police took it from our shop. You'll have to ask them."

So much for that, Claire thought. If only Nick could get his hands on it. Who knew what the quiet but spunky Lola could have photographed around Shadowlawn, inside and out? Right now, she'd rather have Lola's amateur photos than Win's artistic ones.

"Have you told Sheriff Parsons this new theory that maybe Bronco staged the ghost picture? And that he might have hurt Lola?"

"I'm going to tell him tomorrow. I—somehow I trusted you. I wanted to run it by you first."

"Why don't you call him right now while I'm here with you? If he's not there, just leave a message on his phone or tell whoever is on the night desk what you told me about Bronco? Won't you sleep better then?"

Claire felt increasingly desperate. How she wished she could ask Nick on the phone if she was doing the right thing. Of course, it was possible Bronco had killed Lola. He was strong and could be volatile. Had Lola suspected him of more than trying to stage a ghost scene—maybe harming Francine—and accused him of that? Or did they just have a lover's quarrel? She still thought Neil—or even Lola—was more likely to have tampered with Francine's medicine than Bronco. But if Bronco was taken in and formally questioned, it could help Jasmine.

"Sleep?" Cecilia challenged. "I can't sleep. And you—you look like you can't, either. But yes, all right, I'll call the sheriff."

"I'll talk to him or his lieutenant when you're done, so he realizes I know what you said," Claire added.

When Cecilia went to pick up the wall phone in their kitchen, Claire turned away and said to Nick, "Did you hear all that?"

"She's definitely distraught and maybe delusional. But let her call in. I'll make the same call just after to

give our background for being here, but not mention
I heard it all over the phone. Their looking closer at
Bronco will at least muddy the water, so Jasmine's
not the only A1 suspect. Sit tight with Cecilia, try to
calm her."

Great, Claire thought. Finally, Nick was on her
side about this. But Claire was starting to shake, and
her stomach kept cramping from nerves. She should
have taken her meds and been in bed an hour ago. So
who was going to calm *her*?

She paced a bit, keeping the line open to Nick but
eavesdropping on what Cecilia was saying on the
phone. Standing there, her gaze skimmed a series of
framed documents on the wall. She'd been so busy
concentrating on the puppets that she hadn't noticed
these before. Leaning closer to read the print, she
saw Cecilia had won statewide four-hundred-meter
dashes in high school. The others were certificates for
her participation and placements in the St. Augustine
sprint competitions the last three years. She'd placed
quite high, and there was one picture of her dashing
across the finish line.

Claire's head jerked, and she clutched the phone.
When Nick had chased the person who was spying on them at Shadowlawn, he'd said it couldn't
be a woman, that Jasmine could never have run fast
enough to elude him when he'd chased her.

So besides the people they suspected, could they
be chasing a killer who was an outsider to Shadowlawn?

23

After the night she'd had so far, Claire couldn't sleep, which was weird. Usually, by now, she'd have measured out and taken her first dose of nighttime liquid medicine and be dead to the world. But her mind was racing. She was sitting up reading Francine's diary long after she should have gone to bed, but she couldn't even keep her mind on that as thoughts and doubts pounded her.

Bronco was not all on the surface, as Win had claimed. As a matter of fact, "dumb" Bronco Gates might have pulled one over on Neil, who seemed to look down on him or even on the "brilliant" Dr. Win Jackson. Had Bronco planned to manipulate both men into thinking a puppet was a ghost, so they'd agree he had ties to the land and secure him a place at Shadowlawn if it was sold? That, at least, Claire could believe, but she had real trouble thinking Bronco could have hurt Francine, even if he had struck out in anger at Lola.

And Lola had evidently had more backbone than anyone knew. Her sister Cecilia did, too. Claire had told Nick about her skills as a runner, but he still thought the person spying on and knocking their car in the water had been sent by Clayton Ames. As for Neil, he was obsessed with his freaky museum, so what did that say about his state of mind?

And Jasmine...?

The notes Claire had given to Heck to type up tonight now might be way off base. But still, who killed Francine? Her meds, herself or someone else? Nick seemed so grateful for what Claire had done here, but right now it looked like a screwed-up mess to her. She was starting to feel she was the master of disaster. If only something in this diary would help!

She kept coming back to a part Francine had starred for some reason, but it wasn't about her own life. It evidently concerned Rosalynn Montgomery, and it was on the pages where Claire had also seen mentioned the name of Bronco's Civil War–era relative, William Richards, the indigo expert the family had brought in to oversee their cash crop.

Claire ran her index finger along the tight rows of Francine's writing and whispered aloud the words she could read, *Maybe no ghost, but surely W. Richards was hanged from that tree. It was passed down that he ran the entire plantation when R's husband was away serving the Confederate cause. Rumors she was...*

Here Claire was stumped again at a blurred word. Rumors she was *pretty*? Of course she was. Stunning in that portrait. Rumors she was *precious*? But neither of those things would be spread by rumors and *precious* didn't make sense.

Then, when Claire glanced up at the small, framed

photo of Lexi she'd placed on the nightstand, she knew. *Rumors she was pregnant.* She'd read earlier something about *with child.* That had sounded so old-fashioned. But now Claire knew: during the war when Rosalynn's husband was away, fighting for the cause, Rosalynn had become pregnant. And from what Claire had read on the previous page—she flipped back to it—the rumor must have been that the father of her child was William Richards!

The rest fell into place. The husband came home after the war. Rather than face him and admit betrayal, Rosalynn threw herself off the second floor gallery to her and her unborn baby's deaths on the flagstones below. Either before that or after, Rosalynn's husband and lover fought each other. In a duel? With fists? Her husband died in that confrontation, and William Richards was either lynched or legally hanged.

"Shadowlawn reeks of tragedy," Claire whispered. "It has to end."

It made her very angry that the historic deaths of Rosalynn and William were solved but not the ones she and Nick were obsessed with now. Claire had only one more day at Shadowlawn, then Nick was driving her home with Heck following, though the men were coming almost right back.

She couldn't wait to get home, yet her work here seemed unfinished. Praying she wouldn't be haunted by dreams of death, past or current, that maybe she could decipher more of what she really needed from this diary, she slipped it under the other pillow of her bed.

Her hands trembled when she measured out and

drank the liquid that led to oblivion and renewal. She turned off the light and curled up on her side. Should she tell Bronco what she'd learned? She could try to use that to make him admit he'd argued with, had maybe hurt—or killed—Lola. But it still felt like a stretch that he'd hurt Francine, too…

A PWN always went to sleep fast, especially with that powerful stuff. Thank heavens she had it, could block out her own ghosts. But her mind kept going, thinking about Nick… Jace…

Until she suddenly stepped off the shore into the deep waters of sleep.

"You're not running the Spanish Inquisition, Claire," Nick told her the next morning as they drove toward Shadowlawn. "You do not turn the screws on someone until they scream that they're guilty. It was bad enough to be alone with Cecilia, but you're not confronting Bronco with all that. It's looking like he's guilty of something at least, and, therefore, danger-ous. I hired you for information, not to pull a citizen's arrest on someone."

"If he isn't confronted, he'll clam up and go back to his hillbilly Florida cracker routine—assuming it's fake—if you or, worse, Sheriff Goodrich start to interrogate him. I can be nonthreatening."

"It's amazing we got away with that open-line trick with Cecilia, but it won't work with him."

"How about this? I'll get him to sit with me on that bench and you can watch him as he may have done us when we sat there. There's thick foliage all around there. If things get out of hand, you'll know it or see it and step in. Nick, I don't want to overrule you, but I'm our best chance. I want to get this over and get home."

"I know, I know. Me, too. But I just don't want anything to happen to you."

"Then we're agreed."

"I'm agreed you're a velvet steamroller and I hardly knew what hit me from the first time I saw you in court. It's only gotten worse—and better."

"And we don't want to go to court, defending Jasmine."

"Right. You know, all we've done lately is argue, almost like we're married."

"Very funny. What do you know about being married?"

"True. I made myself a promise I wouldn't consider it until I got Clayton Ames off my back and where he belongs—either in prison or off the face of the earth."

"So you can understand wanting to erase an enemy? Losing control enough to strike out?"

"Yeah, I can understand a murderer, a crime of passion, at least. Which Francine's death could have been. But whose passion? And it's so tragic what you said about her ancestor—and Bronco's."

"I plan to use that on him, too, probably start with that. Nick, this can all be wrapped up today, if you let me talk to him alone—no Heck, no you."

"But I'll be close," he muttered. "Real close."

Jace hated to admit it, but he was really missing Naples. Actually, he was probably missing Lexi. But it was Claire he could still not get out of his mind.

He'd come alone to Sentosa Island near Singapore's

main island. It was one huge amusement park here, but he wasn't amused. He'd bought Lexi a bunch of things, sat on the white sand beach, walked through the oceanarium and watched the musical fountains with their laser light show. The cable car ride over here he'd enjoyed before, but this time it had just bored him. It made him feel lonely since families and couples seemed to be having so much fun. The water between Singapore's version of a theme park and the main island as well as the beach only made him recall happy times with Claire. He had the weirdest feeling, especially after getting those three bizarre photos in the mail, that he had to get home to protect her.

Okay, okay, he told himself. *You still care for her. Want her. Need her.*

But would she ever trust him to let him try with her again? Maybe not so fast this time, not sweeping her off her feet but steady on their feet. He would prove to her that he wouldn't just fly off the handle. He'd try not to be so self-centered and expect her to bend to his crazy schedule. He'd help her through her narcolepsy, encourage her with her desire to go with more natural cures, and if that didn't work, support her when she took those strong medications. All that not just because Lexi needed them both. Because he'd learned the hard way he needed Claire, faults and all. God knows, he had them, too.

He headed back toward the cable car area through the crowd of happy, noisy people. The mix of nationalities and races here made Singapore seem like a great melting pot, the same claim America had made for years. But he could see why Claire didn't want Lexi raised here or in LA. Singapore touted its values of harmony and the family as the basic unit of society, but that would never salvage his broken marriage. He had to get back to Florida, to Claire and Lexi, even if it meant taking unpaid leave for a while.

He ducked into a jewelry store, one that had great-looking bracelets in the windows. He'd bought enough stuff for Lexi. He wanted a peace offering for Claire, a love gift.

"You like bangle bracelets?" the attractive Asian saleswoman asked with a smile and a clatter of metal as she raised her slender arm to show him her shop's wares.

"No, something more…well, conservative. Something very nice. Something gold."

Claire was amazed the setup with Bronco was so easy. That must be a good sign, she thought. When he took a break from helping Win arrange his equipment in Francine's bedroom—Rosalynn's room—the next morning, Claire told him she'd learned something from Francine's writings that might throw light on his ancestor. He'd readily walked out to the river with her.

But Bronco didn't sit on the bench. Instead, he started fussing with his airboat. He'd obviously been out in it or was going soon since it was headed upriver and not pulled up on the bank. She wondered if he'd thought to make a quick escape if she said something he didn't like. He kept coiling the mooring line in the square prow of the boat and wasn't looking her in the eye.

"I recall," Claire said, "you tried to learn why William Richards was hanged."

"'Specially since he was important 'round here."

He stepped out of the boat and put one foot up on the edge of the bench. "You found somethin' on that?"

"Yes. And it ties to Rosalynn Montgomery's suicide."

Jaw clenched, hands fisted, Bronco looked as if he'd go ballistic. She was glad they were not in a closed interview room and that Nick was nearby.

"He didn't kill her, no more'n I hurt Lola!" Bronco insisted. "He didn't get hanged for that. No way!"

"I didn't say that," she said in a steady, quiet voice, hoping that would calm him. His voice level would sure help Nick, hiding not far down the way, to hear him. She realized she should keep her voice louder, too, but keeping Bronco under control was more important right now. She hoped she hadn't made a mistake to try this.

"As a matter of fact this story is about love, not hate," she tried to assure him.

That seemed to settle him some. "Like Lola and me. Why can't people get that's how it was for us? Sheriff Goodrich sent a detective out to talk to me early this morning, crack a dawn. Lola's sister been accusin' me of fightin' with Lola, maybe hurtin' her."

"But you didn't. You wouldn't, right?"

"'Course not! Why won't folks believe me—'bout William's ghost, 'bout Lola and me gettin' on, not fightin'?"

She actually thought the big bear of a man was going to cry.

"Tell me, then, 'bout Willliam," he said.

"So Sheriff Goodrich's man told you that Lola's sister is saying Lola made you a marionette and an old-fashioned outfit to hang in the tree to take pictures of, posed as William's ghost? Can you tell me why? Was it so others would believe that your ancestor was important here, so you could stay?"

Bronco just stared at her—past her—glassy-eyed. She felt she'd been so close to his admitting something. She had to refocus him, get some answers for Nick.

"Bronco, he was important but in a tragic way. Francine's diary says that William and Rosalynn Montgomery were lovers and she was pregnant with his child when her husband came back from the war. She evidently killed herself rather than face him, then William killed him in some sort of duel, so—"

She didn't see it coming. Was he even listening? He muttered, "I din't kill Lola, don't say I did," and lunged at her.

It all happened so fast. He picked her up, wedged her facedown into the airboat under his elevated seat there. The motor behind them roared to life. She tried to right herself, she screamed, but the sound drowned her out. Bronco put a foot on her back so she couldn't get up. She thought she heard Nick's voice, a distant shout.

She yelled, "Bronco, stop! Don't do this!"

The boat lurched, the propellers roared, and they were off on the river.

24

Nick shouted, but the airboat noise drowned him out. It also disturbed a pair of gators who scuttled into the river. He ran along the bank but the boat with Bronco riding high and Claire unseen, flitted behind tree limbs heavy with Spanish moss, then disappeared. The roar of the boat echoed in his ears and head, then muted to a distant hum.

"Damn it! Damn!"

His heart pounding, he saw she'd dropped her purse. He scooped it up and ran for the house, pulling out his cell, dialing 911. It must have been Bronco all along, at least who killed Lola. And now Claire had stepped over the edge, but Nick had let her.

"Heck!" he shouted inside the house. "Bronco's got Claire!"

"What?" Neil cried as he appeared from his small apartment at the back. Heck ran out of the library.

Nick shouted, "He's got her prisoner in his airboat, heading south."

"Dear God, he must have broken," Neil said. "He's

been so obsessed with the ghost and losing Shadow-lawn, and then with Lola's death—"

Nick held up a hand for silence when an opera-tor answered. "If this is not an emergency, hang up and…"

"It's an emergency! At Shadowlawn Estate, south-east of Palatka, just beyond Devil's Elbow, a woman's been kidnapped and is in an airboat, heading south on the St. Johns River. Can you scramble a chopper? I'll pay for it or air patrol, though it's thick along the river there where cars can't get in. We don't have a boat here to give chase, so can they bring an airboat?"

"Please keep calm and talk slower, sir. Your name is?"

He gave all the pertinent information, then handed his phone to Heck to fill in other details. He turned away and checked in Claire's purse. The diary was there, her cell phone—and her medicine, some liquid in a bottle, a vial of pills.

Jasmine came downstairs wearing a robe, looking like she just got out of the shower with her hair wet and no makeup on.

"Bronco's snapped," he told her, closing the purse but keeping a hold on it. "He took Claire in his air-boat when she told him about William Richards fa-thering Rosalynn's child and that being the reason she killed herself."

Jasmine gasped, pressing both hands over her mouth. "But that's—that's horrible."

"It was in your mother's diary with who knows what else."

Neil had come close and was hovering, but Nick ignored him. "I was nearby," he plunged on, "but couldn't get to them in time. I'm not even sure if he knew I was there."

Neil put in, "Outside, he has eyes in the back of his head."

"She thought he might confess to harming Lola at least," Nick said. "There's more to tell but not now. I've called for a search party, but is there a place to access the river, if I drive that way down the road?"

Neil said, "If Bronco hurt Lola, maybe he hurt Francine…"

Jasmine grabbed Nick's arm. "I can't believe it. But he's got a lot of spots out there where he gigs frogs or gators. Best let the authorities search and—"

"I can't just sit here. It's my fault!"

Win appeared from upstairs. "What's all the ruckus?"

Heck interrupted everything by shouting, "They're sending the only chopper they have, and officers will be here soon. Cops in patrol cars are coming, the sheriff, too."

"Sorry, Jasmine," Nick said, pulling away from her grip. "The last thing I wanted was the cops—maybe the sheriff—out here, but if Bronco… Hell, we've got to find Claire fast."

Win spoke up. "I know some spots along the river where you can walk down. What say I drive you and Neil can take Heck, so that will give us two pursuits, plus the authorities whom Jasmine can fill in from here. If they make this a staging point, don't let them near my equipment. But Bronco?" he said, shaking his head. He stared at Neil. "I would not have suspected *him*."

"All right, let's go," Nick ordered, stepping between Win and Neil before the personality politics took over again. "It's been barely ten minutes, and he can't get far."

"Sorry," Win said, fishing his car keys out of his pants pocket, "but the St. Johns is the longest river in the state."

Nick felt coiled tight inside, like his head would explode. He wanted to break things. He should have sent or taken her home after that plunge in the water-filled ditch. And now she was out there without him. She was maddening when she got the better of him, but she mattered, suddenly, so much.

Claire wasn't sure how far they'd gone or for how long. Everything blurred. The roar of the motor. The bouncing, turning. The rush of air, even here in the bottom of the boat. Sometimes she felt and heard scraping sounds as they went over vegetation and sped on. She was shocked she had misjudged Bronco and he had either set this up or just panicked. Stupid, stupid, stupid. Had she ruined things for Nick? Would he ever forgive her, hire her again—if she got out of this? But she had to, for him, for herself—for Lexi. And then she had to go home and be safe forevermore.

Safe on the South Shores forevermore. Wasn't that what Nick said his father had written just before he died?

She tried to wriggle free to get to her purse with her cell in it, but she realized she must have left it—dropped it—on the bench or the ground. Her phone. The diary. Her meds!

So it was just her and Bronco, and she was going to have to use all her skills to talk him down and make him let her go, whether or not he was the one who hanged Lola just the way his ancestor had ended up hanging from a tree. He obviously felt trapped, panicked, but so did she.

Worse, if he decided to get rid of her out here, there must be a hundred walls of tall grass, of gators to clean up a body, of places to wedge someone under a cypress knee.

Oh, Lexi, sweetheart, sorry. Darcy, Jace, Nick, too, so sorry.

As they raced along, her brain threw at her the image in Neil's museum of the *Creature from the Black Lagoon*, taking the frightened woman down into his dark, underwater lair.

As Nick and Win raced for Win's SUV, Jasmine got a call that Sheriff Goodrich himself would be here soon to set up a command post. What a disaster, Nick thought. One of his goals had been to keep Goodrich away from Jasmine and Shadowlawn—and another had been to keep Claire safe.

He wasn't sure why, but he kept Claire's purse with him. When he found her, she might need her meds. He wanted to keep an eye on the diary. Her phone was here, though what good would that do? Truth was, he just wanted to have something of hers with him.

Win Jackson drove fast, but not fast enough for Nick. He was glad to get out on the paved road, heading the way Bronco had taken her. Heck and Neil were somewhere behind them. They were going to hit the places closest to the house, the ones Neil knew.

"In places the river twists away from the highway," Win told him, "but I've set up shots in a couple of spots I know."

"Speaking of shots, wish I had a gun," Nick admitted.

"She's more to you than an employee," Win stated. It wasn't a question. "You rely on her to help find who killed Francine. I can tell she's running herself ragged over this. She's on edge, and you two are getting so desperate that you misjudged."

"I ought to hire you as a psychologist."

"Hold tight on these next curves. At least this road has little traffic out this far. We'll probably have the cops on our tail here, but—all right, I see the first turnoff I was thinking of. It's a good lookout for a distance up and down the river."

He drove into a bumpy turnoff spot on the west side of the river. The track was muddy, and Nick heard thunder rumble in the distance. That was all they needed, a downpour. And a strange mist—almost a low-lying fog—hovered over the river here.

"We'll have to watch for gators," Win warned, pointing. "They're fairly thick along here as I recall."

Nick almost dry-heaved. He'd never forgive himself if Claire was harmed. Though she'd been adamant about setting up the interview with Bronco, he'd agreed. But, from the first, she'd insisted on doing things her way, and he didn't want to come on like the boss from hell with her. Now he wished he had and that he hadn't compromised things by falling for her. But too late for that. Hopefully, not too late for Claire.

Watching where they walked—the only gators they saw were on the opposite bank—they leaned out and looked up and down the river. Nothing. No sounds of an airboat. Nick would never forget the roar as Bronco took off with Claire. Now, just bird calls and more thunder. Nick could have cried.

But then they heard a sound. "An airboat?" Nick choked out.

"Helicopter," Win said, pointing up.

Thank God, Nick thought, at least help was here.

Claire knew she was going to have to get herself out of this mess she'd made. She lay still until Bronco stopped the motor, and they coasted under a screen of trees into a small cove along the west side of the river. He gave her a hand up. She fought to keep calm when he touched her, even to steady her.

She glanced around in the river mist. An anhinga speared a fish, then tossed it up so it went down his open bill. A gator lazed a few feet away, eying them. Birds screeched in the trees. Cypress knees and drapes of Spanish moss made a curtain hiding them here. So isolated. Lonely. Scary.

Bronco spoke first. "I din't mean to hurt you, but you can't be sayin' I hurt Lola or thinkin' I killed Miss Francine. I can't let you tell the lawyer or the police that."

Didn't he realize that by running, he looked guilty, of something, at least?

She moved as far away from him in the boat as she could, sitting on the blunt prow. Despite that gator, she'd leap into the water if he produced a knife or made a move toward her. She felt so utterly alone and vulnerable out here. She tried to stop shaking and to steady her thoughts and voice.

"I was only asking if you knew what her sister was

claiming. I wanted to hear your side of it. I'm sorry if I surprised you with that information about William Richards's death, but I knew you would want to know what Francine had written in her diary."

"'Cause he was hanged—and Lola, too—you think I did it?" he repeated. "And maybe hurt Miss Francine, too? Now why would I do anything to either of them? 'Cause they was good to me."

"That's what I was thinking. My point exactly. Since Miss Francine was good to Lola, I think you must have been good to both of them."

"Well, I wasn't. And I'm sorry."

Claire's heart pounded. Dear God, was he going to confess and then kill her? Drown her? Hang her from this big cypress tree limb overhead with that rope he'd so carefully coiled in the bottom of the boat? He'd have to go on the run then, but he knew this river and land and he had a damn good start.

She waited for him to say more, fighting to keep control of her own body language when she wanted to jump for the bank and flee. But this was his territory. He'd chase her, get her.

"See, I had a big fight with Lola, no matter how much I—I loved her. Miss Francine scolded me bad for that. Then the night Lola died, I went to see her again—"

A *whack, whack* sound echoed overhead. Ibis in the tree flew out. They both looked up. A helicopter was low, following the river. Bronco frowned and started the motor to push them back farther under the tree cover.

Was this her chance? Despite the gators, jump into

the river to wave to the chopper? Was it here looking for her, for them?

"Stay put," Bronco shouted, "'cause I'm not done yet."

To Claire's dismay, the chopper pivoted almost overhead, then kept going, low, dipping now and then. Yes, Nick must have sent for help. But what did Bronco mean he wasn't done yet?

Once the chopper noise became a mere buzz, she said, "Bronco, I don't think you killed Lola or Miss Francine. But if you don't take me back or at least let me go, people might think that. Tell me what happened so I can help you, support you. My job is to learn what people really think and explain that to others."

"To your lawyer and the cops?"

"To anyone I have to."

"Really, Miss Jasmine's the one in big trouble, isn't she?"

"Yes, but we hope to help her, too."

"Help her by accusin' me?"

"Absolutely not. You know you are important to Shadowlawn, and she knows that. You, in your own way, are just as important as your ancestor William was. He helped build the plantation through overseeing the indigo, then fell in love with someone he should not have. But Miss Rosalynn obviously loved him, too."

"Like Lola did me. But Miss Rosalynn let him have her, if she carried his child."

"So that's what you argued about with Lola?"

"She said, let me make you a puppet so you can take a photo of your relative that got hanged. But when Miss Jasmine told her he got hanged for murdering someone, she got real upset."

"I'm sure she didn't blame you for something that happened to other people long ago. I don't blame you now—for anything. But since you understand the power of love, I hope you will understand that I have a little girl who needs me. Her father lives away and she's missing me, so I hope you'll let me go. If you say you didn't harm Lola or Miss Francine, that's what will be in my report."

"I can't go back. They'll say I kidnapped you, that I hurt Lola no matter what you tell them. I can't go back to Shadowlawn."

"Just put me out where I can walk back on the road and be on your way then. Or, if you want to come back with me and state your case, part of my job is testifying in court and—"

"No court! Oh, hell, I got to get rid of you one way or the other now!"

Nick was so distraught he had trouble focusing. He was grateful to Win for driving him from place to place. Twice police cars had passed them on the road, lights flashing but no sirens. A storm was closing in. This was a nightmare. Claire had suffered from them for years, but this one was real and it was his.

He would have picked Neil over Bronco, if someone at Shadowlawn was guilty. But Bronco had the connection to Lola. How easy it must have been for the big man to lift her into that noose. Claire was slender, too. Damn, he was tormenting himself, when he had to hold it together. Where was she in this labyrinth of dangerous river?

"One more place to look I can think of." Win's voice cut through his agonizing. "We'll have to hike back in a ways. I've got two more light poles in back. We'd better carry them because I spotted copperheads around there when I was working."

"Thanks, Win, for sticking with me through this. Gators, snakes—and Bronco. Anything to find her."

"I understand your fear," he said. "Bronco must have killed two women already. I understand."

25

"Look," Bronco said, suddenly distracted. He pointed at the river. "A snake in the water."

Better than a snake in the grass, Claire's frenzied mind chattered at her as she glanced at the sinuous swim of a long snake. She was feeling dizzy and sick to her stomach, close to losing control. But she had to hang on, keep him talking, stall for time. With gators and snakes swimming past, what were her options about diving in and making it to the other bank?

"You know, I do good things," Bronco told her. He leaned back against his elevated seat instead of standing, but he still seemed to tower over her.

"I know you do. You have meant a lot to Shadowlawn and Miss Jasmine, just as you did to Miss Francine."

"She was kinda a loner like me, Miss Francine. Was on a lot of committees, had friends, even men friends from time to time, but I think she really felt alone. Tell you the truth, she didn't get along with Miss Jasmine that great."

Thank God, Claire thought, he'd calmed down

some. If she only had Heck here to jot all this down for her interview logs. She needed to keep Bronco on things that didn't set him off. As badly as she wanted information from him, she had to let the police interview him now, because, surely, he must have hurt at least Lola.

"So what kind of snake is that?" she asked, trying to sound interested.

"Not the kind I been huntin' in the Glades down by where you live, that's sure."

"Were you part of that python hunt? I can't believe someone let their pets loose, and they're breeding like—"

"Like pythons. Yeah, I been volunteerin' with the so-called Swamp Apes patrol that's tryin' to keep Burmese Pythons from takin' over. Now you're thinkin' Swamp Ape's a good name for me."

"I'm not. I'm thinking that's a helpful and brave thing to do."

He nodded as if they were having a chat on Everglades conservation. "Those snakes are a-killin' native birds and mammals, gonna be movin' into people's backyards, changin' the balance of nature, like they say. You just keep a close eye on your daughter if she's out playing."

A ray of hope! "Oh, yes, I will," she said. "I'd like to head home tomorrow to do just that."

Claire's heartbeat kicked up again as he leaned closer. "That's what scares me 'bout Shadowlawn, see?" he went on as if he hadn't heard what she'd just said. "If Miss Francine woulda sold it, that upsets the balance of everything, the way it's been for years. But some snake should not have killed her—if she didn't mess up her own medicine. I wish't I'd been there to call for help, rush her to the doctor, something."

For one moment, Claire almost forgot her own predicament. This man was not all on the surface, as Win had said. Bronco had used the word *snake* as a symbol. He saw a connection between upheaval in nature and at Shadowlawn. One moment she was certain he had killed Lola and Francine; the next, she was sure he would never have done that, however much he'd argued with Lola and been upset with Francine. He simply loved Shadowlawn and had a strong emotional tie to his ancestor who had died there so tragically.

Just when it started to rain, she heard the helicopter coming back. It would never spot them under these trees, and its *thwack-thwack* was a dead giveaway that might set Bronco off again. She had to risk all. Now or never, but her strength was not in running fast like Cecilia. She had to use words, meager, feeble words.

"Bronco, if you take me back, I'll say we had an argument and you just thought it would be better if we talked away from the plantation."

"Nick Markwood was spyin' on us, wasn't he, so he'll know better."

Claire's stomach knotted even tighter, but she had to keep going with this.

"You need to let Nick help you. A good lawyer like Nick knows that just because someone argues with a person like you did with Lola or scolds a person, like Miss Francine scolded you, that hardly leads to murder. Of all the people I've talked to who would have access to Miss Francine's medicine to make her overdose, your duties outside of the mansion make you last on the list."

"You don't think Lola did it!"

"No, I don't. They were close, and Francine had helped her and Cecilia buy the Party Puppets Shop."

"If you're tryin' to clear Jasmine, who's left? Monster-lover Neil?"

"I'm not sure yet, but you can help us, if you'll just take me back."

Huge raindrops bounced off the leaves over them, then started to get them wet. But Bronco nodded, ignoring both the chopper noise and the rain. He said, "Not counting Lola, Neil, even Dr. Jackson were closer to Miss Francine and her medicine than me."

"Win Jackson? Because she let him take pictures at Shadowlawn?"

"No, it was more than business. Told you she had men friends. He was one until she ended it, I think, kinda like me and Lola. It made her sad."

"So sad she might have killed herself?"

"I thought of that. Plus her and Miss Jasmine havin' problems, so could be. But don't think she would have done that 'til she saw to Shadowlawn's future."

Claire's brain went into overdrive again. Win and Francine in an aborted romance? He was younger than her, but so what? They had interests in common, had served on committees and charities together. It didn't mean anything, except that Win had never mentioned that, nor had Jasmine. Why had that not come up? Had Jasmine even known? If she had, would that have worried or upset her?

Claire blinked rain from her eyelashes and slowly, carefully swiped water from her face, so she wasn't making any sudden movements. But she felt she was crying, even that the sky was crying.

"Bronco, you are a good man. I'll tell them what you've told me, but you need to tell them, too."

"Don't trust cops, not lawyers neither, but Markwood gave me some good advice."

"He did, and he can help now when we explain things to him. He advised you not to go along with Neil and play the monster—and you don't want to play the monster today. Take me back, and that mere fact you've returned me will show them your good heart. Shadowlawn needs your help, and I do, too. Let's do everything we can to find who hurt Lola and Miss Francine, and we can't do that if I'm dead and you're on the run."

"Dead?" he said, looking shocked. "I was just goin' to leave you somewheres here and keep goin', hide out in the Glades down south. I didn't and I won't kill no one!"

Despite it all, in that moment, she believed him.

"So let's head back and convince everyone of that," she told him as the skies absolutely opened up to pour rain.

The sound of the helicopter faded as it headed back toward Shadowlawn. Rain came straight down, thudding into the river while thunder rumbled. Why, when she had thought he might take her back, did this have to happen? And what would he do when he had a few moments more to think?

As the bottom of the boat filled with rain, she sat down in it and feebly bailed water with her cupped hands. At least the deluge disguised her tears. Bronco began to bail with a tin coffee can. She prayed the lightning wouldn't hit the tree over them, that their sitting in the water wouldn't fry them. She pictured

Lexi and sent her love silently to her. She hoped that Nick wasn't losing his temper. And she prayed most fervently that she wouldn't lose her life out here one way or the other.

Nick and Win sat in Win's SUV while the rain pummeled it. They were at their third stop, but the downpour had kept them from getting out. Except when he'd found his father shot in the head with a gun in his hand, Nick had never been more distraught, and he was trying desperately to hold himself together. He was usually good under pressure, but not now. He was so scared he couldn't think straight.

"Deluges like this don't last long," Win said. "Can't see a damned thing. I hope we don't get mired in this turnoff."

"I still can't believe this is happening. Claire convinced me to let her talk to Bronco about what happened to his ancestor, why he was hanged, that's all."

"I hope she was going to work up to how Lola Moran was hanged. How did she find out about that tragic history? That old diary of Francine's?" He turned toward Nick with one hand still at the top of the steering wheel.

"Yeah. It's in bad shape, but yeah. I've got it here in her purse, but the trouble is, her meds are here, too."

"Jasmine mentioned that Claire has narcolepsy. I know that needs heavy medication. Will she be all right without her drugs?"

"She'll be okay for a while," Nick tried to assure himself as well as Win. He'd left her purse on the floor of the seat behind him. He ran his hands up over his face and through his hair. "Until tonight, when she needs the heavy hitter liquid one, I think."

Slowly, as they sat there in silence, the rain let up.

Nick said, "Maybe you should back out onto the pavement so you don't get stuck here. I've got to go check this last spot, hope to see something. They may have stopped in the rain." He got out. Win had gone with him at the other stops, but he just nodded.

"Take that pole in case of snakes again," he called so Nick opened the back door and took one from the seat.

As Win backed out and waited along the road with his emergency lights blinking, Nick slogged through muck and water over his ankles. Saw grass snagged at his pants and cut his ankles. Stabbing their long beaks in the ground, a group of ibis already poked around for food. Warily watching for snakes, Nick held the pole in front of him like a weapon. Where was that river?

He saw it through the trees and then the miracle of his life. A gift from God! He glimpsed Claire sitting in the airboat and Bronco, both bailing water on this side of the river. Was he hallucinating? Dreaming? Should he call out to them, sneak up on them—no, they'd see him first.

Suddenly Bronco turned and spotted him. "Well, look who's here," he said, as if this were some sort of *Survivor* TV show and Nick had just won.

"Oh, Nick, thank heavens you're here," she called to him. She didn't sound like herself; her voice was shrill. "Bronco's going to need a lawyer, so we hope you're willing to help out. He argued with Lola and Miss Francine scolded him but he didn't hurt either of them, and I believe him."

Nick was still stunned. Wasn't sure he could even speak.

Claire went on, "There's room for you in the airboat, and we can plan our strategy on the way back. All right, Bronco?"

To Nick's utter amazement, the big man nodded. "You drive out here on the road?" he asked Nick.

Hell, he must be dreaming, Nick thought. Had Beauty tamed the Beast?

"Ah—Win brought me, let me off, thought you two might have had engine trouble or a problem in the rain." Well, sometimes lawyers lied, but he felt he was really over the edge now.

"You send up that chopper?" Bronco asked.

"I was hoping they could spot you and that you hadn't had an accident. Gators and all—I know it can be dangerous out here," he stumbled on, sounding like an idiot, but this was so unreal.

"Dr. Jackson doesn't like to wait for anything," Bronco said with a shake of his head. "But just walk out on the tree roots there and get in. You can send someone for him when we get back. We'd better go 'fore it rains again or that chopper wastes more gas."

And more of his money, Nick thought. But he didn't care. Claire was all right. Bronco was calm, and Win had helped out. He'd just step away a second and motion to him to head home. All was well unless Bronco planned something dire on their way back. But then, wouldn't Claire sense that, manage to make everything all right? As awful, dangerous and insane as all this was, he realized he needed her in more ways than one.

* * *

Jace phoned Claire's cell from Singapore. Three times and it still wasn't a charm. Each time, he got only her voice mail. The second time, he'd thought she picked up and heard breathing, but he must have been wrong. Finally, he decided to leave a message. She'd see who had called anyway.

He cleared his throat and said, "Sorry for some of the things I said recently. I'm really missing you and Lexi. If you think it might be a good idea, I'll inquire about openings or postings for Canadian or Caribbean routes—not be gone so much for so long. I hope your work there is going okay, that you've figured out for Nick who the murderer is by now. You won your last court case, and I know you'll win this one."

On a roll, he didn't want the connection to die and plunged on, "I'd like us to consider that family trip to Disney. If Darcy, Steve and their two want to go, that's fine, but I hope you'll spare me some private time. I'm flying back in about eighteen hours and can't wait to see you—both of you. Call me back if you can, but otherwise, see you soon. And speaking of seeing things, I'm taking a good look at myself because I know I'm to blame for a lot of what went wrong with us. Okay—soon. Hope everything's okay."

He talked so long that her phone beeped to tell him message time was over. Again, he thought she might be listening and then ended the call, which worried him. He'd fought telling her he realized he still loved her, wanted her back. Better to say that in person—work up to it with good behavior, so to speak. Besides, she was the one who was good with words, with talking, psyching people out, so his actions would have to speak louder than that.

26

Nick had never seen a more chaotic scene than when Bronco took him and Claire back to the Shadowlawn river landing. Emerging through the gloom of mist and rain dripping off the trees, a small crowd of people surged forward.

Police patrolled. Nick saw several guns drawn and pointed at them before he held up his hands and shouted, "It's all right! I found them but they came back on their own."

He'd had to put off comforting Claire for her ordeal. With this audience, he couldn't scold or hold her, either. She'd screwed things up big-time, but he was so thankful she was unharmed. It had upset him even more to see a big, blurred footprint on the back of the shirt she wore over a sleeveless tee. Although they were all soaked and cold from a breeze that had sprung up, he'd told her to take off the shirt so the police wouldn't see the footprint.

The two of them had managed to put on a calm and steady show for Bronco, as if all this was no big deal. Now Nick almost panicked that the nervous man would just speed away, but he nosed the airboat into the muddy bank.

Flashlight beams stabbed through the graying gloom. A guy who must be a police cameraman snapped pictures, blasting his flash at them. Thank God nearby Palatka wasn't a big city or they'd have a media mess here, too.

Afraid Bronco would bolt, Nick kept hold of his arm and put his other around Claire, who was shaking, however calm she appeared. He was impressed with her again. The girl had guts.

Two officers stepped forward, one with handcuffs, obviously waiting to apprehend Bronco. Worse, Sheriff Goodrich stood there, legs spread, with his Glock drawn.

"You can put the guns away," Nick called out to him. "There's been a misunderstanding. It was an argument, not a kidnapping. I jumped the gun and hope you won't."

"Is this your idea of one big damn joke, Markwood?" the sheriff demanded as everyone pressed forward. "This whole thing reeks to high heaven! This man's under arrest, and you're lucky you're not, too."

"I'm Bronco Gates's *pro tem* lawyer. He'll be glad to answer questions, but you need to ask Claire Britten here if she wants to press charges."

"No. No, I don't," she said. "Bronco and I had an argument, then a talk. Everything's settled."

"Like hell it is," Goodrich insisted, but he gestured for his men to holster their pistols, then put his away, too.

Nick could tell Claire almost wavered on her feet. He couldn't let her be taken away for questioning, even if they did take Bronco. Nick noticed Jasmine was here. She came up and stood on Nick's other side as the three of them climbed out of the airboat onto the riverbank, slippery from the rain. He steadied Claire again. Suddenly Win Jackson appeared from the back of the small crowd.

"I can tell you it looked bad but it wasn't," Win told the sheriff. "I'm the one drove Nick upstream so he could check on them, but everything turned out calm and quiet."

Silently, Nick blessed Win. He surely hadn't seen that, but he was trying to back them up. "Let's hear more from the so-called victim," Win said with a nod at Claire.

"I know you, don't I?" the sheriff interrupted, swinging around to face Win.

"Dr. Winston Jackson, photographer from St. Augustine. I'm working here to memorialize Shadowlawn as a historic site in your area. There will be a book, articles, photos. You know, this would be a great site for you to kick off your campaign if you run for office, and I could photograph it, beginning to end. Jasmine Montgomery Stanton and I could set that up for you."

Despite his frustration, Nick almost burst out laughing. That ploy was so blatant, so ludicrous— and so damned welcome. Goodrich didn't reply but he nodded as if all that was his due. Again Nick was grateful to Win for stepping in to help. He'd made it back fast through the rain and growing fog. Better yet, he had a camera trained on the sheriff as if to counteract the police department cameraman.

"This isn't going to be washed away by the rain

and this swollen river," Goodrich muttered. "Everybody inside. I need statements."

As they trailed toward the mansion, Nick wished he hadn't claimed to represent Bronco, but he'd get him another lawyer fast. No way he could defend Jasmine and Bronco, too. The sheriff's questioning would have to eventually get to Francine's death. Could what had set Bronco off today be related to that? God forgive him, at first he'd hoped Bronco *was* guilty of harming Francine but now he had to see this through, get him some pro bono help.

But he was really worried about Claire. She'd have to hold herself together at least long enough to give her statement. He wasn't worried she'd say something wrong, but that she'd collapse.

"Jasmine, can you get Claire some dry clothes and help her out?" he asked. "Something to eat—a hair dryer. You know what I mean."

"Yes, of course. Can I take her upstairs for a few minutes, sheriff?"

"Come right back down. This isn't over yet, not by a long shot on my watch."

As Jasmine led Claire away, wishing he was going with her, Nick realized he was shaking, too.

Jasmine's long skirt and peasant-type top were too big on her—even the slippers—but Claire didn't care. She was safe. Nick seemed not to be mad, but then *seemed* was a big word for a Certified Fraud Examiner.

When she saw the back of her wet shirt still had the faint outline of a muddy shoe on it, she washed it out with some liquid soap next to the basin in the upstairs bathroom. So she'd stooped to this, she told herself with a sniff, trying not to cry: destroying evidence, slanting the truth. As much as she wanted to help Nick, to be with Nick, she just wanted to go home.

Ignoring the hair blower, she toweled her hair partly dry, though she looked like a specter of herself in the mirror. This bathroom was near Jasmine's bedroom. It must have been shared with Rosalynn's bedroom, so it was probably the one where Francine had kept and taken her fatal dose of Propranolol.

Then a thought hit her hard. Her own meds! Had someone found her purse she'd dropped outside or had it washed into the river in the rain? She needed her day pill and, soon, in her exhaustion, her double night dose—and sleep. She shouldn't carry all those meds with her, but she was afraid to leave the pills and bottle in her hotel room. Who knew if the maid would think it was drugs, which actually it was— drugs she couldn't stay sane without.

She hung her wet blouse over a towel rack and braced herself with both hands on the basin, staring at herself in the mirror. She was getting goofy, crazy. She wanted to hide, hide in Nick's arms like she did after they escaped from his car in the water. She washed her face again, blew her nose and went out into the hall where Jasmine was waiting.

When they were downstairs, before they could join everyone in the parlor—an officer stood guard at the entry—Neil appeared. "I've made a cup of tomato soup and a grilled cheese sandwich for you," he told her. With a nod, Jasmine went on into the parlor, but Claire saw he'd put a tray on the dining room table. "Let them wait," he told her. "Jasmine asked me to feed you, and Nick Markwood's handling things right now. He's telling Bronco which questions he can answer."

"Oh, Neil, thank you. Can you sit here a minute, too?" she asked, almost collapsing into the chair he scooted closer to the table for her. "You haven't heard anyone say they found my purse, have you? My phone and meds are in it," she told him, intentionally omitting mention of the diary.

"Sorry. Maybe the police have it. If it has any interview notes in it, they probably think all that's their property now and could try to use it against Jasmine in court."

She didn't think she could have ruined things much more for Nick, but what if Neil was right about that? Even though Heck had the final write-ups, she did have notes in the purse that could compromise everything. And, without her meds, she could have one of those waking, horrid nightmares which would make this real-life one pale by comparison.

But she could not pass up the chance to interview Neil now, again. His museum, his masks—had he been the one who tried to scare them en route from Naples? Did he wear his helpful concern like a mask to disguise the face of a killer, one who'd harmed Francine and maybe even Lola?

Neil sat—almost perched as if he would flee— across from her. "Thank God you're all right, and Bronco, too," he said, gripping his fingers tightly together but twiddling his thumbs as if he were bored, without a care in the world. "But she can't keep him on here. He's a loose cannon to say the least. And who knows if he isn't really guilty? You've seen him up close and personal, as they say, how he can snap. Go ahead," he urged. "Eat something."

The hot soup helped some, but she still felt light-headed. Cold, too, but she was warmed by the thought Nick had done everything to look for her. Yet *strike while the iron is hot,* one of her favorite professors had always said when he taught interview techniques at the university.

"So you do think Bronco could have harmed Lola?" she asked.

"Can't put it past him. Can you, after all this?"

He looked smug. She didn't want to have to answer that. "Not to change the subject," she went on, "but do you believe in the ghost here, the one that's so important to Bronco?"

"Not really, but I get why he did—or wanted to. It gave him ties to the place, made him feel important."

How astute that comment was impressed her. Neil was clever. He'd matched her assessment of Bronco exactly. "We're all like that a bit, aren't we?" she asked as she took a big bite of the grilled cheese. It had some kind of sharp mustard in it.

"I suppose so. In my case, my museum, you mean?"

She nodded and took a drink of the glass of milk on the tray. "I hear you have some theatrical masks, too. You should put those on display."

"I intend to. Did Bronco tell you that?"

"Win mentioned it. Look, Neil, tomorrow's probably my last day here before going home. Could you show the masks to Nick and me before I leave?"

"I don't really have them on display. I just showed

Win so that he'd help me promote my museum." His voice rose. His posture stiffened.

She'd obviously found his sore point. So did that mean he had been the one in the scream mask the day they left Naples to come here and was afraid to show it to her? She would be wary of him right now, except for the open door and that officer nearby.

Claire ate more soup, while, despite her exhaustion, her mind raced. Jasmine could have told Neil that Nick and she were coming from Naples. If he was guilty of Francine's murder, maybe he would have looked up Nick's or her address and stalked them. Had he tried to stop Francine from selling or donating this place? It might have ruined his hope for some fame with that museum as well as his longtime employment here. However, since Jasmine wanted to keep Shadowlawn, Neil wanted things in her control. Maybe he hadn't realized what was supposed to look like Francine's accidental drug overdose would turn into a murder investigation with Jasmine in the crosshairs.

"Neil, I can't thank you enough for this food," she said again.

He stood, nervously wiping his hands on his shirt as if they were dirty. "Don't thank me. Jasmine agreed when Markwood requested it. The power always comes back to Jasmine, so don't forget that in your reports," he added and went out.

Now what was that supposed to imply? Suddenly the soup and sandwich tasted strange to Claire. How a mood change could affect her. And, whatever else anyone did here tonight, whatever the demands on her, she had to find who had her purse and get her long-past-due pill.

* * *

Despite her Gypsy look and wild hair, Nick thought Claire looked a lot better when she joined them in the parlor. He'd staked out a corner with Bronco sitting beside him, both facing the sheriff. He'd advised Bronco to answer only the questions he'd cleared, and the guy was doing amazingly well. More than once, Claire had warned him not to think Bronco was as backwoods and dense as he managed to sound.

Nick was surprised the sheriff had let Win stay in the back of the room, but maybe he'd gone for his blatant bribe about publicity and a media-friendly place to announce his candidacy. Nick trusted the sheriff about as far as he could throw him.

"Nick, could I talk to you for a minute?" Claire asked. She remained standing next to the officer in the entry. "Or Sheriff Goodrich, too, has anyone found my purse? I have my cell phone there and some other important things. I'd like to call home."

"I found it where you left it on the river bench," Nick told her. "With all that's going on, I forgot it. I think it's still in Win's car."

"I didn't notice," Win said, "but I'll go check. I'll be right back."

"May I go with him, sheriff?" Claire asked. "It won't take long."

"Officer Armstrong, you go along with them," Goodrich ordered. "Then I'll meet you in a front room, Ms. Britten, and we'll talk there. And not with Attorney Markwood, who suddenly seems to be everybody's lawyer. You need protection and counsel, Ms. Britten?"

"Of course not, though I must tell you, as a Certified Forensic Fraud Examiner, I'm used to asking the questions."

Nick sat back down as she followed Win from the room. As scared as he'd been that she'd be hurt or even killed today, her independent streak that drove him nuts was back in force. Damn, but she was going to mess up this case and she'd already played havoc with his life.

27

Claire had been surprised to find Win in the interview room, sitting quietly at the back. He had a small camera in his hand, not his large one. She felt so grateful to him, like he was on Bronco's side and helping Nick.

But, besides being desperate to find her purse, she wanted to find out if he'd admit to an affair with Francine that Bronco had mentioned, so that was why she'd asked to go with him. But would he turn against Bronco? Maybe she could imply she'd guessed it from the diary he already knew about.

The officer following them opened the front door and stood there watching. The rain was starting again, so she waited on the covered front veranda as Win went out to his SUV, popped on the lights, opened the doors and searched.

Oh, no, she thought. *It must not be there.*

She gripped her hands together. She'd missed a Provigil, and was exhausted from last night, not to mention the terror of today. Worse, she really needed her nighttime double dosage soon. She'd have to take it in Nick's car on the way back if they had to stay here late—if Win could find her purse. And then, four hours later, she'd need that second dose.

"Got it!" he called to her. He slammed the back door and jogged toward the house.

She could have hugged him! Thank heavens, Nick had found it and kept it safe. The moment they stepped back into the house, she opened the purse and looked inside. Yes! Her meds safe, her notes, the diary here! She'd made such a mess of things today that Nick might never trust her or want to work with her again, but this helped.

"I've got to take a pill, Win."

"Settle your nerves?"

"For my narcolepsy."

"No kidding? That's tough. I never knew anyone with that. Do you need some water?"

"I've got a glass of milk in the dining room. You know that diary of Francine's I mentioned?"

"Yeah, saw you reading it. I'd love to include it in the photos—maybe a close-up, inside and out."

"I've been reading it, as I said. Forgive me for asking this, but I get the idea that you and Francine were, maybe briefly, more than friends."

He glanced back at the police officer still following them, though the man went back to his position at the entry to the parlor. Win followed her into the dining room, leaning against the wall, arms crossed as she gulped down her pill. She wondered if he was going to answer. He looked sad, but not really upset or angry she'd asked.

"*Briefly* is probably the operative word," he told

her. "It was a weak moment for each of us. Needy. Mutual. Intense. Over."

"Just a parting of the ways, but not over anything?"

He shrugged. "I thought she should not lose control of this place, but it was her place."

"But how could she have afforded to keep it—to keep control?"

"She was a fine fund-raiser for other causes and charities. I ran the idea of the book I'm doing now past her and would have split the profits with her, though, I admit, that would have been a drop in the proverbial bucket to restore and keep Shadowlawn."

"I suppose," she said, avoiding mentioning her and Nick's interview with the Montgomery family's old lawyer, "you could have helped Francine or Jasmine try to oversee the funds and the running of this place even if she sold it or it went to the state."

He pushed away from the wall and propped his hands on the edge of the wide table across from her. "You know, Claire, the real ghost at Shadowlawn is the burden of Shadowlawn, hanging on, peering out of every dark corner. I think that just weighed Francine down so much she couldn't share it with an outsider like me or, worse, the mass market public, the gawkers, those who love ghost stories and tabloid type scandals. Although she may have just been careless with her medicine—and you understand that, since you lost yours today—I think she just decided it was all too much, including her arguments with Jasmine, and she deliberately took too much of her medicine. You know, like that big line in the 1976 movie *Network,* 'I'm mad as hell and I'm not going to take it anymore.' Only, she was not mad, but burdened. Sad but—"

The police officer appeared in the door, and Win stopped talking.

"Ms. Britten, the sheriff wants a statement from you before he leaves. Mr. Markwood is going to be there, too."

That surprised Claire as the sheriff had told Nick he couldn't sit in. Would he attend as her employer, friend or her lawyer? But she could do this, she told herself. She'd been through worse, the terrible scenes with Jace, losing him, being shot in Naples. At least Neil's food had helped her, and this stimulant pill would, too. Win's calm admission and astute explanation of things had boosted her. Jasmine could be innocent, Francine's staff, too. Win had just provided the best proof she'd heard yet that Francine could have killed herself, and that would solve and save so much here at sad Shadowlawn.

"I realize you've had a tough day of it, Ms. Britten," Sheriff Goodrich began.

He, Nick and Claire were sitting at the dining room table. Neil had cleared her tray away. She felt exhausted, almost dizzy, but she had to stay alert, then get some sleep. Evidently, the lengthy interview with Bronco had gone all right, though an officer was still keeping an eye on him in the parlor.

"Frankly," Goodrich said, "I and my resources have had it tough, too. Markwood, you owe the citizens of Putnam County a pretty penny for that chopper."

"I can write you a check before you leave."

"Is that Hector Munez who searched for the airboat with Neil Costa another lawyer?"

"A tech assistant."

"Running a pretty fancy, expensive operation here—your personal Certified Fraud Examiner, too, in Ms. Britten. Talk about a pretty penny. From what I hear, Jasmine Stanton and Shadowlawn don't have the means to pay you."

Nick looked all business. "Did you have questions for Claire before we head back to St. Augustine this evening?"

"I have to run Bronco Gates into Palatka for the night, and you said you'd go with him," the sheriff said. Then he turned toward Claire. "I still think Bronco Gates took you under duress today, didn't he, Ms. Britten—by force?"

"Please call me Claire." She sat up straighter and steadied herself, not looking at Nick but directly at the sheriff. She tried to buck herself up for this ordeal. She was on the other side of what she usually did, but this was just like facing a prosecutor or defense attorney in court.

She said, "Bronco and I were both under duress. I assume he told you I'd just explained what had happened to his ancestor here. That was a tragic story in itself and not what he wanted to hear. In a way, he identified with the man."

"The guy he thinks is a ghost come back to haunt the place? Yeah, he told me. I'm just hoping Bronco didn't think he had to avenge that loss by getting back at anyone here."

Nick cleared his throat but didn't speak. Strange, but Claire could sense what he was thinking. The

sheriff now had two suspects for Francine's murder—
if it was murder.

Looking the sheriff dead in the eye, even leaning
forward a bit to show she didn't fear him, she said,
"So the case you've been putting together against
Jasmine Montgomery Stanton for allegedly harming her mother could have holes in it? Frankly, after
hours of interviews here, I'm coming to the conclu-
sion that Francine had enough problems—and the
means—to commit suicide without any interference
from either Jasmine or Bronco. Do you really think
Bronco would hurt Francine?"

"Damn it," he exploded, slapping his hand on the
table so hard the nearby candlestick shuddered, "I'm
asking the questions here! The man was upset by
what you told him, why this, ah—" he glanced down
at the notes in his lap—"William Richards was hung.
For hanky-panky with the lady of the manor, when
it should have been strictly a business relationship."

He glared at Nick, then looked back to her with
a pointed glare. She steeled herself not to sit back,
waver or so much as blink at that barrage. Just as
she'd done with Bronco, she'd underestimated this
man. He knew that Nick would happily pay for the
helicopter to search for her. Maybe he sensed how
attracted they were to each other. All they needed
was to have that come out in court to detract from
the real issues.

Claire said, "To answer your question about Bronco,
you are absolutely correct. Hearing about his ancestor
is what upset him."

"Hell," he said, jumping to his feet, "I know you're

going to toe the party line here and say he didn't harm you."

"You can see he didn't."

"He some kind of charity case for both of you? Counselor, you ought to be doing everything you can to nail him to get the heat off Jasmine. Imagine that, a lawyer with a heart. Well, if you're still defending her, you better get Bronco another lawyer because I'm not charging him for harming Francine, but— with the sheriff of St. Johns County—for the murder of Lola Moran. The sheriff there has two witnesses spotted them arguing in Heritage Walk in Old St. Augustine shortly before she was drugged and murdered. Sheriff Parsons there interviewed Lola's sister earlier today, and she blames him for an argument he had with Lola."

Nick sat forward in his chair. "You're arresting Bronco for Lola Moran's murder?"

"You heard it here. Be grateful. Maybe, once I get him away from you two, I can pry a second woman's murder out of him."

Nick said, "I'm going with him, calling someone in the area I know for his counsel. Are you finished with Claire then?"

"For now. She looks like she can use a good night's sleep."

Now Claire felt really shaken. Nick was going into Palatka while they booked Bronco? She hoped he didn't think she'd accused him of killing Lola, because she didn't believe that. She mustn't panic. But she needed to take her night meds, to be in Nick's car back to St. A, then go home, back to Lexi. Oh, well, Heck would have to take her back to the hotel now.

Night had fallen, and the weather made it seem even darker outside. Rain streaked the windows as if the entire house were crying.

"Claire," Nick said, reaching down to help her up when the sheriff walked out on them, "I swear he just wanted to shake us both, throw his weight around. He hoped you'd turn on Bronco to help him solve the Lola murder."

"I still don't think he killed her."

"Motive, opportunity, proximity."

"I know. I know! But this is what I do, Nick—though sometimes not very well. Despite Bronco's temper tantrum, I still don't think he killed Lola or Francine. I'd just as soon blame the hanging tree ghost."

"Step outside with me a minute before I drive to Palatka behind the squad car taking Bronco. I'd better be there while he's booked. I'll make a few calls, get him representation and come back here as soon as I can. I detest authorities who jump to conclusions about murders when nothing's proven," he gritted out.

She knew he was thinking about his father's death again. She wanted to comfort him. He led her outside, moved away from the door and window light and pulled her into his strong embrace at the far corner of the veranda. She clamped him to her, arms around his waist. He leaned his shoulder against a pillar. Her head fit perfectly under his chin.

They stayed that way a moment as the rain rattled down. "I was so worried," he whispered. "I was going nuts to get you back, to find you."

However light-headed she still felt—it wasn't just the Nick-effect this time—she leaned back slightly and looked up into his face. Her hips tilted into his. His eyes seemed silver in the reflected window light.

She told him, "I managed to mess up today, but you did find me—and I've found you. I'm so sorry I misjudged Bronco. But then, in the end, I don't think I did. He is not Francine's killer, probably not Lola's, either."

"I'll work on that. But onward and upward for us, no matter what we have to face?"

She nodded. They bumped chins as he tilted his head and took her mouth in a crushing kiss. For one moment, nothing else mattered. All their troubles seemed so distant, out there in the river or the rain. He lowered his hand to grip her bottom, to almost lift her to him. Her breasts crushed against his chest. She felt dizzy, even faint, so sleepy and exhausted, but her body responded and her spirits soared.

Voices nearby. They stepped apart, though Nick still held her arm. The sheriff's stern tones, Jasmine's voice, pleading.

"They must be bringing Bronco out," Nick said. "I don't want Heck driving you back in all this. Jasmine said you can stay the night in a room down the hall from hers, and Heck will sleep on the sofa downstairs. She knows you need your sleep. You and Heck shouldn't be out in this rain, especially after what happened to us in the dark the other night. In the midst of all this, Clayton Ames and his lackeys are still out there somewhere."

"Yes. All right. I need to sleep fast. I'll take my night med and be out."

"I'll be back as soon as I can, and we'll head to St. A in the morning. Then I'll take you home tomorrow, though I'll have to come back and forth for a while. I hate that I have to run off, but I'll be back as soon as I can," he repeated as he dug his car keys out of his jeans pocket.

She followed him back down the veranda toward the cluster of four officers who surrounded Bronco at the open front door. He looked solemn and resigned. She still didn't think that was guilt on his face as he stared out toward the hanging tree. He frowned, then squinted at it, so she turned to look, too.

Was she seeing things in her exhaustion, or was that old ghost figure hanging there in the tree in the dark and rain? And—and a woman's form, a woman with long loose hair—just beyond the tree, half hiding behind it! No way, not Rosalynn's ghost!

She heard a huge clap of thunder, then a second.

Nick pushed her down behind the pillar nearest to the front door and shouted, "Gun! Gun!"

28

Jace arrived early at the Changi Airport, eager to be off on the flight. This might even be goodbye to Singapore, if he could get a change of assignments. He'd emailed that request to the airline office onsite at LAX.

He ducked into the news store, bought an international paper and scanned the books, almost as if he were going to be a passenger and needed something to read on the flight home. A display rack of books caught his eye: *The Simple Guide to Customs and Etiquette in Singapore*; *Singapore: Enchantment of the World*; and one touting Singapore as *The Garden City*.

When he noted that the enchantment book was for juveniles, he bought it for Lexi. Despite Claire's problem with her mother reading to her and Darcy all the time, she did read to Lexi. But he'd read this to their daughter, because he'd never really taken time for that. Someday he'd bring her here for a visit—Claire, too, God willing.

He sat in a restaurant, ordered sweet-and-sour pork

with lemon rice while he flipped through the newspaper. That Malaysia Airlines plane that had been missing for over six months had not been found, though Australia was heading up the search now. It must be somewhere at the bottom of the ocean, but where? Worse, it was suspected the pilot might have diverted it and brought it down.

A chill raced up his spine, and he shuddered. That airliner had been flying to and from exotic places, too—Kuala Lumpur heading for Beijing. He hated to admit it, but pilots obsessed about airline accidents. Not being ghoulish, but reading about others dying because they were doing what they loved—the same thing all pilots loved—was a horrible but effective way to learn what *not* to do in the air.

Private pilots sometimes committed suicide or mass murder by deliberate crashes, too. He recalled a suicide flight in Indiana about four years ago where some guy flew a Piper Cherokee into an Internal Revenue Service office building, killing someone on the ground, too. Man, no one liked paying taxes, but that was really over the edge. And yet, lately—and with the way his father had treated him and his mother— he could almost grasp desperate despair.

But this crash detailed in the newspaper was a Boeing 777 with only two-hundred-twenty-seven passengers compared to his large Airbus which carried over five hundred. One loss was too many, though. And all those people, never to see their loved ones again…

Man, he couldn't wait to get home. He could honestly say that for the first time in a couple of years. He pictured Lexi bouncing off the walls and screaming,

"Daddy's home! Daddy's home!" Then Claire would come to the door, on edge at first until she heard him out, that he wanted a second chance and was willing to change his life to earn that.

He was pretty sure Claire would be done with her assignment for that slick lawyer Markwood by now. He pictured her back in Naples, safe, catching up on cleaning the house, laundry, yakking on the phone to Darcy, checking out her anti-fraud website for her new business Clear Path that meant a lot to her, so it would to him, too, now.

Clear Path. Yeah, he could see his way home now, home to Naples and back to her.

Nick sprawled half beside, half on top of Claire when the gunfire started. Adrenaline poured through her. Her pulse pounded, jolting her alert for the first time in hours. Her brain flashed back to the shooting at the courthouse when all this started. It was so clear, like a moving picture: heat, bright sun. Fred Myron sprawled in grass and blood, another shot, her arm hit, people shouting, then Nick there...

Nick's shout was echoed by the sheriff's to his officers. "Gun! Gun! Shooter at ten degrees north. Behind the tree. Running now! Pursue!"

Claire lifted her head. The officers drew their guns and almost vaulted off the veranda. Keeping low, running, they scattered into the darkness. Only one of them seemed to have a light. She saw one officer pick Bronco up off the ground where he'd shoved him and push him inside their vehicle. Another officer fired back in the dark and rain.

A shot shattered the police car window in the vehicle where they'd put Bronco.

"I saw a woman," Claire whispered to Nick. "And that puppet back in the tree, see? Forget Clayton Ames this time, unless he's hired Cecilia."

"Put nothing past him but—you saw her?"

"Her silhouette—her hair."

They watched as Jasmine and Neil crawled on their hands and knees into the house and began to turn off the lights that made them easy targets. Nick didn't let Claire budge. Was Win still here? Yes, she saw him hunkered down behind a pillar on the other side of the door. Evidently, everyone had been out here to see Bronco taken away.

The wait—silence now—seemed endless. The rain still thudded down; the wind picked up. From time to time, they heard men's shouts, calling out positions. The voices became more distant, then came closer. "Got her!" someone yelled.

Yes, Claire could see in the bouncing light of an officer's big flashlight that she had been right. There was a form—a puppet, no doubt in a familiar outfit she'd seen at Cecilia's house—hanging in the tree.

"It's Cecilia for sure," she said. "The puppet she made for Bronco is back in that tree. Maybe she decided to avenge her sister's death by shooting him, or by mocking him with that puppet. Or, if she's this reckless—and she does seem unbalanced—could she have been so angry with Lola since she spent so much time with Bronco that she killed her? Maybe she saw her own close relationship with Lola threatened. But I'm not sure she could have boosted Lola up high to hang her. Nick, I'm so out of it and rattled I can't think straight."

"Yes, I see the puppet. If she came out here to kill Bronco, she was crazy and desperate to try it with all these cop cars here. And if she's nuts enough to try this, who knows what else she'd do."

From the misty dark came two officers, their guns still drawn, half dragging, half carrying a slight form between them. It was Cecilia, limp, sobbing but evidently not hurt.

"Sheriff, she had the gun," an officer shouted.

Jasmine's voice rang out as people rose to their feet. "That's Cecilia Moran, my mother's maid's sister," she told them.

"Ah," Sheriff Goodrich said. "I recognize her, too. The plot thickens."

Nick whispered to Claire, "If I hear one more cliché out of him, I'm going to have to push it back down his throat."

"Counselor Markwood," the sheriff's voice boomed out, "I don't think you need another client, but now I'll have two very interesting suspects to take in."

Cecilia shouted, "Bronco killed my sister. I know he did. And he'll get away with it—murder, just like Jasmine did for killing her mother!"

"Damn!" Nick muttered.

"That's a lie!" Jasmine cried. "Sheriff, I admit I fired her sister, but this woman's demented!"

"You know, Mr. Gates," the sheriff called to Bronco as the officers pulled him from the car with the shattered window and walked him to another of their vehicles, "this just isn't your day. And," he told his officers, "we'll book Ms. Moran for assault with a deadly weapon with intent to kill for starters. I swear, there's just something about this place that doesn't make it sound real sweet for a gubernatorial announcement, Dr. Jackson, but I thank you for the earlier offer."

"Bastard, and I don't mean Bronco," Nick told Claire, still talking under his breath.

Despite her defiance, Cecilia looked like one of her own limp marionettes as she was handcuffed and put in another of the police vehicles. In spite of what Cecilia had done tonight, Claire's heart went out to her. She completely grasped being so close to a sister that her cruel loss tilted the world.

Bronco was put into another car. Nick hugged Claire, walked her to the door as if they'd been on a date and told her, "Take your meds and get some sleep. I'll get you to St. A, then home to Lexi tomorrow, whatever else comes up—promise."

Pressing her lips tight together, with a sniff, she nodded. Tears she could not control started, and she tried to blink them back. With his thumb, Nick captured one and put it to his lips. He went over to say something to Jasmine, then Heck, and headed for his car.

Though Jasmine was tugging at her arm, Claire stood watching the parade of cars, including the one with the shot-out window, as they made their way down the long drive toward the road. In their passing headlights, she saw the marionette was gone from the tree, so they must have taken it. When Neil turned the porch lights back on, the shattered glass under the hanging tree glittered in the rain.

* * *

Claire thought the walking dead must feel this way. She hated those zombie books and movies, but she felt she was the main character in one now. She was glad to see the small but pretty bedroom Jasmine had given her near the back of the hall.

"It was once a housemaid's room," she'd told Claire, "but Mother fixed it up for a guest room, then had Lola stay there sometimes. So—servants' quarters, but I'll never think of you that way. You've been a big help to Nick and to me. If—if it turns out that Mother killed herself, so be it."

After Jasmine had gone to her own room, Claire plodded to the small bathroom near the back servants' steps—ones that also went up to the attic—used the toilet, washed her face again and took a glass of water with her to mix with her dosage of Xyrem. Every PWN hated that prescription if they had any form of cataplexy. It was horribly expensive and ridiculous that the user had to take one dose of it at bedtime and one four hours later. Nothing like waking a narcoleptic up in the middle of the night to take more meds. More than once, like others with the disease, she'd slept through her second dose and suffered for it the next day.

Trying to steady her hands, she used the syringe to draw the 2.25 gram dosage out of the orange bottle, then mixed it with the correct one-fourth cup of water. She could almost do it in her sleep—ha, that was funny, she told herself. She was losing control, all right, had to get in bed, fall asleep fast. She set her cell phone alarm app to wake her up for the second dose, then started laughing again when she remembered the long list of possible side effects with this. One of them was suicidal thoughts, so was that insane?

For once, the dose didn't taste as bitter as usual. Years ago, she used to feel she'd throw up from taking it, but she soon learned to gulp it down fast. Mind over matter, mind over matter. Talk about Sheriff Goodrich using clichés… She was going to use her mind to tell Nick that she was opting for Francine taking an overdose—possibly by mistake, but more likely intentionally. And it sounded like Jasmine would accept that. The thing was, then Nick still might have to prove it in court.

She jumped when a knock sounded on her door.

She stumbled across the hooked rug to the door but didn't open it. There was a keyhole under the knob but no key.

"Jasmine?"

"It's Heck, Claire. Just want you to know I got a sleeping bag and I'm bedding down out here in the hall to keep an eye on things. Too far away downstairs."

"Oh, thanks. That makes me feel better. Don't worry if you hear an alarm in about four hours when I take my second meds."

"Sure. Okay. I'm expecting Nick back by daylight. He said he'd call me if he needs me, so I got a phone out here, too, in case you hear it go off."

She padded back to the bed and fell into it. Those meds always hit her fast but gave her a great night's sleep. Tomorrow she'd see Lexi. Tomorrow Nick was taking her home.

She comforted herself with her favorite saying from years past: *surely, nothing else could go wrong now.*

29

Claire swam upward through thick, foggy water. Where was she? In the river? Trapped in a car that crashed?

At first she couldn't move. She kept her eyes tight shut. Had someone tied her up, that man who was a ghost? She tried to roll over to see if it was time for her second dose of medicine. But she couldn't move.

Oh, dear Lord in heaven, had her paralyzing cataplexy come back? Maybe she had spilled her medicine in the river. Her bedside clock wasn't where it was supposed to be. Where was she?

She fought to move her feet, a hand. Slowly, slowly. *Don't panic.* She was sure she took her medicine. Yes, her first night dose. She'd take her second one now. She might have slept through her alarm.

She felt so stiff but she finally moved her muscles. When she was first diagnosed, she was so young and so scared. Horrible nightmares.

But where was she? Oh, yes, she knew now. At Shadowlawn where darkness was as thick as black water.

Keep calm. Keep calm. Get that second dose of medicine down. Stop shaking. Steady hands.

She clicked on the bedside light and saw the bottle and mixing cups. And a flashlight. She still heard the rain, scratching on the window like a creature wanting to get in. Despite the lamplight, the fog from the river was swirling around in this room and in her head.

She measured out the dose and mixed it with water. See, she knew what she was doing. *Claire,* she told herself, *don't be afraid.* But it was midnight, and she'd been asleep for three hours. That was good, wasn't it? This second dose was early, but she had to go back to sleep. So exhausted. She downed the liquid in one gulp the way she'd learned to do because it tasted terrible.

But like the earlier dose tonight, it wasn't as sharp as usual. At least she was finally getting used to the stuff after all these years. Just when she had planned to wean herself off this drug and try some of the herbals. It still hurt her that Jace had accused her once of being so out of it that she might drop her baby. She would never drop her baby. What was her baby's name, and why hadn't she brought her along?

Oh. Oh, because Darcy was keeping her for a few days. Darcy didn't like to read to her son and baby girl during the day either, because that's all Mother used to do. Even when they needed her. Sometimes when they were crying like Claire was crying now.

She put her feet to the floor and her head in her hands. Why did she keep losing people? Her mother and father were dead. Someone had thrown herself off the balcony because she was in love with the wrong man or maybe just in love with Shadowlawn. But could she be in time to save that woman if she got up now, if she could stop her in time?

Was she dressed? Yes, she wore a wrinkled blouse and long skirt she didn't recognize. She lurched toward the door. When she opened it, she saw a dark hall, so she went back for the flashlight someone had left on her bedside table.

Oh, good, she thought, when she reached for it. It looked like she must have taken her second dose of medicine so she could go to sleep without bad dreams. The water in the glass was all gone.

She opened the door into the pitch-black hall and clicked on the flashlight. Wasn't there supposed to be some guard out here to look for ghosts? She couldn't think of his name, but she knew who it was. Maybe his name was Nick, because she was pretty sure he'd taken care of her before, after someone was hanged from the tree.

She padded down the wooden hallway trying to stay on the rug runner. Not this first bedroom, but the front one, she was pretty sure. Either her mother and dad slept there or someone named Francine. Francine had argued with her daughter, just the way Darcy had argued with their mother. But right now, she had to keep Francine from jumping out the window, from throwing herself onto the pavement stones.

Claire knew she had to hurry, but her feet, like her thoughts, were not moving well. There was a key in the lock of the door. She turned it and the brass knob. The door swung inward at a little push. She could hear the wind outside and some light rain throwing itself against the windows.

But where was Francine? She had to hurry now to stop her from killing herself if her daughter didn't kill her first.

Her beam of light skittered across the room and skimmed the tall picture of the woman. "Don't jump," she told her, but she might just be thinking the words. "My medicine has the side effect of thoughts of suicide, but don't jump. I can prove someone else killed you if you don't kill yourself!"

Claire's legs gave way. She tried to reach for the corner of a dressing table but she went to her knees on the floor. It was as if she were worshipping before the shrine of Shadowlawn. Shadows. Shadows everywhere here.

Claire got to her feet and stumbled to the long glass doors that went to the gallery outside. Had Francine gone out already? Claire had to be sure she didn't jump.

She twisted the lock on the doors until one opened. It swung inward with a moan the rain almost drowned out. Drowned—a better way to die than this, jumping to the pavement below. And taking her unborn child with her? Jace never should have said Claire would drop her baby. Alexandra called Lexi, that was her name. And she wasn't a baby anymore, was she?

Suddenly Claire was too scared to go out onto the gallery and look for the body on the wet pavement below. What if her knees gave way again and she fell? If she got soaked outside, could that be like drowning in a car? She had to get back to Lexi, to her doctor.

Where was her doctor? He'd promised if she took her night meds without fail, her legs would not fail and no more nightmares. But now the room was spinning, and the storm outside was inside her head again. She had to find the doctor!

She wasn't sure where his office was, but she staggered back out and down the hall, looking for him. Why weren't her meds working, that's what she'd ask him. She'd tell him that Francine's didn't either because that's why she'd killed herself, just like the woman in the picture.

At the very back of the hall, she saw a narrow staircase that went up and down. Hadn't there been an elevator here before to go up to the doctor's office? She heard the hum of it, didn't she, voices in the wall, maybe old dance music like they played in elevators?

She started up the narrow stairs, pulling herself along by the wooden banister. Hadn't someone told her there was a guard on the sofa on the first floor, that handsome man she maybe loved?

Oh, a body here on the stairs! A man! Blood on his head. He was probably looking for the doctor, too, but didn't make it. She knew this man, didn't she?

Though she almost lost her balance, she grabbed the banister and leaned toward him. She tried to say, *Are you all right?* but nothing came out. She must be dreaming this! Her meds made her have crazy dreams if she missed them or took them wrong.

Had she done something wrong? Had she let someone down? The man she loved? But was that Jace or Nick? At least she was better now, remembering names, but not this man's on the stairs.

She knelt on a step and put a hand to the side of his neck. He was alive. Then she must be, too. Dreaming. Just dreaming, but not a nightmare yet, thank heavens.

She flashed her light beam up and down the stairs. Only this slumped man. If she went up to the doctor's office, she could send someone down to help him. Oh, heck—that was his name. Heck, but she couldn't remember where she'd met him.

She began to climb, but her legs weren't working right any more than her head was. At the top of the stairs, she could have cried when she saw only a big, dark attic and no doctor's office.

She needed help. She needed help right now and so did that man whose name she could not remember. But she did know one thing about him. Someone had told her that man had lost his grandfather's big house and wanted it back. So this place must be it! At least that would make him happy when he woke up. She'd just go to tell him that she'd found it.

More than once, she nearly fell on the way down. He wasn't there anymore, which proved she was dreaming. But she knew where she had to look next. She'd promised someone she'd look for masks, and she knew now where they were hidden.

Everyone had a mask, especially murderers. She looked behind masks—that was her job. That was what Clear Path was for. Nick had South Shores but she had Clear Path. Stumbling, she unlocked the back door of the house and went out into the mist and light rain down the path toward where everyone kept their masks.

She was barely outside when a person—someone she knew but couldn't place—came out of the darkness. He—or was it a woman?—wore a baseball cap with hair slicked back and pulled up under it. A slicker raincoat, wet too, the collar pulled up high as if it was cold out here. The wall of wet night hid the face, and she was so dizzy she felt almost blind.

"I was about to come get you," the person said in a whisper. "Where are you going?"

Though her mouth seemed numb, she tried to say the words carefully. "To see the masks. I have to write d-down about the masks."

"I'll take you there."

The person steadied her elbow and moved her farther into the darkness of memory, taking her flashlight and clicking it off, but that was probably all right because he or she seemed to know the way. Oh, yes, this was a dream for sure.

"How are you feeling after taking your night meds?" Claire was asked so politely, but why did this person keep whispering? She should ask who it was, but she wanted to be polite. That was the best way to get people to trust her—be positive and polite.

"Not so good," she said. "I th-think I'm dreaming, but I don't want it to be a n-nightmare. That hurt man disappeared, you know."

"Yes, I know. People disappear, one way or the other, sometimes for a good reason. He'll be back there later. In the morning, people will think you hit him over the head."

"But I didn't—did I? He disappeared like the g-ghosts here," she said, hoping her guide didn't think she was sick or crazy, even if she was. "Like Francine," she added, "but she's up in her room. Just like her d-daughter, I didn't want to believe she killed herself on purpose."

"And so, here we go again, powerful chemicals, another strange death, so maybe this place is cursed and haunted. But first, let's get one of those masks you're looking for, then go down by the river."

"But why? Is the b-boat still there, the airboat that goes in the air?"

"Just step in here a moment." The person produced a key that, even in the dark, fit the lock. She knew who this was now. It had to be that man that owned the monster.

Dizzy, almost floating, Claire went in. She collapsed on a bench in the dark room, lit only by the single flashlight—her flashlight the person had taken. Claire tried to keep her eyes open to watch. Her guide lifted a cushion from another bench like the one she sat on. Claire slumped against the wall, half asleep, but sat up straight when, from that chest, a very terrible mask leaped out, one that looked like it was screaming.

Which is what she wanted to do, because she was thinking this person was someone she didn't trust. But it wasn't Sol Sorrento. No, he'd pretended to be dead, but she'd helped to prove that he wasn't and then her client was killed and she was shot. She had to do everything she could to keep that from happening to her and Nick.

She gripped her left arm with her right hand. Yes, she was remembering true things now, that she had been shot and her arm still hurt.

"I don't like that mask," she said, still trying to remember his name. Or could this be Jasmine with that whispery, husky voice?

"Let's take it outside with us anyway. I'll let you throw it in the river, drown it."

She didn't like the sound of that. She didn't want to

be near the river, on the river, in the river. She forced herself to her feet and tried to flee, but the person grabbed her arm and pulled her back. Off balance, she fell to her knees against the finned feet of something tall. And looked up at a finned face and clawed hands.

The monster reared up over her, no, two of them. The slick skin of the creature looked like the raincoat on the person. Claire started to scream, but the mask was pressed over her mouth.

She couldn't breathe, and ghosts grabbed her to hold her down. No, she was being tied with her hands behind her back. Tied with something soft like strips of cloth. And something was put in her mouth to gag her.

"Don't fight and don't be afraid," the whispery voice said. "Those ties won't leave any marks. I think I hear someone. I'll be back in a few minutes. You just rest until I get back, but I'm going to have to lock you in to keep you safe."

When the door closed and the lock clicked, Claire huddled against the wall as far away from the creature as she could get. She curled up in a ball. It was time to wake up now, time to end all this, end it once and for all.

_30_

Nick fought to stay alert on the way back from Palatka in the rain. The wet streets made other headlights seem to leap at him. Right now he totally understood Claire's tendency to get tired. He'd had trouble putting one foot ahead of the other, forming one more thought.

As he pulled into the curved driveway in front of Shadowlawn and killed the rental car's engine, he just sat there a moment in the dark silence. Win's SUV was gone, but, of course, Heck's vehicle was still here.

Nick's headlights, which stayed on a few minutes with the interior dome light, illumined the hanging tree through the light rain. He saw someone had taken down Cecilia's marionette, no doubt the police for evidence. Someone had cleaned up the shattered squadcar window glass, probably Neil. Other than that, the house and grounds looked unchanged—timeless.

He ran his fingers through his hair and gripped his skull as if to hold inside all he'd thought, all he'd been through. He'd managed to get Bronco a pro bono lawyer who would drive in from Daytona Beach in the morning. A contact of a contact, a good guy. He'd briefed the attorney on his cell phone before he'd left Palatka. He'd also assured Bronco that he and Claire believed he had not drugged and murdered Lola. It had cut deep when the big, rugged man grabbed his hand and thanked him with tears in his eyes. His gut told him Bronco—real name Charles—was not a murderer. After all, his walking, talking conscience Claire had said the same.

Despite the blessing of getting her back in one piece today, Nick felt he was about ready to cry over the chaos of this case. Claire had messed things up, yet her help and insights had been invaluable. He wanted desperately to protect her, even more than he wanted to protect Jasmine. That tear of Claire's he'd tasted before he left hours earlier tonight was salty, but sweet on his lips. That was Claire, and he wanted more of her.

To his surprise, when his car lights went off, the veranda lantern over the front door came on. Jasmine—that is, he thought it was Jasmine through the wet side window of his car—came out to meet him. She had either been out or knew it was raining again, because she wore a shiny raincoat. Her hair looked wet, and she'd slicked it back. He wished it could be Claire but he knew better. Right now she must be dead to the world.

"Aren't you coming in, stranger?" Jasmine asked when he opened his door to get out.

"Too exhausted to move."

"So much has happened. I'm going crazy. Can't sleep. Despite the rain, Win left a long time ago. Neil says he's getting a sore throat from picking up all that broken glass out here in the rain and he went to bed. Heck's in the hall upstairs in a sleeping bag I gave him instead of on the sofa, so that's all yours. I haven't even been to bed—been in the parlor, trying to read and pacing until I knew you were okay."

She took his hand and tugged him toward the house. "So the sofa's waiting for you, unless you'd like a shower and a real bed. None of the other bedrooms are set up but I wouldn't mind sharing, I'd— I'd really like it." To his surprise, because she hadn't made a move like in the old days when she'd often been the aggressor, she pressed against him at the door. Man, where was this coming from all of a sudden?

"The sofa will have to do," he told her. "Was there some problem that Heck went upstairs?"

"He was just worried that Claire might sleepwalk or something— I don't know."

Nick could tell she was upset, at him, at the happenings here tonight. He was almost too tired to care for once but was glad to hear Heck had gone upstairs to protect Claire.

As they went in, Jasmine kept her arm around his waist. "Nick, am I going to be all right now? Do you think Bronco killed Lola over a lover's quarrel? It wouldn't be the first time, that's for sure. But Claire believes my mother might have actually ki— Damn, I hate the words *murder*, *kill* and *suicide*. Oh, sorry, I know you do, too—your father, and all. What a coincidence for us, right? We do have a lot in common."

She was babbling. She was panicked. He sank onto the sofa and kicked off his shoes. "We can go with a suicide defense for you if Goodrich still indicts you," he said, trying to stick to business. "We'll make a case that she was depressed and overwhelmed by the problems here. And one side effect of her meds is depression and even suicidal tendencies. When Claire's herself again—and I am, too—we'll sort it all out and decide—"

"Why Claire?" she interrupted. "I'm the one with everything at stake. Hasn't she finished around here?"

"Because, even if we call you to testify, the jury will want to hear calm, professional testimony about everyone's state of mind. That's part of what fraud examiners do."

"I haven't asked, because—well, it's your and Claire's business to examine a dead woman's state of mind—but was there anything in Mother's diary Claire had that would throw light on that? I have a right to know—to have possession of it when she's finished with it."

Nick rubbed his eyes with his fingers. Bright colors exploded in his head. "Some of it's really hard to read," he said. "She's deciphering it but slowly."

"It's where she figured out the tragedy between Rosalynn and Bronco's ancestor, isn't it? But what about current things that could help us build a case to protect me?"

"We have time, especially now that Goodrich is focused on Bronco and Cecilia. We'll show the diary to you—translated, so to speak—when we've examined it."

"When *she* has, you mean. But Bronco and Cecilia, poor souls. Amazing how desperate people are capable of—of anything and everything. Okay, I get the message. I'll leave you to sleep off your exhaustion. You know where there's a restroom off the library near Neil's quarters if you need it."

"Thanks, Jasmine. I just need to recharge my battery right now," he said and lay down just the way he was.

She touched his shoulder once—almost a caress—then went out. Just before he drifted off, he didn't hear her climb the front staircase but head out toward the back of the house.

Claire wandered between fear and exhaustion, trying to stay awake. She knew where she was now—Neil's creature museum. She had to get up, get out. Find a way to take her gag out, go to the door and scream. But that scream mask—it wasn't still on her face but here somewhere.

She rolled into the darkness, hurting her left arm. Trying to keep her balance, she got to her knees, managed to get to her tied feet. Still so dizzy. Why hadn't her meds worked? But at least, for some reason, her thoughts were a little clearer now.

Then a terrible thought: If someone had tampered with Francine's meds, could someone have tampered with hers?

She fought to clear her memory even more. That food Neil gave her, which Jasmine had ordered? That sharp taste to the cheese sandwich. Maybe that was what had thrown her taste off later when she took her night dose. But it had tasted sweet, not tart as it should. When she was in the bathroom, had Jasmine—or Neil—tampered with her Xyrem?

She had to find something in the dark to dislodge her gag so she could scream. But who would there be to hear her? That person, whether it was Neil or Jasmine, was coming back. She had to hurry. Hurry now.

She tried to recall the layout of the museum when Neil had showed it to her and Heck. She'd seen Heck unconscious, hadn't she, though he wasn't tied, and it looked as if he'd simply fallen down the stairs. At least her thoughts were better now. Adrenaline rush. Desperation.

Though she hated to do it, she shuffled toward where she thought the Creature from the Black Lagoon must be. Its finned hands and feet had sharp edges and claws. Maybe she could hook something to pull her gag out, but she'd have to guard her eyes. She could try to saw the ropes around her wrists there. But that could take a lot of time.

She'd barely started rubbing her wrist ties against a sharp fin behind her back when she heard the key in the lock. The door opened, and a beam of light swept the room, blinding her. The light came closer; hands pulled her away.

"Got to move fast now," her captor said, shoving her ahead, perhaps so she wouldn't look back to recognize a face. "Sorry about this, but you got in the way. I can't read that damned diary either, but you're sharp. And your ex-husband says you know the murderer and are going to tell, and we can't have that."

This person had read the diary and talked to Jace? But he could not be in on this! Was she hallucinating again, hearing voices that weren't there? No, this was real, too real.

"You'd figure it out," her captor said. "Messing with meds worked twice before, so hope the third time's the charm."

This phantom—this person—had killed Francine! And drugged Lola, too, before hanging her!

She realized a corner of the gag had been snagged loose and tried to shove it out with her tongue. Struggling to dislodge it, she almost choked. Should she spit the gag out, then try to scream? Or trust her psych-and-talk skills which had saved her once today already?

She spit the gag out and said—amazed at her steady voice—"Neil, just let me go. I'm going to testify that Francine killed herself, and Bronco's going to prison for killing Lola, if you had anything to do with that, so—"

The sharp laugh was a man's, but his own voice. And not Neil's.

"Sorry you got caught in this, Claire, honestly I am. Another strange death will keep the sheriff busy, won't it? Maybe break Markwood, get him out of here. And then who's left to advise poor, broken Jasmine, right? There must be a death curse on this place—that and the phony ghosts will help to save Shadowlawn when I finally control it and the wealth it can bring if handled properly. Really—again, sorry I can't save you, though."

Her insides cartwheeled. How could she have been so trusting and so wrong? She knew who this was now and that words would never save her.

Someone shook Nick awake. Damn, but he could have decked the person—Jasmine?

"Nick, Nick! I finally went upstairs. Your man is missing. There's blood on the floor, and Claire's gone! The diary's missing, too, unless she hid it, and I swear I didn't take it!"

He was on his feet in a second, didn't stop for his shoes. She thrust a flashlight in his hand. He took her at her word, didn't consider it a trap—at least not one she'd set.

"Go knock on Neil's door to see if he's there," he ordered. "And be careful. He still could be behind this."

He sprinted for the front staircase. Even in the darkness, probed only by his beam of light, he took the stairs two at a time. His socks made them slippery. Upstairs, every door was open and squares of light crisscrossed the hall. Jasmine must have searched every room for Claire.

He wasn't even sure which room had been hers until he saw the blood. Heck's? Claire's?

He looked in the small room. Yes, her meds on the bedside table. Her purse there, opened. Had Jasmine done that? He wasn't sure, didn't have time to ask. His heart pounded so hard from exertion and fear he could hear it thumping in his ears.

He thought of two places Claire could be, especially if she'd gone out on her own. If she'd been taken by Neil—who knew? He cursed himself for even thinking the other possibility—that Heck could have turned on them, but he'd always feared the long, rich reach of Clayton Ames.

31

Claire could not get her gag out to make more than a murmur as Win Jackson carried her toward the river. If only she could get her feet down to make drag marks, anything to leave evidence she did not walk into the river to drown herself because she'd messed up her meds today.

Win was vocal and clearly a manipulative mastermind, so she knew she could not outtalk or outpsych him. He was the one doing the talking, as if his righteous reasons for murders would make things all right. He'd been so clever through all this. So she had one chance, one choice. Keep calm, she told herself. Stop fighting until he didn't expect it. Wouldn't he have to take out her gag and untie her to make it look as if she'd drowned herself in her drugged state?

Through mist and light rain, she saw the water. The silhouette of Bronco's airboat emerged, then faded as they passed it. What if there were alligators? She'd seen them here!

Thoughts bombarded her. Lexi, Darcy. She should not have been so resentful of her mother. People had to cope with their lives, and she had to cope with this so she would not lose her life. If her head would only clear more, if the gag would come out and—

Win slipped once in the mud, and they went thigh-deep in the water. It seemed warm, welcoming. He drew a knife. Was she wrong he meant to drown her? But he only cut the ties around her ankles and shoved her to her knees in the current which swirled almost up to her chin.

"Sorry, really," he said again. "I'm afraid you're collateral damage. After Francine realized I was faking my feelings for her, she changed her mind about letting me help guide Shadowlawn, but I think Jasmine will. Lola knew I loved the place and not the woman and talked against me—accused me of messing with Francine's meds. You were eliminating others, and you'd get to me, so I have to—to eliminate you. When Markwood left your purse in my car, I had a look at the diary, and your ex-husband called on your phone to say you were on to Francine's killer. Just relax now, relax and breathe..."

He meant breathe in the water! He thrust her head into the river with her feet free but her hands still tied behind her. Jasmine's long skirt kept her from kicking. Her gag finally came out, but what did it matter now as he held her down, down, down.

Nick was completely panicked. He tore into what Francine had called Rosalynn's room. The portrait loomed large, and one door to the balcony was open. He ran out onto the wet surface and looked over the railing.

He bellowed, "Claire?"

He glanced down at his car, at Heck's SUV, then toward the hanging tree. Nothing amiss. River fog had sifted in, and light rain pelted down.

"Claire!"

He didn't wait for Jasmine to report in. No way—he hoped—that she was in on any of this because she wanted to get her hands on the diary. Had she—like Win Jackson—been too helpful lately?

He tore down the front stairs and ran toward the back of the house. Claire had said her meds—or lack of them—could give her nightmares, but he was living one now. He prayed that getting her back safe today was not one miracle too many.

Claire went limp and held what little breath she had. With that gag still in when he'd first dunked her, she hadn't taken a big breath. The river current seemed to carry her away, but he hadn't let her go. Still, he seemed to slip again, to relax his hold a bit. She felt her hair tug at her scalp, floating above her head. "Doesn't your little girl have beautiful red hair?" she heard a voice asking her mother. Lexi's face...Darcy's...even Jace's floated past.

Now. She had to do something now before her lungs burst and she sucked in water. The current had lifted, twisted her skirt higher, almost to her knees. One kick was all she would get.

Wait, he was untying her hands. Her left arm still hurt from being shot. Hold on, hold the last bit of breath. Yes, her hands free. Should she just pretend to float away if he loosed her? But then she'd have to keep her head under, couldn't do that anymore, had to lift her head, had to be herself, stand on her own, take a clear path to life and…

She slowly raised her right leg almost to her chest, then slammed it back. Her foot connected with his stomach. She tried to yank free, reared up, sucking in air through the heavy curtain of her sodden hair.

She screamed but not loudly. Out of breath, gasping, then screamed again. The sound seemed to echo, echo as if another woman had screamed while falling to her death. Behind Win as he slipped, staggered and reached for her again, she thought she saw a woman in a white gown pull him back. No, not a woman, only river mist that looked like the merging of a woman's form with that of a man reaching for her, reaching for her and holding her…

She clawed at Win's face and, off balance, hit at him, but she only struck his shoulder. Screaming again, she scrambled for the slippery bank.

Suddenly, Nick exploded into the water, hitting Win, kicking him, shouting. Claire clung to the riverbank, clawing at it to get a handhold.

Jasmine appeared, pulled her out, helped her up the bank where she fell to the ground. Kneeling, Jasmine steadied her, patting her on the back, screaming curses at Win.

Claire gasped in huge breaths as Nick dragged the bloody, soaking man from the river. He grabbed rope coiled in Bronco's boat and tied him to it. He stuffed a ripped piece of Win's shirt in his mouth.

Jasmine called to Nick, "Neil was in his room, but your man Heck was dumped by his door, we think to make it look like Neil did it. Heck's alive, and we called the squad for him. They can help Claire, too."

Claire shook her head. "All—right—now," she wheezed. Yes, she was all right now.

"Okay," Nick said. "Then go call to get the sheriff back here, Jasmine. I'm not letting this bastard out of my sight until they get here, but Claire needs something then—blankets, hot tea, something."

"I think," Jasmine said very quietly with a little sob, "she just needs you." She hugged Claire's shoulders and ran back into the house.

Claire breathed deep but trembled from shock as she watched Nick nudge Win with his foot.

"I'll let you tell it all to the sheriff and then a jury," he said. "I hope you get a good defense lawyer because Claire and I—and Jasmine—are going to testify against you."

Nick stumbled to Claire and, panting, pulled her to her feet and picked her up. He carried her a little way toward the house, then collapsed on the grass with her in his arms. As weak as she felt, she curled against him, her head on his shoulder. He was shaking, too, and she could feel his heart pounding.

"He admitted he killed Francine and Lola," she whispered.

"But not you! And I saw an alligator go into the river when I did."

"But I saw the ghosts, Nick. I swear I did. Rosalynn and William together. They helped me before you came, after I kicked him."

"All right, all right," he said, holding her even tighter. "My Superwoman in word and deed. I knew you'd turn up the murderer, but don't ever do it this way again."

She knew he didn't believe her about the ghosts.

But—screwed-up meds or not—she did now, at least she believed in people from the past and present who made mistakes and paid for it with their lives. Thank God, she did not have to do that. And it wasn't listening or talking or thinking that had saved her this time, but fighting. Fight over fright.

She sat up straighter. Her voice was rough, but she had to say this, so she took a big breath. "Nick, I think Win hit Heck over the head and dumped him in the stairwell to the attic, before he must have moved him to Neil's door. He messed up my meds when my purse was in his car and he said something about talking to Jace, so I'll bet he listened to a phone message of mine. I should have checked my messages when I got my phone back."

"Let's save all that. Save it for when we put things together—for the prosecution this time, not the defense. The only thing that bothers me is we're handing Sheriff Goodrich a lot of publicity to make his future." He set her aside, got to his feet, then lifted her in his arms again.

"But," she told him, "you've made my day—maybe made my life."

He bounced her once in his arms and held her tighter. "Yeah, let's do what we have to do here, get home, and then we can really work on that."

32

At LAX, Jace popped into the airline scheduler's office between the flight from Singapore and his cross-country jump to Miami. He'd emailed ahead to request a change in his schedule, and he had to admit he'd probably given them fits lately. In the scheduler's office, he was surprised to find the doctor who did the annual psychological well-being tests for pilots. Dr. Carson gave him a thin smile and gestured him into the empty office of the scheduler he'd been hoping to see.

"Hey, Jason—oh right, you go by Jace—sit down for a minute," the young doctor said, indicating a chair across from the scheduler's desk.

"You know it's not time for my yearly interview," Jace said, hoping this wouldn't take long.

"I know, but I just wondered if there's something on your personal horizon that's behind your asking for assignment changes when you were so glad to get the Singapore run not long ago. And you took a sudden leave for a week recently. I hope to be of help to pilots who have gone through separation or divorce.

It can wear on anyone. Sit, sit. This won't take long. So, have you been sleeping well lately?"

This guy should hire Claire, Jace thought. She'd be great at this Q and A stuff. He had to admit he was a bit distracted lately—not that it would reflect on his work at all.

"Well, you know, time zone changes, but that's about it," Jace told him, but he realized that was a lie. He'd thought he'd mastered jet lag until lately. He felt kind of woozy right now.

"So, I have here," Dr. Carson said when he sat down across the desk, "your recent inquiry about getting a Miami-Caribbean assignment or even Miami-Toronto. I know you like foreign places, but can you elaborate on your thinking here? Is it more than wanderlust? You don't feel like you're running from the home situation, do you?"

"Just the opposite, if I can get a Miami-based assignment."

Jace tried to watch his body language. He'd learned that from Claire, too, but he was longing to get out of here. Wanderlust? Claire was the only thing he lusted for right now. He tried to keep his voice level.

"Staying close to my family is a consideration. I'm hoping for reconciliation and that takes proximity."

"That and family consistency is a tough one for pilots. Have you ever considered private piloting, say for a corporation?"

"Not for a while. I love flying the big boys."

"And, of course, compensation is better. You haven't felt depressed over this, have you, not being able to coordinate your professional life and keep the family situation stable? Don't consider this an official interview, but I just want you to be sure you know what you want to do, career-wise, family-wise."

"I can assure you of that, Doctor," he said and went on to explain that he felt steady and sure in his course of life, just like he did in the cockpit of a plane. But, truth was, he was thinking that, finally, family had to come first.

The moment she saw Lexi run out of Darcy's house to greet her, Claire ignored the fact that her left arm was hurting again. She picked the squealing child up and spun her around.

"Mommy, Mommy, I'm glad you're here before preschool started!" Lexi screeched so loud that her ears rang.

"Me, too! No more traveling, at least not for a long time."

"Maybe to Disney! Daddy said on the phone maybe to Disney!"

"Well, maybe."

Claire kept kissing Lexi's face and felt tears of gratitude on her own. Nick was still watching, leaning on the car door he'd opened for her.

"Oh," Lexi said. "It's Mr. Nick. Do you have some kids, too, Mr. Nick?"

"Not yet," he said, "but I'm starting to wish I did."

"Better get them a mom first," the child said as Claire put her down but kept a good hold on her hand.

"Right. I'll need to work on that. Claire, since you want to see your family here, I'll drop your suitcase off on your screened lanai, then see you tomorrow, okay? I'm going to head to the office, take care of things there. I hope our statements to the sheriff were enough to keep us ahead of the hounds for now. At least it won't be Jasmine on trial, so I can concentrate on things here—and that's what I plan to do," he added with an intense look that rattled her poise.

"Yes. All right. Call tomorrow before you come over."

"Will do. And don't be accepting other clients, all right? The law firm and South Shores still need you. And I promise it will be closer to home."

She wanted to kiss him goodbye, but Lexi was all eyes, and Darcy had appeared in the front window. He'd talked to her about a possible assignment only twenty miles from here. It was something about a Southwest Florida cosmetics corporation that was claiming eternal youth products and had experienced corporate theft and fraud, but beyond that she'd hardly been listening.

Home. She was home with Lexi and her family and Nick said he'd call her and come over tomorrow.

She and Lexi waved as he backed out and disappeared down Lakewood Boulevard. But despite the late-afternoon September sun and the fact she was safely home, Claire had a strange premonition she tried to shake off. Sometimes she felt the river was still pulling at her, trying to drown her, suck her in, yank her away into nightmare oblivion.

Nonsense, she told herself. She was home where she had fresh meds, she had her normal life back, her daughter, so she was in control now. And Nick—boss or not, it was clear he wanted to keep seeing her, and that excited her totally.

"Let's give Aunt Darcy's family a big hug and

bigger thanks and then we'll walk home together," she told Lexi, and the child skipped along at her side.

Everything, Claire thought the next afternoon, was looking bright. Nick had phoned at noon to tell her that Win would be indicted today. Of course, she'd have to testify, but that could be months away. Win had admitted to everything except running them off the road, knocking Jace out and spying on them on the grounds of Shadowlawn. Since Win had confessed to murder, claiming he was trying to protect Florida's historic heritage, Nick was certain he would have admitted to the lesser charges. Therefore, they feared, Nick's nemesis, Clayton Ames, had been behind those acts. Nick was hoping the man would crawl back into the international woodwork for now since Jasmine was determined to both keep Shadowlawn but share it with others.

On the home front, things looked promising, too. Claire had several potential jobs waiting for her that had come through her website, ones that could be done locally. She'd slept well with fresh meds and no bad dreams. Lexi and Jilly were excited about preschool at the start of the new year, so Darcy and Claire were, too. And with Nick, her future seemed good and new.

After Nick's call, the early afternoon at home blurred by in a rush—doctor's visit for her arm, grocery store, all with Lexi in tow. Nick called again between meetings and asked if he could stop by mid-afternoon. He said Bronco had been released and was back at Shadowlawn. Nick had arranged another pro bono lawyer for Cecilia to try to get her charges reduced, though they could hardly be dropped. Jasmine had already hired another photographer to take pictures of the mansion for a book and a brochure for future visitors, and, starting with her mother's elderly lawyer, she was looking for investors to help her keep the place private.

"How about I bring three McDonald's Happy Meals?" Nick had asked. "I remember you mentioned Lexi liked those."

"Sure. Great," she'd said, though it was way off the time they should eat. And those Happy Meals were something Jace and Lexi had often shared.

At three thirty, she'd prepped Lexi not to say that food now would spoil their dinner, or that her daddy had always bought her Happy Meals, in front of Nick.

"I wouldn't say that, Mommy. I can always eat fries and a shake. I know you like him, so I do, too. He's pretty cute."

Claire's eyes widened. What to say? Well, he was pretty cute. His car, not the rental car, but one that looked to be a shiny new one with a temporary license plate, pulled into the driveway. Smiling like someone in those You-Just-Won-A-Million-Dollars ads, Nick came up the walk with two big sacks of food.

Lexi led them in as Claire's cell phone on the kitchen counter rang. "I'd better get this," she told Nick and darted out into the kitchen.

"Claire, it's Jace. I'm about a half hour away. I'll just pop by briefly, then see both of you longer tomorrow. I'm bushed and I want to make a good impression—a new, good, first impression."

"Could we make it tomorrow? Things are crazy here."

"Yeah, well, I'm crazy to see both of you. Tell Lexi. Traffic's bad, see you soon," he said and hung up.

"Everything okay?" Nick asked as she went back out to the screened lanai where she'd set up place mats on the table. Lexi had taken over, unpacking the food and laying it out.

"Yes. Just that Jace is going to stop by to see Lexi in a little while."

"So we should make this quick?"

"No, we should sit right here and enjoy ourselves. After we eat, Lexi can watch for him. He said he wouldn't stay long. I've asked him not to just pop in, but Jace is Jace."

"He flies planes," Lexi told Nick, zooming a French fry toward her mouth.

"That's an important job," he told the child.

As they ate, Claire silently blessed Lexi that she didn't carry on about her father. Why did things have to be so complicated?

"Mommy, can I go look for him out the window now?" she asked, after gulping down her milk shake and about half of her fries.

"Sure. All right," Claire told her. When the child scampered off, she told Nick, "Sorry about the timing for all this."

"How about I leave, and we can do something else later? I've been gone so long, I need to meet with the office staff. I actually had to send Heck to lease that car for me. I don't mean to mess things up for you, but I wanted to see you and get to know Lexi, too. Can you and I go out some evening soon? I got the idea your sister's a second mom to her, and I'd like to meet her, too—Darcy."

They held hands over the corner of the glass table, interweaving their fingers. "We've been through so much in such a short time," Claire told him, her voice soft and shaky. "It's hard to believe it's all been so fast, just a bit over two weeks."

"I know." His silver eyes focused on hers like a laser. "Intense, all the way."

He leaned forward. She did, too. He tipped his head and took her lips. As ever with him, she felt that down to the pit of her belly and up to the stars.

"Mommy, he's here! He's here!"

Reality. They broke the kiss, the touch. Claire heard Lexi's feet on the tile in the entryway. She was opening the door to fly to Jace's arms as usual. Claire and Nick stood slowly. Lexi opened, then slammed the front door.

"I'd better go," Nick said, "but I'll call. I'll be back. I understand all this," he said with a sweep of his hand toward the front of the house. "It's okay."

"Let's hope this goes better than last time in the hotel room," she said as they walked toward the front door. "He's been hinting he wants to turn over a new leaf, but I don't know."

"With you?"

"I just think you can't put broken eggs back together—too scrambled."

Claire opened the front door, expecting to have to face Jace with Lexi in his arms. But there was no Jace. No car. No Lexi!

Oh, a car that looked like his was just disappearing

around the curve in the street. But—but he wouldn't take her for a ride without clearing it with Claire first. Would he? He'd never done that before!

33

"I—I don't think he'd just take her somewhere," she repeated, running out to the street and looking down it with Nick right behind. "He usually comes in."

"She was only out here a minute or two. Do you know that neighbor down there? The silver-haired older lady," he said, pointing. "I can go ask her."

"Oh, Margaret. I'll ask her."

Claire ran across the driveway and two doors down. "Margaret, did you see Lexi in our front yard a minute ago?"

"Oh, yes. How are you, Claire? I believe you two have been on vacation after that terrible accident where you got shot."

"But did she get in a car?"

"Yes. She was shouting 'Daddy, Daddy,' and he pulled her into his arms and right into the car. So, did you two go very far and have a good time?"

"I can't talk now," she cried and tore back toward Nick.

"She got in a car with him! But Jace wouldn't take her. That couldn't be what he meant about things changing! Oh, thank heavens! Here he comes right now. I recognize the car. He must have just taken her for a little ride, but he scared me to death! That's his car he keeps in town, but he uses rental ones from the airport sometimes."

Nick started back toward his car as Claire went to meet Jace. She wouldn't scold him in front of Lexi, but he was going to hear about this. Was he trying to teach her a lesson not to go off on distant assignments?

"Hey, I like the personal welcome!" Jace called out the open driver's-side window. "And the fact he's leaving but not that he's been here."

Claire could see Lexi wasn't in the front seat with him. "Where is she, Jace? This isn't funny! Is she hiding in the backseat?" she demanded, covering her eyes from the sun's glare and squinting in his back window, which reflected her silhouette like a dark mirror.

"What are you talking about? Where's Lexi?"

"You tell me. I hear she just got in your car for a little ride."

He got out and slammed the car door. "Says who?"

"A neighbor who saw it."

Jace's eyes widened, and his lower lip set. "No, I swear it."

Claire hit his shoulder with her fist before he grabbed her wrist. "It has to be! Where is she?" she screamed.

Nick got back out of his car and strode toward them. "What is it?" he asked. "Where is she?"

"You two cozy here in the middle of the day, so maybe she ran away!" Jace roared. "Is that it?"

"Didn't you listen to me?" Claire cried. "She got in a car that must have looked like yours with a man who—who maybe looked like you!"

Jace would not have done this as a sick joke, not with Lexi at stake. Lexi…

"I'm calling the police," Claire said and started toward the house but stopped when she saw the drone. It hovered about twelve feet in the air, then set down perfectly on the lawn just ahead of her. She hurried to it. "There's an envelope here!" she called out. Her stomach cramped so badly she almost doubled over, but she snatched the note off the thing and ran into the house with Nick and Jace close behind.

Her hands shaking so hard the paper rattled, she pulled a note from the envelope and read aloud, "Lexi's going on a nice vacation to Grand Cayman Island. Nick and Claire must come get her. She will be safe if you obey. No police. No one else! You will be contacted there."

To Claire's horror, Nick turned and ran out the front door. "I've got to follow that drone!" he yelled back.

"You SOB!" Jace roared and ran out, too. "I swear, if you set this up to get them off alone…"

Claire collapsed onto the floor. She wanted to tear the note, scream, beat the tile. But this note was evidence—of—of her daughter's kidnapping. No police. No one else.

This could not be happening. It was worse than any nightmare she'd ever had.

Nick ran back in with Jace close behind him. Nick reached down to Claire's shoulders and pulled her to her feet, then sat her on a tall counter chair. He got right in her face. "The drone is gone, but we know who sent it. We've been watched, set up. I'm so sorry. I—I should have known not to get close to someone that way to give that bastard leverage. It's why I've changed—changed close friends so much."

"Who sent it? Who the hell took my daughter?" Jace roared and reached for Nick.

Claire stood and wedged herself between the men. "Stop it! Stop it, Jace. It won't help. We'll explain!"

But would Nick go into what was obviously a trap set up for him? If not, if she went alone, would this Clayton Ames who must be behind this give Lexi back? Or if he thought Nick cared for her or her daughter, would they be in danger, too?

"I'll go, do what he says," Nick said in a deadly calm voice. It was as if he'd read her mind. "It's time I faced him. I've crossed him so many times, and he kept dancing out of reach, but it's time now. I'll go."

To her amazement, he put his index finger by his lips to get them to keep quiet. He gestured for them to follow him out of the room. He quietly opened the door to the closed garage and motioned them out. Once they were inside the dim garage, he closed the door to the house but still spoke in a whisper.

"I've had my house bugged more than once, but I do regular sweeps. I didn't think of it here, but it's time to trust no one and no place. If there's a listening device, it's more likely to be in the house. No time to look for it now. Time to act."

"This note says it has to be both of us," Claire insisted. She still had the envelope and note clutched in her hand. Tears streamed down her cheeks. "The drones—it's obvious we, or you, have been watched from the day of the courthouse shooting."

"And with all the trees at Shadowlawn," Nick said, "a drone wouldn't work, so he sent someone to watch us, someone I chased that day. Maybe someone who hit Jace over the head when he showed up there."

"Who the hell are you two talking about?" Jace demanded. "And why would he take Lexi if he wants you, Markwood?"

"I'll explain, but only if you swear you won't go to the police, that you'll let me—"

"Us," Claire put in.

"—play this his way—or at least seem to until I can figure out what to do—how to get your daughter back. She'll come first, not me…"

Nick stopped speaking. He shrugged. When Claire reached out to grip his arm, Jace said, "You know, I got some photos of you two together at a park, another of you near the hotel in St. Augustine, and one of when Claire was shot at the courthouse and you were bending over her, Markwood. I'm sure they were shot with drones. I couldn't figure out how someone knew to find me at the airport in LA. And it came with a handprinted note, kind of like that one, that told me not to trust you, and to get back to get Claire away from you. I should have heeded the warning."

Claire cried, "He's been watching all of us! Who does he think he is—God?" She crunched the envelope she still held. It seemed stiff. She looked inside, then pulled out more papers. She gasped. "A printout for two airline tickets, Nick, in your name and mine, Miami to Grand Cayman Island—first thing tomorrow morning. And your name's here for ordering the tickets."

"Which I didn't."

"And," she said, shuffling to get to the third sheet, "a copy of an online reservation it looks like you made for a place called the Reef View Club, oceanfront suites on the north end of Seven Mile Beach." Crying again, she showed them to Nick, then Jace snatched them.

Nick muttered, "Look, I swear to both of you I'll get Lexi back, and I didn't set any of that up, even if it looks like it. If it costs me everything—my life—which it well could, I'll get both Lexi and Claire back safe. Knowing how he thinks, it would be just like him to stage my suicide. He—he likes to torment me, so I'll have to hope, after he lets them go, he'll let me go, too. But I doubt it. I've tightened the screws on him again, so I—doubt it."

Jace slammed his fist down on the hood of Claire's car. "All right, since this guy, this enemy, seems to know everything you do, I'm going, too—to ride shotgun. It will screw the career I've worked so hard for, but I'm going. You two can look like you're following orders, and I'll fly down in the plane I can borrow. When we're all there, I'll tail you—change how I look, keep out of sight but be there if you need me or we need a fast escape. I know a place I can stay."

"Even out here, keep your voice down," Nick said, raking his fingers through his hair. "I can't stop you, but I can't advise it. You can see how this guy operates. Okay, here's the thing. He framed my father, ruined him, and I think murdered him, but set it up to look like a suicide I've never been able to disprove—so far. You can see he's rich and powerful. If you insist on going south on your own, let's go back into the house and stage a loud scene where you say you're giving me—both of us—forty-eight hours to get your daughter back or you're going to the cops. Then storm out and do your damnedest to be sure you're not followed to wherever you keep your plane. Maybe fly down ahead of us, but steer clear of contacting us there. We'll no doubt be watched, but maybe—if you're careful and lucky—you can watch the watchers."

"Yeah, got it," Jace said. "Believe me, I know how to follow orders, and I get it about carrying a dead dad around with you for years. Then, let's get this show on the road—or die trying."

Claire pulled her hand back from Nick's arm. He was shaking. His usual tan complexion looked bleached out with fear. "Claire," he said, "I repeat, we'll get her back, no matter what it costs."

She nodded. Jace looked as shell-shocked as she felt. Nick, devastated. No, he looked determined and as quietly angry as Jace was openly fuming. Despite it all, she didn't hate Nick, never could. Or Jace. God help her, the three of them were a team now, a desperate but daring team.

* * * * *

Author's Note

Since I have lived the last thirty winters in the lovely city of Naples, Florida, I had always wanted to set another story there. (I did use that Southwest Florida setting for two earlier books, *BLACK ORCHID*, 1996, and *BELOW THE SURFACE*, 2008, which has recently been rereleased with a Heather Graham novel in a book entitled *STILL WATERS*.) So was born the SOUTH SHORES series, set in cities, states and countries—and beautiful beaches!—which I have lived, loved and visited. Although we are dedicated Ohioans, I figured out by adding up our Florida months that we have lived there for a total of ten and a half years.

For this first SOUTH SHORES novel, I owe a great deal to my stepson and daughter-in-law Bill and Sunny Harper for their help with St. Augustine sites. Although we have visited them there numerous times, it took someone living in the area to answer all my questions. They own and operate two stores in Old Town St. Augustine in Heritage Walk off St. George Street. Their shops are Nautical Watch, which specializes in leather goods, and Mara's Hotter

Side, which features salsas and other spicy delights made from the regional datil pepper. If you're in that historic city, stop by to see them and say hi.

Except for its cash crop of indigo, Shadowlawn Plantation House is greatly based on the beautiful antebellum Oak Alley in Louisiana, which we visited on a Mississippi River boat trip. For a look at this historic home, please visit its website at www.OakAlleyPlantation.com and think of fictional Shadowlawn. However, indigo plantations once flourished in northern Florida, and Kingsley Plantation, mentioned in this novel and located near Jacksonville, is a great example of this. Kingsley has a fascinating story of its own, including its claim to being haunted. It is operated by the US National Park Service.

All the characters in this novel are fictional. The sheriffs who appear in the book are strictly creations of my imagination and no way reflect on the actual government or police forces in Florida.

Thanks as ever to my team at MIRA Books, especially my editor Nicole Brebner and publicist Lisa Wray. As ever to my agent Annelise Robey and the Jane Rotrosen Agency staff, especially Meg Ruley who has been with me through thick and thin. My husband Don has been my travel companion for years as well as my proofreader.

Please say hello and take part in the various questions and contests on my Facebook page at www.Facebook.com/karenharperauthor or visit my author website at www.karenharperauthor.com. You can also drop me a note at Karen.Harper.Author@gmail.com.

Karen Harper

If you enjoyed CHASING SHADOWS,
don't miss the next story in Karen Harper's
SOUTH SHORES *series...*
DROWNING TIDES
Coming soon from MIRA Books!
Turn the page for a sneak peek...

<u>1</u>

"I'll get her back, Claire. I swear to you, I'll get your daughter back."

"We'll get her back together," she insisted, turning toward Nick as he drove the rental car across I-75 to Miami where they would catch their plane.

Thank God, Claire thought, Florida was narrow west to east, but the drive across the state on what Floridians called Alligator Alley seemed endless. Claire's four-year-old daughter, Lexi, had been kidnapped, taken to the Caribbean island of Grand Cayman. They had round-trip Cayman Airways tickets, leaving this morning from Miami and getting into Grand Cayman early afternoon. They also had reservations for a place to stay on the island—all provided by the kidnapper who wanted much more than Lexi.

Claire clenched her hands so tightly in her lap that her fingers went numb. She frowned at the canal where alligators basked like logs in the early morning sun, and white herons and ibis fluttered in the tops of mangrove trees. Early October was just past the rainy season, and the air seemed crystal clear. But nothing looked beautiful to her anymore.

How could she ever have imagined when she went to work for criminal lawyer Nick Markwood that it would come to this? The two of them had been through hell enough already, but this horror was so much worse.

"Let's go over some things again," Nick said.

Ever clever, seemingly calm, even in the chaos of his own life, and now hers and Lexi's, too, Claire thought. But she clung to that. She needed that—and him.

"Yes. Yes, all right," she agreed. "I know we have to go along with him, play by his rules. But we have to find his weakness, a way to save Lexi and you, too—if he lets any of us go."

"Clayton Ames controls people the way he does his international business empire," Nick said of the sixty-four-year-old billionaire business mogul.

"Except for you. He found he couldn't control you, that you would pursue him for your father's murder, even if he had it staged to look like a suicide. You'd think by now he'd ignore your attempts to prove that, since he always just slips out of reach. Nick, that's what terrifies me about him having Lexi—and soon having us. He can make people disappear."

A noisy semi went around their car with a deep honk of its horn. They passed the exit to the Miccosukee Seminole Indian reservation on the edge of Everglades National Park. The lush foliage merged with the saw grass prairie of the Glades with its tree-filled raised mounds called hammocks. At last a scattering of west coast buildings appeared along with green and white highway signs to Fort Lauderdale and Miami.

She stared at Nick's profile, seemingly set in stone. She was grateful he was as obsessed with saving Lexi as she was, and she loved him all the more for it. It seemed the long night they'd spent planning and packing had etched deeper lines on his chiseled face. The silver streaks along the temples of his dark hair seemed more pronounced and his gray eyes more intense than even during the days they'd struggled to get answers and stay alive on the St. Augustine murder-suicide case. He suddenly looked older than thirty-nine, but then, she felt far beyond thirty-two today.

How ironic she'd decided she would not work as his forensic psychologist again if an assignment took her away from Lexi, and now her daughter had been taken away from her—from her own front yard. Claire had vowed she'd stay home in Naples and stick to more mundane investigations through her Clear Path fraud-fighting website, but here they were, more desperate than ever.

"As I said, expect the worst from Clayton Ames," Nick told her, his voice hard as it always was when he spoke of his archenemy. "We have to watch what we say at all times, in the airport, on the plane, even once we get to our Grand Cayman hotel, because he could have places bugged or his lackeys hovering. Expect to be under invisible surveillance day and night. We'll walk on the beach away from others if we want to be sure we're not overheard. Nothing about Jace, especially. He's risking his neck to fly down on his own in case we need him."

It went unspoken between them that they couldn't have stopped Jace Britten anyway. Her ex-husband had arrived at Claire's house just after Lexi was taken and saw the threatening note the drone had delivered. Lexi's abductor had evidently driven a car like Jace's and even resembled him to a degree, to get the child close enough to grab. But Claire had to agree with Nick that Jace could be a loose cannon in all this.

"Jace and I may be divorced, but he'd do anything for Lexi."

"And for you," he said, turning to shoot her a sudden stare before looking back to the road. "He still cares for you a lot."

"I'll never forgive myself if his plan to fly down there on his own blows up. He's a skilled pilot and used to jets, so it's not that. But rather if he's harmed once he's there or ruins our chances of getting Lexi back."

"At least he knows the stakes. But as I said, Ames likes to know exactly what his competitors, even in business, are saying and thinking, what's going on. I wouldn't have rented this car at the last minute if I didn't think he'd manage to bug my other one."

"I know," she said, her voice shaky. She looked at the narrow, deep waterways that ran along this four-lane highway. "I'll be careful what I say and when." She turned toward him, tugging her seat belt out to give herself room to sit sideways. "Nick, I can't thank you enough for risking yourself to get Lexi back. I know Ames means to harm you."

"He does, but I'm banking on the fact he likes to exert his power, make his enemies twist and turn, control and ruin them, torment them. I'm hoping he means to make me toe his line somehow, not just trade my life for hers."

Claire broke into tears again when she'd tried since yesterday to keep calm. But she felt she was spiraling down into a dark hole. At least she didn't have a horrible dream last night from her narcolepsy in the half hour she'd gone to sleep. Right now, she didn't need her so-called "sleeping disease" or her powerful meds that controlled it. Despite her deep exhaustion, for once, she couldn't sleep.

"Sorry. I'm okay. I mean, not okay, but holding up. Really," she tried to assure him as she grabbed for a tissue in her purse on the car floor and swiped under her eyes.

"I'm sorry, too, sweetheart," Nick said, reaching over the console to grip her knee with one hand. "But, despite all this, I can't be sorry we met, that we—we care for each other. Again, I swear to you on my life, we will get Lexi back and get through this. Then I'll leave your life so that bastard doesn't try to use you and those you love to get to me again."

A tear trickled down Nick's cheek from under his sunglasses, but, focused on the road again, he ignored it. She loved him desperately despite hating him, too, over this—didn't she?

Claire made herself look away from him. Fear was on his face but fury, too. Did he know her heart was broken not only over Lexi but over what he'd just said—that once they got her back, Nick would leave their lives?

As Nick took the turn south toward the Miami Airport through a maze of curved and elevated ramps and overhead signs, the horrible day he'd found his father dead came back to him. That waking nightmare crashed in on him sometimes when he least expected it. His attorney dad whom he adored and had later patterned himself after, dead. His head partly gone. Pistol in hand. Blood spatter and brain matter on the wall behind his desk.

He heard again his own shrill, young voice. "Dad! Dad! Dad!"

Obviously a suicide, the coroner ruled: late at night, wife out of town, son supposedly asleep upstairs, trajectory of the bullet, spatter pattern, only the deceased's fingerprints on the gun. And the fact his father had recently lost huge real estate investments, ones he'd made on the advice of his trusted friend, Clayton Ames, Nick's "Uncle Clay." Later, in his teens, Nick had found papers stashed in a metal box that showed his father had meant to expose Ames as a cheat and fraud.

But Nick had known even then—his mother did, too—that Dad would not have killed himself and left them broke and bereft like that. The only good thing that had come from their public family tragedy was Nick's dedication to becoming a criminal lawyer. Eventually to found two entities to help distraught people: Markwood, Benton and Chase, LLP, the law firm in which he was a senior partner; and South Shores, a secret, separate enterprise which sought out and defended those who were wrongly accused of or ruined by murder or suicide.

Once he'd seen forensic psychologist Claire Britten testify in court about interviewing witnesses and suspects, he'd known he needed her on his South Shores team. The problem was, it hadn't taken him long to learn he needed her in other ways, too, though he'd tried not to mix purpose with pleasure. They had not yet made love, but he wanted her desperately. Before this chaos, he'd had hopes he could convince her they should be seriously looking at a life together. Now, he might even lose his life, but he was not going to forfeit hers—or Lexi's.

"You need to try to sleep or at least rest now, on the plane, too," he told Claire. "We're going to need, as they say, our wits about us."

"I can not only do my best, but what is necessary. My mother used to say that. I suppose she got it from one of her books she always had her nose in. My sister and I say it sometimes to get through tough times. Nick, I wish I could have told Darcy what happened. She's going to think I'm nuts, that I've taken Lexi and run off with you, like I stupidly eloped with Jace. But I had to leave her that note about us taking time away so she wouldn't call the cops. *No cops*, Ames's note said."

"She'll understand when you get Lexi back, when you can explain the truth, or some of it. We'll be there soon. Trust me, Claire. Again, on my life, I swear we'll get her back. Close your eyes. I've got to keep mine on this heavier traffic."

Out of the corner of his vision, he saw her settle back in her seat. But a big Boeing 747 jet taking off overhead from the Miami Airport made her open her eyes again, sit forward and look up. Her ex was an international airline pilot, so what was she thinking in that beautiful head of hers? He was afraid to ask because he knew in his gut that she and Jace still cared for each other and not just because of the endangered child they shared.

Besides, unfortunately, Jace was blond and raw-boned handsome, a real take-charge guy. Emotional, even volatile for a former navy pilot, Nick thought, so that could spell more trouble if the guy was frustrated or cornered in Grand Cayman. Still, even when Jace Britten was angry, he radiated that top-gun charisma women probably went for. Evidently, Claire had fallen for him and hard. She'd said she'd eloped with the guy.

After she settled herself again in her seat, Nick stole one more glance at her. Her body stayed tense. Here in south Florida, she always seemed slightly unworldly, out of place with her porcelain complexion and stunning red hair—natural red hair, the color of a sunset over the gulf. Most tourists and Floridians were tanned like he was, and her hue of hair was so—so Irish, or like a painting of an angel.

But her delicate appearance was deceptive. She was strong, great at psyching out people's lies and deceits and patching together the truth. She performed what lawyers called forensic autopsies, where a person, living or dead, was dissected through their statements and deeds to ferret out guilt. When he'd hired her, Claire already had a small consulting firm she called Clear Path. He wished he could find a clear path for her and Lexi—and himself—out of this looming catastrophe.

He felt guilty that he'd caused this catastrophe and at how much he still wanted her. He figured she knew that. And he was scared, not at how finding someone he could trust and love had finally come his way, but that, even if he saved Lexi, he had to lose Claire so Ames couldn't hurt her like this again.

Jace cruised over Cuba in the Cirrus SR22 turbo-charged plane he'd borrowed from an old buddy who was a lot richer than he was. It was legal to pass over the embargoed island in a small plane. Several of his hotshot pilot friends had faked engine problems and asked for an emergency landing there just to look around in off-limits Havana. This was one heck of an emergency, but no way he was stopping anywhere but Grand Cayman.

He planned to get there in slightly under the three-hour flight plan he'd filed back at the Marco Island Airport. He'd picked that smaller facility instead of Naples Airport, hoping the spying eyes of that damned Clayton Ames would have more trouble finding him there. Jace had obviously been researched and watched. He'd been sent photos of Nick and Claire together at an address no average outsider should have, but Ames's long arms seemed to pull a lot of strings. He felt really guilty that the guy who had snatched Lexi had resembled and pretended to be him.

The distance was just under 400 nautical miles, and he was pushing the Cirrus near its top speed of 180 knots, hovering just under its ceiling of 17,500 feet since the plane was not pressurized and he didn't want to mess with supplemental oxygen. He wanted to land at MWCR as if he were a tourist. He'd case the area where Nick and Claire would be staying and, no doubt, where they would be contacted. Just as when he'd flown jumbo jets to Singapore and back or when he'd gone on Middle East combat missions, he wanted to be prepared and ready.

He didn't really have a specific plan after he landed, but he'd recon and get one. Anything he had to do to find this Clayton Ames who held his daughter's life in his dirty hands. So what if Nick Markwood said he'd been trying to get the goods on him, even locate him for years because he moved around so much? The guy might be rich, powerful and slippery, but he was going to pay for this, even if Jace had to take orders from Markwood for a while. Even if Claire was staying with the rich lawyer in what were probably luxurious digs on a gorgeous beach on a tropical island. Even if—this really scared him, too— she seemed to trust Markwood, to look at him as if…

Damn, why hadn't Claire been content to just run Clear Path from her home office and steer clear of criminal investigations? She put her life—all their lives—in danger. This whole mess really got to Jace. It would be so easy to just end things up here over this endless blue-green water, to just disappear. Maybe Claire would talk to people he knew to try to find out if he'd been suicidal, why he'd kept changing his work flight schedule, why he'd considered giving up the international flying career he'd worked so hard for. She could use her forensic autopsy skills on him even if they never found his body.

He shook himself loose from that sick daydream. He was going to not only survive, but live. Really live. And with Claire and Lexi by his side.

KAREN HARPER

31735	BROKEN BONDS	___ $7.99 U.S.	___ $8.99 CAN
31504	FINDING MERCY	___ $7.99 U.S.	___ $8.99 CAN
31503	RETURN TO GRACE	___ $7.99 U.S.	___ $8.99 CAN
31502	FALL FROM PRIDE	___ $7.99 U.S.	___ $8.99 CAN
31472	UPON A WINTER'S NIGHT	___ $7.99 U.S.	___ $8.99 CAN

(limited quantities available)

TOTAL AMOUNT	$ _____
POSTAGE & HANDLING	$ _____
($1.00 for 1 book, 50¢ for each additional)	
APPLICABLE TAXES*	$ _____
TOTAL PAYABLE	$ _____

(check or money order—please do not send cash)

To order, complete this form and send it, along with a check or money order for the total above, payable to MIRA Books, to: **In the U.S.** 3010 Walden Avenue, P.O. Box 9077, Buffalo, NY 14269-9077, **In Canada:** P.O. Box 636, Fort Erie, Ontario, L2A 5X3.

Name: _____
Address: _____ City: _____
State/Prov.: _____ Zip/Postal Code: _____
Account Number (if applicable): _____
075 CSAS

*New York residents remit applicable sales taxes.
*Canadian residents remit applicable GST and provincial taxes.

MIRA®

www.MIRABooks.com

MKH08

REQUEST YOUR FREE BOOKS!

2 FREE NOVELS
FROM THE SUSPENSE COLLECTION,
PLUS 2 FREE GIFTS!

YES! Please send me 2 FREE novels from the Suspense Collection and my 2 FREE gifts (gifts are worth about $10). After receiving them, if I don't wish to receive any more books, I can return the shipping statement marked "cancel." If I don't cancel, I will receive 4 brand-new novels every month and be billed just $6.49 per book in the U.S. or $6.99 per book in Canada. That's a savings of at least 18% off the cover price. It's quite a bargain! Shipping and handling is just 50¢ per book in the U.S. and 75¢ per book in Canada.* I understand that accepting the 2 free books and gifts places me under no obligation to buy anything. I can always return a shipment and cancel at any time. Even if I never buy another book, the two free books and gifts are mine to keep forever.

191/391 MDN GH4Z

Name	
	(PLEASE PRINT)
Address	Apt. #
City	State/Prov.	Zip/Postal Code
Signature (if under 18, a parent or guardian must sign)	

Mail to the **Reader Service**:
IN U.S.A.: P.O. Box 1867, Buffalo, NY 14240-1867
IN CANADA: P.O. Box 609, Fort Erie, Ontario L2A 5X3

Want to try 2 free books from another line?
Call 1-800-873-8635 or visit www.ReaderService.com.

SUS15R

Reading Has Its Rewards

Earn **FREE BOOKS!**

Register at **Harlequin My Rewards** and submit your Harlequin purchases from wherever you shop to earn points for free books and other exclusive rewards.

Plus submit your purchases from now till May 30th for a chance to win a $500 Visa Card*.

Visit **HarlequinMyRewards.com** today

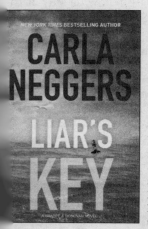

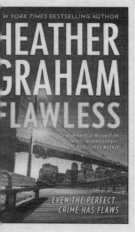